INTENT
TO KILL

INTENT TO KILL

A NOVEL BY
JAMES GRIPPANDO

DOUBLEDAY LARGE PRINT HOME LIBRARY EDITION

MADISON PARK PRESS™

NEW YORK

Published by Madison Park Press, One Penn Plaza, New York, NY 10119. Madison Park Press is a trademark of Bertelsmann Direct North America, Inc.

ISBN: 978-0-7394-9217-8

Printed in the United States of America

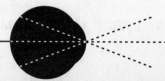

This Large Print Book carries the
Seal of Approval of N.A.V.H.

For Tiffany. My Home Run.

INTENT
TO KILL

CHAPTER 1

The first thing Ryan found was a hand with part of an arm. He guessed it was the left hand, but it was hard to tell. He spotted the right foot on the other side of the kitchen, on the floor, next to the high chair.

God only knew where the missing eyes and ears were.

Some might have said that "Birthplace of Mr. Potato Head" was all the fame a working-class city of seventy-two thousand on the Blackstone River deserved. But Pawtucket, Rhode Island, was no one-spud wonder. It was the minor-league home of one of the most storied teams in baseball.

"Hi Dada," said Ainsley. She was wearing only a diaper and her baseball cap—her daddy's team. The Pawtucket Red Sox—"PawSox"—were the Triple-A minor-league affiliate of the Boston Red Sox, and twenty-four-year-old Ryan James was their rising star. Ryan put his daughter's partially reconstructed toy aside and gathered up Ainsley in his arms.

"What do you want for breakfast?" said Ryan, as he put her in the chair.

"Mama," she said.

"Anything else?"

"Dada."

"Coming right up," said Ryan.

Ainsley had fewer words in her vocabulary than most two-year-olds, and anything that she couldn't say was either a mama or a dada. Ryan didn't want to get Freudian about the whole thing, but he assumed the dada was a banana. He had no idea what the mama was. He selected a ripe one from the bunch, sliced it up for her, and put the pieces on the tray.

"Here you go, gorgeous," he said.

Ainsley ate one bite, then took the biggest piece and threw it right over Ryan's head. It landed in front of the refrigerator, and the real mama had to duck out of the line of flight as she entered the kitchen.

Chelsea sighed and put her hands on her hips. "Ryan, please don't throw food."

"I think you meant Ainsley," he said.

"What?"

"You said, 'Ryan, please don't throw food.' I swear it wasn't me."

Chelsea looked flummoxed. "Oh, God. I'm already stressed."

"Just wait till we have five of these bambinos."

Chelsea froze.

"Kidding," said Ryan. He wanted only four.

Chelsea poured a quick cup of coffee and gulped half of it down.

"Why are you so tense?" said Ryan.

She coughed on her java, and he immediately regretted the question.

As a minor-league player, Ryan made the standard eleven hundred dollars per month plus a twenty-dollar per diem food allowance. It wasn't enough. Chelsea supplemented their income by teaching third-grade English at one of Boston's prestigious private schools. Three nights a week she attended law school classes at Suffolk University in Boston, a four-year program that would earn her a diploma when Ainsley was ready for first grade. If Ryan made it to the majors, she'd keep teaching; if he didn't, she'd start a new career. Either way, money would no longer be such an overriding issue in their future. For now, however, finances were tight, and with her full-time teaching responsibilities, her part-time law studies, and an hour-long commute each way between Pawtucket and Boston, Chelsea was struggling to be the good wife and mother.

Chelsea said, "I have a very important meeting, first thing this morning with the head of school. I cannot be late."

"You should eat something. It will settle your nerves."

"No time."

"At least take a dada for the road," he said, holding up another banana.

The Ainsleyism brought a smile.

"Okay," she said. "I'll have a dada."

She went to him and gave him a kiss, and for a brief instant, it seemed to cut the stress. That was the great thing about marrying the love of your life. People often said "I can't live without you," but when Ryan said those words to Chelsea, he meant it with all his heart. Teammates teased him for being whipped, but deep down they envied him.

"Me, me, me!" said Ainsley.

Chelsea gave her a kiss too.

"Ainsley has speech therapy today at eleven," she said. "Can you pick her up from day care and take her?"

"Sure," he said. "Batting practice doesn't start until three. I'll take her to your mother's afterward."

"If you can't do it, just let me know. I'll have my mother take her."

"No, I'll take her. Are you coming to the game tonight?"

There was a long pause. Chelsea's schedule hadn't allowed her to see many of Ryan's games this season.

"I have a two-hour criminal law class tonight," she said.

"Honey, it's the last game of the season."

"I know. But the semester has barely started, and I'm already getting into trouble for missing too many classes."

"Don't they let you make up the class work for family commitments? Just this one time?"

"Well, I guess I could call the professor and see what he says."

"So you'll come?"

"I will really, really try."

Ryan took an envelope from the kitchen counter and handed it to her. "I snagged you really great seats."

She hesitated, and Ryan could see that he was adding pressure that she didn't need today. But it truly was the biggest game of the season.

Chelsea looked inside the envelope. "There are only two tickets," she said.

"Yeah. One for you and one for Ainsley."

"What about Babes?"

Ryan paused. *What about Babes?*

Babes was the nickname for Chelsea's younger brother, Daniel. Twenty-two years old and still living with his parents, he suffered from Asperger's syndrome, an autism-related disorder, but he rarely missed a PawSox game. He was more of a team mascot than a fan, and most of the players were kind to him. A few weren't. In fact, it was a bad practical joke that had brought Ryan and Chelsea together. For laughs, one of Ryan's teammates asked Babes if he wanted a chocolate bar, but it was really Ex-Lax. Around the seventh inning, the prankster and his coconspirators exploded in laughter when poor Babes suddenly dropped his baseball mitt and cap and went running home, a grown man with a load in his pants. Ryan got a three-game suspension without pay for breaking the nose of the jackass who'd done it. When Babes's sister came to thank Ryan, it was love at first sight.

"I love Babes," said Ryan. "I really do. But you know how he can have these meltdowns around crowds sometimes."

"He goes to almost every game. He sits through all of your batting practices."

"And most of the time he's just fine. But sometimes he isn't. Leaving early is no big deal at most games. But tonight is huge. I don't want you heading home in the second inning because Babes suddenly can't handle the clapping, the shouting, or the sound of the guy sitting next to him cracking his peanut shells."

"Aren't you exaggerating a little bit?"

"No. Babes gets these fixations, and . . ."

Ryan stopped himself. He could have gone on, but it would have come off as an attack on Chelsea's family—how everyone's life revolved around Babes, how Chelsea's parents didn't even seem to know each other anymore because it was all about Babes, all the time.

"He'll be crushed that you didn't invite him," said Chelsea. "We can't leave Babes out. He's my brother."

"Honey, that's kind of the point. He's *your* brother. He's not Ainsley's brother. I want this to be a special night. It's about *our* family."

She bristled. "Didn't know the Townsend family was such a burden."

He went to her, but she pulled away. He stopped.

"They're not a burden," he said. "It's just this one night. I promise you I will do something really special for Babes. Just him and me."

She seemed to be considering it, but it still felt pretty chilly in the room from where Ryan was standing.

Ainsley threw a banana slice that sailed over Ryan's head and landed on the other side of the kitchen.

"Whoa! Did you see that? Sign her up. The kid's got an arm!"

Chelsea couldn't help but laugh. Ryan seized upon her smile, and this time she didn't resist his embrace. There seemed to be more stress than usual in their lives, but some things still felt perfect.

"Lucky for me I'm irresistible," he said.

"Lucky for you I have a heart of gold."

"So you'll come tonight?"

"Yes," she said with a sigh. "I'll be there."

"Let's go, Baaaabe," came the lone voice from the grandstands.

The PawSox's biggest fan—with his incessant chant—was for obvious reasons known affectionately as Babes. A virtual fixture at McCoy Stadium since his middle-school days, Babes was now old enough for a brewski with his Pawdog and cheese fries, but alcohol never touched his lips. He looked like a big kid dressed in his lucky Sox cap and jersey, his treasured old baseball mitt, autographed by the entire PawSox team, resting in his lap beneath a well-thumbed stat book. Today, as always, he came to watch his favorite player take afternoon batting practice before the evening game.

"Come on, *Baaaabe.*"

Ryan tipped his helmet and stepped into the batting cage. At six foot three and 220 pounds of athletic ability, Ryan had once been in the enviable position of fighting off football and basketball recruiters before accepting a baseball scholarship to the University of Texas, where he then had plenty of fun fighting off the women while leading the Longhorns to a national title. The Red Sox selected him early in the Minor League

Baseball draft. He skipped over the Single-A and Double-A teams, where every player could hit a fastball, and went straight to Triple-A, where breaking balls separated the men from the boys. He probably would have advanced quickly to the majors but for the ifs: *if* he hadn't destroyed his shoulder in his first spring training, *if* he hadn't missed his entire first season in rehab, *if* the team doctors hadn't labeled him damaged goods. But even if the big leagues passed over him again this year, Ryan knew he was a lucky man.

As long as he had Chelsea.

"Come on, *Baaaabe.*"

Babes sat through every batting practice before PawSox home games. His favorite seat was right above the Sox dugout. He always sat by himself. Often he was the only fan in the entire stadium. That was the way he liked it.

Babes had never been one for team sports, teamwork, or team anything. His interest in baseball was purely as a spectator, or more accurately, as a walking baseball encyclopedia. He knew the batting lineups, not just of every major-league team, but of nearly every major-league team that had ever existed. He memorized batting averages, box scores, all sorts of trivia that for other baseball fans was a source of amazement and amusement.

What blew people away, however, was his ability to work anagrams in his head.

"Hey, Babes," a Sox player called out. It was Ivan Lopez, an ace pitcher, the team jokester, and Ryan's best friend. Ivan cupped his hands over his mouth and shifted to his stadium-announcer voice, as if it were suddenly the bottom of the ninth inning at famous Fenway Park: "Next batter for the Boston Red Sox, the designated hitter, number thirty-four, David Ortiz."

The wheels immediately began to spin in Babes's head, and he worked it out aloud, rearranging the name of one of the most famous Boston Red Sox sluggers into something else entirely: "David Ortiz, David Ortiz—Diva or ditz?"

That one just about had Ivan and the rest of the boys rolling on the grass. Babes and his anagrams were a steady source of entertainment for Ryan and his teammates. The possibilities were endless. A diehard Sox fan, Babes, of course, hated that team in pinstripes from the Bronx: Yankee Stadium became "Nauseate my kid." The great Ted Williams was "I'm still awed." And on it went, usually well beyond the point at which most people ceased to consider it amusing. It was such a compulsion that sometimes he was even forced to insult his own favorite team: "Red Sox win the World Series" became "Ex losers with new disorder."

"Say good-bye to that one," said Ivan at the crack of the bat. Ryan had just parked his third consecutive home run over the left-field wall, this one right between the billboard-sized advertisements for Honey Dew Donuts and Hasbro's Mr. Potato Head. It was only practice, but he seemed to be on fire.

"Little wager on four in a row?" said Ryan.

"Only if I'm pitching," said Ivan. He picked up his mitt, but before he could take step one toward the pitcher's mound, the PawSox manager emerged from the dugout.

"Save it for tonight, boys."

"Come on, Coach," said Ivan. "It's only going to take me three pitches to strike him out."

Ryan howled.

"I said *save* it." His hands were on his hips, a surefire sign that he wasn't kidding around.

Manager Joe Bedford was a foul-mouthed, tobacco-chewing baseball relic who, Ryan guessed, would probably be buried in his uniform. He was usually easygoing, but things were getting serious. They were just three hours away from the final game of minor-league regular-season play—the Paw-Sox against the Toledo Mud Hens. Since 1896 the Mud Hen name has been linked not only to their current affiliate, the Detroit Tigers, but also to the New York Yankees, Philadelphia Phillies, Cleveland Indians, Minnesota Twins, and—perhaps most famously of all—Klinger on the old television hit *M*A*S*H,* who was cast as a diehard Mud Hen fan from Toledo whose dresses and high heels never did get him kicked out of the army. The PawSox and the Mud Hens were the two best teams in the International League, and tonight's game in Pawtucket was seen as a preview of the postseason championship. Ivan was slated to be the starting pitcher. With a wicked breaking ball and the lowest earned run average in the minor leagues, Ivan was without question on his way up to the majors next season. No one begrudged his success. Every Triple-A team had its share of bitterness—players who'd been passed over year after year or, even worse, who'd tasted the major leagues only to be sent back down to the minors. But even the guys with inflated egos had to recognize a future star like Ivan.

"Come over here, you two goofballs." Bedford was smiling now, a more familiar disposition.

Ryan and Ivan ran to the dugout. Ryan said, "What's up, Coach?"

"Got some news for you. Wasn't going to say anything tonight, but you're big-league material, and you can handle the pressure."

Ryan braced himself. It didn't sound like he was being fired, but in the minor leagues you never knew. "What are you telling me?" said Ryan.

"John Henry will be here watching tonight's game."

Ryan felt goose bumps. Henry was the principal owner of the major-league Boston Red Sox.

The manager said, "He's got two players on his short list. I have it on good authority that it's Tweedledum and Tweedledee."

"I think he means us," said Ivan.

"I must be Dee. Which makes you Dum."

The manager rolled his eyes. "I don't know why, but I'm gonna miss you guys. Please, just don't blow it tonight, all right?"

Ryan had a spring in his step as he and Ivan returned to the clubhouse. Ivan hit the showers. Ryan couldn't wait to share the news with Chelsea. First thing, he grabbed his cell phone from his locker and hit speed dial number one.

The call went to her voice mail. He was about to leave a message but stopped himself. He'd pressured her enough. She'd already promised to come tonight. That was a nice change. More than anything, however, he wanted her to *want* to come.

He hung up and put the phone away, hoping not to be disappointed.

Chelsea James was having a bad day.

The Boston area was well known for its prep schools—Phillips, Milton, Roxbury Latin, Groton, Winsor, to name a few—but for anyone who wanted the one-stop option of pre-K through twelve, Brookline Academy was of singular distinction. The upper grades had a separate facility to accommodate boarding students, but preteens attended the day school on the original campus. Built near *the* country club—as in the first one ever in America—the school's ivy-clad halls were among the finest examples of neo-Gothic architecture outside Europe, inspired by the British Houses of Parliament in the mid-nineteenth century. An alumni roster that read like *Who's Who in Amer-ica* funded an eight-figure endowment. Ninety-five percent of the faculty had postgraduate degrees, more than half held doctorates, and the rest (like Chelsea) probably would some day. No class had more than twelve students. Mandarin Chinese was mandatory beginning at age three. Classrooms had the latest SMART Board technology, and any student who didn't have a brand-new laptop every September was living in the Dark Ages. About once every decade, someone made it through the fifth grade without being named a "Duke Tip Kid," but these kids weren't aiming for Duke or any other school south of the Charles River. The graduate immortalized by the century-old bronze statue in the verdant quad was said not to have a diploma in hand, but an acceptance letter to Harvard. Day tuition was a mere sixteen thousand dollars—*per semester.* To families that didn't qualify for financial aid, it was nothing compared to what their children would be asked to donate as alumni.

For Chelsea, today's trouble began at

her 7:45 AM meeting with the headmaster. She had volunteered to assist the parents' association with the all-important fund-raising auction at the school's upcoming gala. Chelsea thought it would be nice if students in the lower grades worked with their teachers and room mothers to create quilts as one of the marquee items.

"I'm excited about it," said Chelsea, "aren't you?"

The headmaster was smiling, but that was not necessarily a good sign. Arguments were not allowed at the Academy. Faculty and administration had "discussions," and they had them with smiles—by edict and by example of the headmaster, a consummate administrator and gifted peacemaker who had the ability to smile through the worst of circumstances, whether she was telling you that your house was on fire or, far worse, that your child wasn't going to be in the math honors program. She reminded Chelsea of Margaret Thatcher with a New England accent.

This particular smile was about as

warm as the Italian ices at Caffè Bella Vita.

"What's wrong?" said Chelsea.

The headmaster folded her hands atop the antique mahogany desk that had served every head before her, and that had been hers for the past twenty-nine years.

"Chelsea, I like you very much. But do you have any idea how much our annual auction raises for the school?"

"A lot of money."

"*A lot* of money," she said, her smile thinning. "Now why don't you start thinking more along the lines of a week at Canyon Ranch or lunch with Baryshnikov? Fast."

"But bidding on our children's own creations strikes me as sweet and charitable. Dropping ten grand on lunch with a celebrity who has absolutely no desire to be there is, well, kind of pathetic. Don't you think?"

"You may have a point."

"So the quilts are a go?"

"No, dear. But when Ryan James is inducted into the baseball hall of fame, we'll be sure to let his lunch go for five grand."

For a moment, Chelsea thought she was serious, but then they shared a genuine smile. As the headmaster escorted her out, she tossed enough bones of praise to keep Chelsea from feeling completely shot down. The quilts were dead, but Chelsea reminded herself that a woman didn't get to be the Margaret Thatcher of Brookline Academy for almost three decades by making mistakes. This was a great school. Chelsea loved it, and she hoped in a year that Ainsley would enroll as a three-year-old in the preschool program. Every institution had its bureaucratic land mines.

But why did Chelsea seem to be stepping on every single one of them *today*?

By late afternoon it seemed that the stars had truly aligned against her. The entire faculty was summoned to the upper-grade campus for "a very important meeting" at 4:00 PM. Unless this turned out to be the shortest meeting ever, getting to Ryan's game on time was going to be next to impossible. Maybe Babes was right: God was a Sox fan. Perhaps this was His way of finally punishing her for the only mean thing she'd ever done to her brother. At the age of six he'd painted red socks onto all of her Barbie dolls. She retaliated by coloring Yankee pinstripes onto his Smurfs. It had made him cry for a week. Chelsea still bore the guilt.

Guilt. With a two-year-old daughter who saw her mother so little that she sometimes called her grandmother Mama, her heart had no room for more of it.

She made a quick stop in the faculty restroom and checked herself in the mirror. Chelsea had the heart-shaped face of a classic beauty, and it wasn't until recently that she worried about lines on it. Late-night law studies had turned her into a real fan of concealer. She fixed her makeup and gave her hair about ten seconds of attention. At her job interview a year ago it had been long and blond, but on the headmaster's advice, she never wore it down on campus, and she'd darkened it to a honey shade of blond. Ryan said he liked it, but she still wasn't sure.

She entered the AV room two minutes early and took the seat nearest the door. She was leaving at 4:30 PM, not a minute later. Chelsea had no doubt in her mind that this faculty meeting was important. Only the truly important meetings at the Academy were convened with no advance notice of the time or topic, no chance for the faculty to shape its collective thought into any form of meaningful opposition. But at this point, she didn't care if the meeting was about the closing of the school. She couldn't let Ryan down. Not again—and definitely not at the last ballgame of the season, with no chance to make it up to him. Tonight's game was not to be missed, and she was determined to get there on time.

Even if it killed her.

CHAPTER 2

Seven-thirty PM was game time in Pawtucket. At 7:29 the choice seats behind home plate were still empty.

The final home game of the PawSox season was a sellout, and Ryan had pulled in favors to score two of the best seats in the stadium for Chelsea and Ainsley. He felt a little guilty about not including Babes, but he'd already figured out how he was going to make it up to him—once he and Ivan were playing up the road at Fenway.

"Play ball!" cried the home plate umpire.

The crowd cheered the PawSox players onto the field. Ivan was all business as he climbed atop the mound and started his warm-up pitches. Ryan and the other infielders scooped up practice ground balls and fired them to first base. The PawSox manager paced nervously in the dugout, chomping on his plug of chewing tobacco while checking his crumpled roster card. The sun had set, the lights were up, and the national anthem had been sung. It was sixty-two degrees, not a cloud in the raven sky, a light breeze blowing out over the left-field wall. The night was perfect for a ballgame.

Where the heck are you, Chelsea?

The PA system crackled with the introduction of the Mud Hens' first batter. A wiry young man from Puerto Rico stepped up to the plate, crossed himself, kissed his gold crucifix, tugged at his crotch, spit in the dirt, and then glared at Ivan with contempt. Ivan wiped his brow into his sleeve. Ryan gave him a little nod for encouragement, and the first two pitches popped like gunshots in the catcher's mitt. A rumble of approval emerged from the crowd, and on the third pitch the batter chased after a knuckle curveball that he couldn't have hit with a tennis racket. Gone in sixty seconds. The PawSox faithful cheered, and one of Ivan's fans started the strikeout count by hanging a card with the letter K on the fence by the bullpen.

Ivan was unbeatable when he started out this strong. If Chelsea didn't arrive soon, she'd miss the entire first inning.

Keep your head in the game, James, he told himself. But it was hugely disappointing, to say the least. The final game of the season. The principal owner of the Red Sox in attendance. Ryan could feel the electricity in the air, the excitement of the fans. Ten thousand people had managed to arrive on time. How many of them were married to a player who had dreamed of baseball since he was five years old and was now on the short list for the major leagues?

Another crack, but this time it wasn't Ivan's fastball hitting the catcher's mitt. A screaming line drive down the third-base line had extra bases written all over it. Ryan went completely horizontal, diving to his right, extending his reach, and snagging it for the out.

"Attaboy, Ryan!" his manager shouted from the dugout.

Ryan dusted himself off and fired the ball off to the second baseman. Ivan gave him a look that said *Thanks for saving my ass.* Half the crowd gave him a standing ovation. It was a defensive gem worthy of the ESPN highlight reel.

And Chelsea had missed it.

Two outs. The Mud Hens sent their third hitter to the plate, a big left-hander who rarely hit the ball to the left side of the field. Ryan shifted a few steps closer to the shortstop, then glanced over to the dugout to make sure the manager was happy with the defensive adjustment. The manager didn't look at him. He was talking on the telephone, which was odd. The only time managers spoke on the telephone was to communicate with the bullpen, which usually meant a change of pitchers. Surely they weren't thinking of taking Ivan out of the game.

Ryan checked the seats behind home plate one more time. No Chelsea.

He glanced into the dugout on the third-base side. The manager was still on the telephone. He was pacing now, but not the thinking man's long, deliberative walk from one end of the dugout to the other. These were spasmodic bursts, no more than two or three steps in one direction before turning and marching back the other way. Clearly he was upset.

Ivan hurled the first pitch to the new batter. Ryan heard the pop, but he didn't see the ball hit the mitt. His focus was elsewhere, his gaze shifting back and forth from the empty seats behind home plate to the PawSox dugout. His fingers tingled with a strange numbness. The familiar game noises—the jabbering of fans, the hawking of vendors, the stadium music—were suddenly foreign to him. Ryan's world seemed to be moving in slow motion. He was picking up a very bad vibe.

The PawSox manager was still on the phone.

Chelsea and Ainsley's seats were still empty.

Ryan knew his manager's mannerisms, and the old man didn't appear to be upset. He seemed distraught. Finally, the phone call ended. The manager signaled the umpire for a time out and called another player off the bench. A surprised kid two weeks out of double-A ball jumped up, grabbed his cap and mitt, and ran from the dugout. He went straight to Ryan.

"Coach needs to see you," he said, never looking Ryan in the eye.

Ryan knew this was no routine substitution, not with the owner of the Red Sox in the stadium to watch Ryan and the other players on his short list. Ivan stepped off the mound, confused. Ryan's teammates looked at one another and shrugged, and the wave of speculation carried over with equal force to the opposing team's dugout. The fans, too, seemed baffled, and a few started booing the decision to pull Ryan from the game. The umpire behind home plate removed his mask and planted his hands on his hips, as if to say that someone owed him an explanation.

Ryan jogged to the dugout, slowly at

first, then faster, reeled in by his manager's seeming refusal—no, inability—to
look at him. Finally, his gaze met Ryan's,
and the expression on the old man's
face was unlike any Ryan had ever seen
before. His lips moved, but it was as if
no words would come, and when this
big bear of a man could hardly find the
strength to put his arm around Ryan, it
was painfully obvious that something
terrible had happened.

"It's bad, son," was all the old man
could bring himself to say.

CHAPTER 3

Ryan rode shotgun as the company car sped toward Memorial Hospital, the major trauma center in the area. There hadn't even been time for him to retrieve his own phone and car keys from his locker. One of the PawSox trainers drove while Ryan tried to gather information on a borrowed cell.

"Faster, you gotta go faster," said Ryan.

They were already doing seventy in a forty-mile-per-hour zone. The driver edged it up past seventy-five.

"Let me call you back," Ryan told his

father-in-law. "I want to check with the hospital again."

The only thing he knew for certain was that there had been an automobile accident, a serious one. Both Chelsea and Ainsley had been in the car, both alive when the ambulance had arrived at the hospital. The ER nurse had shared all that information in the previous phone conversation, minutes earlier, and she had nothing new for him yet. She could only confirm what he already knew. He closed the flip phone.

"How much farther?" Ryan asked.

"Two minutes."

"Make it one."

Ninety seconds later the car screeched to a halt at the emergency entrance. Ryan jumped out, the pneumatic doors parted, and he ran straight into ER pandemonium. A drug addict paced across the waiting area, arguing with the television set. An old man with an icepack on his head was mumbling about some kid who'd gotten away with his dog and his wallet. A homeless woman with mouth agape, no teeth, slept in the chair beside him. A single mother tried to make her boys stop kicking the soda machine for a free Pepsi. Pawtucket wasn't Newport, and while violent crime no longer riddled neighborhoods like Pleasant View and Woodlawn the way it had in the 1980s and 1990s, 30 percent of families with young kids lived below the poverty line. The crowded ER waiting room was graphic testimony of the city's continuing problems with crime, drugs, and general hard living.

Ryan threw a quick glance at the mob scene around the registration desk and just kept running. He'd visited this same ER last year for his shoulder, so he didn't need directions to the examination bays down the hall and beyond the double set of doors.

"Sir!"

He tried to keep going, but the intake nurse practically tackled him.

"I need to see my wife and daughter! Where are they?"

The PawSox uniform left no doubt as to his identity. The nurse checked her clipboard. "Your wife is in surgery right now."

"How's Ainsley?"

"Your daughter is going to be fine," she said in a voice that tried to calm him.

"I didn't ask how she's going to be. I said how *is* she."

"Fortunately, your daughter was in the rear seat in a child safety restraint. Her injuries are minor."

"Thank God." Never before had Ryan felt such relief and terror simultaneously, afraid to ask the next question. "What happened to Chelsea?"

"Right now I think you need to be with your daughter."

"What *happened* to Chelsea?" he said, completely unaware that he was shouting.

The nurse didn't flinch. It wasn't callousness. She was a pro. "Her injuries were more serious. As soon as I have any news at all from the OR, we will let you know."

"I need to be with her," he said as he tried to push past.

She took his elbow. "You can't."

"Which way is it?"

"Please, Mr. James. It's a sterile environment."

Ryan's uniform was covered in red clay from his diving catch at third base. "I can scrub."

"And then do what?" she said. "She's anesthetized. Your wife won't know you're there."

Ryan was torn, and for a moment he couldn't move.

"Come see your little girl," she said. "She's getting the best of care, but I'm sure she's scared. I can take you to her."

The nurse was pushing all the right buttons, and Ryan trusted her. It was a maze of hallways to the pediatric ER, which gave Ryan a chance to call his father-in-law. They were still five minutes away. Ryan didn't ask, but he presumed that difficulties with Babes—either in bringing him to the hospital or in trying to leave him behind—were slowing them down.

The sound of his baseball cleats on the tile floor pushed the moment into the surreal. An hour earlier he'd had nothing on his mind but PawSox and Mud Hens in the big game. Two hours from now he

and Ivan might well have received a personal "welcome to the Red Sox" from
the team's principal owner. Sandwiched
between those bookends were some
very painful chapters, a few still being
written: the way he'd doubted Chelsea's
promise to come, his anger at her for
being late, and the crash he still knew
nothing about except that it had left his
twenty-six-year-old wife fighting for her
life on an operating table.

"Dada!"

If Ainsley only had a few dozen words
in a growing vocabulary, that particular
one always lifted Ryan's spirits. She was
standing at the bed rail, her arms reaching for him from beneath the green hospital gown. He went to her and gathered
up the little bundle in his arms.

She looked perfectly fine, and the
pediatrician confirmed as much. The
plan was to keep her in the hospital
overnight just to make sure the crash
hadn't given her a concussion. It looked
as though Ryan would be there at least
that long for Chelsea anyway. The pediatrician moved on to the next patient.
The nurse was putting fresh paper on

the examination table, and Ryan was seated in the rocking chair in the corner and holding Ainsley in his arms when a doctor wearing surgical scrubs appeared in the doorway.

"Mr. James?" he said.

Ryan looked up. "Yes?"

"I'm Dr. Weinstein. I'm the hospital's chief surgeon."

The chief surgeon. Ryan wasn't sure if that was a good sign or a bad one. "Do you have any . . . is Chelsea going to be OK?"

He glanced at the nurse, then back at Ryan. "Could we talk alone?"

It was suddenly harder to breathe.

The nurse lifted Ainsley from Ryan's arms, and he reluctantly let her go. His little girl screamed as she was carried from the room, and the nurse made such a point of closing the door on the way out that Ryan wanted to shout right along with Ainsley—*No, no, no*!

The news was all over the surgeon's face.

"I'm sorry," the doctor said. "There was nothing we could do. She passed away on the operating table. I'm really very, very sorry."

Ryan was listening, but it was as if his mind could process only a few words—*nothing . . . do . . . passed . . . sorry*—until a tsunami of emotional devastation washed over him, and he launched himself from the chair. His scream could only be described as primal, and in a blind fury he kicked the chair across the room. The doctor grabbed him. Ryan nearly collapsed in his arms, and the tears came immediately.

"It's all right," said Dr. Weinstein. "It's good to let it go. But you're going to have to pull yourself together here. Not just for yourself."

Ryan glanced through the little diamond-shaped window in the door. Ainsley was pummeling the nurse outside the room, trying to break free and get back to Dada. He stepped away from Dr. Weinstein and collected himself.

"When can I see Chelsea?"

"I recommend you give that a few minutes. When you're ready."

Ryan nodded. The door opened and Ainsley ran into the room. The nurse had finally lost control of her. The kid had her father's strength and athleticism.

Ryan did a quick change of face and scooped her up. "There's my big girl!"

She laid her head on his shoulder, threw her arms around his neck, and in a cute little gesture that Chelsea had taught her, gently patted Ryan on the back.

The doctor and nurse left the room.

"I wan Mama," said Ainsley, her face buried in his big shoulder.

Ryan struggled to hold it together. He knew he would somehow have to find a way to live without Chelsea. But as he stood there alone with his daughter in the quiet hospital room, clutching her, trying not to let her see the tears streaming down his face, he wasn't at all sure he could.

"Me too," he whispered.

THREE YEARS LATER: BOSTON

CHAPTER 4

"This is *Jocks in the Morning*; you're on the air. What's up, knucklehead?"

It was 6:00 AM, and Ryan James was kicking off another day in his new life as cohost of Boston's hottest talk-radio sports show. Originally it had been just *Jock in the Morning,* but when the legendary Jock Grogan hit fifty, the station brought in young blood to reach the key underforty demographic. It was nonstop jokes and jabbering, which only masked the fact that Ryan's life had spiraled downward.

The PawSox had overlooked the dip in Ryan's performance the year after

Chelsea's death, but by the second season, the lack of focus proved to be too much. Ryan was cut from the team. He gave up on baseball. At his lowest, he was even fired from his job as assistant manager of a sporting-goods store. Life was hard enough without Chelsea. It was almost impossible without sleep.

"Yeah, dis is Tony from Wattahtown," said the caller.

"Go ahead, Tony in Watertown."

"Hey, chief, I know Ivan Lopez is your good buddy, but in these last two games, does he look like the most overpaid pitcher in the major leagues or what?"

Ivan was the newest star pitcher for the Boston Red Sox, having just signed a seven-figure contract, and he was far more than Ryan's "buddy." Ryan had been best man at Ivan's wedding the year before, and to Ainsley he was still Uncle Ivan.

"Okay, Tony from Wattahtown. First off, you're an idiot. Second, it's not *Eye*-van, like *Eye*-talian. It's Ivan, like—"

"Like Trump's ex-wife?"

"That's Ivan*a*. You got too many A's.

Just like this phone call. One too many dumb-A's." Ryan hung up and pitched the next call to his cohost.

Being surly and putting morons in their place was good for ratings. Jock Grogan was particularly good at it. Ryan was raised to be polite, and insults didn't come naturally, so he had to work at getting in touch with his inner Yankee, as his Texas grandma would have called it. Today, however, it was hard for him to work at anything, and not just because he was functioning on only one hour of sleep.

The sixth day of September was the anniversary.

Three years after Chelsea's death, Ryan's love endured. He knew she would have wanted him to date, but he had declined most well-meaning attempts to set him up with single women. The few dates he'd agreed to weren't total disasters, but he just didn't feel it in his heart to pick up the phone and call any of them for a second date.

The insomnia didn't help.

For the first few months, Ryan had resisted prescription sleep medications.

An athlete on pills seemed wrong to him. Drugs of any sort just weren't part of the James family culture, and Ryan didn't believe anyone who said that sleep aids weren't addictive. The difference between real sleep and drug-induced sleep would reveal itself anyway, like the difference between making love and having sex. His daddy—a man who plowed a Texas field by day and slept like a log at night—told him to suck it up, work through it. But the demons kept him awake, and he was showing up at the practice field exhausted every morning. When he started nodding off in the middle of team meetings, he took the doctor's advice and tried the meds. They gave him everything from diarrhea to blurred vision, and the dosage he required left him in a haze all day long. His hitting slump worsened. Rightly or wrongly, Ryan blamed the medication and quit taking it. He tried relaxation therapy instead, which helped for a while, until the nightmares took over.

Not long after Chelsea's death, Ryan had watched a television news story about corpses literally piling up at the morgue. Shelves in the cadaver cooler, designed for only one body, held two or three stacked one on top of another. Others were kept in disaster-response vehicles parked outside the building. The plumbing had also backed up, and the medical examiner admitted that effluent from autopsies was clogging the pipes. That was in Boston, not Pawtucket, but the mind runs wild when disturbing news breaks anywhere, and the thought of his beautiful Chelsea lying naked on a shelf and stacked beneath unidentified vagrants, of Chelsea being part of the "effluent" that was backing up in the pipes, kept Ryan awake for two days. When he did finally find sleep, the nightmare came. And it kept on coming, night after night, always ending with his waking up in terror—just as Chelsea woke in his dream, surrounded by cadavers.

What made Chelsea's death so difficult for Ryan to accept was that so many things had needed to go wrong in order for her to die. She would have been at her evening criminal law class in Boston if Ryan hadn't forced her to drive home for his game. The collision with the tree would not have been fatal but for the low-hanging limb in exactly the wrong spot. She could have dialed 911 in her final conscious moments and probably saved her own life—but she didn't have her cell phone with her. In fact, it was never found. Chelsea *never* went anywhere without her cell, so it was one of those flukes that cut Ryan to the core: had Chelsea not lost her cell on that day, of all days, Ryan would not have lost his wife.

And the real kicker in Ryan's emotional slide, of course, was the drunk driver who had run her off the road— and who was never caught by the police.

"Ryan, what do you think?" Jock Grogan asked his cohost.

Ryan had zoned out. Sleepless nights made for foggy days. He could tell from Jock's tone, however, that it was time to sling an insult. Insomnia was an asset there. Ryan once read about a clinical study involving sleep-deprived rats. On the sixth day they all died. Ryan

guessed that on the fifth they'd all become talk-radio hosts. *Grrr.*

"Let's ask Tony from Wattahtown,"
said Ryan in Bostonese. "He's wicked
smart."

Jock laughed way too loudly and kept
the on-air banter going with his next
call-in victim. Ryan took another swig of
coffee. The doctor had told him to avoid
caffeine, but after a night of little or no
sleep, the only way to stay alert for a
four-hour show was on the jet fuel in the
station's lounge.

Jock said, "What do you know, sports
fans? It's Tony from Watertown, calling
on his cell."

The producer had her hand on the
bleep button. Angry callbacks definitely
jazzed things up, but they were always
dicey.

"Hey, I heard what you said, James.
You think I'm a know-it-all? Well, lemme
tell *you* something. You are nothin' but a
washed up wannabe who couldn't even
cut it in the minor leagues. You are
a *bleep-bleep-bleep* loser, you know
that?"

This was a total lob, Ryan's chance to

slam a complete dope like Tony and
make his audience howl. But he didn't
have the fire today. Not on the anniversary of the worst day of his life—the day
that should have been his best.

"Yeah," he said. "We all know."

At 3:30 PM Ryan picked up Ainsley at
school. He usually looked forward to it,
but today the mix of emotions was complicated.

When Chelsea died, Ryan knew he
couldn't stay in Pawtucket. He considered moving back to Texas, but he
couldn't put a thousand miles between
Ainsley and Chelsea's parents. He settled on Boston, where Ainsley would attend Brookline Academy, the school
Chelsea had always wanted for their
daughter.

The South End was their neighborhood, a diverse and lively community
adjacent to the utterly unaffordable
Back Bay area. Ryan loved their old
bowfront Victorian row house—there
were more of them in the South End
than anywhere else in the country—and
the variety of good restaurants on

Tremont Street was unbeatable. Ryan liked Boston more than he ever thought a boy from Alpine, Texas, possibly could, and he supposed that his grandmother would have taken solace in the fact that he'd at least chosen a northern city that hated the Yankees with a passion.

The verdict was still out, however, on Brookline Academy. No doubt, the education was first rate. The social component was what worried Ryan—was the school even remotely the real world? The Academy was the kind of place where the nannies drove better cars than Ryan did. There was a technical degree of ethnic diversity, though the lower school lost 20 percent of its African American students when the Boston Celtics traded two of their players to the Chicago Bulls in the off-season. Families had to go on a waiting list to pay an extra fifteen grand per year for a reserved parking space. At morning drop-off it was virtually impossible not to spot someone who was not only a parent but also rich and famous—a professional athlete, a local television anchor, a best-selling author, a college president, and on and on.

Today of all days, Ryan had to run into Conradt Garrisen.

"Ryan James, how're you doing, my friend?"

Garrisen was one of those old friends who came with emotional baggage. Losing Chelsea and then losing his shot at baseball had been devastating for Ryan. He'd let down himself, his daughter, his parents, his best friend, his teammates, and thousands of baseball fans who were pulling for him. Worst of all, he let down Chelsea's parents, who never said the words, but who, Ryan knew, wanted to see Ryan make it in the majors "for Chelsea." The organization had given him every chance to salvage his career, and probably no one believed in him more than the owner of the Paw-Sox, Connie Garrisen.

Dr. Garrisen was one of the most prominent physicians in Boston, where he was chief of staff at Massachusetts General Hospital. His specialty was plastic surgery for skin cancers, which afforded him a nice living, but the kind of money that made it possible for him to own the PawSox came from the commercial development of his own line of skin and antiaging products. The word on the financial street was that he and his partners were on the verge of selling their company to a major cosmetics manufacturer for nine figures. For Ryan, letting down a man like Garrisen had been no small matter. Their relationship ran deeper than baseball. Not only was Garrisen married to the assistant attorney general in charge of the state's criminal division, who was overseeing Chelsea's vehicular homicide case, but it was Garrisen, as chairman of the Board of Trustees of Brookline Academy, who had gotten Chelsea her teaching job. When she died, he established a scholarship with his own money to make it possible for Ainsley to attend school there.

"How's that beautiful Ainsley doing?" asked Garrisen. Kindergarten was always safe ground, a way to avoid talking about topics that were no longer happy. Like everyone else, Garrisen had long ago stopped asking Ryan if he was ever going back to baseball.

"She's great," said Ryan. "Really great."

"Good to hear," he said.

The polite thing would have been to ask him about Mrs. Garrisen, but since her office's investigation into Chelsea's accident had gone absolutely nowhere in three years, it seemed awkward to bring her into the conversation on the anniversary of Chelsea's death. Ryan didn't go there, which created an un-comfortable moment of silence.

"Well, it was good to see you again," said Ryan.

"Likewise," Garrisen said as he patted Ryan on the shoulder. "And don't be a stranger. Call me sometime; let me know how you're doing."

It was one of those things that old friends always said to Ryan, partly out of concern, but mainly because they didn't know what else to say.

"I will," said Ryan, knowing that he never would.

Garrisen headed toward the school's administrative offices.

Ryan continued across campus to the playground, where Ainsley was in after-care. For most of the academic year, pick-up would be in the gymnasium or library, but this was one of those beautiful September days in New England that could almost make a southerner forget about the coming winter, and kids got to play beneath a cloudless blue sky until a parent or nanny came to get them. Ryan was completing the sign-out log with the teacher's assistant when Ainsley sneaked up from behind and jumped on his back.

"Guess who!" she said, covering his eyes with her little hands.

"Uh, Beyoncé Knowles."

"No!"

"SpongeBob SquarePants."

"Daddy!"

He pulled her up and over his shoulders and turned her upside down until she giggled, her pigtails reaching for the ground.

"Oh, it's *you*," he said.

They held hands while walking to the parking lot. The school uniform for kindergarten girls was a plaid skirt,

navy-blue knee socks, and a blue ox-
ford-cloth shirt, but Ainsley was in complete violation of the dress code at day's
end, her shirttails hanging out, her
socks down to her ankles, and her
loafers scuffed from running and tus-
sling with the boys on the playground.
Ainsley loved her school, and like her
daddy, recess was her favorite subject,
but Ryan always had to drag the details
out of her.

"How was your day, sweetie?"

"Good."

"Did you have fun?"

"Yes."

"What did you do?"

"Daddy, I'm hungry."

He shook her hand. "Hi, hungry, nice
to meet you. I'm Ryan James."

Ainsley rolled her eyes. Two months
ago she would have thought a joke like
that was hilarious. She was growing up
fast.

He buckled her into the booster seat
in the car and drove out of the parking
lot. Normally, they turned left to go
home. This time, they went right.

"Wrong way, Daddy."

"We're not going straight home to-day."

"Where we going?"

"Pawtucket," he said.

"Why?"

Somehow, the word *cemetery* wouldn't come. "We have to deliver some flowers."

CHAPTER 5

The adrenaline was still pumping as Emma Carlisle left the Licht Judical Complex in Providence. Her closing argument had been flawless, the case was now in the hands of twelve jurors, and she could smell another conviction coming.

Emma was a trial attorney in the Criminal Division of the Rhode Island Office of the Attorney General, which was the prosecuting authority for all felonies throughout the nation's smallest state. Emma had joined the office right out of law school, and in five years—the last two in the Domestic Violence and Sexual Assault Unit—she had yet to lose a case. Her record was a source of pride, though admittedly it was somewhat artificial. Prosecutors didn't take losing cases to trial. Sometimes they knew who did it but couldn't prove it. Other times, the investigation failed to turn up a single suspect. It was difficult to say which scenario was more frustrating. Either way, there was still a victim, still a suffering family. Occasionally, on days like today, Emma was able to deliver a sense of justice, but the thrill of victory was short lived and, in the end, her courtroom successes only seemed to remind her that many cases were never solved. Some, she knew, would haunt her for years.

One, in particular, seemed to follow her everywhere.

"Another brilliant performance, Counselor. Any predictions?"

A microphone was suddenly in her face. The handsome courthouse reporter from the local news had ambushed her at the base of the granite staircase. Doug Wells had no cameraman with him, however, and Emma knew that the mike was just a prop.

"Predictions," she said, stopping to ponder the question. "Maybe just one: you and I will never have a second date."

"Aw, come on," he said with the smile that had won him two local Emmy Awards. "You know I don't take no for an answer."

"That was the problem with the first date."

"Fair enough. I came on too strong, I admit. But we've seen each other around the courthouse for so long that it just didn't feel like a first date to me. I said I was sorry."

Emma felt a mild sense of irony. She'd just spent the last three days prosecuting a case of date rape in which her final words to the jury were "No means no."

"And I accept your apology," she said. "But let's leave it at that, all right?"

His smile faded, his feelings obviously hurt. "Okay. Sure. I can keep it professional. But you do realize what this means, don't you?"

"What?"

He smiled again. "My cameraman will now film you only from your bad side."

"I can live with that," she said.

"Catch you later, Emma."

"Later," she said, happy to part amicably.

Rush-hour traffic was crawling toward the interstate entrance ramps, and Emma was in a hurry to return to the office before her division chief left for the day. Emma was still at that stage of her career where an integral part of the trial experience was recapping the drama for her boss, which was much more fun to do in person than over the telephone.

She stopped at the corner before crossing the street. Several copies of the *Providence Journal* were still in the self-service newsstand. In today's world of real-time reporting it contained nothing but old news by five PM, but she bought a copy anyway. The man who'd hired her out of law school was on the front page. Brandon Lomax had served as Rhode Island's attorney general before launching his campaign for the United States Senate a year ago, and he was the front-runner heading into the fall election. Emma missed him. But it was the date on the newspaper's masthead that had caught her attention: September 6.

The three-year anniversary of Chelsea's death had not been lost on her. Emma was the prosecutor on the Chelsea James vehicular homicide investigation.

Public outcry over the accident had been considerable, especially when it became apparent that Chelsea was the victim of a drunk driver. The community wanted justice, and for a time it was a high-profile investigation at the attorney general's office. She worked her contacts at local papers and used the Providence television media to appeal for leads. It turned out to be one of those frustrating cases that never turn up a suspect, never come close to the filing of criminal charges. Emma even felt mocked by one of the state's most well-known bumper stickers: IN RI DRUNK DRIVERS GET COURT. It was a play on words rooted in a dialect where the letter *r* appeared out of nowhere—where a soda was a "soder" and an idea was an "idear." Did it literally mean "court," or did drunk drivers get "caught," which in Rhode Island—"Roe Dyelin"—was pronounced "court"?

In the Chelsea James case, it meant neither.

After two years without a single lead, Emma still fought to keep the case active. Last year, when she was transferred to the sexual assault unit, all of her DUI prosecutions were reassigned to other prosecutors. All but one. The James case she held on to. Or perhaps more accurately, *it* held on to her.

Emma stood at the busy street corner flipping through the pages. She didn't even realize that the traffic light had cycled from red to green and then back to red. Today's local section contained not a single word about Chelsea James. Not that she'd expected to find one. It was as if the world had forgotten.

But Emma hadn't.

She tucked the newspaper away and crossed the street. She was just a few steps from her building when she spotted her car in the public lot across the street. The citation on the windshield

was what really caught her attention.
She'd parked the same car in the same
spot at the same time every day for a
year and never gotten a ticket. She was
sure that she'd fed the meter plenty of
change.

Meter maids on steroids strike again.

She jaywalked across Main Street to
read the bad news. But it wasn't a
ticket. Someone had neatly folded a
page from the newspaper into a rectan-
gle and left it on the driver's side. She
slid it out from under the wiper and saw
that it was the front page of the *Pawtucket Times.* The date was September
7, but she didn't have to check the year
to know that it wasn't an early edition of
tomorrow's paper. The headline read:
TRAGEDY FOR PAWSOX STAR. The beautiful young woman in the color photograph staring back at her was Chelsea
James.

Emma had seen it several times, but it
still chilled her—chilled her more than
ever before. She wasn't sure if the impact stemmed from the fact that today
was the third anniversary of Chelsea's
death, or if the added creep factor came

from the thought of someone going to the trouble of leaving an old newspaper on her windshield.

Emma checked for a signature or a note that would reveal the sender's identity. She found only a few curious markings. Certain words on the front page were underlined, and each underlining was numbered one through five. Three of the words were from the article about Chelsea, but two of them were from another front-page story. The numbers were not sequential—if she read left to right, top to bottom, the number sequence was three-one-two-four-five. But when she read the words in the order of the assigned number, one through five, it created a sentence.

" 'I know who did it,' " she said, reading aloud.

She checked again for a signature, but there was none. Someone was being cute and clever, but Emma still had to take it seriously for what it might be: a note from an anonymous tipster who claimed to have seen the car and the drunk driver who ran Chelsea off the road.

She put the newspaper into her trial satchel, careful not to smudge any possible fingerprints, and headed back across the street to the Office of the Attorney General.

CHAPTER 6

It was up to Emma and the chief of the Criminal Division, assistant attorney general Glenda Garrisen, Dr. Connie Garrisen's wife, to decide what to do about the anonymous tip.

"Use the media," said the chief.

"I'm not suggesting that we reveal the tipster's unusual MO—the way the message was crafted from underlined and numbered words in a newspaper. That would just trigger copycats."

"Agreed."

"The media is the only way for us to communicate with this source. If he's for real, we want to encourage him to keep talking to us. If this is a hoax, we want to remind him that giving false tips to law enforcement is a crime we will prosecute."

"Emma, I said go for it. So go."

It was the green light Emma was hoping for.

The Chelsea James investigation might have been cold for some, but for Emma the details remained fresh: the make and model of the car, the street name, the official time of death. She didn't even have to retrieve the file to draft the press release. By 6:45 it was finished. It was time for dinner.

She chose to eat crow—and call her *Action News* "friend" Doug Wells.

"I need a favor," she said.

"Well, isn't this an interesting turn of events?"

Somehow, she just knew he was grinning on the other end of the line.

"This is important," she said. "There's a possible break in one of my cold cases. The Chelsea James accident."

"Oh, yeah. The ballplayer's wife. Very sad. I did a story on that."

"Can you run an update at eleven?"

"If it's newsworthy."

Good answer. She'd almost expected him to say "If you'll have dinner with me."

Chelsea said, "I'll e-mail you the press release."

"Press release? You mean you're not giving me the exclusive?"

The guy never stopped pushing buttons. "You're the first one I called," said Emma. "Does that count for anything?"

"Not really. But I'm a pushover. Send it to me. I'll see what I can do."

She thanked him and hung up before he could take the conversation in the usual direction.

What other talking heads owe me a favor?

She gazed out her office window, thinking. The sun was setting, the long shadows of downtown Providence ushering in darkness. It was a beautiful sunset, but an eerie feeling came over her as she realized that three years ago, to the minute, Chelsea was driving to the PawSox game with their two-year-old daughter in the backseat. They had to have been excited about going to see

Ryan play. Maybe Chelsea was even a little anxious about running late. Without question, she was completely unaware of how defenseless she and Ainsley were against another driver who'd had too much to drink, who'd dared to feed his addiction at the cost of a young mother's life. Emma was suddenly thinking about Ryan too, inside the stadium wondering why his wife and daughter weren't there for such an important game.

Ryan. He needs to know.

She couldn't let him hear about this latest tip on the eleven o'clock news. The same went for Chelsea's parents. From a professional standpoint, a phone call from the Victim Services Unit would have sufficed. On a personal level, however, it didn't seem like enough. Emma grabbed her briefcase and hurried downstairs to her car. She made a few more calls to her media contacts while on the road. At the freeway exit she dialed Ryan's number on her cell. He was pleasant enough, given the anniversary, but he did seem puzzled by her call.

"I'm in the neighborhood," she said. "I'd like to stop by, if that's okay. We may have a break in the case."

He didn't hesitate to invite her over.

It was after eight PM when Emma knocked on the door. The curtain in the bowfront window moved, and through the shining pane of glass Emma saw the glinting eyes of a young girl who checked her out and then disappeared.

"Daddy, somebody's here!" the little voice from inside called.

The door opened a minute later, and Ryan greeted her. Emma didn't answer right away. He'd sounded very together on the telephone, but the look in Ryan's eyes and the sadness in his smile only confirmed that no homicide had only one victim.

"Are you sure this is a good time?" she said.

"Of course."

He took her coat as she entered, and Emma heard the patter of Ainsley's little feet scampering up the stairs. They went into the living room, which was way too small for the sixty-inch big-screen television in the corner, but that kind of thing was to be expected from an ex-jock with no woman in the house. The place was otherwise furnished nicely in a Rooms To Go kind of way. The framed photographs lent a homey feeling. Emma noticed about a dozen of Chelsea.

"Did you eat supper yet?" asked Ryan. "Ainsley never touched her grilled chicken breast. Five-year-olds, you know. They live on the bag of Cheetos they eat ten minutes before coming to the dinner table."

"I'm fine, thanks. I don't want to intrude. I have some important news for you."

She removed the press release from her purse and showed it to him.

He read it once to himself, then reread the key language aloud: " 'Assistant attorney general Glenda Garrisen announced that late yesterday afternoon a trial attorney in the Criminal Division was contacted by an anonymous tipster who may have information pertinent to the ongoing investigation into the death of Chelsea James.' " He looked up from the release and said, "I assume that 'trial attorney in the Criminal Division' means you?"

"Yes."

"What did he tell you?"

"Well, I don't know if it's a he or a she. But as for what was said, I think it's easier if I just show you."

She opened her briefcase and gave him a photocopy of the newspaper. Just the sight of the three-year-old headline and Chelsea's photograph seemed to take Ryan's breath away.

"I'm sorry," she said. "I want to keep you informed as much as possible."

"It's okay," he said.

Ryan studied it for a moment, reading aloud once again—" 'I know who did it' "—as he decoded the tipster's message.

"Why the cryptic word game?" said Ryan.

"I don't know."

"Why would it take three years for him to come forward? And why anonymously?"

"Don't know that either."

"Any possible leads on his identity?"

"Fingerprints can remain intact on

porous surfaces like newspapers for
decades, so I sent the original down to
the state crime lab to check for prints.
I'll have results in the morning."

He handed the copy back to her. "I'm
glad you're going public with this.
Somewhere out there is a drunk driver
who probably thinks this case has gone
away."

"That's the way I see it," said Emma.
"Getting this back in the news puts the
heat on him again."

"Maybe he'll do something stupid to
make sure his tracks are still covered—
something that will finally get him
caught."

"That's possible."

"Maybe Chelsea's death has been
weighing on his conscience for three
years. This could be the thing that finally
makes him come forward and confess."

She didn't want to crush him, but she
had to keep his expectations realistic. "I
wouldn't get your hopes up about that."

"You never know. There was a story
on the news not too long ago about
a forty-something-year-old guy who
cleaned himself up through Alcoholics

Anonymous and wrote a letter of apology to a woman he raped back in college."

"I saw that too."

"So those things do happen."

About once every generation, she thought. "Yes, they happen."

Emma tucked the copy of the newspaper back into her briefcase. "I was going to drop by to see Chelsea's parents as well," she said. "I didn't want any of you to hear about this on the news."

"I don't think that's a good idea tonight," said Ryan. "I'll call them. I don't see any need to show them the actual newspaper with the coded tip anyway. Seeing that headline again with Chelsea's picture . . . well, that's just tough on the anniversary."

"I understand."

Emma took another look at his tired expression. The man probably hadn't slept in two days. Her heart went out to all victims but, without question, Ryan was the survivor she worried about most.

They looked at each other not knowing what to say.

"Daddy, will you read to me?" Ainsley was standing at the top of the staircase, dressed in her pink pajamas with the clashing Red Sox logo.

Ryan seemed to welcome the interruption. "In a few minutes, sweetheart. Can you come down here? There's someone I want you to say hello to."

Ainsley laid her book on the top step and walked slowly down the carpeted staircase. Emma tried not to do an obvious double take, because she knew the uncanny resemblance must have been a source of joy and pain to Ryan. His wife had been an astounding beauty, and although this gorgeous little girl was as much his daughter as hers, she was all Chelsea.

Ainsley went straight to her daddy and curled up in his lap.

Ryan said, "Do you remember Ms. Carlisle?"

Ainsley shook her head.

Emma said, "I'm not surprised. She was probably three the last time I saw her."

Ryan said, "Ms. Carlisle is a lawyer."

"You're pretty."

Emma blushed. "Thank you."

"Ms. Carlisle is also a very smart woman."

"How smart?" said Ainsley.

Ryan said, "One of the smartest people I've ever met."

Ainsley looked at Emma as if to quiz her. "Do you know the song 'Twinkle, Twinkle, Little Star'?"

"Sure I do. Would you like me to sing it?"

"No," said Ainsley, her tone making it clear that she had another question in mind. "Do you know what star is closest to Earth?"

Emma had to think about that one. She seemed to recall from the old Jodi Foster movie *Contact* that it was in the Alpha Centauri system, but she was somewhat surprised that a child would have learned that in kindergarten.

"It's the sun," said Ainsley.

Emma laughed at herself for having made the question so complicated.

"As usual, the answer is much closer than I thought it was," she said, and for some reason, she looked at Ryan when she said it. And he was looking at her.

It was as if they could feel Chelsea's presence in the room.

Not in a creepy Sixth-Sense-I-see-dead-people kind of way. It was more of a simultaneous recognition of the deep bond of trust that defined their unusual friendship. And it was unusual—in ways Emma probably could never explain to Ryan. Emma was committed to all victims, as well as their families. Driving an hour to Boston to soften the blow about a development in a case typified the deep sense of humanity she brought to her job as a prosecutor. That kind of commitment didn't leave much time for a personal life, but Emma had always been perfectly happy to keep her career on track and her relationships uncomplicated. In all honesty, living in her world of sexual assaults and domestic violence, prosecuting rapists and wife beaters on a daily basis, Emma had almost given up hope that true love existed. The overwhelming love that Ryan felt toward his wife touched Emma deeply. For that she felt strangely but profoundly indebted to Ryan.

And to Chelsea.

"Daddy, can you read to me now?"

It was the voice of innocence, another bit of comfort.

"Sure he can," said Emma, rising. "I should be going."

Ryan carried Ainsley in his arms as he escorted Emma to the door.

"Thank you for driving all the way up here," said Ryan.

"It's the least I can do. I want you to feel assured that even though I've transferred to the Domestic Violence and Sexual Assault Unit, I'm still on the case, following up every lead."

"I appreciate that."

They shook hands—more in friendship than a purely professional relationship—and Emma said goodnight.

Ryan read the story of the stray dog to Ainsley three times until she finally fell asleep.

He reached for the bedside lamp and switched it off. The way she breathed in and out so gently, her little hand against her cheek, she looked like an angel beneath her Bambi-and-Thumper blanket with the white lace trim. Ainsley seemed much younger to him when she slept. She was growing up fast. The things that came out of her mouth continually amazed him. *Do you know what star is closest to Earth?* Her mother would have been really proud.

I'm so sorry, Chelsea.

Ryan kissed his daughter on the forehead, then tiptoed out of her room and went downstairs. It was dark in the living room, but he didn't turn on the lights or the television. He just lowered himself into the armchair and sat in silence, staring out the bowfront window. Sometimes when he was up late at night, unable or afraid to fall sleep, he could see Chelsea walk up the street and smile at him as she passed by the apartment. She was not a ghost. Whenever he was alone, away from Ainsley, Chelsea was the only thing that made him feel alive.

Anniversaries were the worst. People always told him that things would get better, and at times he even believed them. But not on Chelsea's birthday, not on their wedding anniversary, not on the anniversary of the day they met—and definitely not on the anniversary of the day she died.

Ryan checked his watch. Nine-thirty-three. Chelsea had been dead exactly three years and ninety-seven minutes.

The one-year anniversary had been much worse. He had opened a bottle of bourbon and dragged out every old photograph of Chelsea, every love note she had ever written to him, every memento that could possibly increase his suffering. Those were the bad old days when he was still asking why, a question that tumbled round and round inside his heart like a shard of glass. Ryan had not yet been released from the PawSox, but he knew the ax was coming at the conclusion of that horrendous season after Chelsea's death. When he got the official word in mid-September, his friend Ivan drove him to Roxbury the following Sunday to listen to a minister who had lost his son, sister, brother, nephew and niece—all murdered. "God is telling me—He's telling all survivors—that we need Him," was the preacher's message. It helped a little. Perhaps the meaning would have stuck if Ryan had been able to get a decent night's sleep.

The insomnia, his grief counselor had told him, was partly about guilt. At least a million times Ryan had replayed in his mind the things he could have done differently—things that might have kept Chelsea alive after the accident, things that might have kept her from getting into the accident in the first place. He should have made a nuisance of himself in the emergency room, whipped those doctors into shape, let them know that they had better not let his wife and Ainsley's mother die young. He should never have insisted that Chelsea come to the PawSox game, should have let her go to her night class at Suffolk, should have arranged for someone else to drive her after such a stressful day at work, should have made her buy a bigger and safer car, should have asked for a damn trade to the Dodgers and moved the whole family to Los Angeles—should have, should have . . .

Three years of guilt. But it was the fear that kept him walking the floors at night.

Ryan rose from his chair and went to the closet. On the top shelf, in a shoe box, was a collection of old DVDs. He grabbed one at random and shoved it into the DVD player. Chelsea suddenly appeared on-screen, smiling and wearing a white veil. It was the video her maid of honor had taken before their wedding.

Ryan's counselor had told him to put the old movies away, but on anniversaries and other milestones—the nights he *knew* would be sleepless—he couldn't let go. It was all tied to the fear, which in some ways felt a lot like grieving, the panic attacks, the sudden chills and breathlessness. But it was different. Emma had no idea how much she had exacerbated that fear tonight by telling Ryan that she had a possible lead on a suspect. Not that he didn't long to find out who had done it.

He feared what he might do once he knew.

I'm gonna kill him.

Ryan went to his chair, fighting back tears in a lonely, dark room where the only source of light was the recorded on-screen image of his beautiful bride-to-be.

I'm sorry, Chelsea. But I just know I'm going to kill that son of a bitch.

CHAPTER 7

Ryan woke with only a semiconscious awareness that someone was nudging his arm. He grumbled, and the nudge turned into a shove with the force of a linebacker.

"Mr. James," said the soft voice of a woman. "Mr. James, wake up."

Things slowly came into focus. He was still in his living room, slouched in the armchair. The light from the lamp across the room was only sixty watts, but it assaulted his eyes like lasers.

"You have to get up, sir."

The bowfront window was black with night. "What time is it?"

"Five-thirty."

Only upon her mention of the ungodly hour did Ryan recognize the voice.

Claricia Castillo had been Connie and Glenda Garrisen's full-time housekeeper for years, but they'd offered her services to Ryan when he and Ainsley moved to Boston. At first, it was merely a second job for Claricia, but soon she was like a grandmother to Ainsley—*la muñeca,* she called her, "the doll," *un regalo de Dios,* "a gift from God." Claricia arrived with a smile every weekday morning at five-thirty sharp to straighten up the house, get Ainsley ready for school, and drop her off at Brookline Academy by eight. From there Claricia went to the Garrisen's brownstone on Beacon Hill for her regular day job. The arrangement gave her extra money to send to her five sisters in Bogotá, and it was the only way Ryan as a single dad could do a morning radio talk show at six.

"You're going to be late," said Claricia.

Ryan was in a daze. The last time he'd checked the clock, it was almost four AM. He'd finally broken down and taken one of the sleeping pills his doctor had prescribed.

"I can't do the show this morning."

Claricia shot him a reproving look and said something in her native tongue that needed no translation.

"You're upset," he said.

"Upset? Why would I be upset? *La muñeca*—of course she needs a father who is a drunk. What little girl doesn't? I'm not upset."

"I wasn't drinking," said Ryan.

"You said that last time."

She was right. The police had stopped him on suspicion of drunk driving. It was the lingering effect of a sleeping pill that had made his driving so erratic, but the media reported, "Radio talk-show host and former PawSox star Ryan James was arrested on drunk-driving charges." He was eventually vindicated, and the charges were dropped. But it didn't stop people—even Claricia—from suspecting a drinking problem. Never mind the studies showing that people who stayed awake for upward of twenty hours drove worse than people with a blood-alcohol level above the legal limit. Ryan could only imagine where he would have fallen in that study—awake for twenty hours or more *every day* for the past three years.

"I'm going up to bed," he said.

Claricia was already busy straightening up the living room.

"*La muñeca* needs a father without a job too," she said, never looking up from her work.

Ryan climbed the stairs slowly. On some level he appreciated her well-intended tough love, but going to work in this condition was more likely to earn him a pink slip than not showing up at all. Upstairs, Ryan found his BlackBerry on the dresser and fired off an I'm-not-feeling-well message to his cohost. His head hit the pillow, and he hoped the sleeping pill he'd swallowed ninety minutes earlier would kick in and carry him off to dreamland. He worried that it wouldn't. He worried that worrying about it would keep him awake.

Just close your eyes, relax, breathe in and out, relax, think happy thoughts, relax.

This was such bullshit. Falling asleep

was like hitting a baseball—the insomniac who tried to break down a good night's sleep into its component parts was no better off than the hitter who tried to break out of a slump by overanalyzing his swing.

Ryan's eyes popped open. The clock said 6:25 AM.

Shit! Why did Claricia have to wake me?

The sleeping pill he'd taken at four was now an official waste of time.

Ryan rolled out of bed, unplugged the alarm clock, and hid it in the closet. The clock was to night as the cattle prod was to sadists. His mattress beckoned, but he hesitated before sliding back beneath the covers. Reconditioning rule number one: Never climb into the bed until you are ready to go to sleep. Ryan had been ready for three years. It didn't seem to matter.

He returned to the closet. There was an assortment of pillows on the top shelf, from extra soft to extra firm, goose down to synthetic. It brought to mind his wedding day and the old Dominican saying that Ivan had shared about the inverse relationship between the number of pillows on the bed and the number of times a couple used it to make love—Ivan's way of saying "don't let the things you accumulate in a marriage get in the way of what's really important."

Ryan grabbed a dozen pillows from the closet and tossed them onto the empty side—Chelsea's side—of the bed. One of them was sure to do the trick. Or not. He chose one made of "memory foam" and forced his eyes shut. They didn't want to stay closed, but he was not going to let those single, tiny muscles in his upper eyelids win this battle again. Tonight, or this morning—whatever the hell time it was—the eyes were going to shut and stay shut, and Ryan James was going to the land of nod, damn it.

How can I be so dead tired and not fall asleep?

The telephone rang. It seemed like a minute later. Or a day later. Maybe that sleeping pill had worked after all, and he had only dreamed about not being able to fall asleep.

Fat chance.

Ryan grabbed the phone from the nightstand and checked the caller ID display for the time—8:10 AM—and the number. It was his in-laws. Rachel probably wanted to know why he wasn't on the radio. He let it ring through to the answering machine. All hope of falling back to sleep was lost, but he didn't feel like talking on the telephone. He didn't feel like getting out of bed. He didn't feel like turning his head three inches to the right to avert the annoying ray of sunlight that was streaming into his left eye. He didn't feel like anything.

He just couldn't believe that Chelsea had been dead for over three years.

"No answer," said Rachel Townsend.

Her husband shrugged it off. "Let's just get this over with."

"If we're going to talk to the police, I'd like Ryan to be here."

Paul Townsend went to his wife, looked her in the eye, and rested a reassuring hand on each of her shoulders— the near embrace that had come to define their marriage.

"It will be fine," he said. "Come on."

Paul led her into the living room. A nice-looking man dressed in a blue suit and white shirt rose as they entered. He'd been waiting only a short time, while Paul tried to pry his nervous wife out of the kitchen.

"Rachel, this is . . ." Paul stopped himself. "I'm sorry. Your name again?"

The man offered a courteous smile and a business card. "Benjamin. Lieutenant Keith Benjamin. Rhode Island Sheriff's Department."

He shook Rachel's hand as Paul checked his business card.

"This won't take long at all," said Benjamin. "It's just routine follow-up to the tip the attorney general's office received. I'm sure you saw the report on the news last night."

"Actually, our son-in-law called to tell us about it before it aired."

"Good. Basically we're just trying to do everything we can to determine if this is legitimate or not. If you don't mind, I'd like to ask a few questions."

"Well—" Rachel began to say.

"Sure," said Paul.

Paul and Rachel took a seat on the couch. Benjamin seated himself in the armchair. A framed photograph of Chelsea rested on the cocktail table between them.

"I'll keep this short and sweet," said Benjamin. He took a pen and notepad from his coat pocket. "Any idea who this tipster might be?"

"No," said Paul.

Rachel shook her head.

"What do you think of the list of possibilities the attorney general's office has come up with so far?"

"List?" said Paul.

"I don't mean a formal written list," said Benjamin. "I know that the prosecutor's office has some names they're considering."

"If they do, they haven't shared them with us," said Paul. "Isn't that right, Rachel?"

"I haven't heard any names," said Rachel.

"So no one from the AG's office, the sheriff's office—no one—has expressed any thoughts or theories to you as to this tipster's identity?"

"No," said Paul.

"Oh, I see."

"Can you share them with us?" said Paul.

"I'm sort of reluctant to, without Ms. Carlisle's approval. She may want to handle that personally."

"Can you call her?"

Benjamin checked his watch. "It wouldn't do any good. She's in trial. So for now, I don't see any reason to take up any more of your time," he said as he started to rise. Then he sat back down. "But, hey—is your son at home?"

"Yes," said Paul. "He's upstairs in his room."

"I have a few questions for him too."

Rachel sat up, and Paul could almost see the mother bear's protective claws emerging.

"What kind of questions?" she said.

"Along the same lines I asked you."

"I'm sure Babes doesn't know anything," she said.

Benjamin gave her a polite but firm smile. "If it's all the same to you, ma'am, I'd like to hear it from his own mouth. It's just me—I do things by the book."

Rachel matched his polite but firm smile—and then some. "You obviously don't understand. Babes—Daniel—has Asperger's syndrome."

"So . . . is he deaf?"

"No."

"Mute?"

"No."

"Mentally incompetent?"

"Not at all."

Benjamin shrugged. "Then what's the problem?"

Rachel was now at the edge of her seat, almost leaning over the cocktail table. "The problem is that—"

"There is no problem," said Paul.

Rachel raised a hand, blinking slowly to emphasize her annoyance at the interruption. When it was clear that the men had deigned to give her the floor, she continued. "Asperger's syndrome is a pervasive development disorder that is often grouped under the unofficial term *autism spectrum disorder.* Daniel was not diagnosed until . . ."

Blah, blah, blah. Paul Townsend had heard Rachel's speech a thousand times, and he'd been tuning out for as long as he could remember.

"As a child with higher than average intelligence," said Rachel, "he appeared to be developing normally in terms of expressive speech and motor development: sitting, crawling, standing, walking. He was on schedule for basic self-help skills, toilet training, self-feeding, and manipulation of common objects."

Good Lord, the woman talks like a textbook.

Paul longed for the fun and spontaneous Rachel who used to tell jokes and make him laugh. Not that they hadn't enjoyed Babes. When their little boy stood up at his third birthday party and not only recited but spelled the names of all fifty states, Paul was the proud daddy. When Babes heard the story of the infamous Chicago "Black Sox" and transformed part of the Shoeless Joe Jackson dialogue—It ain't so, Joe—into "Is too, Jane," Paul laughed right along with everyone else. Paul even went out and bought baseball equipment. That didn't fly. None of the plans Paul had for his son worked out. By elementary school it was obvious that something was different—*really* different—and that Babes was never going to change. Rachel changed. The life that Paul, Rachel, and Chelsea had known and hoped for was forever changed.

"Babes!" Paul shouted.

"What are you dong?" said Rachel. "I haven't finished."

"Yes, you have," said Paul. "Babes, come down here!"

"Leave him be," said Rachel.

"If Detective Benjamin wants to talk to him, he can talk to him."

"What, Dad?" said Babes. He was standing in the hallway, as if afraid to enter the room.

"Come in here," said Paul.

Babes took a half step forward.

"All the way in. Sit down."

Babes shuffled more than walked across the room, his head down, making eye contact with no one. He went to the armchair closest to his mother and almost slid into the sitting position, his posture perfectly erect, his knees together, the palms of his hands flat atop his thighs.

"This is Detective Benjamin," said Paul. "He has a few questions he'd like to ask you."

Babes was silent.

Benjamin looked at Paul and said, "I hope this isn't a problem, but I'd really prefer to talk to Babes one on one. Man to man, so to speak, just the two of us."

Rachel dismissed it with a wave of her hand. "Well, I'm afraid that just isn't poss—"

"It's fine," said Paul. "Rachel, let's go. We'll wait in the kitchen." He rose, started out of the room, and then stopped. Rachel hadn't moved.

"Rachel, I said we'll wait in the kitchen."

She breathed out her anger, then leaned toward Babes to pat the back of his hand. He withdrew, and she backed off, giving him only verbal support.

"If you need me, sweetheart, I'll be just a few feet away."

Rachel rose, and Paul pushed open the swinging door that led to the kitchen. He went to the counter and took a seat. Rachel stood at the door, leaving it open a crack, and watched her son.

"You have always coddled him," said Paul.

"Shush. I'm trying to hear."

"Don't shush me. Look at yourself. Do you think that's good for Babes?"

She shot him an angry look. "Don't pretend to know what's best for him. You don't even know his doctors."

"How could I? How could *anyone*? Let me see, would that be his psychologist? His psychiatrist? His neurologist, neuropsychologist, psychotherapist? The family doctor? Or maybe you're still in the world of pediatrics, which I say he should have left behind when he turned eighteen. His developmental pediatrician, pediatric psychologist, pediatric psychiatrist, pediatric neurologist, general pediatrician? Which one do you mean, Rachel?"

"Lots of young people continue to see their pediatric physicians into their twenties. The important thing was for Babes to find the right doctor."

"It was important for Chelsea to go to a good school too. It was important for

us to give her and Ryan a decent wedding. It was important to take a family
vacation every now and then. But there
wasn't ten cents left for any of those
things. I run a stinking little hardware
store, not a bank."

Rachel was still peering through the
crack in the doorway, but she was apparently listening. "A family does what it
has to do."

"Yes, I agree with that. But you have
always *over*done it. Do you remember
those business cards you printed up to
hand out to people in restaurants? 'My
son has an autism-related disorder.
Thank you for your patience.' People
thought you were nuts."

"I was just ahead of the times. I'll have
you know that some of the top experts
in the world recommend that parents
have a card like that handy."

"Yes, to pass out *after* your child has
an embarrassing meltdown in a public
place. Not to hand out to everyone in
the restaurant as you walk in. I swear,
sometimes it seems like you *prefer* having a son with AS."

Rachel let the door swing closed. She

turned slowly to face her husband, her expression stone cold. "You wish it had been him, don't you."

"What?"

"Don't you think Babes can sense it? If you could ask God to rewrite history, you'd have Him take Babes instead of Chelsea."

"Oh, please," he said, his voice rising. "Don't bring God into this."

"Mom!" Babes shouted.

"See, now you've upset him."

"Me? What did I do?"

Rachel shoved the door open and dashed into the living room. Paul started after her, but then he stopped. He'd had enough of this.

He paced angrily across the kitchen floor, not sure how to vent. That was a cruel thing for Rachel to have said—to suggest that he would ever wish for something like that, wish for one life over another, wish his own son into the grave. Wishing was for fools, anyway, at least when the wish was for things that could never come true. In that respect, Paul Townsend was as foolish as the next guy.

He wished that Babes didn't have Asperger's.

And more than anything, he wished that Chelsea were still alive.

Paul grabbed his coat and went out the back door for the one thing that had become the hallmark of his marriage.

Time alone.

CHAPTER 8

Around eleven-thirty Ryan emerged from the bedroom and grabbed the newspaper from the front step. He thumbed through the *Herald* in the open doorway. The Boston papers apparently hadn't picked up Emma's press release. He walked back to the computer in the kitchen and checked online. The *ProJo* had the story on page one, below the theoretical flap: NEW LIFE FOR INVESTIGATION INTO DEATH OF PAWSOX WIFE.

Good job, Emma.

He was suddenly hungry, but not just for anything. These old pangs were calling out for Juan in a Million, an unfussy

Tex-Mex joint in Austin that was famous for its award-winning breakfast tacos. The key ingredients were open to debate—corn versus flour tortillas, whole versus refried beans, bacon versus chorizo, real cheese versus processed, potatoes or none—but one thing was settled: breakfast tacos were the de rigueur morning-after grub at the University of Texas. The aftereffects of a sleeping pill weren't technically a hangover, but they were a pretty fair excuse for something sinfully delicious.

Ryan found one waiting for him in the refrigerator. Claricia had made it for him before taking Ainsley to school. Breakfast tacos weren't even remotely Colombian cuisine, but Claricia was a fast learner and always eager to please. It was her way of letting him know that she wasn't mad at him anymore.

God bless you, Claricia.

The phone rang as he popped his breakfast into the microwave. His mother-in-law was not about to go away quietly. This time he answered.

"Why weren't you on the radio this morning?" she said.

"I think I've got the flu."

Ryan expected a challenge to his obvious lie, but Chelsea's mother had more important news: "A detective came to see us."

That seemed odd, after all the talk of how Emma was too sensitive to the anniversary of Chelsea's death to visit them last night. Sending a cop—a total stranger—the next morning didn't seem like Emma.

"What was his name?"

She answered in a voice that sounded as though she were reading his name from a business card. Ryan had dealt with several detectives over the years relating to the accident, but the name Benjamin didn't ring a bell.

"What was the other guy's name?"

"What other guy?"

"His partner."

"He came alone," she said.

That seemed strange to Ryan, but maybe it was just because they didn't do it that way on *Law & Order.*

"This isn't right," said Rachel. "Emma should have at least called one of us to say that a detective was coming."

"You're right. That isn't like Emma."

"And he was so rude. He insisted on speaking alone to Babes. Naturally, he's all upset now. Paul's angry. This family can't operate like this."

"I understand. Let me give Emma a call and see what this is all about."

"It won't do any good. Detective Benjamin said she's in trial all day."

"How does he know that?"

"I don't know. I just assumed he would know."

Ryan's suspicions were growing, but he didn't want to sound paranoid. "Hold on a second," he said. "I'll dial her on my cell now."

After three rings, Emma answered.

"Emma, hi. It's Ryan James. Did I get you at a bad time?"

"No, this is fine."

"I thought you might be in trial."

"No, not today. I'm waiting on a jury verdict."

Apparently, Lieutenant Benjamin had bad info. "Hey, do you know anything about the detective from the Rhode Island Sheriff's Department who visited Chelsea's parents this morning?"

"This morning?" she said, surprise in her voice. "No."

"I have Rachel on the phone now. She's pretty upset."

"Ryan, I am truly sorry about that. But this is news to me. What were their names?"

"That's another weird thing. There was just one guy. Lieutenant Benjamin."

"Benjamin?" she said. "Not anyone I know. Hold on a second, let me pull up my directory."

Ryan waited as she scrolled down her computer screen, muttering "Benjamin, Benjamin, Benjamin" into his ear.

"Are you sure about the name?"

"Hold on," said Ryan. He double checked with Rachel and then got back on the line with Emma.

"Rachel tells me she's reading straight from the business card he gave her— 'Lieutenant Keith Benjamin, Rhode Island Sheriff's Department.' "

There was silence.

"Okay," Emma said finally. "Here's the thing: we don't have a Lieutenant Benjamin."

CHAPTER 9

Emma was an hour closer to Pawtucket than Ryan was, and she arrived while he was still on the road.

Paul and Rachel Townsend had been married twenty-eight years, and they still lived in the brownstone flat that Chelsea had grown up in. They were wearing sweaters—the chill in the air was a reminder that the official start of autumn was only days away—and were seated in patio chairs outside on the covered front porch. Babes was off by himself at a small round table in the corner of the porch. An open newspaper was spread out before him. His elbows were on the table, and his hands were in his hair, as if he were trying to pull the thoughts out of his head. Babes read his newspaper the way Emma studied her legal research. He didn't look up, didn't move a muscle as Paul and Rachel rose to greet Emma.

Emma said, "Sorry to pull you out of your own house. A forensic team will be here shortly. We didn't want you walking around touching things, possibly destroying fingerprints. I'm determined to find out who this impostor Lieutenant Benjamin was."

"This is really scary," said Rachel.

Paul said, "Babes, say hello to Ms. Carlisle."

Emma didn't take it personally that Babes didn't respond. She understood him better now. To see Chelsea's brother laughing at her funeral had been a shock, but Rachel had pulled Emma aside to explain that Babes wasn't cold, mean, uncaring, and unsympathetic. "It's not that Babes doesn't feel at all," she'd told Emma, "it's that he feels too much. It's confusing for him." At first, Emma simply took Mrs. Townsend's word for it. As the investigation wore on, Emma had no doubt in her mind that this mother was right about her son, and that Babes loved Chelsea with all his heart.

"Oh, never mind," said Paul.

Rachel tried a sweeter tone. "Babes, Ms. Carlisle is here."

No answer. Emma guessed that he truly hadn't heard his mother, though it had nothing to do with a hearing disability. If Babes stared at the newspaper any harder, he might burn a hole in it.

Emma said, "He's quite the voracious reader."

"Yes, anything sports. He loves to collect information. That's his AS."

Paul rose, suddenly annoyed. "I'm going to get a root beer. Anybody want something?"

"Don't go through the living room," said Rachel.

"I'll walk around back. The good lieutenant didn't go into the kitchen. Emma, something to drink?"

"No, thank you."

"Babes, you want a soder?"

No answer. Paul shook his head,

climbed down the front steps, and headed around to the back of the house.

"Paul's a little out of sorts," said Rachel.

"I understand. This impostor in your house has us all concerned."

"Honestly, it started before that. Yesterday marked three years since Chelsea passed. The anniversaries don't get any easier."

"I'm sure that's very difficult for everyone."

"But it's even harder than you might imagine for Paul. From the day she was born, Chelsea was her daddy's girl. That became even more true with Babes and his special needs. I had less and less time for Paul or Chelsea, which seemed to draw them closer to each other. No regrets. It's just a fact."

Her concern for Paul was interesting. Emma couldn't help but notice how much Rachel had aged in the three years since her daughter's death. Some of the lines seemed carved in wax.

"How is Babes holding up?"

Rachel breathed in and out, as if taken

by the size of the question. "It depends on which doctor you talk to. One thinks he's taking on aspects of obsessive compulsive disorder."

"How so?"

"He obsesses about keeping people safe. But if you talk to other doctors, they will say it's not OCD. It's persever-ation of thoughts."

"What does that mean?"

Rachel glanced across the porch at her son. He was still absorbed in his newspaper. No way was he listening. "He can get stuck on a certain event or situation and be unable to let go. It was really bad right after Chelsea died. Get-ting Babes to ride in a car was virtually impossible. He walked or took the bus everywhere. Sometimes he walked a mile out of his way just to avoid cross-ing certain busy streets."

"Is that still the case?"

"Not as bad. But in other ways, he's worse. I'm sure you remember how he's totally into anagrams, right?"

"Yeah. Baseball, as I recall."

"His anagrams are less about sports these days. They're more about danger and violence—particularly against women."

Emma's gaze shifted toward Babes. He was still reading the same page of the newspaper, but his hands were out of his hair. He was squeezing a Koosh ball, one of those squishy stress relievers.

"That looks to be the sports page he's reading now," said Emma.

"Baseball is still his special thing. He probably reads three or four sports sections a day. Babes also says it's important to know your enemy," she said with a wan smile, "so we got him a subscription to the *New York Times*. And he never throws anything away. Like I said, he reads to collect information. You should see his bedroom. Stacked floor to ceiling."

"He saves newspapers?" said Emma.

"And magazines. Everything from the *Pawtucket Times* to *Sports Illustrated*. Paul says that one of these days the floor will collapse from all that weight."

Emma suddenly had a thought. "Did this Lieutenant Benjamin speak to Babes?"

"As a matter of fact, he seemed determined to speak to Babes alone. Paul and his tough love for Babes—he insisted that we leave the room and let that impostor have his time alone with Babes. Poor boy is still traumatized about it."

"What did he and Babes talk about?"

"I don't know. I was in the kitchen with Paul, and I can't get Babes to open up about it."

Emma glanced in Babes's direction. "Do you mind if I talk to him?"

Rachel bristled.

"I won't push," said Emma. "I'll keep it light."

"Well," she said tentatively, "I guess that would be okay."

Emma crossed the porch and sat in the ice-cream chair at the little round table opposite Babes. He was so into his newspaper that he didn't notice her. She took her BlackBerry from her purse and laid it on the table beside his newspaper.

"You have one of these, Babes?"

His gaze slowly shifted from the sports page to the BlackBerry.

Emma said, "I can get the Internet on that. You want to pull up some baseball scores?"

He picked it up and pushed a few buttons, but his focus remained unchanged. "Can I get the *Times* article I'm reading?" he asked.

"Absolutely. What's it about?"

His posture straightened, his eyes brightened. He was suddenly engaged; they were talking about what he wanted to talk about. "The San Diego Padres are in New York to play the Mets this week."

"Are you a Mets fan?"

"Heavens, no."

Heavens, no, thought Emma. She had forgotten how stiff and formal Babes's speech could be.

Babes continued, "The article is of particular interest to me, however, because it is about former Boston Red Sox catcher Josh Bard, who was a career .240 hitter with the Red Sox and has batted an astonishing .338 in 231 at bats since being traded to the National League Padres."

"I see," said Emma. It was precisely

the kind of statistical detail that would captivate Babes, recited exactly the way he'd read it and committed it to memory. He continued to summarize the article in language more suitable for the printed word. It was more of a monologue than a conversation. Emma pretended to be interested, but then something really did catch her attention. It was a curious item that bore out the earlier comment from Rachel about the change in Babes's anagrams—the shift in focus from sports to danger and violence.

In the newspaper's masthead, each of the printed letters in *The New York Times* was crossed out in pen and rearranged by hand into "They strike women."

"That's an interesting anagram," said Emma.

"Oh. Just something I came up with."

Emma noticed another anagram in the body of the article. "What's that one say?"

"Nothing, really."

"Can I see?"

He shrugged, seemingly reluctant to

share. But he didn't physically stop Emma from looking. In paragraph two of the article about the Padres and Mets, former Boston Red Sox "catcher Jason Bard" was circled in ink, and in the margin appeared the handwritten anagram "Crash hard object."

"That's a rather stupid one, actually," said Babes.

Emma was still impressed. Anagrams were not a skill she possessed.

Babes said, "If I really thought about it, I'm sure I could come up with something better."

He took the newspaper back from her, clicked his pen, and turned his laserlike stare back to the newsprint. Just like that, he was completely disengaged from their conversation and absolutely refocused on the *New York Times.*

Emma watched him work, the wheels turning in her head.

"I'm back," said Paul, as he climbed the steps.

Emma rose and stepped away from Babes before Paul could sit down. "Could we talk in private?" she said to both him and Rachel.

Paul glanced toward his son, then back at Emma, as if to tell her that they already were in private. Emma wasn't comfortable. Paul led them down the front steps, and they followed the sidewalk to where Emma's car was parked at the curb.

Emma said, "I was going to wait for Ryan to get here before we discussed anything important, but something just hit me, and I need to talk about it. What exactly did this Lieutenant Benjamin ask you?"

Paul answered. "He was actually very to the point with Rachel and me. He wanted to know who we thought the tipster might be."

"And he said you have a list of people who you thought might be the tipster," said Rachel. "He wanted to know if you had shown us that list."

"I don't have a list," said Emma. "But that's all he asked?"

"Yes," said Paul. "To be honest, he seemed more interested in getting Babes alone and talking to him."

"That's what Rachel told me," said Emma. "Which is interesting to me."

"In what way?" said Rachel.

"Last night, all the Providence news stations and two stations in Boston ran the story about an anonymous tipster coming forward in the investigation. It's possible that the media attention pushed this tipster even more into his game, and he showed up here this morning pretending to be a cop."

"That's a really sick puppy. He should just help us."

"That goes without saying, but there's another possibility. It could be that the driver who caused the accident saw the report on the news and freaked. He could have come here himself or hired someone to find out exactly how much the police know."

Paul's expression turned to disgust. "That's a stomach-turning thought— that we were sitting in our living room with the man who killed Chelsea."

"Either way, you satisfied him rather quickly that you didn't know anything. But something made him zero in on Babes. He needed to get Babes alone. The question is, why?"

"I can't answer that," said Rachel.

"I can't either," said Emma. "But something just came to me—it may sound screwy, but hear me out."

"Go ahead," said Paul.

Emma said, "We didn't go public with this information, but you know that the tipster used a three-year-old copy of the *Pawtucket Times* to communicate with me. It was the paper that reported Chelsea's death, and the message was in code."

"Ryan told us," said Paul, "but we haven't actually seen it."

"The point is that the tipster used coded messages in an old newspaper to send his message. I find that very interesting, particularly since I just watched Babes decode words in the *New York Times,* and Rachel tells me that he has a collection of old newspapers in his room."

"Are you saying that our son is the anonymous tipster?" said Paul.

"I would just like to ask him some questions."

"This is crazy," said Rachel.

"I have to agree with Rachel," said Paul. "If you think that for three years

Babes has been sitting on useful information about the driver who caused his sister's crash, I'm afraid you're way off base. Maybe I'm overreacting, since Rachel has already laid into me once today for letting Lieutenant Benjamin have Babes to himself. But this kind of interrogation you want—anything that dredges up the memory of Chelsea's death—is too much for Babes right now."

Rachel took a breath, trying to steady her voice and downplay her anger. "You see, Emma, people with AS often have prodigious memories, but unhappy memories are particularly vivid, and the replaying of unhappy moments in their life can persist for years and—"

"Oh, knock off the psychobabble, Rachel," he said. "The bottom line is that Babes isn't up for it. Just look at him, for Pete's sake. We had to give him that Koosh ball to make him stop pulling his eyelashes out."

"It's a tactile release that his therapist encourages in order to keep him from engaging in socially unacceptable or destructive forms of self-stimu—"

"I said stop it, Rachel. My point is this: On his bad days, Babes is barely functional. I'm not one to coddle our boy, but I'm afraid that if you start interrogating him now, you'll undo thousands of dollars worth of therapy and push him back into a world where he has *only* bad days."

"Mom," said Babes, "it's getting cold out here. I want to go inside."

"I'll take him," said Paul.

Babes kept his nose in his newspaper as his father took him by the arm and led him down the front steps. He handed Emma her BlackBerry as he passed, and the men walked around to the back of the house. Emma and Rachel returned to their patio chairs, waiting on Ryan.

"I'm sorry," said Rachel. "We have to do what's best for Babes. I hope you understand."

"I never judge in situations like this."

They sat in silence for a minute. Then Emma heard a faint noise coming through the open window that sounded like the back door opening. A howl emerged from inside the house—defi-

nitely Babes—followed by Mr. Townsend's shouting.

"Enough with the damn newspaper,
Babes! Now give it to me, damn it!"

Babes screamed like a child.

Rachel looked away from Emma nervously, and those carved-in-wax worry
lines in her face seemed to deepen right
before Emma's eyes.

There was another howl from inside
the house, this one louder than the last.

Rachel's gaze drifted off vacantly
toward the street, and her voice weak-
ened, as if she were speaking more to
herself than to Emma.

"We always do what's best for
Babes," she said.

CHAPTER 10

For a guy who hadn't rolled out of bed till lunch time, Ryan's day was surprisingly full.

The two hours he spent in Pawtucket seemed like theater of the absurd. Paul and Rachel were in their usual form. Babes peered through the window in silent fascination with the forensic specialists as they checked the living room for prints. A real detective showed up from the sheriff's department to take written statements from Paul and Rachel. Paul left for work at the hardware store, and Emma headed off to the crime lab to see if an in-person appearance might expedite the forensic analysis.

Then Rachel got her time alone with Ryan.

"Emma Carlisle thinks Babes might be the anonymous tipster," she said, and Ryan listened carefully as she recounted her earlier conversation with Paul and Emma.

Ryan said, "The newspaper was placed on Emma's car sometime after she parked there in the morning. Was Babes home all day yesterday?"

"Well, not all day. He was out for a couple hours."

"Do you know where he went?"

"No. He was with his friend Tom."

Tom, thought Ryan. And the thought was sobering.

"I'll look into it," he said.

"What do you mean 'look into it?' " she said, her tone uncharacteristically sharp. "You don't actually think Chelsea's own brother is playing this game, do you?"

Ryan's head was throbbing again. Sleeping pills were just not worth the side effects. "Honestly, I'm not capable of thinking anything at the moment."

"He was with Tom, for heaven's sake. It's not possible."

Ryan didn't say anything, but he disagreed with her on at least one point: with Tom, *anything* was possible.

By 3:30 PM Ryan was riding the MBTA Red Line out of Boston and under the Charles River, to a city that was on just about everyone's list of "most livable," as long as you were looking for an education and not a job.

Cambridge is for most people synonymous with the ivy-clad halls of Harvard University, but it is also home to the Massachusetts Institute of Technology, the science and engineering mecca of the world. The 168-acre campus stretches for about a mile on the north riverfront, the land converted from swamp and industrial tracts with the help of an anonymous donor who was later identified as George Eastman, founder of Kodak. Fitting for the nation's first school of architecture, MIT is defined by a variety of distinctive and stylistically inconsistent buildings, from its

Great Dome designed by William Welles Bosworth to the twenty-first-century "starchitecture," from the postwar modern designs of alumnus I. M. Pei to the controversial containment building for an on-campus nuclear reactor. Its academic distinctions are stellar, but it is equally well known for its meritocratic work ethic. Not once since its creation in 1861 has MIT awarded an honorary degree, and its motto is a five-letter abbreviation, IHTFP, which, depending on one's course load, could be decoded as "I Have Truly Found Paradise" or "I Hate This F—ing Place."

It so happened that the current student body included Babes's best friend.

Tom Bales was, without a doubt, the smartest person Ryan had ever met. He was also the only man in Cambridge who wore short-sleeved Hawaiian shirts year-round. He'd even worn one with his tuxedo at Ryan and Chelsea's wedding. Tom was Babes's only guest. They had been friends since early childhood, though as they grew older it was obvious to everyone but Babes that Tom was more often acting out of kindness than friendship in the conventional sense. That was particularly so after Tom went away to college where, to his credit, he made a point of finding paid work for Babes. Professors or students who needed raw data inputted into a re-search matrix could count on Babes to do it by computer in the comfort zone of his own bedroom. It was the perfect way for Babes to fill a chunk of his day with a meaningful task, and the only hu-man being he ever had to deal with di-rectly was his boyhood friend.

Through an exchange of text mes-sages, Ryan and Tom agreed to meet outside the famous domed library on Killian Court, the picturesque green space facing the river where com-mencement was held every spring. Ryan arrived to find Tom flat on his back relaxing on the lawn, hands clasped be-hind his head, eyes closed, and his bearded chin pointing toward the late-afternoon sun. Scores of students were cutting across the court on the way to and from classes, but Ryan had no trou-ble spotting Tom in his trademark Hawaiian shirt.

"Aloha," said Ryan.

Tom sat up to greet him, and Ryan took a seat on the lawn facing him. A stack of textbooks lay between them. On several occasions Babes had told Ryan what his friend was studying, but Ryan could recall it no more than Tom could have hit a ninety-mile-per-hour fastball. All Ryan could say with any degree of certainty was that this walking brain in the Technicolor shirts would very likely own fifty U.S. patents before his thirtieth birthday and end up selling his company for nine figures. It was just the way things worked on this side of the Charles River.

"So you're worried about Babes," said Tom.

In vague terms, Ryan had told him that much in the text message. "Yeah. The three-year anniversary was yesterday."

"I know. I'm sorry."

"Rachel tells me that you and Babes spent some time together."

Tom looked confused, but only for a moment. "Rachel, right. She's still Mrs. Townsend to me. She called me around nine-thirty in the morning and said she didn't know where Babes was."

"She called *you*?" said Ryan.

"Yep. Mr. Townsend was at work and she couldn't reach you. Babes did his usual morning walk over to the diner for coffee at seven, but over two hours later, he still wasn't back and he wasn't answering his cell. You know how routine he is, and this was not his usual pattern at all. She was getting worried."

"So you came down?"

"Sure. I don't mind the drive. Turned the heat on and put the top down on the Mini Cooper. Good way to clear my head."

"You went looking for him?"

"Yeah. It's not as daunting as it sounds. There are only so many places Babes feels comfortable going. I found him, no sweat."

"Where?"

He paused to choose his words. "At the scene."

"Of Chelsea's accident?"

Tom nodded.

Ryan said, "What was he doing there?"

Tom sucked down a couple gulps of his extra-large double café grande. "You ever seen his crash box?"

"No. What is it?"

"I'd say it's his personal way of grieving. It's where he keeps things about Chelsea's accident."

"What kind of things?"

"Anything and everything. When I caught up with him yesterday, he was pacing from one end of the crash site to the other, like a detective. He had a couple of glass pellets in his pocket. Maybe from a shattered windshield or a busted headlight. Every accident scene has little pieces of debris that aren't cleaned up. He's collected dozens of little mementos like that."

"Does he go there often?"

"All the time," said Tom. "Sometimes just to sit and think. But he's also collected lots of stuff."

Ryan's gaze drifted across Killian Court toward the frieze of a marble-clad building that bore the name NEWTON. It was as if the proverbial apple had just fallen on his head. "What about newspaper clippings?"

"What about them?"

"Are they part of Babes's crash box?"

"I don't know. Could be. Why?"

Ryan didn't want to share the details about the anonymous tip. "No reason."

Tom let it slide, his attention having turned to a passing coed. Her backpack and matching denim handbag were Tommy Bahama. He gathered up his books and sprang to his feet, seeming to sense a match made in Hawaiian-Caribbean heaven.

"I'm off to six."

"Sex?" The New England accents were still a challenge for Ryan.

"No. Building six. All but the residences are referred to by number around here, not names."

"Ah," said Ryan. *Would a campus full of human calculators have it any other way?*

Ryan thanked him, and Tom hurried after the Tommy Bahama brunette—close encounters of the nerd kind. He was a good guy, Ryan supposed, even if he did have a decade-long crush on Chelsea. After too much champagne at the Townsend/James wedding, Tom si-

dled up to Chelsea and told her that if
her new husband ever broke her heart,
he'd be waiting for her. Chelsea laughed
it off, but Ryan sensed that it hadn't
been just liquor talking.

The midday clouds had completely
dissolved, and it was turning into a
beautiful September afternoon. The
rowing crews on the Charles River
seemed to skim the waves toward Harvard Bridge. Ryan watched for a few
minutes and then walked off campus.
He was a block away from the Kendall/
MIT subway station when his cell rang.
It was Emma. She was apologizing for
the way things had gone with Chelsea's
parents before Ryan got there.

"Rachel told me about it," he said.
"It's all right."

"So you're not angry?"

"No. I understand how they might be
upset about your questioning their son.
But I also understand that you're just
doing your job."

She sounded grateful for that, but she
quickly turned to business.

"I know it's a long shot," she said,
"but the fact that this phony Lieutenant

Benjamin seemed so determined to talk to Babes, away from his parents, has me really thinking."

"I understand what you're saying," said Ryan. "I just spoke with Babes's best friend. Seems that Babes has spent countless hours at the scene of the accident since Chelsea died, just puttering around. If the drunk who ran Chelsea off the road lives anywhere around Pawtucket, maybe he's seen Babes there."

"And if he has any fear of getting caught, maybe he'd really like to know what Babes knows."

"Bad enough to play phony detective and interrogate Chelsea's parents?"

"Depends on how much he has to lose by getting caught, I suppose."

"Which is why I don't take offense at the questions you asked Paul and Rachel. We need answers."

Emma hesitated, then said, "I hope you don't think I pushed it too far by taking it to the next step."

"What next step?"

"I just left the crime lab. We were able

to pull a latent print off my BlackBerry. I let Babes use it before you got there."

"You're checking Babes's prints?"

"We got a ton of fingerprints from the newspaper that the tipster left on my windshield. At some point in time, the newspaper must have been in a library or bus station, where it was handled by a number of readers. But not a single one of them turned up a match in the database. So I asked our analyst to compare Babes's print from the Black-Berry to the prints on the newspaper."

"And?"

"No match."

"So Babes is definitely not the tip-ster?" said Ryan.

"I wouldn't go that far," she said. "It could mean nothing more than the fact that Babes's right index finger showed up on my BlackBerry and somewhere on that newspaper is the print from his left thumb, right pinky, or whichever. Or it could mean that he wore gloves to handle the newspaper, or that for what-ever reason the old newsprint just didn't pick up a clean set of his fingerprints."

"It doesn't bother you that Babes lives

in Pawtucket and your car was parked in Providence?"

"Not at all. The two cities are so close together that Babes could have walked. It's definitely an easy bus ride."

"So your bottom line is what?" said Ryan.

She paused, as if fearful that Ryan could still be as protective of Babes as his parents were. "I can't rule out Babes as the tipster," she said. "I'd like to get a complete set of his fingerprints, but I'm going to let your in-laws cool down a little before I make another approach."

"That's probably a good idea," said Ryan.

"Meanwhile, if you think of anyone else I should talk to, you call me, okay?"

Tom Bales came to mind, but putting Babes's friend on the police radar just because Ryan didn't like the way he used to look at Chelsea seemed petty.

"I've got your number," Ryan told her.

CHAPTER 11

Emma had promised herself she would never do it. But she did it.

On Wednesday she met Doug Wells for lunch on Federal Hill.

For some, it was the College of Culinary Arts at Johnson & Wales University that put Providence on the culinary map. For Emma, it was Little Italy. Doug said he'd take her anywhere that didn't serve broiled haddock or Yankee pot roast, and while that left a plethora of choices in one of America's best small-restaurant cities, Emma chose Andino's on Atwells Avenue, the main drag on the hill. It was a pleasant and sunny afternoon—perhaps one of the last of the year to see temperatures climb into the seventies—so they took a table for two on the quiet back patio and sat in the shade of a big umbrella. Emma's Chicken Andino was excellent, as usual, and Doug was all the things she hadn't expected: charming, funny, attentive. So charming, in fact, that he didn't lose any points when he had to excuse himself to take a call on his cell.

"It's fine," Emma said with a smile.

The waitress came to clear their plates. Emma could have eaten every last bit of angel hair pasta, but that would have meant another half hour on the treadmill. She restrained herself and let the waitress take it away.

The lunch crowd was thinning out, most patrons at the coffee stage. The man at the table beside hers was alone and reading the *Providence Journal*, which she noted only because Brandon Lomax was on the front page again. He seemed to be everywhere lately, and by all accounts his campaign for the U.S. Senate was becoming a veritable juggernaut. Emma was happy for him, and not just because he was her old boss. His daughter was Emma's age, and once upon a time, they had been insep- arable girlfriends. Not too far south of Providence, along the Block Island Sound out to Point Judith, a teenaged Emma had spent many a weekend on the Lomax family sailboat.

Doug returned to his seat and seemed to be in a playful mood. The phone call must have gone well.

"So I'm just curious," he said. "What made you give me another shot?"

Emma was deadpan. "Complete and utter desperation and loneliness."

"That's what I thought. Which leads to my next question. When you said we could start over, clean slate, did you mean that literally?"

"What do you mean?"

"Is this our second date, or our first?"

"Why does it matter?"

"Well, a year from now, I just want to know the anniversary of our first date."

"Doug?"

"What?"

"Cut the bullshit. Now you're trying too hard."

"Damn. And I was doing so well."

The waitress came and offered coffee. Emma wasn't trying to cut things short, but she did have to be back in court. Doug handed the waitress his credit card.

"We'll split it," said Emma.

"My treat."

"I should have ordered lobster."

"Next time?" he said.

She smiled. "Yes. Next time."

The busboy filled their water glasses, then left.

"Not to talk too much business," said Doug, "but how much play did you get from your media pitch on the anonymous tipster?"

"Your eleven o'clock segment was great. Thank you again for that. Really, the Rhode Island media jumped all over it. Coverage extended into Massachusetts as well, fueled I'm sure by the Red Sox connection and by Ryan's semi-celebrity stature as a Boston radio-show host."

"Congratulations. You worked it hard."

"I did. But the emergence of an

anonymous tipster after three years without leads was legitimate news."

"I agree. That's why our station ran with it."

"Unfortunately, it's only news for a day. Then once again—silence."

"Nothing more from your tipster?"

She paused. The sheriff's department had not yet gone public with the Lieutenant Benjamin impostor. Until they officially determined that he wasn't one of their own current or former officers, they were treating it as an internal affairs matter, so Emma couldn't mention it. "No new tips," said Emma.

"Any leads as to who it might be?"

"One," she said, meaning her own theory about Babes. "But a fingerprint check took some of the steam out of that theory."

"He might still come around."

"I'm hoping. But I feel like I've taken my best shot, and already the media have moved on to the next car accident, the next homicide, the next middle-school teacher to have sex with a student, the next Hub cop to get drunk and shoot a fellow officer in the ass. Chelsea James is old news all over again."

The waitress brought Doug's credit card. He signed, and they started the walk back through the interior of the restaurant to their cars on the street. Doug seemed pensive as they joined the flow of pedestrians along Atwells Avenue.

"What are you thinking?" said Chelsea.

"This James case seems really important to you. And I want to help."

"That's sweet of you, but you've done your part."

"Here's a thought. How about giving me an exclusive on the next anonymous tip?"

"Why on earth would I want to do that?"

"A little quid pro quo. You give me the exclusive, I give you sex. You drive a hard bargain, but hey, I really want that exclusive."

"Very funny."

"Sorry, bad joke. But I'm serious about the exclusive."

"Am I missing something, or does that

sound more like me helping you than you helping me?"

"Not at all. You believe you need another jolt from the media to draw out your tipster. Unfortunately, media interest is now down to zero. But if you give me an exclusive on the next tip, I could probably talk the producer into giving the Chelsea James story more coverage. We could maybe even do a feature on the tireless prosecutor and the three-year-old unsolved case that still haunts her."

And the story of the phony detective who went knocking on Paul and Rachel Townsend's front door—if she could talk Internal Affairs into going public.

"That's kind of interesting, actually."

"So what do you say?"

"I like it," said Emma. "Let me run it by Chief Garrisen."

"Great," he said. They stopped at Emma's car. "Business is closed. Now for the important stuff. Do you kiss on the first date?"

"Only if I like the guy."

He smiled, leaned closer, and gently kissed her on the cheek.

"This was fun," he said.

"I'll call you," she said, then got into her car. Doug watched and waved good-bye as she pulled away.

Emma was smiling as her car passed beneath the big arch with the symbolic Italian pinecone that marked the entrance and exit to Little Italy, but just crossing the river put her back in a business mind-set. She stopped by the office before heading over to the courthouse for jury selection in her next trial—another fun-filled afternoon of "Juror number seven, can you be fair and impartial; will you return a verdict of guilty if the state proves its case beyond a reasonable doubt; will you please not hold it against me when I walk over and strangle the defendant's scumbag attorney?"

"Mail call," her secretary said, as she dropped a bundle on Emma's desk.

Emma thanked her and thumbed through the stack. Bonnie was old school—still called herself a secretary, not an administrative assistant. "More organized than the Rhode Island mob," she liked to say of herself. As always, the court orders were on top. Letters from lawyers were next. MC—miscellaneous crap—was on the bottom. It was the MC that caught Emma's attention—specifically, the manila envelope with no return address. It was postmarked Providence.

Had she not been waiting for the tipster's next move, she probably would have thought nothing of it. Her antennae were up, however, and she had a hunch about this one. She took a pair of latex gloves from her top drawer—she always wore them when handling evidence—and pulled them on. With the envelope flat on her desk, she sliced across the top with her letter opener and peered inside.

Her heart skipped a beat. It contained a page from the newspaper.

She picked up the envelope by one corner, gave it a little shake, and let the contents slide out onto her desktop. It was the front page of the *Providence Journal.* Two days old.

Emma remembered having stopped on the sidewalk to buy a copy of this same newspaper after her trial on Monday, on the three-year anniversary of Chelsea's death, right before she had found the tipster's first message on her windshield. The big color photograph of her old boss, Brandon Lomax, was staring back at her again. "FRONTRUNNER," was the headline, followed by the lengthy article about his steamrolling campaign for the U.S. Senate. In this copy, however, certain words were underlined and numbered by hand, just as they had been in the first newspaper— the tipster's "I know who did it" message. This time, the message contained just two words. Emma put them together in the numbered sequence, and in the context of the tipster's previous message, it made her stomach churn.

"It's him," she said, reading in disbelief.

CHAPTER 12

Ryan picked up Ainsley after school and took her to see the Emerald Necklace. At least that was the promise.

"We're here," said Ryan.

"Where's the necklace?" said Ainsley.

"You're standing on it."

Boston's Emerald Necklace consists of an eleven-hundred-acre chain of nine parks linked by parkways and waterways. Considered a shining (green) example of Frederick Law Olmsted's genius, it was designed to connect the Boston Common, scene of everything from colonial-era hangings to hourly duck crossings, to Olmsted's crown jewel "in the country," Franklin Park.

Ainsley didn't much go for the history lesson in landscape architecture.

"You owe me a green necklace, Daddy."

Ryan smiled. Good thing he hadn't promised to show her the Green Monster. He'd owe her a ballpark.

The Public Garden was across the street from the Common, and together they formed the northern terminus of the seven-mile chain of parks in the necklace. The area west of Charles Street was once a salt marsh, so the nation's first botanical garden came with tons of fill and an equal amount of planning. The manicured look didn't exactly conjure up memories of Texas rodeos and dusty cattle drives on the plains, but it was still one of Ryan's favorite places. The summer before Chelsea died, they had brought Ainsley here, and Ryan would never forget the way their little girl giggled herself silly on the famous swan-boat ride.

It was also convenient to the Ritz-Carlton Residences, where in the fine tradition of Manny Ramirez, the newest Red Sox star enjoyed the penthouse lifestyle.

"Uncle Ivan!" Ainsley shouted, and she ran to him.

Ivan scooped her up and whirled her around. "How you doin', munchkin?"

"I can't believe you're here!" she squealed.

Ryan gave him a quick wink to keep the game going. Ryan had set up the "chance" encounter, but he wanted it to be a surprise for Ainsley.

"What luck," said Ivan. "How weird is this?"

Ivan's wife and young son were with him, and Ryan greeted them warmly. Ivan had been a true ladies' man when he and Ryan played ball together, but he settled down with a Boston Brahmin who astounded her blue-blooded family by marrying a first-generation Hispanic American to become Jacqueline Ward Lopez.

Jacqueline said, "I'm going to take the kids to see the swans."

Before Ryan could say "I'll come with you," Ivan said "You go ahead."

Ivan seemed determined to get Ryan alone, and Ryan braced himself for a lecture as the two men continued their walk around the pond.

"I got a call from your housekeeper," said Ivan. "She tells me she found you passed out drunk in the living room."

"I wasn't drunk. I took a sleeping pill at four AM."

"If you're going to take the meds, take them at bedtime, fool."

"I know. I tell myself that I can beat this stupid insomnia without drugs, and then before I know it, it's one o'clock in the morning and too late to take a pill. Then it's four o'clock, and I can't stand it anymore, so I take one. Then I'm screwed."

"You have to get past this son-of-a-Texas-preacher idea that taking medicine is a sin or something."

"My dad wasn't a preacher."

"He might as well have been."

There was truth in that, but Ryan didn't want to go there.

At the bend in the path, they stopped at the concession cart for frozen lemonade. September weather in Boston

could mean cold drinks or hot chocolate. Today was one of those in-between
days where you could go either way.

"Here's something for your radio
show," said Ivan. "My agent brought me
another six-figure offer this week."

"For what?"

"Advertising. On my crotch."

"Right," said Ryan, scoffing.

Ivan swallowed a heaping spoonful of
the slushy lemonade. "It's totally legit,
dude. You remember George Brett?"

"Only one of the greatest third base-
men to play the game."

"Good looking guy too, which is why
a market research group decided to
show his photo to a group of women.
They focused on his face. Then they
showed the same picture to a group of
men. Guess what they focused on."

"The group of women?"

"No. Men actually split their time between his face and his crotch."

"So naturally your agent put your
crotch up for sale."

"We got an offer too."

"But do you really want a bunch of
men looking at your crotch?"

"That's the thing: It's got nothing to do with me. The same study showed that the male crotch fixation was just as strong with pictures from the American Kennel Club as it was with the *Sports Illustrated* swimsuit issue. Men just can't help it."

A woman jogged past them with her poodle on a leash. Ryan averted his eyes, fearful of putting Ivan's crotch theory to the test.

They crossed Charles Street and entered the historic Common, where everything seemed to be marked by a plaque—trees, benches, flowerbeds, statues, monuments, walkways. Bostonians sure loved signs. Ryan's favorite was actually just up Beacon Street, right in front of the state legislature: GENERAL HOOKER ENTRANCE. Ryan thought that every state capitol should have one; politicians got into so much trouble whenever they were too specific about that sort of thing.

"Sorry, dude!" shouted a passing skateboarder.

A line of death-defying teenagers was surfing on wheels down the paved hill at the very southern end of Beacon Hill. Ivan led the way toward the baseball diamonds, and they stopped at the chainlink fence behind home plate. A man was on the field with his teenaged daughter, and Ryan suddenly saw the future that had been stolen away from him and Ainsley when a drunk driver had sucked all the enjoyment out of the game. The man on the pitcher's mound was wearing a Red Sox jersey with Ivan's number on the back. A five-gallon bucket of baseballs was right behind him. His daughter stood strong in the batter's box, smacking everything that came close to the strike zone.

"Pretty good hitter," said Ivan.

Ryan didn't answer. He had a bad feeling about the direction of this conversation.

Ivan said, "How about I throw you a few pitches?"

"I don't think so," said Ryan.

As if on cue, Ivan's wife showed up with the kids.

"Are you and Uncle Ivan going to play baseball?" said Ainsley. She had an ice-cream cone in her hand and chocolate smeared all over her lips.

"Not today," Ryan told her.

She licked her ice cream. "Why not?"

"Yeah," said Ivan, "why not?"

Ainsley put her head against his hip. "Daddy, I've never seen you play baseball."

That hit Ryan hard. It wasn't technically true—Ainsley had seen him play. She just didn't remember the old Ryan James, before Chelsea died. Thankfully, she also had no memory of the horrible year afterward, which had marked the end of his career.

Ivan's wife chimed in. "Come on, Ryan. What can it hurt?"

"*Please,* Daddy?"

He couldn't say no to Ainsley.

"You're lucky I don't kick you in the advertising," he told Ivan. "Let's get this over with."

Ivan smiled and walked out to the mound. The girl's father immediately recognized the newest Red Sox star, and he was more than happy to lend his equipment in exchange for Ivan's signature on a ball, a bat, a mitt, and a cap.

"Batter up," said Ivan.

He stepped into the box, tapped the plate with his bat, and assumed his stance. Ivan went into his windup and threw the first pitch at batting-practice speed. Ryan whiffed.

"That was ugly, dude," said Ivan.

"The bat's too small."

The girl's father had a bigger bat in his equipment bag. It was the one Ivan had signed, but he lent it to Ryan in exchange for a signed jersey to be delivered later.

"No more excuses," said Ivan.

He hurled another pitch. Ryan connected, and Ivan had to hop over a hot ground ball that sizzled past his ankles.

"Base hit," said Ryan, and it actually felt good.

"No more Mr. Nice Guy," said Ivan.

His next pitch was a legitimate major-league fastball. Ryan fouled it off. Ryan readied for the next pitch, and out of the corner of his eye he noticed that a crowd was starting to gather. Obviously word was spreading throughout the park that Ivan Lopez, the Boston Red Sox sensation, was pitching to "some guy" over on the north diamond. Ryan foul-tipped another fastball.

"Come on, Daddy. You can do it!"

Ryan dug in. Up against a major-league pitcher, his daughter cheering him on—he was almost standing too close to an evaporated dream. Ivan went into his windup. Ryan guessed curveball. And he was right.

A screaming line drive went deep into the gap in left center field.

"Double," said Ryan.

Ivan smiled, then pointed at Ryan, as if to say "no more." He went back to the fastball, and Ryan creamed it. Dead center field.

"Shit, man," said someone behind the batting cage. "That one was to the warning track in Fenway."

The crowd of onlookers was growing. A group of kids started a chant: "Ivan, Ivan!" The Red Sox ace reared back and threw some serious heat.

The crack of the bat silenced the Ivan fans. Ryan sent the ball on a towering ride to left field. Ivan turned to watch it go—and go, and go.

"Wow!" said Ainsley.

"That one would have cleared the Green Monster," Ryan heard one of Ivan's fans say.

Ivan was no longer smiling. Ryan knew that his friend was too much of a competitor not to be angry. It only spurred Ryan on. Ivan dug another ball out of the bucket, and then another, hurling one pitch after another at his old teammate. Kids lined up in the outfield to flag fly balls, but Ryan was hitting them well over their heads. They climbed over the left-field fence and stood in the next field. One kid was all the way in the Central Burial Ground, the historic old cemetery on the Boylston Street side of the Common, south of the playing fields. Ivan was working up a sweat, and Ryan continued to knock the cover off the ball. They kept at it until the bucket of balls was empty.

Ivan stood on the mound with his hands on his hips. "That's it, man."

For the first time in a long time, Ryan had a baseball bat in his hands and a huge smile on his face.

Kids swarmed onto the field. Ivan took a few minutes to sign hats, T-shirts, arms, legs, and tennis shoes. Ryan gave the bat back to its owner and went to Ainsley. She leaped into his arms and hugged him around the neck.

"You should play baseball," she said.

"Nah, that's not what I do." Ryan turned to give her a little twirl in the air, but he almost stepped on a little boy who had come up behind him.

The boy looked up and said, "Can I have your autograph?"

Ryan put Ainsley down. "You can," he told the boy. "But I'm not a baseball player."

"Yes, you are," said Ivan.

Ryan turned to disagree, but Ivan's dead-serious expression silenced him.

Ivan said, "You need to get back in the game."

"Yeah, Daddy. You're good!"

Ryan drew a breath. This whole thing was beginning to feel like an ambush. "We need to go. Your Uncle Ivan has a game tonight."

"I'm in no hurry. I don't pitch again till Saturday."

"We have to go," said Ryan.

"Why?" said Ainsley.

"Yeah, why?" said Ivan.

"Because we *have* to," said Ryan. He picked up Ainsley and started away, but Ivan stepped in his path.

"I want you to think about coming back."

Ryan suddenly felt the weight of the week's events—the three-year anniversary, the anonymous tip, the relapse into insomnia. The fact that his deepest home run had rolled all the way to a cemetery hadn't helped matters. It was all too claustrophobic.

"You need to get out of my way," said Ryan.

"Just think about it."

"I can't."

"Why not?"

"Because I *can't.* Now will you get out of the way?" he said, his tone harsh.

Ivan stood there, his expression showing confusion, anger, and disappointment. "Fine. Go."

With Ainsley in his arms, Ryan made a beeline for the path toward Frog Pond.

"Why do we have to go?" said Ainsley.

"We'll talk about it later."

They were almost home free when he heard someone in the crowd ask "Who is that guy?"

Ivan answered in a voice loud enough for Ryan to hear: "That, ladies and gentlemen, is a major-league Hall of Fame quitter."

Ryan stopped cold. The inner voice of reason told him to keep going, but he was overpowered by a sudden surge of painful memories and a strange mix of emotions, not the least of which was anger. He put Ainsley down on the jogging path and told her to wait there. Then he walked back to Ivan, invaded his personal space, and looked him squarely in the eye.

"Don't you ever call me that again. Not in front of my daughter."

"What're you gonna do about it?"

The anger swelled, and only the fact that they were surrounded by children prevented Ryan's fist from flying. He turned and went back to Ainsley.

"Are you and Uncle Ivan fighting?" she said as he picked her up.

"Let's go," he said.

As they started down the path, he heard Ivan call to him, but they weren't fighting words.

"I wasn't holding back," said Ivan.

Ryan kept walking.

Ivan shouted louder. "That was a ninety-mile-an-hour fastball I threw, and you hit it four hundred feet."

Ryan didn't answer.

"You still got it, man. You hear me? You still got it."

Ryan tried not to listen. The urge to get away was overwhelming. He walked faster, almost running. Mercifully, Ainsley somehow sensed that this was not the time to talk. The anger was giving way to regrets and confusion. Maybe Ivan was right; maybe he did still have it. But that didn't matter.

Irrational as it was, baseball was at the core of Ryan's guilt over Chelsea's death.

"Daddy, you're hurting me."

"What?" he said, still hurrying down the path.

"You're holding me too tight."

"Sorry, sweetheart."

He eased up—but only a tiny bit, because Ryan's heart and mind were in complete accord: it was impossible to hold on to Ainsley too tight.

CHAPTER 13

Emma arrived at Toll Gate High School in Warwick around seven o'clock that evening. All two hundred seats for the first of five Senate debates were reserved, but Emma had enough pull to snag one at the last minute. It had nothing to do with the fact that Brandon Lomax was her old boss.

It was much more personal than that.

Emma couldn't remember a time when her real father hadn't been sick. On occasion he had found the strength to give his little girl piggyback rides or play with her on the swings, but mostly he watched her from his armchair or lawn chair and rested. It was often frustrating for Emma. Once, she had even called him lazy. Not until after the funeral did she understand that it was a three-year battle with cancer. Five days before her sixth birthday it finally killed him. They had the cake two weeks early so that he could watch her blow out the candles. Emma would never forget the sympathy card she had made for her mother. On the outside, she colored a giant yellow flower with black pistils for eyes, tears falling to the ground. Inside she wrote "I'm sorry your husband died," unable to say "Daddy died."

Summers with the Lomaxes were as close as Emma came to family vacations. Brandon and Sarah Lomax had one child, Jenny, who was Emma's best friend from the third grade through high school. Each school year, Jenny somehow managed to get the same teacher Emma got. (Jenny's dad had more than a little something to do with that coincidence.) They took dance classes together and played on the same soccer team. And when summers rolled around, Emma felt as if her last name could have been Lomax. The weekend sailing trips started in late May with Nantucket Sound's annual Figawi Race—so named for the New England sailor's foggy-day refrain "Where the f—— ah we?"—and continued through the first week of August. Then Emma would spend three weeks with the Lomax family in their home in the Berkshires. Emma and Jenny told everyone in Great Barrington that they were sisters. One summer, she kept the ruse alive by calling Brandon Lomax Dad. It was a game, but she liked playing it.

"Ladies and gentlemen," said the moderator, his voice filling the auditorium, "welcome to the first televised debate between the candidates for the United States Senate. To my right is the incumbent, Senator Shelby Broadhouse. To my left is Mr. Brandon Lomax . . ."

Emma's gaze tracked the shift of the television cameras. The lights were up, the audience was utterly silent, and the tension was palpable. Two candidates dressed in dark blue suits stood at wooden lecterns, the image of the United States Capitol projected on the blue backdrop behind them with an American flag at each side of the stage.

Silver haired and movie-star handsome, Rhode Island's two-term former attorney general stood tall as a man on the rise. The most recent WPRI-TV poll showed Lomax in the lead, but it was only September, and things can change quickly in politics. As the candidates readied to square off in their first debate, Emma realized how potentially explosive the latest anonymous tip was. Public outcry to find the man who'd run Chelsea off the road had long ago subsided, but it wouldn't take much for the press to whip up a new frenzy about the front-running Senate candidate who got drunk and killed the star baseball player's pretty wife while she was driving to the big game.

Talk about breathing life into a cold case.

The first forty minutes went the way of most political debates, with the exchanges between candidates slowly but

steadily devolving from intelligent discussion of the issues toward the more
tried-and-true tactics of mutual assured
destruction through all-out mudslinging.
Then came the bomb—or at least the
fireworks.

"I do not raise this issue lightly," said
Broadhouse, as if character assassination were an issue. "But any man who
uses his power and influence to avoid a
DUI charge is simply not fit to be an
elected senator from the state of Rhode
Island."

Emma went cold. She thought that
she alone knew that the tipster had
named Brandon Lomax in Chelsea's
crash. She had no intention of hiding
any legitimate lead in the investigation,
but it would have been irresponsible to
go public with an anonymous tip before
the AG's office determined that it was
indeed legitimate and not merely a vicious campaign smear tactic.

Lomax kept his composure, and even
though Emma was seated in the back
row, she watched his expression closely
as he spoke.

"Senator, I believe the incident you are mischaracterizing occurred some twenty-two years ago."

Twenty-two? Emma was even more confused.

Lomax continued, "I was cited for drinking a beer on the beach in Florida. Through some computer glitch it ended up on my Rhode Island record as driving while intoxicated. I did not pull any favors. I simply pursued my rights to clear my name and eliminate a bureaucratic mistake from my record. End of story."

Emma felt relief—until the moderator interjected: "Having said that, you have spoken publicly about a time in your life when alcohol became a problem."

"Yes," said Lomax. "I'm not proud of that, but I am proud of the support I received from my family and friends, who helped me to put that chapter behind me many years ago. Senator Broadhouse knows what I've overcome. He knows the truth. The truth is that I have not had a drink stronger than root beer in over fifteen years. Coincidentally, it has been at least that long since Senator Broadhouse was honest with the people of Rhode Island."

The rules prohibited applause, but Lomax's barb drew a standing ovation. It was way overdone, a well-choreographed stunt by his supporters. Emma didn't join in, but she did rise up from her seat. As the noise swelled, Emma squeezed her way out to the side aisle and broke for the exit.

She had gone to the debate intending to talk with the candidate afterward, but that would have to wait. Now Emma felt the need to get out, to get away. Getting a tip naming Lomax as the drunk driver who had killed Chelsea James was distressing enough. Watching the senator dredge up his past battle with alcoholism doubled the pain. But what had pushed her over the edge was Lomax himself. She had heard him say that he hadn't had a drink in over fifteen years. And she knew that was a lie. A barefaced lie.

Emma had firsthand knowledge of his brief but dangerous relapse, and it had nothing to do with the anonymous tip about the Chelsea James crash. Or maybe it had *everything* to do with it. Emma had smelled alcohol on his breath at the office. On more than one occasion.

Three years ago.

CHAPTER 14

Ryan took Ainsley for pizza after the park and then to the toy store—for a green necklace, of course. It was eight o'clock when they got home. Ainsley took a quick bath, brushed her teeth, and put on her pajamas. A brief disagreement over sleeping in her necklace followed, which Ryan won, and she crawled into bed. Ryan slid beneath the covers beside her, and they took turns reading—for the tenth night in a row— the story about the stray dog. Ryan knew it was only a matter of time before Ainsley asked for a puppy. Ainsley was fading by page eight, and by page twelve Ryan thought she was out cold. He switched off the lamp and kissed her on the forehead. Her eyes blinked open.

"Daddy, why did Uncle Ivan call you a quitter?"

That one hit him like a left hook to the chops. Kids were often direct, and any child of Chelsea's couldn't help being *that* direct. Ainsley didn't just *look* like her mother.

"I think he was just mad," said Ryan.

"About what?"

Her face was barely visible in the shadow of her Scooby-Doo night-light, but Ryan could see the inquisitiveness in her expression.

"That's really a long story."

"I got nowhere to go," she said.

He chuckled. An only child could sound so grown up, so fast.

"Is it about Mommy?" she said.

That drained the smile from his face. Ainsley, too, was very serious.

"In a way, yes."

Ainsley sat up, her back against the headboard. "We had red ribbon this week in school. You know, when they tell you how bad drugs are."

It seemed like an abrupt change of topic, but he knew somehow Ainsley was going to tie this all together. "That's a good thing."

"Do you know Amanda Hearst?"

"No, I don't."

"Amanda's a fifth grader. She's really smart. She's my reading buddy. We read together every Thursday during second period."

"That's really nice. But it's a school night and—"

"She told me that Mommy got killed by someone who was drunk. Is that true?"

Another left hook. This one had Ryan on the ropes. He had talked with Ainsley about the car accident and explained that Mommy lived in heaven. But he had been saving the part about drinking and driving until Ainsley was a little older. He didn't want to lie to her, however, and he definitely didn't want her to think that her reading buddy at school was a liar.

"Yes, Amanda is telling the truth. The police have always thought it was a drunk driver who ran Mommy's car off the road."

"So, Mommy died because somebody drank too much?"

He squeezed her hand and said, "I know that sounds so unfair. But yes, I'm afraid that's what happened."

She glanced away for a moment, toward the ducks and rabbits on her wallpaper. Finally, she looked back at him and said, "Then how come you drink so much?"

"Where did you hear *that*?"

"Claricia."

"She told you I was drinking?"

"Not exactly. I heard her talking on the phone to Uncle Ivan."

This was getting out of hand—like the media frenzy after he'd nearly fallen asleep at the wheel from the lingering effect of a sleeping pill and was stopped for suspected drunk driving. Even though he wasn't guilty, he'd spent hours on his radio show explaining to callers that he hadn't thrown away his career to booze.

"Claricia means well," said Ryan. "But I don't have a drinking problem."

"Do you drink at all?"

"Well, yes. Occasionally."

"Why?"

Good question. "It's something that some grown-ups choose to do. Unfortunately, even grown-ups don't always know when to quit."

She lay back on her pillow. He wished he could find the right thing to say, but more than anything he wanted the conversation to end.

"I love you," he said.

"Love you too."

He lay there, wondering if she was going to ask another question. The silence was almost more than he could endure, but finally she was asleep. Ryan didn't want to wake her, so he stayed in the bed with her. His eyes grew heavy. He needed sleep, but the more he wanted it, the more elusive it became. His mind would not shut off, not even with the calming breath of his little girl caressing his neck. She was deep into dreamland.

Good thing insomnia isn't contagious.

It wasn't a disease in its own right, his doctors had told him. It was "symptomatic."

Symptomatic of what? That was what Ryan wanted to know. The death of his wife? The thought of the drunk bastard who'd killed her still going out every night and tipping back drinks? The fact that no matter how hard he tried, he could never be the father Ainsley deserved, let alone the father *and* the mother.

Daddy, why do you drink?

It's something that some grown-ups choose to do.

What kind of a lame answer was that? And Ainsley was only in kindergarten. The really tough questions were yet to come! Why is my body changing? Did you and Mommy actually do *that*? How old were *you* the first time you had sex? What business is it of yours what I do with my boyfriend?

Sorry, Chelsea. I just wasn't cut out to do this alone.

By 1:12 AM he could no longer stand staring at the ceiling. In less than five hours he had a radio show to do.

Ryan tiptoed out of Ainsley's room and went down the hall to his own bed. He stripped down to his boxers, slid under the covers and closed his eyes, hoping that sleep might come easier in his own room, away from Ainsley, away from that angelic reminder of the way he used to sleep so peacefully at Chelsea's side. But it was useless. It was destined to be another one of those nights where "rest" would be one or two good yawns, at most.

And in the darkness, his closet beckoned.

He switched on the light and went to it. The box he wanted was behind his golf clubs. He dug it out, placed it on the floor and sat down beside it. Opening it wasn't easy, but it wasn't about strength. He needed courage.

He removed the top, and the journey began.

Right on top was a five-year-old copy of *Sports Illustrated.* LONGHORNS REIGN was the cover story. Ryan and his University of Texas teammates were on the field, a human pile of celebration after they'd won another College World Series in Omaha. Ryan was voted series MVP—eleven hits with three home runs—which no one would have predicted. Ryan had been in a batting slump going into the playoffs. His confidence was shaken. He tried everything to snap out of it. In the end, a simple talk, man-to-man, turned him around. He remembered his coach telling him that it wasn't a game about balls and bats. Baseball was like life, a thinking man's game, a matter of the mind. Ryan had a career batting average of .305 in college, which made him a star, and which meant that he failed seven out of ten trips to the plate. "You have to put the last failure behind you," his coach had told him. "If you don't, it's over."

Ryan laid the magazine aside, and the open box called to him like a portal to the past. Things didn't get any easier. Underneath the magazine was a plaque that had been mounted over his locker. The same plaque hung over every Longhorn player's locker, and a large painted sign with the same message was the first thing players saw when they entered the clubhouse from the dugout: THE PRIDE AND WINNING TRADITION OF THE TEXAS LONGHORNS WILL NOT BE ENTRUSTED TO THE WEAK OR THE TIMID.

The realization was painful, but Ryan felt as though he had broken that trust.

It would have been easy to blame it all on Chelsea's death, but the groundwork for this downward spiral had been laid long ago. Perhaps if he had taken the sleeping pills his doctor had prescribed after the funeral, he would never have started on the slippery slope of insomnia. But he was afraid of them—afraid of his own addictive personality, which he had discovered in college. He and his buddies at Jester Hall would start at Buffalo Billiards on Brazo and Sixth Street, share a pitcher of beer or two in one of the cowhide booths. Next was the Blind Pig Pub, then across the street to Shakespeare's Alehouse (HELPING UGLY PEOPLE GET LAID SINCE 1991), back across the street to Darwin's Pub (survival of the drunkest), and then finally over to The Drink, where athletes broke training. Too much drinking, way too easy. It was amazing that he'd never ended up at the Black Cat Tattoo Shop for a lifelong memory of another forgettable night. He'd finally straightened himself out, but an experience that bad was enough to make him choose sleepless nights over sleeping pill addiction.

Ryan could have sat all night beside his box of mementos and drowned in the past. Instead, he picked himself up from the bedroom floor and headed downstairs. This was a journey he'd made before, usually late at night, bearing his load of regrets like a Mount Everest Sherpa. But he felt different this time.

He went to the phone and dialed Ivan's number. It was late, but Ryan needed to do this—now.

"Hello?" Ivan answered in a sleepy voice.

"It's me," said Ryan.

"Dude, what time is it?"

"I'm ready," was all Ryan said.

He knew that Ivan had been waiting a long time to hear those words, and Ryan had vowed never to say them unless he truly meant them.

"I believe you," said Ivan.

Ryan smiled to himself. He believed too.

Emma was becoming an addict, she was sure of it.

Once upon a time she'd been able to

brush her teeth, shower, do her makeup, get dressed, maybe even have break-fast—all before checking e-mails. Her BlackBerry had changed all that.

The sleep was barely out of her eyes, and she was scrolling down her list of messages.

Most of them had short subject lines ("Re: Carver Sentencing"). The third one from the top sent chills down her spine. The "Re" line read like a message in and of itself: "Why haven't you arrested him? Are you going to LET HIM GET AWAY WITH THIS?"

The sender's screen name was a jum-ble of numbers rather than an actual name. Emma didn't waste time trying to figure out if there was any significance to the number sequence. She opened the message.

It was only one paragraph, but the print was small.

One quick reading was enough to tell her that it was no prank. It was real.

She would have her tech experts try to trace the e-mail, but probably it had been sent from an airport kiosk or busi-ness center under an untraceable address. It could have been from anyone. Except that she knew it wasn't just anyone. It was her tipster. He'd abandoned the cutesy format of underlined words in newspapers, but his anonymity was preserved.

She dialed her new boss and gave assistant attorney general Glenda Garrisen the news.

"We need to meet," said Emma. "First thing."

CHAPTER 15

Emma entered her boss's office to discover that it was going to be a three-way meeting: Emma, Glenda Garrisen, and Brandon Lomax.

Division Chief Garrisen was seated in the oxblood leather chair behind her antique mahogany desk. She was an exceptional lawyer who referred to herself as a Radcliffe woman, which was only technically correct: she'd enrolled in 1976, the year before Radcliffe placed all of its undergraduate women in Harvard College. Whatever her alma mater, she was a refined woman with exquisite taste. The impressionist oil paintings on the walls were of museum quality, and someone long ago had sacrificed five years of living, one knot at a time, to the priceless Sarouk rug on the floor. History all but spoke from her collection of leather-bound law books on glass-encased shelves, several volumes predating the election of Rhode Island's first attorney general in 1650. Nothing in Glenda Garrisen's office was government issued. While such displays of wealth might have raised suspicions about some lawyers on the paltry salary of a civil servant, the four-carat diamond ring on her finger explained all, even if she chose not to clutter her office with pendants, photographs, or other memorabilia of her husband's beloved Paw-Sox.

The chief said, "I thought it was time to let Brandon respond to the anonymous tips."

Emma agreed—in theory. Her relationship with the Lomax family and her respect for Lomax as a former boss, however, raised an internal red flag. Layered on top of that history was the fact that Lomax had appointed Glenda

Garrisen to her position as chief of the Criminal Division—a position he had once held himself—and it was the last appointment he made before leaving the Office of the Attorney General to run for the U.S. Senate. Glenda's wealthy husband, Connie Garrisen, had known Brandon Lomax for many years, and while Glenda never made campaign contributions, her husband was among the biggest fundraisers for the Lomax campaign. Emma could only assume that the chief had taken all that into consideration when she invited Lomax to join them.

Emma also assumed that Chief Garrisen had advised him of his right to be represented by an attorney.

"Where would you like me to start?" said Emma.

"Actually, *I* would like to start," said Lomax. "This is character assassination, pure and simple."

Emma said, "From the very beginning, I have suspected the timing of this tip."

"It's bogus," said Lomax. "What conceivable reason could anyone have for not coming forward with this evidence

three years ago? Why would they implicate me anonymously unless the tip is
nothing but a scandalous lie started by
political enemies to disparage me before the election?"

"I've asked myself the same questions," the chief said.

"So have I," said Emma. "But this latest tip presents a bigger problem."

"Tell me about that," said Lomax.

Emma glanced at her current boss.
The chief nodded, giving Emma the go-
ahead. Emma said, "The e-mail message included information that adds
serious credibility to the accusations
against you."

"What does that mean?" said Lomax.

"The message contains important details that only someone who had actually seen Brandon Lomax at the scene
of crime would know."

Lomax glanced at the chief. "I can't
respond if you aren't going to get specific."

"Tell him," she said to Emma.

"According to the e-mail, the tipster
saw Brandon Lomax stop his car and
walk over to the crashed vehicle. When

he saw how badly Chelsea was injured, he vomited. That version of events jibes with the evidence found at the accident scene three years ago."

"I don't recall hearing anything about vomit at the scene while I was attorney general," said Lomax.

Emma said, "That was a matter of investigative strategy that wouldn't have found its way all the way up to the attorney general's desk. You can't get a blood-alcohol reading from the contents of someone's stomach, but vomit does contain saliva, and that saliva could provide enough DNA for the police to do a DNA test on a suspect. The idea was to keep the DNA a secret—our ace in the hole to be played only after the prime suspect had been identified, interrogated and locked into his story."

Lomax shot her a look that only a father could give. "Is that what you intended to do with me, Emma? Lock me in?"

"No, not at all. In fact, now that all of this is out in the open, the quickest way to exonerate you is to do a simple DNA—"

"Hold on," said the chief. "I am not going to ask the former attorney general for a DNA sample."

Emma paused to choose her words. "With all due respect to both of you, why not?"

"Number one, I'm sure there will be no match. Number two, simply asking a man like Brandon Lomax for a DNA sample sends a message to the press that the attorney general's office considers these anonymous tips credible. I don't care to send that message. Even after the lab comes back with no match, a cloud of suspicion will hang over him for the duration of the campaign."

"So, it's a political decision?" said Emma.

"No," the chief said firmly. "It's a question of fairness and prosecutorial discretion. This isn't the Duke-Lacrosse rape case. I don't ruin people for no reason."

Emma suddenly felt the combined weight of the stares from her current boss and the former one. But she was not going to let personal feelings—hers or the chief's—stand in the way of professional judgment. "Okay, no DNA sample. But I have to go somewhere with this investigation. How about an alibi?"

"What about it?" said Lomax.

"Do you have one?" said Emma. "I don't mean to insult you, but you could put the whole controversy to a quick end by establishing your whereabouts at the time of Chelsea's accident. We don't even have to involve the crime lab or the police department. I'm simply asking you to give me some objectively reasonable justification for closing the door on this anonymous tipster."

"You're talking about three years ago. Off the top of my head, I couldn't tell you where I was three weeks ago."

"Check your records, your calendar, whatever you need to do," said Emma.

"All right," said Lomax. "I'm sure I'll be able to dig out something or someone who can tell you exactly where I was." He looked at Chief Garrisen and said, "But let's not lose sight of the big picture here. Like I said at the beginning: this is politically motivated character assassination. While that might not be a crime in most situations, providing false information to law enforcement *is* a crime."

"You're absolutely correct about that," said the chief.

"I know I am," said Lomax. "Emma knows I'm right too. Don't you, Emma?"

She suddenly felt like a teenager. "Yes. I do."

"Good. Since we're all on the same page, I think it's time we come up with a plan to lure this scumbag out into the open. And then we can expose him for what he is—an anonymous fraud who is trying to ruin my good name and reputation."

"Do you have a specific plan in mind?" the chief said.

"I do," said Lomax. "It involves Emma."

"Me?" she said.

"Yeah," said Lomax. "You."

CHAPTER 16

On Saturday afternoon, Ryan entered the Gilded Age.

It was actually a political fundraiser for Brandon Lomax, and Ryan was the personal guest of none other than PawSox owner, Connie Garrisen. If he squinted, however, Ryan could well imagine that an engraved invitation had come from Alva Vanderbilt and that he was among Newport society for a champagne toast to woman suffrage, the exploitation of the masses, or some other robber-baron cause de jure.

Built as a summer "cottage" at a nine-teenth-century cost of eleven million dollars, Marble House stands on the Atlantic shore as a monument to an era when industrialists got insanely rich and architects went completely wild. Railroad baron William K. Vanderbilt spared no expense, drawing on the talents of Richard Morris Hunt, architect of New York's Metropolitan Museum of Art and the pedestal for the Statue of Liberty, to design a neoclassical masterpiece that mimicked the great palaces of Europe. The cottage's half a million cubic feet of marble, a ballroom covered in 22-karat gold leaf, and four years of handiwork by more than three hundred European artisans made it the most lavish house in America when it opened in 1892.

That afternoon it was filled with Brandon Lomax's most loyal and generous supporters—and there was none more loyal, or generous, than Connie Garrisen.

"Ryan, so glad you came," said Garrisen.

"Thanks for inviting me."

He shook Ryan's hand and put his left arm around him in a friendly half embrace. "It's the least I can do for my re-turning third baseman."

Ryan smiled, but at lunch the previous day he'd been all jitters. He'd managed to set it up through Connie's secretary without saying what it was about, but the venue should have been Connie's first clue. Of all the great lunch spots in Boston, Ryan chose a sandwich shop on the corner of Huntington Avenue and Forsyth Street—diagonally across the street from the original home of the Boston Red Sox. Before Fenway Park, it was Huntington Grounds that had brought baseball fans the first World Series, the first modern perfect game, the first (and last) major-league ballpark with a tool shed in deep center-field that was in play. For Ryan, the significance went beyond baseball: four years earlier, seated at a table by the window and looking at Northeastern University and the law school that had sprouted on Cy Young's footprints at the old Huntington Grounds, Chelsea had told him that she wanted to study law.

"I'm asking for a tryout," Ryan had told him. "I understand I have to earn my spot on the roster, no guarantees. I'm just looking for another shot."

"I have just one thing to say about that," the PawSox owner had replied. "I'll be pulling for you."

With that, it was settled. Ryan would get his shot, and he'd give it his all— even if tonight's champagne was a break in training.

Connie said, "I hope you don't mind, but I've been telling everyone about yesterday's talk. It's very exciting news for the PawSox family."

"That's great," said Ryan, though part of him wished Connie weren't spreading the word so freely. Lots of things could happen between September and April— many of them not so good.

"Let me introduce you to some folks," said Connie.

"I'm fine," said Ryan. "There must be plenty of people you need to talk to without me tagging along. Enjoy yourself."

Connie gave him another smile and a friendly punch to the bicep. "See you around, number eleven."

Ryan gave him a mock salute and

watched him disappear into the crowd. The hors d'ouvres were being passed, and Ryan tried to snag something that didn't involve fish eggs and that wouldn't make him look like Tom Hanks spitting out his caviar in *Big.*

Strangers. I'm in a roomful of total strangers.

A woman across the room looked vaguely familiar. She was standing with her back to him, and he caught only glimpses of her profile as she spoke to the guests in her circle of conversation. She was wearing a black spaghetti-strapped cocktail dress, and her hair was up in a twist to show the curve of her slender neck. Finally, Ryan got a good look at her.

It was Emma.

And she was gorgeous.

"Champagne?" said the waiter.

Emma took a flute from the silver tray and thanked him.

The bubbly was surprisingly drinkable. The violin player was a nice touch too. Lomax fund-raisers were rarely this exquisite. It was easier to be a man of

the people among Boy Scouts at a pan-
cake breakfast or the obligatory Rhode-
Island *fundraiza* at Lombardi's 1025
Club. But every politician in a state-
wide, multimillion-dollar campaign had
to show his appreciation for the way the
other one-half of 1 percent lived—and
for their check-writing abilities. Smart
politics dictated no tuxedos until *after*
the election, but to Emma it seemed
that it was more than just the semifor-
mal attire that distanced modern wealth
from old Newport and the days when
society really worked for the label "rich."
Alva Vanderbilt's fascination with Louis
XIV of France was evident everywhere in
Marble House, from a grand entranceway defined by massive Corinthian
columns and ten tons of bronze and
crystal, to hallways made entirely of yellow Sienna marble, to palatial rooms
with eighteen-foot ceilings reminiscent
of Petit Trianon at Versailles.

Moments like these made Emma
wonder about her government salary.

Doug returned with her drink. "Oh,
you already have one."

She accepted his and placed hers on

a passing tray. "Thank you for being so thoughtful."

Emma was a guest of Brandon Lomax's daughter. Jenny and Emma had been inseparable as school girls, but Jenny had married and moved to New York right after college. They tried to keep in touch, but as the years passed and Jenny became a stay-at-home mother of three, it seemed that she had less and less to talk about with Emma the single career woman.

"Find Jenny yet?" said Brandon Lomax. Connie Garrisen was with him.

Emma smiled. "No, not yet."

"I know she's eager to see you. Who's your friend?"

"I'm sorry," said Emma. "This is Doug Wells."

The men shook hands, and Doug seemed to make a point of introducing himself as "Doug Wells, *Action News.*"

"No wonder you looked familiar," said Lomax.

"I don't typically do political events," said Doug. "I cover the courthouse. That's how Emma and I met."

"Doug is here *off* duty," said Emma, reeling him in. "Right, Doug?"

"Uh, sure," he said, but Emma could tell that he was already in reporter mode. His radar was fixed on the candidate.

"So any truth to the rumors that Dr. Garrisen will be the next U.S. surgeon general if you're elected to the Senate?"

Lomax chuckled. "Not that he isn't qualified, but where did you hear that?"

He smiled thinly. "It's no secret that Rhode Island is one of the key states the president needs to gain a friendly majority in the Senate. I imagine he'd be quite grateful to Dr. Garrisen for all the support he's given your campaign."

"Talk like that is very premature. You know how unreliable rumors are."

Doug trained his sights on Connie Garrisen. "Speaking of rumors, I heard some guys at the bar talking about Ryan James coming back to the PawSox."

Connie smiled. "Now *that* rumor is actually true."

"Really?" said Emma.

Doug looked at Emma, his face alight

with an idea. "Hey, maybe we can tie
that into the segment we're airing."

"Segment?" said Lomax.

"Yeah," Doug said. "Emma wants
more media coverage on the Chelsea
James case, hopefully to encourage her
anonymous tipster to come forward.
Yesterday afternoon we shot a short
piece on her three-year pursuit of the
drunk who ran Chelsea off the road. It
will air tonight. We could follow up with
something about Ryan James and his
comeback."

"That would be so nice for Ryan," said
Garrisen.

"Yeah," Lomax said flatly, "that all
sounds just great. Good luck to you with
that. Enjoy the party."

Lomax turned and left, taking Garrisen with him.

"What was that about?" said Doug.

"What was what about?" said Emma.

"The brush-off Lomax just gave me.
From the get-go, he seemed terrified
that you were with a reporter. Then
when I mentioned that I was covering
the Chelsea James case, he looked like
he was going to pass out."

"I'm sure he just has a lot on his mind. Would you mind getting me more champagne?"

"You have a full glass."

Emma guzzled it. "Not anymore."

He smiled, took her empty flute, and headed toward the bar.

Emma surveyed the distinguished guests. Across the ballroom, speaking to a retired congressman, was Jenny Lomax. Emma didn't rush over. Doug had been right on target in picking up the negative energy from Brandon Lomax. As eager as she was to see Jenny, Emma worried that the chill would carry over to the candidate's daughter.

Emma stepped outside to the canopied terrace. Night had not yet fallen, and the setting sun's afterglow cast a magnificent magenta hue on the Chinese Tea House at the foot of the lawn. Beyond was the Atlantic Ocean, and Emma watched and listened to the waves break against the rocky seashore. A server brought her another glass of champagne, and as she turned to reenter the ballroom, she ran straight into Ryan James—literally.

His shirt and tie were soaked with her champagne.

"Oh, my God!" she said.

"It's all right," he said.

She grabbed a cocktail napkin and started dabbing.

"Ow," he said.

"Sorry. Did that hurt?"

"I did about a thousand sit-ups today. I'm back in training."

She handed him her napkin. "Training? Oh, yes. I heard about the comeback. Congratulations."

A server brought him a cloth napkin, but Ryan had already given up trying to dry himself. It was futile. Emma needed to make him laugh—fast.

"Some house, huh? Did you know that this was a present from William Vanderbilt to his wife on her thirty-ninth birthday?"

"Is that so?"

"Yes, and three years later she divorced him, married the neighbor, and moved into the Belmont mansion down the street. Men just don't get it: if it doesn't sparkle, it's not a gift. Go with jewelry."

"I'll try to remember that," said Ryan, and he was smiling.

The awkwardness had passed, and he seemed to have forgotten about the spill.

"Are you here with anyone?" he asked.

In the three years she'd known him, it was the closest he'd come to inquiring about her "status."

"I'm here with Doug Wells. The *Action News* reporter."

"Oh, yeah. I still watch the Providence stations every now and then."

"How about you?" she said.

"Just me and Asti Spumante," he said, meaning the spill on his shirt.

She could have pointed out that they were serving champagne and that Asti was actually a sparkling wine, but to his shirt it was a distinction without a difference.

"There's Doug now. Let me introduce you."

"No, that's okay. I actually need to be on my way back to Boston. Babysitter has a hot date. Early night for me."

Emma wasn't sure if her read was correct, but Ryan didn't seem to be himself, and she wondered if he would have darted off so quickly if she'd been without a date.

"Well, it was good to . . . *run into you* again," she said, alluding to the champagne.

He smiled, they said goodnight and she watched him disappear into the crowd.

Now, where the heck did Doug go?

The music stopped, the crowd fell quiet, and Connie Garrisen was making a toast that would have made the average State of the Union Address seem terse. The candidate was at his side, his jacket off in signature Lomax style. Every speech was a photo op, and he wasn't going to lose his roll-up-the shirt-sleeves-and-get-to-work look for anyone, anywhere—at least not this close to the election.

Emma slipped away but stopped halfway down the hallway at the entrance to the Gothic Room. It was a private area set up as a staging room of sorts for the candidate and his en-

tourage. But it was empty, all of his supporters out listening to the speech.

Emma noticed a blue blazer draped
over a chair—Lomax had removed his
jacket for the speech—and the wheels
began to turn in her head.

Emma had been given no choice but
to accept the division chief's decision
not to subpoena Brandon Lomax and
force him to submit to a DNA test. But
Emma feared that both she and, to an
even greater extent, Glenda Garrisen,
were letting personal feelings to stand in
the way of prosecutorial objectivity. To
Emma, a comparison of the Lomax's
DNA to the DNA found at the scene of
Chelsea's accident made sense, even
though she might not like the answer.

And Doug had been absolutely right:
Lomax *did* seem to freak at the mere
mention of added publicity for the Chelsea James case.

Emma entered the room and walked
toward the jacket. She had an idea in
her head, but with each step it became
clearer that no matter how close she felt
to Brandon Lomax, she would never
find the nerve to reach inside his jacket

and remove his comb. But there it was, right beside the powder his makeup artist had applied to take the shine off his forehead: A hair brush.

It would require only a few silver hairs to know the scientific truth.

She plucked several strands from the bristles and tucked them into her handbag.

"Emma?"

She turned with a start, her heart in her throat.

It was Jenny Lomax.

Before Emma could even begin to wonder whether her old friend had seen anything, Jenny hurried over and gave her a huge hug. Obviously, none of her father's chill had spilled over to Jenny and, fortunately, she'd seen nothing.

Jenny pulled a flask from her sparkling evening bag and filled Emma's glass.

"Vodka and cranberry," she said. "Somebody has to get this party off the ground."

Emma laughed, and a memory flashed of two rebellious teenagers drinking themselves silly on the lawn at

Tanglewood after Jenny had sneaked too much of her father's bourbon into their cherry Cokes.

"Cheers," said Jenny.

"I can use it," said Emma, her hand still shaking.

Arm in arm, the two old friends stepped out onto the terrace to join the crowd and give their enthusiastic applause for "the next United States Senator from the great state of Rhode Island."

The guests were gone by ten o'clock. Brandon Lomax was in the Gothic Room, resting in the Louis XIV–style armchair. His campaign manager was still too wound up to sit.

Both men understood that the proverbial gloves were off from now to election day. The newspaper photograph of the candidate with the coded message "It's him" was dangerous enough. But it was the recent e-mail that really had Lomax worried. The timing of the anonymous tip suggesting that he had run Chelsea James off the road and killed her could hardly have been coincidence. This kind of scandal could cost him the election.

"That Doug Wells from *Action News* is trouble," said Lomax. He was massaging between his eyes, as if staving off a migraine.

His manager was staring at the patterns in the red silk wall upholstery, his expression tired. Josef Weimer was a Princeton graduate with the political cunning and finesse of Otto von Bismarck but the television persona of a frankfurter, which in the modern world left him perfectly equipped to live vicariously through men who were gifted with the total political package. For the past eighteen months he had worked twelve hours a day, seven days a week with one mission: get Brandon Lomax elected.

"He's just one reporter," said Josef.

"A reporter who's trying to impress a woman."

Josef looked away. "A dangerous combination, I admit."

"Wells is not going to let go of this Chelsea James investigation. Even if Emma backs off now, Wells won't. Not after his TV segment on how Chelsea James is the unsolved case that still haunts her three years later. If she suddenly loses interest, that will only make him more inquisitive. That's the way the journalistic mind works."

"What do you want to do?"

"We have to find out who this anonymous tipster is before Wells finds out that the son of a bitch is pointing the finger at me."

"If the AG's office can't find him," said Weimer, "I don't see how we can."

"I don't care how," said Lomax. "Make it a priority. Make it the *top* priority. The top fucking priority, you hear me!"

The order came with so much force—indeed, desperation—that Josef paused to collect himself. His voice quaked, but he had to ask the question.

"Sir, I don't mean to be impertinent. But are we talking about saving an election here, or are we worried about going to jail for vehicular homicide?"

Lomax delivered a chilling glare. "Just find him," he said. "Fast.

CHAPTER 17

He did it in the black of night, alone, in the parked car. Total darkness and total silence. As if that would help conceal his identity.

He had absolutely no intention of giving up his anonymity.

The *Action News* segment on Emma Carlisle and the Chelsea James case had aired midway through the eleven o'clock news, right before the weather. It concluded with Doug Wells's direct appeal to the anonymous tipster: "Law enforcement is waiting to hear from you on your terms. Please visit the Rhode Island attorney general's Web site for more information."

At 11:25 PM, after the sports update, he logged on to the AG's Web site from an iPhone. The phone was still linked to the pirated wireless account that he had used to send Emma the anonymous tip by e-mail. The police hadn't shut it down—obviously, because they wanted to hear from him again—but there was no way to trace the wireless activity back to him. It wasn't exactly ingenious, but he was definitely feeling clever.

Anyone who could fly under the police radar this long deserved some credit.

The attorney general's Web site came up on his screen. On the far left side, directly below the attorney general's shield, was a menu. At the bottom of the list, below the button marked "Media and Information," was a link to "Chelsea James Investigation." It looked different from the other menu buttons and was obviously a new addition.

He clicked on the link, which led to another Web page.

"Please enter your password," it read.

His first thought was that he didn't

have a password, but the directions at the bottom of the page cleared up the confusion.

"Earlier this month, an attorney in the Criminal Division of the Office of the Attorney General received an e-mail from an anonymous tipster. The password is the e-mail address from which that e-mail was sent."

Smart, he thought. Without a password, no one visiting the attorney general's Web site—including the media— could see whatever special instructions law enforcement wanted to give the tipster. The chosen password was one that only the tipster would know.

He entered it.

The Web site took him to another page. The message there was short, directly to the point: Emma wanted to meet. She promised it would be just herself and the tipster—no police. It laid out everything he needed to know. It told him where to go. It told him when to be there.

But he already knew all that.

His visit to the Web site had nothing to do with gaining information. He'd gone through the motions for one reason only: to alert the authorities that their special Web site had received a hit from the man who knew the correct password, the man who had sent them the last e-mail. The cops would spring into action, even if Emma had promised no police involvement. They would all be waiting for the anonymous tipster to show up at the proposed meeting on Monday morning.

He logged off his Internet connection and switched off the iPhone, returning to total darkness.

He wondered who Emma expected to see when she got there.

He couldn't wait for it all to go down.

CHAPTER 18

Brandon Lomax was getting nervous. The meeting between Emma and her anonymous tipster was set for Monday at nine AM. The countdown had begun: T minus thirty-one hours.

"Go to sleep, honey," his wife said.

She lay in the bed beside him. After thirty-two years of marriage, he didn't have to do much to convey his restlessness to her. Even in a dark room at midnight, lying on her side with her back to him, she could sense when his eyes were open.

"I'm trying," he said, but it was futile.

The question his campaign manager

had put to him after the Marble House fund-raiser was replaying in his mind, threatening to keep him awake all night: "Sir, . . . are we talking about saving an election here, or are we worried about going to jail for vehicular homicide?" His response—"Just find him"—must have seemed cryptic, even incriminating. But he wasn't playing games.

The truth was, he *didn't know.*

Lomax had indeed suffered a relapse into alcoholism three years ago and, for him, there were no slight relapses. He had a drinking *problem,* and it was a problem because he didn't want just one or two drinks. He wanted ten or twelve. When Emma had asked him if he had an alibi for the night of Chelsea's death, he said he would have to look into it. That afternoon he and his wife had reported back to chief Garrisen.

"Brandon was with me," Sarah told the chief. "The entire evening."

Glenda Garrisen was too respectful to probe, which was fortunate. Sarah was a good wife but a lousy liar. Her story would never have held up under real cross-examination. Lomax hated himself for putting her in that position, but it wasn't as if they were covering up a crime he knew he had committed. The honest truth was that he had no idea where he was on the night of Chelsea's death.

He had been drinking. That was all he could say. His lack of any memory of what actually happened that night left open a sickening possibility: he very well could have been the drunk who had driven Chelsea James off the road.

"Honey," his wife said in the darkness. "Your alarm clock is going off in five hours. Please shut off your mind."

He sighed heavily, then rolled over and kissed her on the cheek.

"What was that for?" she said.

"You know."

She withdrew just a bit, as if ashamed by the lie she'd told to construct his alibi. He held her in his arms for a minute, just to reassure her. Then he peeled back the covers and climbed out of bed.

"Where are you going?" she said.

"I'll be right back," he said. He pulled on his robe and slippers, found his way in the darkness to the hallway, and walked to his study. With the door closed, he sank into his worn leather desk chair and stared at the ceiling.

What if it was me?

The question would have seemed bizarre to most people—to anyone who had never begged an alcoholic to get up off the floor and stop ruining his life, never watched a friend fall slave to the disease, never seen Brandon Lomax at his dead-drunk worst.

What if I killed her?

He closed his eyes tightly, trying to deal with that painful possibility. His drinking had hurt many people before—his wife and daughter for sure. But the wounds had been entirely emotional. Never had his alcoholism inflicted physical injury on any living thing, save for his own liver. The thought of his problem having caused the death of a young mother made him hate who he was, hate himself for his weakness.

It made him want a drink.

Be fair to yourself, Brandon.

That was what Sarah would have told him. It was a self-help strategy to deal with the fact that as long as he was an elected official, at least 50 percent of the people were going to hate him, and many of them would be downright vicious. Internalizing every insult and every mean thing anyone ever said about him gave him no chance against the bottle. His wife taught him to ignore his critics, to question his accusers, to stand up for himself. Sarah's advice made sense here too. He couldn't ask that question—*What if I killed Chelsea?*—without addressing the flip side.

What if this tipster was lying?

The flow of guilt shut off like a faucet. Suddenly he was the victim. Self-loathing gave way to anger. And he had every right to be furious. On Monday at nine AM Emma would meet with her tipster, some anonymous coward who could ruin him with his lies.

He had to seize control.

Across the room the grandfather clock chimed once, marking the half hour. It was 12:30 AM. His campaign manager was on call around the clock, but this was not a job for his usual political geniuses. This was a fight for survival.

Lomax returned to his bedroom and got dressed inside the walk-in closet, careful not to disturb his wife. On his way out, as he crossed the room in the darkness, she sat up in bed and asked, "Where are you going, honey?"

"I need some warm milk. We're out of two percent. I'll be back in fifteen minutes."

He felt like the Grinch, the way he'd thought up that lie and thought it up quick. He wasn't sure if little Cindy Lou Who believed him, but she didn't pursue it. Lomax grabbed his keys, got in his car, and drove three blocks to a convenience store. He would have to remind himself to buy the milk. First things first: the pay phone. This was a call that there could be no record of on his home or cell phone.

He paused to wonder if he was doing the right thing. Perhaps he had jumped the gun earlier in the week by hiring a private investigator to find out what Paul and Rachel Townsend knew about the tipster. He had no idea, however, that the cowboy was going to pose as a police officer and visit their house. And even though the tipster had not named him by name in that first tip, Lomax had long felt a bad vibe about the night of Chelsea's death. The accident had occurred not far from his house. He had no memory of his whereabouts for the better part of that night, but he did know that somehow he had gotten from a bar in South Boston to his house in Providence. He'd driven by the scene of the accident several times over the years, and each time it was strangely—eerily—familiar to him. Once or twice, he'd even seen Chelsea's brother there scrounging around for evidence.

Now that the tipster had implicated him directly, it was time to take things to another level.

He dialed information for Sid's Nightclub in Lincoln. It was long distance, but he had enough quarters to place the call. A woman answered, and there were bar noises in the background. It was a lively Saturday night at Sid's, gamblers tanking up before hitting the slot machines at Twin River.

"Is Sal there?" he said.

"Yeah, just a sec."

In his twenty-two years as a prosecutor, Lomax had come up against plenty of unsavory characters—Olneyville gangs, Valley Street drug traffickers, Mafia, even hitmen. Sometimes, however, he had decided not to seek indictments. His prosecutorial discretion was always based on the law and the facts—except once. One time in two decades, in a racketeering case that could have gone either way, he gave the benefit of the doubt to a friend of a freind. Never did he dream that he would call in that favor, but he was smart enough to recognize when it was time to cash in the chips. Someone had to intercept this anonymous tipster before the face-to-face meeting with Emma on Monday.

It wasn't a mob-style hit he wanted. Lomax hadn't gone completely mad. Like any seasoned politician, however, he knew that everyone had a price. Surely this tipster could be bought off. Particularly if the bribe was offered by someone skilled in the ways of making the proverbial offer that couldn't be refused.

"Sal here," said the voice on the line.

"Sal, hey it's me. POTUS."

POTUS was the Secret Service abbreviation for President of the United States. It was a little trivia Sal had picked up watching the old TV show *The West Wing.* It was the code name he had told Lomax to use if ever he needed to call on a guy like Sal Vanelli.

"How you doing, my friend?"

"Not so good," said Lomax. "I need a favor. A big favor."

"Talk to me," said Sal.

CHAPTER 19

At nine AM Emma entered the Modern Diner in Pawtucket.

Emma had put a lot of thought into the place to meet her anonymous tip-ster. The Modern Diner made sense, and not just because it served breakfast all day and had great pancakes. It was in the Oak Hill neighborhood, true blue-collar Pawtucket, where satellite dishes adorned old but colorfully painted frame houses, and sidewalks still bore the shield of the Works Progress Administration to mark their construction in 1939. The Modern Diner was of the same era, the dining portion of the

restaurant built to resemble an original
Sterling Streamliner, a railway dining car
manufactured in the late thirties and
early forties. More important, it was a local landmark (the first of its kind ever to
be placed on the national register of historic places), so Emma figured it would
be a familiar destination and a non-
threatening setting for anyone from
Pawtucket.

It was also within walking distance of
Babes's house, and even though the fingerprint analysis had failed to link him to
the first newspaper tip, she had not
completely given up on her theory that
Babes was the tipster.

"Just one?" said the waitress.

"For now," said Emma. "I'm expecting
someone."

The diner was bustling, as usual, and
the waitress invited her to take any
available booth. Before heading down
the narrow center aisle, Emma grabbed
a discreet read of every customer, trying
to determine if her anonymous tipster
had already arrived. A man drinking coffee at the counter seemed like a possibility. Apart from Emma, he was the only

customer dining alone. He looked up from his newspaper as she passed, and Emma quickly stole a closer look.

She'd never seen him before, but she'd seen men like him many times over. They would sit on the other side of a courtroom next to their high-priced criminal defense lawyer, all cleaned up in a suit and tie, trying to look legit. Jurors were sometimes fooled, but Emma could spot the little badges of fraud—the shiny new wedding band that had been purchased the day before, the hole in the earlobe that normally held a big diamond stud, the bloodshot eyes that said "I work nights and rarely see the light of day." This "businessman" was clearly pretending to be someone he wasn't.

Emma slid into a booth and positioned herself with a clear view of him.

"Something to drink?" said the waitress.

"Iced tea—no, wait," she said. Something about being in a diner made her yearn for her favorite part of Rhode Island school lunches. "Make it a coffee milk."

"And for your friend?"

"What?" said Emma, fearing that she had been too obvious in checking out the impostor at the counter.

"You said you were expecting someone," she said, her gum cracking.

"Oh, right. He can decide when he gets here," said Emma. *Unless he's already here.*

The waitress left two menus on the table and walked away. Emma picked up one and pretended to read, keeping one eye on the man who was looking more and more like her anonymous tipster.

Seeming to sense her gaze, he cast a slow, confident look in her direction.

Emma hid behind her menu. Then she dug her cell phone from her purse and placed it on the table beside her. Safety was on speed dial. The police were on alert, ready to swoop in if anything went wrong.

The waitress brought her coffee milk. The secret to the state's official drink was in the syrup, of course, a molasses-like substance made of sugar-sweetened coffee extract. The oldest brand name was Eclipse, and Emma had fond memories of her grandmother smiling and saying, "You'll smack your lips when it's Eclipse."

Emma drank slowly and watched as the man rose from his stool, placed a few bills on the counter, and took his briefcase. Emma wondered what might be inside of it—more damning evidence against Brandon Lomax? Her pulse quickened as he stepped away from the counter, but instead of coming down the aisle toward her, he started toward the door. Emma's gaze followed him, and as he left the restaurant, she slid to the end of the booth for a view out the window. He crossed the parking lot, and then she lost sight of him. Maybe he wasn't the tipster after all.

Or maybe I scared him away.

She was about to dial her police contact to put a tail on him when her gaze shifted to a man standing on the sidewalk across East Avenue. He was wearing a hooded sweatshirt with a baseball cap underneath. Emma couldn't see his face, but the longer she looked, the more he resembled Babes.

Suddenly he turned and ran.

Emma jumped up from the booth and tried to rush after him, but the old diner was so much like an old railway car that it had only one narrow aisle and little room to maneuver. By the time she made it out the door and into the parking lot, the man across the street had long gone.

She opened her flip phone but stopped short of hitting the speed dial button that would have sent the police chasing after him. The man's run was awkward, uncoordinated, and the baseball cap was no coincidence. It had to have been Babes, and something had frightened him enough to make him run for it. Maybe Emma's police protection wasn't as low profile as promised.

Sending the cops after him would only have pushed Babes over the edge.

The waitress was suddenly standing right beside her, waving a bill. "You owe us for a coffee milk," she said.

"I'm good for it," said Emma, as she dialed Ryan James on her cell phone.

CHAPTER 20

Run, run, run!

Babes started running the minute he spotted the cop coming out of the Modern Diner. The man wasn't dressed like a cop, but Babes knew an undercover agent when he saw one. The briefcase was a dead giveaway. That's where undercover agents carried their weapons and surveillance equipment. Babes knew. He'd seen it on television.

Run faster!

He was breathing heavily. His side ached. He checked over his shoulder to see if the undercover cop was following him, tripped on a buckle in the sidewalk, and fell to the ground. Running was not his thing. But he had to keep going. He'd been led to believe that the purpose of the meeting was to avoid trouble with the police. Obviously, that was a lie. Police chases never ended well for people like him.

People with secrets. Dark secrets.

He couldn't go home. That would be the first place the cops would go looking for him. He took a shortcut through an alley and raced to the bus stop. The door was closing and the number 99 bus was pulling away just as Babes reached the corner, but he hit the window with his fist and got the driver to stop.

"Hey, easy on the glass there, pal," the driver said.

Babes jumped aboard, flashed his pass, and found a seat.

His heart was pounding, but the familiar rumble of the diesel engine as the bus pulled away was strangely comforting to him. He looked out the window to see if the cop had followed him. He saw no one.

Lost him.

Then a wave of panic struck. Babes
looked around the bus to see if there
were other undercover agents carrying
briefcases. He saw only two other pas-
sengers. The black woman with her
baby he'd seen on this route many
times before. Nothing to worry about
there. But the old man with the walker
was not above suspicion. Babes had
taken the bus all the way to Providence
at least a thousand times before, and
he'd never seen him on it.

Better keep an eye on that guy.

The brakes screeched as the bus
reached the next stop. Babes shud-
dered, fearful that the undercover agent
from the Modern Diner had somehow
caught up and was about to board. No
one got on. The old man with the walker
got off.

Thank God.

The bus rumbled on. Babes was no
longer winded from the run, but he
could still hear himself breathing. He
had to get his anxiety under control. He
drew his knees up to his chest, wrapped
his arms around his shins, and gently
rocked back and forth. His mother

would have scolded him for putting his dirty shoes on the seat, but this was his comfort zone, and if he didn't do something, he was headed for a full blown panic attack. It got him through two more stops.

"North Providence," the driver said, as the bus reached the next stop.

Babes jumped from his seat and ran off the bus. He hadn't seen any sign of the undercover agent since leaving Pawtucket, but he was certain that the cops were still after him. He kept running until he reached Dr. Fisch's office. If he couldn't go home, his most trusted physician would know what to do.

Homicidal cows flirt. Anytime Babes got near his doctor's office, the letters in "Doctor William Fisch" tumbled around in his brain to produce that rather unflattering anagram.

Babes burst through the door. His legs were moving way too fast for him to control his movements, and he stumbled toward the reception desk.

"Is Dr. Fisch here?" he said, breathless.

The receptionist was clearly startled by his entrance—even a little fearful.

"Calm down, Daniel," she said.

"Is he here? I need to see him! I must see him right now!"

The door to Dr. Fisch's office opened, and the doctor stepped into the reception area.

"What's all the shouting about?" he said.

Babes went to him and stood as close as his anxieties would allow him to stand, which was still highly respectful of the doctor's personal space. Not even in a crisis could Babes get right in his face and look him in the eye.

Babes lowered his voice, not wanting the receptionist to hear. "I have to talk to you," he said.

The receptionist overheard. "Your next appointment will be here in ten minutes," she said.

"All right," said Dr. Fisch. "Come on in, Babes. Susan, hold my calls."

Babes entered the doctor's office. His steps were tenative, even though he'd visited many times before. Morning was not his usual appointment time, and the lighting in the office was different. More sunlight. Very unfamiliar. Highly distracting.

"Have a seat, Babes."

The doctor sat in the armchair. Babes didn't like the recliner other patients used. The leather felt icky against his fingertips. Knowing what an issue it could be for his patients, Dr. Fisch had several other chairs to choose from. Babes pulled up the oak chair with the straight back and no armrests. He sat with shoulders rigid, legs together, the palms of his hands flat atop his thighs.

"Tell me what's the matter," the doctor said in a soothing voice.

"I did something," said Babes.

"Something good? Or something bad?"

Babes didn't answer. The lighting in the room was all wrong. It was so bright. He wished it were four o'clock in the afternoon, his usual time.

The doctor said, "Did you do something good or something bad?"

"Something . . . bad."

"Okay," said Dr. Fisch. "You want to tell me about it?"

It was like a spotlight, all that light coming through the window. Like a white-hot light of interrogation.

"Babes, can you tell me about it?"

Where the heck is all that light coming from?

"Babes?"

It was that damn morning sun. The sunlight was reflecting off the windshield on the white van in the parking lot, cutting through the office window, and hitting Babes right in the eye.

I wonder if that's a police van.

"Babes, I need you to focus for me, all right?"

An unmarked police van, shining that light in my eyes.

"They're here," said Babes.

"Who's here?" said the doctor.

The light was getting brighter—at least it seemed brighter to Babes. But he couldn't move. He could only sit there in his chair and take it.

"Babes, tell me who's here."

I can't take it anymore!

Babes launched from his chair and dove toward the window.

"Babes, don't jump!"

The doctor sprang into action and tackled him. The two men collided like sonic jets and tumbled toward the window. Their momentum carried them straight into the glass, and suddenly a thousand pellets of shattered safety glass were showering down on Babes. The doctor fell to the floor, and Babes landed on top of him.

The door flew open and the receptionist hurried into the doctor's office. The piercing sound of her scream made Babes cringe.

Babes tried to help Dr. Fisch to his feet, but the old man needed a moment, and Babes was too apoplectic to give it to him. The blood on his brow sent Babes into a panic.

"Don't touch him!" said Susan, a look of horror on her face.

Babes was shaking uncontrollably. "I think—Dr. Fisch thought I was going to jump through the window. I just wanted to close the blinds."

"Get away from him! Go sit in the corner!"

Babes did as she instructed, and she went to her boss.

"Dr. Fisch, are you all right?"

"I . . . I don't know," he said, grimacing. "Oh, my head."

She was calling the doctor's name and asking him how many fingers she was holding up. Babes heard only fragments of what she was saying. He was trying to listen, struggling to focus, but that light from outside stole his attention all over again. Now it was shining on the pellets of glass on the floor, making them glisten like diamonds. It was all wrong. All this light, the doctor down on the floor, Dr. Fisch's receptionist now blaming Babes for something he didn't mean to do.

And the unmarked police van was still in the parking lot.

"Daniel, stop!" he heard her shout, but his legs were moving and his mind was made up as he raced out the door.

Run, run, run!

CHAPTER 21

Ryan's cell phone vibrated. He recognized Emma's number, but he was on the air with no cohost, and he couldn't take her call. He was eager to hear about the meeting at the Modern Diner, so he returned her call at the commercial break. She didn't answer.

"Thirty seconds to air," said his producer.

"Come on, answer the phone, Emma."

The door opened, and Jock walked in from his doctor's appointment.

"Thank God you're here," said Ryan.

"What the hell?" said Jock, shielding his eyes from the light. "Is this talk radio or a tanning salon? I need sunglasses in here."

Ryan switched off the sunlamp. "Sorry. It's part of my bright-light therapy."

"Your what?"

Ryan's doctor had theorized that he was having trouble falling asleep at night because he was cooped up in a windowless studio all morning, not getting enough bright light. But he didn't have time to explain.

"Never mind," said Ryan. "Can you cover? I have to make a phone call."

Jock took over. Ryan stepped out into the hall and kept punching Emma's number until she answered.

"How did it go?" said Ryan.

"I think it was Babes who showed up," she said.

"What do you mean *think*? Was it him or not?"

"He was standing across the street and ran away before I could get a close look, but I'm almost certain it was him."

"So you're saying Babes is your tipster?"

"The posting on the AG's Web site

said to meet at the Modern Diner on Monday at nine AM. The only way for Babes to get that information was to enter a password that only the tipster would know—the sender's address for the Brandon Lomax e-mail."

"The *what* e-mail?" said Ryan.

The line went silent.

"Are you telling me that the drunk who killed my wife is Brandon Lomax?"

There was brief silence, and Ryan could almost feel her backpedaling.

"That e-mail came from an anonymous tipster," she said. "We're a long way from verifying that Brandon had anything to do with it."

Ryan fell back in his chair, not quite believing. "Why didn't you tell me this before?"

"Because I wasn't supposed to tell anyone. Ryan, you have to keep this between us. I slipped. Please, be professional about this."

The door opened, and the producer popped her head into the studio. "Two minutes," she said.

"This is important," Ryan told her.

"Run the taped interview I did with Coach Belichick."

She groaned, but Ryan gave her a look that said he had both the pope and the president on the line. "Fine," the producer said. "But the last segment is live. I'm not closing out with tape."

The door closed. Ryan could talk again.

"I'm on your side," he said, "so don't worry about the slip. I can help you with Babes, but I want to know more about Lomax."

"Well, we need to slow down a little," said Emma. "So far we have no one but an anonymous tipster saying that Brandon is guilty. To be totally upfront with you, he actually has an alibi. His wife says they were together at the time of the crash."

"I'm no lawyer, but I'm sure prisons are full of guys whose only alibis were their wives."

"That's way too cynical. Brandon and Sarah Lomax are two amazing people."

"Is that so?"

"Yes."

"How amazing?"

"Two of the finest people I've ever met."

"Really? Just how close are you to the Lomaxes?"

"Are you suggesting that it's clouding my judgment?"

"Have you considered that possibility?"

"Have you considered the possibility that the accident was Chelsea's own fault?"

Ryan's mouth fell open, but no words came. He'd never seen that side of Emma. He'd obviously hit a nerve by attacking the Lomaxes.

Emma breathed away some of the tension on the line. "I'm sorry. I didn't mean that."

"It's okay. I probably deserved it. As dedicated as you've been to this case for the past three years, I shouldn't have questioned your professionalism."

"No, I was out of line. Please, don't let what I said make you question my commitment to the case."

"I won't. But . . ."

"But what?"

"I want to see the e-mail. After three

years, we should be able to operate on that level of trust."

"All right," she said, her voice laden with only a hint of reluctance. "I'll have it hand delivered. But it's for your eyes only. Not even Paul and Rachel can see it."

"Agreed."

Ryan's cell phone blipped, signaling another call. He checked the display. "Speaking of Chelsea's parents, it's my mother-in-law."

"You want to call me back?" said Emma.

"No, hold on for a second." He took the call. Rachel sounded extremely upset, her voice racing. She wasn't making much sense.

"Slow down and take a breath," said Ryan. "Now tell me what the problem is."

"Babes just called on his cell. He was crying and sounded like a scared child. He wouldn't tell me what was wrong. He just said he's not coming home, not ever, and that we sholdn't come looking for him."

"Hold on a second, Rachel. I have

Emma on the other line. I'm going to do a three-way." Ryan patched her in and recapped for Emma.

"Did Babes say where he's going?" he asked Rachel.

"No. But he had just been to see Dr. Fisch. His receptionist called me right before Babes did. Babes had some kind of . . . something went wrong. Dr. Fisch got injured."

"Injured?" said Ryan. "How?"

"It's not clear," said Rachel. "Dr. Fisch swears that Babes wasn't trying to hurt him. He thought Babes was going to jump through the window. Babes was very upset."

"About what?" said Ryan.

"He wouldn't tell Dr. Fisch," said Rachel.

Emma said, "Did Babes say anything about being at the Modern Diner this morning?"

"No, no. Not to me, at least. He was hysterical, talking crazy. He said someone is after him. Some businessman with a big leather briefcase."

"Oh," said Emma, and Ryan picked up on her reaction immediately.

Rachel was still talking, but she was simply repeating herself. Ryan said, "Anything else, Rachel?"

"No, I think that's everything."

"Okay. Have you tried calling Babes back?"

"Yes, of course. It rang once and went to his voice mail. That means he turned his phone off."

"If Babes calls again, you call us immediately. We'll take it from there."

"All right."

They said good-bye, and as quickly as he could disconnect Rachel, his question for Emma popped out of his mouth: "What's up with the guy and the briefcase?"

She told him about the man at the counter in the Modern Diner, the one who looked like he was trying way too hard to look legit.

Ryan said, "So it definitely was Babes you saw across the street from the diner."

"I'd say so."

He shook his head. "I'm still having trouble buying Babes as the tipster. Why has he stayed silent all this time? Why did he come forward anonymously?"

"Those are good questions," said Emma.

Ryan ran his hands through his hair. "I need answers."

"We need to find Babes."

She was right. Whatever it was that had scared him off, Babes was now like a big kid on the run, a grown man living in the distorted world of Asperger's syndrome who was fighting to stay one step ahead of his parents, Ryan, Emma, the police, and everyone else who was searching for him—including, perhaps, Brandon Lomax.

And maybe even that guy with the briefcase whom Emma had seen at the Modern Diner.

The door opened. It was the show's producer again. "You're live in one minute," she told Ryan.

He was about to protest, but then a thought came to him. "I'm ready," he said.

She smiled, a little surprised, as if she had expected a quarrel. "Good."

As the door closed, he told Emma, "I've got an idea."

"Why does that make me nervous?"

"No, this is perfect. Babes never goes anywhere without his earbuds and portable radio. He listens all day long. And he never misses my show."

"You're going to talk to him on the air?"

"Live," said Ryan. "Just like the producer ordered."

CHAPTER 22

Babes didn't stop running until he reached one of the oldest cemeteries in Rhode Island, a good two miles away.

He was headed for his favorite hiding spot.

Listed on the National Register of Historic Places, the North Burial Ground dates back to the eighteenth century and was the final resting place for everyone from the founders of Brown University to former governors and senators. Babes's destination was a huge nineteenth-century stone crypt that was like a small chapel. Everyone buried there was named Dawes. The last member of the Dawes family to be laid to rest there died in 1921, and the surrounding graves were even older, so no one ever visited. Only Babes.

Please, God. Make Dr. Fisch be okay.

Unfamiliar places were generally tough for Babes, especially after an event as stressful as his visit to Dr. Fisch's office. But the Dawes family crypt was like his home away from home. Babes had been going to the crypt since he was eleven years old, and it was his secret. He happened upon it after a particularly brutal day of teasing in the sixth grade. He wished he were dead, so, he had walked to the cemetery to select a burial plot. Soon he was fascinated. He started memorizing names and dates on tombstones, and this special (albeit morbid) interest eventually led him to the oldest part of the cemetery, where he first laid eyes on the impressive Dawes family crypt. It was the most quiet, beautiful place he'd ever seen, completely removed from the chaos of the real world, with no one to tease or bully him.

Babes enjoyed his time alone. While

other kids had play dates or after-school activities, Babes would come to the Dawes crypt alone and design for himself a highly complex fantasy world. As a teenager, he pretended that the Dawes crypt was an individual town, and he populated this town with make-believe people and characters, some from TV sitcoms and cartoons, and others from the tombstones he saw in the cemetery. Throughout high school, these people were Babes's *real* friends, and he liked them because they were exactly what he wanted them to be. He pretended that he was popular, owned a car, and had a girlfriend. The fantasies changed as he moved into adulthood— he dreamed of being a successful adult, married with children, living in a perfect world where everything was exactly the way he wanted it to be, providing him a surefire escape from the hardships of reality. He always fantasized about the future, hoping for a better life in a better town with a woman who loved him and a job that paid him immense amounts of money. But one thing in the crypt remained the same throughout his childhood and into adulthood: his baseball card collection. He would spend hours memorizing the statistics on the back of each card and converting the players' names into anagrams. One that still made him giggle was the fabled inventor of baseball, Abner Doubleday. "A barely nude bod," he said aloud, bringing back the memory.

Babes adjusted the volume on his pocket radio. Babes loved his radio. It had cost him all of twenty dollars, and he would never get rid of it. Every morning he clipped it onto his belt, connected the earbuds, and went off. A single double-A battery lasted forever. He could have purchased a more expensive digital model with a more precise tuner, but those were for music freaks who liked to change channels. Babes listened to AM all day long, two or three different stations at most, nothing but sports talk radio. *Jocks in the Morning* was playing at the moment, but he was only half listening to Ryan's interview of Coach Belichick. Babes knew it was taped. Ryan had e-mailed it to him the

previous week, and he'd already listened to it a dozen times.

"We're back live, knuckleheads," he
heard Ryan say over the air.

Babes surveyed the crypt for a place
to sit and listen to the last fifteen minutes of Ryan's show. Rain from the night
before had left the marble floor wet in
spots. He found a dry corner near the
rose-shaped window of stained glass,
drew his knees up to his chest, and listened.

"Got a special message for a special
friend of mine," said Ryan. "This goes
out to my brother-in-law. We call him
Babes."

Babes stiffened.

"Babes, if you're listening, we love
you and we miss you. We want you to
come home. There's nothing to be afraid
of. We'll even come get you, wherever
you are. So, come on, buddy. Give us a
call."

Babes switched off the radio, drew up
his knees even tighter, and began to
rock on his tailbone while biting down
on his lower lip.

Come home, says Ryan. There's nothing to be afraid of. *Yeah, right.* Then why was that undercover cop waiting for him at the Modern Diner? Ryan would deny it, of course. He'd say the guy wasn't a cop. But Babes knew he was one. He just knew it.

And now Dr. Fisch was hurt.

Babes screamed at the top of his lungs. It was one of those long and shrill screams that could curl a person's hair—the kind that, as long as Babes could remember, had forced his mother to grab him by the hand and run for the exit at restaurants and movie theaters.

He felt better now. But he still didn't know what to do.

The secret is coming out.

He was sure of it. It was a terrible, dark secret. He was tired of living with it, and he wanted it out. Why else would he have contacted Emma Carlisle in the first place?

Don't know what to do.

The rocking started up again. It wasn't as if he could control it. Like a reflex, his knees came up to his chest again, his arms wrapped tightly around his shins, and his body was in motion. He was biting down on his lip so hard that he could taste a little blood in his mouth.

The secret is coming out soon.

He might have been okay with coming clean, except for one person. His father. Babes knew his father loved him. At least he thought so. But neither of his parents had been the same since Chelsea's accident. Sure, it was a tragedy. They had lost their daughter. But in a weird way, it simply drove home the point that a big strapping man like Paul Townsend deserved someone like Ryan James as a son, not a grown man who threw a baseball like a sissy and couldn't even look another man in the eye when he shook hands. He should have been the one, not Chelsea, who'd been killed in a car accident.

Babes closed his eyes tightly, very tightly, until he finally forced himself to stop rocking. He checked his watch. Almost ten o'clock. Ryan would be on the air only a few more minutes.

Babes drew a deep breath. Weird, but even though thousands of people would be listening, the idea of calling Ryan at the station and talking live on the air—

letting his secret be known that way—
was less scary than speaking to him
face to face. Especially when he could
call from the safety and familiarity of his
favorite hiding spot.

He removed his earbuds and let the
radio play through its loudspeaker. Ryan
was still jabbering, and the sound of his
voice was comforting too.

Babes knew the call-in number. He'd
heard Ryan say it so many times on the
air, he could have repeated it in his
sleep. He took another long breath and
reached for his cell phone.

Slowly, one fateful digit at a time, he
punched out the studio phone number
for *Jocks in the Morning*.

CHAPTER 23

Emma tuned in to *Jocks in the Morning* just in time to hear Ryan's on-air appeal to Babes. Some of her favorite FM stations were out of Boston, but this was her first visit to this end of her AM band. Sports talk radio was not her thing.

Sorry, Ryan.

Apologies seemed to be the order of the day. That mean retort about Chelsea—"Have you considered the possibility that the accident was Chelsea's own fault?"—was completely unlike Emma. But Ryan had no idea how much it had hurt to hear him question her objectivity, to have him throw the Brandon

Lomax conflict of interest in her face. It stung for so many reasons. Because it mattered to her what Ryan thought of her. Because she was committed to finding out what really had happened to Chelsea. Because she prided herself on her professionalism. And because she feared that personal feelings for Brandon Lomax might really be getting in the way. Childhood memories aside, Lomax had hired Emma right out of law school and groomed her to be one of the top felony prosecutors in his office. Their lives were so intertwined, personally and professionally.

"We're back, knuckleheads," she heard Ryan say after the commercial. "Shake out the cobwebs, light up the phone lines, tell me what's on your mind."

She stopped her car at the red light and listened. Oddly enough, hearing Ryan on the radio made her feel good. Just the sound of his voice—even though he wasn't talking to her—was enough to make her forgive him for bringing up the Brandon Lomax issue. And that worried her. Ever since the party at Marble House—when Ryan had asked if she was with someone, and then looked so disappointed when she'd told him that she was—she'd felt somewhat off balance about Ryan. It had already gotten her into trouble when she'd slipped and mentioned Brandon Lomax and the tipster's e-mail in the same sentence.

Maybe that was a blessing.

Ryan had forced her to be a little more sensitive to her biases. He was right about the alibi: Sarah Lomax was beyond reproach, but plenty of good wives have lied to save their husbands. Now, thanks to his wife, Sarah, Brandon Lomax had an alibi that was airtight. *Too* airtight.

"Lines are still open," said Ryan. "Let's talk sports and corporate sponsors. TV announcers are forced to say the full name of stadiums every time they mention a venue: AT&T Park, Coors Field, and so on. It's no longer the Home Run Derby, it's the State Farm Home Run Derby. We don't have replays, we have Aflac replays. Sometimes I think we're on the verge of hearing routine plays called something like this: 'Top of the first Holiday Inn-ing. Josh Becket on the Boone's Farm strawberry hill. He shakes off the 1-900-ASTROLOGY sign from the catcher, hurls a Jiffy Lube slider, and it catches the outside corner of the Wedgwood china plate for a Don-Carter-Bowling-Lanes strike.' "

Emma wasn't listening. Her mind was busy trying to heed Ryan's earlier words and to be more objective about Brandon Lomax. Her effort suddenly brought to mind a strange conversation with the case manager right before the attorney general left office to run for the Senate. Emma had felt pushed to send the Chelsea James vehicular homicide off to the cold case unit sooner than normal. Maybe the pressure hadn't been coming from the case manager. Maybe it was from Lomax himself, trying to make sure that the case didn't rear its ugly head after he was gone.

"Dude, you there? You're on *Jocks.*"

There was garble on the radio.

Ryan said, "Caller, you have to turn your radio off. I can hear it in the background."

There was silence.

"That's better," said Ryan. "Now what's your question, pal?"

Finally, the caller spoke. "Hi, Ryan. It's me."

Ryan froze. He had been keeping an eye on his cell phone, hoping for Babes to call. He hadn't expected him to dial into the station. Obviously, the producer had put him through without realizing who it was.

"Hold on one second, Babes. We're going to take our listeners straight to a commercial, and then you and I can talk in private."

"No! I want this on the air."

His shrillness both chilled and worried Ryan. "Okay, Babes. Take it easy. We'll stay on the air."

"Don't think you can lie to me! I turned my radio down, but I didn't turn it off. I'll know if we go off the air."

Ryan could hear the echo of their conversation in the background. "That's fine," he said. "But you need to turn the radio way down, Babes. There's a few second delay between our phone conversation and what you hear on the radio. I don't want you getting confused."

The producer barged into the studio, nostrils flaring, her face red with anger. She flashed the CUT sign across her throat.

Ryan spoke into the microphone. "Bear with me, Babes. My producer wants me to hang up, but I'm not going to let you go. I know she wouldn't want it on her hands if you were to hurt yourself."

She glared at Ryan, but she was shrinking before his eyes. She flashed two fingers and left. Ryan had control of the airwaves for that many minutes.

"Babes, where are you?"

"I can't tell you," he said, his voice quaking.

"Why not?"

"Because I *can't.*"

"Where are you going?"

"I—I don't know."

"Why don't you come home?"

"No! I can't."

"Why can't you?"

"Because . . ." His voice cracked. Ryan could tell that he was crying.

"Babes, why can't you come home?"

"Because I did something bad."

"Dr. Fisch is going to be fine. He knows you weren't trying to hurt him. You don't have to worry about that."

"Well, that's good. But that's not what I'm talking about. I did something else that's even worse. Much, much worse."

"That doesn't matter," said Ryan. "You can always come home, no matter—"

"No, you're wrong! You don't know, Ryan. You just don't know!"

"You're right, Babes. I don't know. Why don't you tell me about it?"

"I—I'm trying."

"Do you want to go off the radio?"

"No! This is how I want it."

Ryan wasn't sure what to do. Part of him wanted to take the call private. But Babes had his radio playing in the background, and Ryan was afraid he'd hang up if they went off the radio. Babes obviously had something bottled up inside of him, and he wanted it broadcast for everyone to hear.

Babes was ready, Ryan realized, to lose his anonymity.

"Babes, was that you outside the Modern Diner this morning?"

"Yes."

"How did you know to go there?"

"Because I got a phone call yesterday."

It wasn't the answer Ryan had expected. He knew about the link on the attorney general's Web site—and that there was a password that only the tipster would know.

"Somebody called you?"

"Yes, on my cell. They said that they knew what I had done, and that if I wanted to stay out of trouble with the police, I had to go to the Modern Diner at nine o'clock Monday morning."

"Who called you?"

"I don't know."

"He said he knew what you had done. What does that mean? He knew you were sending Emma anonymous tips?"

"Well . . . no. Maybe that is what he meant. But that's not what I thought he was saying."

"What did you think he was saying?"

"I can't tell you. You're going to hate me."

"I will never hate you, Babes. I love you. Your mom and dad love you. We're your family. We will always love—"

"No, you won't! You'll hate me. You *should* hate me!"

"Babes, what did you do?"

"I . . ." His voice broke again.

The sobbing was audible, and in his mind's eye, Ryan could see the tears streaming down his brother-in-law's face. Babes seemed to be slipping beyond reach. The only person Ryan had ever known to calm Babes in a meltdown like this one was Chelsea, and for the millionth time since her death, Ryan wished she were there.

"Babes, I'm listening."

"I did it," he said softly.

"You did what?" said Ryan, gripping the phone tighter.

More sobbing. Finally, Babes answered in a booming voice that shook Ryan to his core.

"I killed my sister!"

CHAPTER 24

Brandon Lomax was nowhere near a radio on Monday morning. He had a very private meeting in his home with Dr. Calvin Overstreet. Dr. Overstreet didn't normally make house calls, but a candidate for the U.S. Senate couldn't be caught visiting the office of a psychiatrist. Their relationship went back almost twenty years, and Overstreet had never breathed a word to anyone about Lomax's battle with alcohol.

"Have you slipped again?" said Overstreet. He was a slight man with a soft voice and a salt-and-pepper beard that was neatly groomed.

He checked his watch. "It's ten-forty in the morning, and I've had only four scotches. Is that a slip?"

"Sounds like we need to get with the program."

"Screw the program. That's not why I called you."

"Okay. Then how can I help you?"

Lomax paused. He hated to sound desperate, but he was exactly that. This morning's attempt to bribe the anonymous tipster had been poorly conceived. He'd hired Sal the thug, who seemed street smart in the ways of bribery and extortion. But there were too many logistical problems in meeting up with a target who could be identified only after revealing himself to Emma. The plan was doomed the minute Sal had entered the restaurant with a briefcase full of cash and waited at the counter, in Emma's plain view. Fortunately, the dope had the good sense to get up and leave before she became too suspicious. It was the kind of half-baked plan that flowed from a position of weakness—worse than his decision to hire a private investigator to ply Chelsea's parents. Knowledge was strength. If Lomax was going to be strong, he needed to know the truth about the night of Chelsea's crash.

"I want to talk to you about the recovery of lost memories," said Lomax.

"Intriguing. From your childhood?"

"No. There's a night—" he said, then stopped himself. As much as he trusted Dr. Overstreet, he still didn't feel ready to pinpoint his possible involvement in Chelsea's accident. "There's a night in my fairly recent past when I drank too much and simply can't recall anything about it."

"Well, let's dissect that a little. When you say you can't remember *anything,* do you remember whom you were with?"

"I know I started the night alone. Drinking."

"Do you remember what triggered it? The drinking, I mean."

Lomax phrased his answer carefully. "I had an important business meeting with some men in Boston. It went very badly."

"Then what?"

"I left in my car and was driving home to Providence. Didn't get far. I stopped in the first bar I saw in South Boston."

"Do you remember the name of it?"

"No. It was just a place to get drunk, and the name wasn't important. I started drinking scotch, and from that point on, my memory is gone."

"What's the next thing you can recall?"

"Waking up the next morning in my house."

"Was your car in the driveway?"

"Yes."

"So you left the bar in Boston and somehow drove to Providence, and you have no memory of it."

The doctor had zeroed in on the heart of the problem. Lomax said, "I know that must sound unbelievable."

"No, it's more common than you can imagine," the doctor said. "Harvard did a recent study on college students nationwide and found that fifty-one percent of those who drink have experienced blackouts."

"But I was conscious until I got home."

"A blackout and passing out are two different things. In fact, they're mutually exclusive. A blackout is a period of amnesia during which a person is actively engaged in behaviors—walking, talking—but the brain is unable to transfer new information from short-term to long-term storage. You can experience a blackout and appear only moderately intoxicated to the outside world."

"So I'm no different from the average college student?" he said with a sardonic smile.

"Not exactly. One of the most famous studies in this area focused on alcoholics in a laboratory setting. Their blackouts ranged from nine hours to three days."

"You can't get into much trouble in a laboratory setting."

"No, but the literature is replete with wild accounts of things alcoholics do during blackouts. Driving a car, traveling long distances for several days, selling real estate, having intercourse with multiple partners, body piercing, tattooing, self-mutilation. Even committing murder."

The last one on the doctor's list struck an ominous chord. "Do these memories ever come back?"

"It depends. Memory impairment of the fragmentary type can often be recovered with cueing or the simple passage of time. But alcoholics are more likely to have the en bloc form, meaning the complete impairment of memory formation."

"So my memories are gone for good?"

"Not necessarily. But we may have to try some unconventional methods."

"How unconventional?"

Dr. Overstreet paused, as if expecting some resistance. "How would you feel about hypnosis?"

Lomax laughed, but the doctor's expression stopped him. "You're serious?"

"Completely."

"And if it doesn't work, what do we do next? Voodoo? A séance?"

"Hypnosis actually has quite a solid backing in the scientific community."

"All right, doctor. I'll bite. Tell me how it would work."

"The first step is for you to believe that

it will work. So if you'll indulge me a little further, let me give you some background."

He checked his watch. He had lunch with a Rotary Club on his campaign schedule. "You have three minutes."

Dr. Overstreet nodded, then stroked his chin like the professor he was, and Lomax sensed another one of his infamous monologues coming.

"One of the earliest applications of hypnosis was in the reduction of pain during medical procedures . . ."

As the doctor waxed on about Charcot, Freud, and "hysterical" women, Lomax retreated into thought, aching for another scotch and wondering how he had ever gotten himself into this tragic mess. Alcoholism was part of his family, and he was sure he'd inherited it from his father. Four years earlier, he'd thought he had it beat, but he ended up replacing one addiction, alcohol, with another, gambling. Before he knew it, he had a mountain of debt he could never repay on an elected official's salary. Then a year later, when the "bill collectors" came, he came within hours of personal and financial disaster. He finally found a solution—but not before he'd started drinking again.

"Hypnosis today has many practical applications . . ."

None of this drinking was Lomax's fault, of course. Those bastards who'd backed him into a corner on the gambling debts were the ones who'd knocked him off the proverbial wagon. If it weren't for them, he would never have gotten drunk on the night Chelsea James was run off the road. He never would have been on the road that night . . . if he was on the road. He still didn't know. Couldn't remember. But as the doctor had just pointed out, Lomax had somehow driven his car from that bar in Boston back to his house in Providence.

It must *have been me.*

"So tell me," said Dr. Overstreet, "what specific day are you trying to recall?"

Lomax hesitated. "What are the chances of success?"

"There is a danger of false memory. Many recalled childhood sexual abuse cases have been criticized on that ground. But I feel that I have been able to attain reliable results."

There was a knock at the door. Lomax had given his housekeeper a strict order for no intrusions, and she was not one to disregard his instructions lightly. He excused himself and went to the door. His campaign manager was there, his eyes wide with excitement.

"I need to talk to you immediately," said Josef.

"I'm in the middle of something important. That's why I didn't answer my cell."

Josef leaned closer and spoke softly, so as not to be overheard by anyone inside the study. "Chelsea's brother just phoned in to the Ryan James's radio show. He confessed that he was the drunk driver who killed his sister."

"Praise God!" he said, unable to contain himself. He locked Josef in a back-slapping embrace.

Josef broke away, his happy expression evaporating. "You've been drinking," he whispered, but his tone was harsh. "I can smell it."

Dr. Overstreet said, "Do we need to do this another time, Brandon?"

Lomax was smiling so widely that it almost hurt. "No, Doctor," he said, still studying the look of concern on his campaign manager's face. "On second thought, it looks like I won't be needing your services at all."

CHAPTER 25

Emma drove straight to her office. She wanted to believe that Babes's confession cleared Brandon Lomax's name, but she was having a hard time imagining how it could have been true. To sort it out, Emma went straight to the top: Criminal Division chief Glenda Garrisen.

"Did Babes even have a driver's license?" asked the chief.

"He got one at seventeen, but he's never had his own car, and his parents never let him drive alone."

The chief looked across her office, thinking. Her gaze settled on a museum-quality oil painting on the wall directly behind Emma, and Emma knew better than to interrupt. Chief Garrisen searched that seascape for wisdom the way some of the world's greatest thinkers drew upon the ocean itself for inspiration.

"Here's my take," said the chief. "On the night of the accident, only Chelsea and Ainsley had a ticket to the big game, right?"

"That's right. Ryan left Babes out because he was afraid that the crowd and the noise might be too much for him too handle."

"From what I know about the case, Babes probably hadn't missed a home game all year."

"That's true. No offense to your husband or his team, but most games aren't sellouts or anywhere near that level of excitement."

"That's my point. He was probably boiling mad when he found out that he wasn't going to the biggest and final game of the regular season, in which his beloved PawSox, the best team in the International League, battled against the

Toledo Mud Hens, the league's second best."

Her awareness of the standings was impressive, even if she was married to the owner. "I would imagine that's true," said Emma.

The chief continued, "Babes was so angry, in fact, that when Chelsea was driving to the game, Babes ran out of the house, took his father's car and chased her down the road. Plausible?"

"I'd say yes. Ryan, Chelsea, and Ainsley lived rent free in the flat above Chelsea's parents."

"Okay, good," said the chief. "Now, the forensic evidence showed tire tracks on and off the shoulder of the road, suggesting a swerving car. We inferred that those tracks were made by a drunk driver. In light of this confession, however, I suggest that those erratic tire tracks prove that the man behind the wheel was Babes, a driver of limited skills who was in the throes of an Asperger's meltdown. Babes ran her off the road."

"Accidentally?" said Emma.

"Maybe it was an accident. Or in his

rage, maybe it was on purpose. He did say he killed her."

"True. But in this context I think 'killed' means that he caused her death. Not necessarily murder. I'm no expert on Asperger's syndrome, but we do need to take his condition into consideration when evaluating this confession."

"That's why at the very least, he needs to be brought in for questioning. Coordinate with the sheriff's office on that."

"Unfortunately, no one knows where he is."

The chief mulled it over in silence. "Give his parents twenty-four hours to bring him downtown. Be sure to tell them he can have a lawyer present if they wish."

"And if they can't find him—then what?"

"What else can we do?" said the chief. "Get an arrest warrant."

Ryan walked straight into a media storm.

They were camped outside the main entrance to the radio station. Photographers, cameramen, television reporters,

print journalists, the local sports blog-
gers—everybody, it seemed, had either
heard or heard about Babes's on-air
confession. Coming out of a windowless radio station was always a bit like
crawling out of a cocoon, no telling what
might be waiting outside—wind, rain,
snow. Ryan would have preferred nuclear winter to this frenzy. Chaos was literally on the doorstep, and it had caught
him so off guard that, instinctively, he
turned around and went back inside the
lobby to plan another exit strategy.

His cell rang. It was Ivan calling from
his hotel room in California.

"Dude, I haven't even had breakfast,
and I'm getting bombarded by reporters. Is this stuff about Babes true?"

Ryan told him everything, and it was
exactly as Ivan had heard it from the
press.

"What are you going to do?" asked
Ivan.

"I'm headed to Pawtucket now to see
Chelsea's parents," he said. "I'll figure it
out from there."

"This on-air confession is so bizarre.

You might want some advice from a criminal attorney."

"The only lawyer I know does wills," said Ryan.

"Call mine. His specialty is sports and entertainment, but in the legal food chain, that's just one shark tank away from criminal."

"I appreciate that," he said. "I think."

Ivan gave him the phone number. "One other thing. The way they're hounding me, this is definitely going to be page one in sports, if not A-1 news. Be careful with the photographers. They will trick you, taunt you, hound you— anything to get the photo they want."

"I hear you."

"I'll be in LA till the end of the Angels series. But if there's anything else you need, you call me, you hear?"

"Thanks, man. I'll do that."

He closed his flip phone and checked the security monitor by the door. A black-and-white video camera provided a fish-eye view of the outside entrance. It was mainly for the benefit of the graveyard DJs who left late at night, and Ryan normally paid no attention to it on his morning shift. The mob outside had actually grown larger. He would simply have to forge through it. Ryan started toward the exit, but his producer stopped him.

Beatrice was out of breath and holding a high-heeled shoe in each hand, having raced barefoot down two flights of stairs to catch him. "You aren't going to talk to the press, are you?"

"Not a chance," said Ryan.

"Good," she said, her tone conveying a curious sense of relief. She put her shoes back on and then laid a hand gently on Ryan's forearm, as if to emphasize her concern. Beatrice wasn't one of those touchy-feely folks, however, so it didn't come across as genuine. "I just wanted to say that I know how difficult this must be for you. As far as the radio show goes, whatever you need to do, you have the freedom to do it."

"Thanks. I may need some time off."

"No!" she said, and then she caught her own overreaction. "I mean . . . *no problem.* On the other hand, don't put the show on hold out of any concern that this is sports talk radio. If Babes calls in again, feel free to talk to him. On the air. If you think that's best, of course."

Best for Babes or best for ratings?

"I'll keep that in mind," he said.

"Great. Now just head for your car, and don't say a word to those reporters."

It was clear that Beatrice smelled a serious and ongoing news exclusive for her station, and Ryan wanted to tell her to shove it. But it suddenly occurred to him that as long as Babes remained on the run, the radio was the only proven way of communicating with him. He kept his feelings to himself, opened the door, and faced the music.

Cameras clicked, microphones were immediately thrust into his face, and questions came from everywhere.

"Have you spoken to the police?"

"Where is your brother-in-law?"

"How did he kill her?"

Those were the ones that Ryan could hear, but mostly it sounded like one person talking on top of another, a cacophony of interrogation. Ryan simply put one foot in front of another, moving himself and the mob of reporters toward the parking lot next to the building.

"I'm sorry," said Ryan, "but I can't talk about any of this."

The questions kept coming, and it was getting harder to make forward progress. This was a hundred times worse than anything he had ever faced as a ballplayer. On the journalistic scale of newsworthiness, being MVP of the College World Series in Omaha was nothing compared to on-air scandal in Boston.

His car was ten feet away. Ryan unlocked it with his key remote and forged ahead, but the photographers pushed back. Ivan had told him stories about the paparazzi, but this was the first time he'd seen them in action. Each was trying to out maneuver the other for the front-page shot of the one-time rising star in the Red Sox organization who had fallen with the tragic death of his wife, and who was falling all over again with a shocking confession.

"Hey, asshole! Was Babes fucking her too?"

Ryan glared with contempt, which was immediately met by a camera flash. It was a tried-and-true paparazzi tactic to get celebrities to look toward the lens and cast the angry, out-of-control expression that ended up on the front page of the tabloids. Ivan had warned him, and Ryan had fallen for it.

Ryan jumped in the car and burned rubber out of the parking lot.

He called Emma on his cell. Of course she had heard everything. Ryan hardly knew where to begin.

"We need to sort one thing out right away," he said. "The phone call."

"What phone call?"

"I asked Babes why he went to the diner, expecting him to say that he got the information from the attorney general's Web site. But he said that someone called him yesterday and said to meet at the diner if he wanted to avoid trouble with the police. That means he wasn't the person who accessed the Web site and entered the password—he didn't send the e-mail tip to you."

"Two thoughts on that," said Emma.

"I'm listening."

"One, Babes is lying. He's afraid of getting into trouble for giving false tips to the police, so he made up a story about some stranger calling him out of the blue."

"Let me hear thought number two," said Ryan.

"Well, there was a guy at the diner who caught my attention. He left right before I spotted Babes across the street. Nothing concrete. I just had a hunch about him."

"I need to read that e-mail," said Ryan.

"I had it delivered to your house."

"Thank you," he said. "That's right on my way to Pawtucket."

CHAPTER 26

Ryan opened his front door and nearly stepped on the envelope from Emma. The courier had slipped it through the mail slot, and it was lying on the floor. He tore it open, not even taking the time to sit before reading it.

The "Re" line was jarring enough: "Why haven't you arrested him? Are you going to LET HIM GET AWAY WITH THIS?" The sender's screen name was a seemingly random sequence of numbers and letters, not a recognizable name. Ryan read on into the body:

The first clue said I know who did it. The second one said it's him. Didn't you see the picture of XXXXXXX?

The name was blacked out. Apparently Emma had taken the added precaution of redacting all references to Brandon Lomax, just in case Ryan carelessly let the letter slip into someone else's hands. The e-mail continued:

What more do you jerk-offs need? Maybe this will help: VOMIT. You know what I mean. That bastard XXXXXXX was so drunk that he vomited when he got out of the car and saw what happened to Chelsea. The cops kept that juicy tidbit a secret, didn't they? I never read anything in the paper about any vomit being found at the scene. But I don't believe for one sec your CSI guys fucking missed it. Soooo . . . NOW DO YOU BELIEVE ME?

There was nothing more.

Ryan put the e-mail down. The vomit made sense—it must have been the reason the police were so convinced that the driver had been drinking. Alcohol would have shown up in the sample, though proving that it was in his blood would have been another matter. Ryan wasn't sure why they had withheld that information from the public, but he had heard of police withholding pieces of evidence for strategy reasons, and the e-mail was right on: nowhere and at no time in the past three years had there been any public mention of the vomit found on the scene. Emma had first suspected that Babes might be the tipster when she sat in his parents' kitchen and saw the circled words and handwritten anagrams on his copy of the *New York Times.* Ryan tended to agree with Chelsea's father that Babes would not have withheld evidence that could have revealed the drunk who had run Chelsea off the road. But the e-mail presented a different problem entirely.

It just didn't sound like Babes.

Ryan put the e-mail in his coat pocket, jumped in his car, and took one more detour before heading down to Pawtucket to see Paul and Rachel.

Fifteen minutes later, he was in the of-

fice of Dr. Fisch, Babes's neuropsychia-
trist.

"Thank you for making time to see
me, doctor," said Ryan.

"My pleasure. So what is it you would
like me to read?"

"This," said Ryan, as he laid the
printed copy of the e-mail message on
the desk before him.

Dr. Fisch picked it up, but he didn't
read it right away. He was Babes's neu-
ropsychiatrist because he was a gentle
human being who took the time to know
his patients and their families. He
seemed to notice that Ryan was wound
a bit too tightly.

"How have you been sleeping,
Ryan?" he said.

"About as well as you would expect."

"A colleague of mine over at Brown
has had very impressive results with
cognitive behavior therapy and insomnia. That's something you may want to
look into."

Everyone always had "the cure," from
counting sheep to melatonin. Even the
receptionist at the radio station had put
in her two cents last week: a coffee en-

ema. Ryan was somewhat more inclined to go with Dr. Fisch's recommendation.

"Thank you, I will definitely check that out. But if you could take a look at the e-mail, I'd really appreciate it."

He read it once, then he looked up and said, "How can I help you with this?"

"The question I have is whether there is any way for you to tell if this e-mail could have been written by Babes."

He removed his eyeglasses, as if to confirm that he had no need to reread the message to answer the question. "People with AS can be very talented writers. Their handwriting is often poor, but as long as they can type, that's not an issue."

"I wish I could address this only in general terms, but I'm afraid I need specifics: Does this look like Babes's written product to you?"

He paused, obviously uncomfortable with specific questions about his patient.

"Doctor, I understand your concerns about patient confidentiality. But I was married to Chelsea, and Babes just went on my radio show to tell the world that he killed his sister."

"I'm aware of that. I spoke with Rachel ten minutes ago."

"Then you understand the urgency."

"I understand," he said. He pondered the matter a moment longer, an internal debate raging as to how much he could say without betraying Babes. Finally, he folded his hands on top of the desk and spoke in a tone that would have been suitable in a courtroom.

"Babes has a highly pedantic way of speaking. That is to say, he uses a far more formal language register than appropriate for a given context. Rarely, if ever, does he use profanity. From what I've seen, his less than conversational manner of speaking is often exacerbated in his written communications. Babes also has a tendency to overpunctuate. For example, he uses far more semicolons than a neurotypical writer, and frequently he uses them incorrectly."

"Anything else?"

"I think that should be sufficient for your purposes."

Ryan reached across the desk and gave the redacted e-mail another read, bearing the doctor's comments in mind. "I don't see any of those traits in this writing," he said. "This is breezy, like barroom talk. Profane in places. Not formal and overpunctuated."

"I would agree," said Dr. Fisch.

"So, your opinion is—what?"

"Between you and me, this e-mail was not written by Babes. Unless . . ."

"Unless what?"

"Unless someone helped him."

The doctor's words gave him something to think about. Ryan thanked him and left his office, his mind abuzz as he descended alone in the elevator.

For whatever reason, collaboration was a possibility that he had not yet considered. An accomplice was certainly an interesting notion.

Perhaps it was one he should discuss with Babes's oldest friend—Tom Bales.

CHAPTER 27

Emma ate dinner alone at home: microwave popcorn, a tangerine, and for dessert, a scoop of low-fat Chunky Monkey ice cream with sugar-free chocolate sauce. It was the only food in the house, and she was too stressed and too tired to worry about nutrition.

She'd tried to reach Ryan and Babes's parents right after the meeting with Chief Garrisen. They hadn't answered her phone calls. Emma wasn't surprised. When a relative confessed to a crime, families often avoided the prosecutor until all the ducks were in a row. She was forced to convey Chief Garrisen's deadline in a voice mail message: "I'm sorry to tell you this, but in light of Babes's confession, we'll have to issue an arrest warrant unless he contacts us and arranges a meeting within twenty-four hours. You and an attorney are, of course, invited to come with him."

It wasn't often that Emma hated her job, but that phone call was definitely one of those moments.

She sank into the couch with her bowl of ice cream, grabbed the remote, and switched on the local evening news. Babes was the top story, and her friend Doug Wells was the crime reporter on the scene. Archived photographs of Chelsea and the crash scene flashed on the television screen as Wells reminded viewers of "the tragic death of the young wife of Boston radio host and former PawSox star Ryan James, whose two-year-old daughter, Ainsley, survived the crash."

Emma's image appeared next—a great photo.

Gotta give the boy points for trying to keep me happy.

Doug's report continued: "Investigators have suspected all along that Chelsea James was run off the road by a drunk driver, but there were no suspects or meaningful leads in the case until the three-year anniversary of the crash, when prosecuting attorney Emma Carlisle received an anonymous tip. Then today, a bombshell exploded when Ryan James received this on-the-air phone call from his brother-in-law, Chelsea's younger brother, during the final segment of *Jocks in the Morning,* the top-rated sports talk-radio show in Boston."

Ryan's publicity headshot flashed on screen as the taped conversation replayed in its entirety, culminating in Babes's dramatic confession: "I killed my sister!"

It pained Emma to hear it again, but it hurt even more to watch the video footage of Ryan fighting his way through a veritable journalistic frenzy, just trying to walk to his car in the station's parking lot. She could see in his eyes how raw the emotions still were, and it was all capped off with a look of utter contempt

that he threw someone as he was getting into his car. There was no on-scene
audio, just the reporter's voice-over, but
Emma knew that a reaction like that
from a guy like Ryan had to have been
goaded by some photographer angling
for the money shot. She'd had to deal
with similar outrageous remarks in her
high-profile prosecutions, though most
of the insults hurled in her direction involved the C word. And people com-
plained about the ethics of *lawyers.*

"Daniel Townsend remains at large,"
the anchorwoman said, as a color photograph of Babes appeared on the
screen. "He is twenty-three years of
age, five feet nine inches tall, one-hun-
dred-sixty-five pounds, with brown hair
and brown eyes. Police warn that he is
armed and dangerous. Stay tuned to
Action News for more on this developing story."

"Armed and dangerous?" Emma said
to the TV, the words coming like a reflex.
"Babes?"

She immediately muted the television,
picked up the telephone, and gave
Doug flak about that.

"Sorry," he said, "I'll double check our facts. But I'm pretty sure that's the way the police described it."

"They shouldn't have. Babes is not a violent suspect. He confessed to the whole world on live radio."

"Which is something I wanted to talk to you about," said Doug. "Remember how I offered to give you more media coverage on the Chelsea James investigation in exchange for some kind of an exclusive?"

Emma had the definite impression that she was now talking to Doug Wells the reporter, not Doug the new boy-friend.

"It wasn't *some kind* of an exclusive," she said. "It was an exclusive on the next tip from the anonymous source."

"Right. But that's a moot point now."

"What are you hinting at?" she said.

"Here's my thought: If Babes calls into Ryan James's radio show again, maybe you could talk Ryan into taking the call off the air."

"Babes wants to be on the air."

"I know. I heard him say that. But as

long as he talks to Ryan on the radio, nobody has a shot at an exclusive."

"Wait a second," said Emma. "You want me to lean on Ryan to take the next call from Babes in private—which would make it harder for police to hear potentially incriminating statements from a vehicular homicide suspect— and then I'm supposed to feed you the exclusive story?"

"Well, not if you're going to put it that way. But a deal is a deal."

Emma's mouth fell open. "I'm going to say good-bye now," she said in an even tone. "Hopefully, when I wake up in the morning I will have decided to let myself forget what you just said."

She hung up, but the doorbell chimed before she could give any serious consideration to her feelings toward Doug. Emma went to the door and answered it.

It was Brandon Lomax. He didn't look happy.

"May I come in?" he said.

She was so surprised to see him, and still so flummoxed from Doug's phone call, that she'd forgotten her manners.

"Of course," she said, showing him inside. She led him to the couch in the living room, but he insisted that she sit first. Then he remained standing—the position of power. Paternal power. Emma felt seventeen again, as if at any minute her best friend, Jennifer, would be sitting beside her on the couch and the two "summer sisters" would have to answer for an empty beer bottle Mr. Lomax had found on the sailboat.

"I heard some disturbing news today," he said.

"We all did."

"I wasn't talking about the on-air confession," he said, his tone taking on an edge. "This has to do with the crime lab down in Kingston."

That one hit her like a brick. "What did you hear?"

"Someone sent a hair sample of mine down there for comparison to DNA that was taken from the scene of Chelsea James's crash. Would you happen to know anything about that?"

Emma swallowed the lump in her throat. Honesty was the only policy. "I sent it in," she said.

"I see," he said flatly. "Have you heard anything yet?"

"No. The lab is backed up, and this doesn't involve a sexual assault against a minor or a violent assault that would get us priority. Officially speaking, we don't even have a known suspect."

Lomax started to pace—something he did only when he was furious and trying not to explode. "Let me save you another phone call," he said. "Apparently, the sample you sent consists entirely of hair strands. What did you do, steal my comb?"

Emma didn't answer. It was awful enough just to be accused.

"Pleading the Fifth, are you?" he said. "As you know, hair shafts are a pretty iffy source of DNA unless the hair roots are included in the specimen."

He was right. She knew from many rape cases that broken bits of hair strands alone, taken from combs or brushes, were always a long shot.

Lomax stopped pacing, and Emma felt the weight of his stare. "So it should come as no surprise to you that the test results are inconclusive."

Emma was looking down at the rug. "How did you find out about this?"

"A reporter. Isn't that a hell of a way for me to hear this kind of news? The story leaked from someone in the lab, and a journalist coldcocked me with a report that Emma Carlisle—my sweet Emma—is checking out my DNA."

Emma closed her eyes in pain. It was exactly the scenario that Chief Garrisen had warned about: a leak from the crime lab that could label Brandon Lomax as a suspected drunk driver, hit the newspapers, and derail his campaign for the Senate. "Are they going to run the story?"

"Fortunately, we're dealing with a reasonable journalist who won't go to print without two sources. We're denying it, and as far as I know, there's no credible corroboration. So the damage is under control. For now."

"I'm so sorry," she said.

"How could you do this to me?"

The question had no anger in it. It was purely disappointment—and it crushed her. "I felt like . . . I had to."

"You *had* to? You've known me since you were eleven years old. I thought of you as my own daughter."

"That didn't make it any easier. But I had to do my job."

He let out a mirthless chuckle. "Taking a hair sample for DNA testing without telling me about it, treating me worse than you would treat a common criminal, forcing me to hear about this from some investigative reporter—that isn't doing your job. If you wanted a DNA sample, all you had to do was ask for it, Emma. I would have given it to you gladly."

Emma could barely speak. "I'm sorry."

"It's too late to be sorry," he said sharply. He started toward the door. Emma followed him.

"Please, don't leave like this," she said.

He opened the door, then stopped and said, "I'm going over to the hospital right now. The lab will have a proper DNA sample first thing in the morning. I'll do whatever I can as former attorney general to get you the results in forty-eight hours. If not sooner."

"That's not necessary," she said.

"Apparently, it is," he said, his expression turning colder as he closed the door in her face.

CHAPTER 28

Inside the Dawes family crypt, Babes had literally retreated into a corner.

He'd barely moved since making the phone call to Ryan on *Jocks in the Morning.* His back hurt, his legs were cramping, and he needed to go to the bathroom. Those discomforts were hardly punishment enough for the secret he'd finally gotten off his chest. It was over. Done.

Now what?

The last vestiges of daylight were streaming through the crypt's colorful stained-glass window. Darkness was not far off. Sunset would come at 6:58

PM, two minutes sooner than yesterday, and two minutes later than tomorrow. The march toward the winter solstice was not always two minutes per day, however. If he stayed here another month or so, the sun would set at 6:06 PM on October 13, and on the next day it would set at 6:05 PM. And if he stayed all the way past Christmas, the sunset would come at the same time, 4:21 PM, on December 26 and 27. It was the kind of statistical trivia that Babes could spend hours committing to memory and spout off at the drop of a hat.

You have to sleep here. In the dark.

He was strangely OK with the idea—except for the cold. All of New England was experiencing sunny days and increasingly cool nights, a weather pattern that would make for the perfect autumn blaze of color in two weeks' time. Babes's hooded sweatshirt had kept him plenty warm during the day, but with nighttime temperatures dipping into the forties, the crypt offered all the warmth and comfort of an unfinished basement with no heat.

Babes climbed to his feet and stood

with his back against the wall. The crypt was rectangular in shape, the open area roughly twice the size of Babes's bedroom. The stained-glass window was behind and above him in the gabled end of the crypt, and he was looking directly at the wrought-iron gate that was the entrance on the opposite wall. Interment niches lined each of the long side walls, and a white marble bench suitable for two or three visitors was in the center.

His sneakers squeaked on the concrete floor as he crossed the crypt and went outside for a quick bathroom break. When he returned, it seemed even darker inside. The lock was broken, but he pulled the gate shut tightly and prepared to spend the night.

Loneliness wasn't an issue. In middle school and as a teenager, Babes had spent countless hours here alone and content. He was always happiest by himself, as long as he was engaged. Boredom was his enemy. He didn't have his baseball cards with him, which was a huge departure from the old days. The crypt hadn't been part of his routine in quite some time, but it didn't feel the same to him without his cards. Babes didn't handle any type of disconnect very well, especially when he was tired and hungry. He could feel his anxiety rising, which frightened him far more than the thought of spending the night alone in a cemetery. In the day's last remaining light, he tried to keep his mind busy memorizing the memorials chiseled onto the stone façades of the niches: Robert Dawes, Leslie Dawes, generations of dead Dawes's from another century, probably whom no one had thought about in decades.

Then he noticed something. Several of the niches in the far column, closest to the gate, had no memorial. In the years since his last visit to the crypt, he had forgotten about his secret hiding spot—the vacant crypt right beside Barbara Dawes. Back in middle school, he used to hide his baseball cards in there.

Maybe they're still there!

He nearly leaped across the crypt and grabbed the stone façade. It was like a dresser drawer with no handles. With both hands, he jimmied it from side to side, wiggled the facing free, and peered inside.

"Whoa!" he said, a reflex.

Inside was a treasure trove of cool stuff, all kinds of things he needed: a coat, a flashlight, a candle and matches, some plastic bags. There was also food: a half-full box of vanilla wafers. He tried one. Still good! And behind it all, way in back, was an old brown shoebox.

My cards!

Babes had hit the jackpot. And he was starving. He gathered up his loot and carried it over to the marble bench. It was almost too dark to see, so he tried the flashlight. No batteries. He struck a match and lit the candle. It was more than enough light.

He devoured the cookies while sorting through the cards. Then he lined them up on the floor in perfectly straight columns, one for each team. He arranged them first in alphabetical order—Baltimore Orioles, Boston Red Sox, and so on—then he rearranged them according to won-loss records for last season, which he knew from memory. He smiled each time he came across one of his old favorites, but seeing them made him realize that it had been much longer than he'd thought since his last visit. He had at least a hundred cards face up on the floor, and the newest one was five years old.

No way were those vanilla wafers five years old.

He was deep in thought, calculating the team on-base percentage for the 1999 Boston Red Sox, when he heard footsteps outside the crypt.

Babes blew out the candle, gathered up his baseball cards, and hid in a dark corner. A man was fidgeting with the latch on the iron gate. He seemed to know that the lock was broken, and the gate swung open. Babes held his breath, but it took every ounce of strength not to freak out. He hoped and prayed that the intruder would just go away. The door closed, and in a sliver of moonlight, Babes saw a man's shadow stretching across the stone floor.

The silhouette stepped forward, found the matches on the marble bench, and struck one.

Babes let out a helpless whimper.

The man looked at Babes and spoke in a voice that chilled him.

"What the fuck are you doing in my house?"

CHAPTER 29

Ryan and his in-laws regrouped in the kitchen for a late dinner.

Ryan had taken Ainsley out of school early and was in Pawtucket by one o'clock. It was always an emotional jolt for Ryan to visit Paul and Rachel Townsend, to see the old brownstone where he and Chelsea had started their life as husband and wife in the apartment above Chelsea's parents. It felt even stranger drawing up a search plan, identifying everyone they should call and every place they should look for Babes. Rachel spent the afternoon at home with Ainsley while Ryan and Paul drove

around town hitting all the likely spots—
near McCoy Stadium, the Modern Diner,
the library, even his favorite sports
memorabilia store all the way down in
Warren.

Babes was not to be found, and no
one Ryan talked to had seen him.

"I want a cheeseburger," said Ainsley.
She was digging in the sack of food that
Ryan had picked up at the drive-thru.

"Cheeseburger it is," said Ryan.

"But no bun," said Ainsley.

That seemed odd, but Ryan was OK
with it. "All right. No bun."

"And no meat," she said.

"So . . . you want a piece of cheese?"

"No! I want a *cheeseburger.* But no
bun. And no meat."

Another lesson in the big picture from
Ainsley: Life's a cheeseburger, and
some people eat just the cheese. Ryan
let her watch *SpongeBob SquarePants*
during dinner so that the adults could
talk, and then he put her to bed.

Afterward Ryan tried Tom Bales on his
cell again. He'd been trying to follow up
on Dr. Fisch's accomplice theory all day
long, but Tom wasn't answering. It was

making Ryan all the more suspicious. But the priority now was to find Babes. The plan was for Paul and Ryan to split up and continue to search for Babes tonight, all night if necessary. Ryan had a list of additional places he wanted to check out in south Pawtucket and northern Providence. By eight o'clock Ryan was ready to hit the road again, but before he could grab his coat, Paul stopped him.

"Rachel has something to tell you," said Paul.

If she did have something to say, Rachel didn't look happy about it.

"Actually, I have something to show you," she said, and she led Ryan down the hall to Babes's bedroom. Paul followed.

She switched on the light, and Ryan was immediately struck by the amount of stuff Babes had collected over the years. But he was even more taken with how organized everything was. Against an entire wall, floor to ceiling, were banker's boxes stacked on top of another in perfect columns. Each box was labeled and dated. Ryan stepped closer to read some of them at random: *Base-ball Daily News* 1995–2000, *Japan Baseball Daily* 2004–2006, PawSox Programs 1989–1996, *Red Sox Magazine* 2001–2005, and on it went, all in alphabetical order. The other side of the room was like a memorabilia store. Posters of Red Sox players, including an autographed "Fathead" of Ivan Lopez, covered the wall like wallpaper. Shelf after shelf displayed neatly organized collectibles, everything from a Boston Red Sox dog collar—Babes didn't have a pet—to a PawSox versus RedWings "33 Innings" pin, which commemorated the longest game in baseball history.

On the nightstand, right beside Babes's pillow, was a baseball signed by Ryan and the rest of his Texas Longhorn teammates from their national championship season, which, for a moment, sent Ryan's mind drifting in another direction entirely.

"I found this while you and Paul were out," said Rachel.

Ryan took a seat beside her on the bed. Paul leaned against the wall, standing near the door. In Rachel's lap was an old wooden cigar box. On the lid, written in Babes's distinctively poor handwriting, was just one word: *Chelsea.*

Rachel opened the box. Ryan looked inside, and he didn't know what to make of it at first. It was almost full, but it contained nothing recognizable. He saw little jagged pieces of plastic and broken metal, all mixed together with shards of glass and chips of paint.

Rachel said, "Babes visits the scene of the accident. I don't know how often, but I think it's a lot. He'll stay there for hours if he has to, until he finds something, like a little piece of Chelsea's car that didn't get cleaned up. Part of a taillight, a chip off the bumper, a pellet of glass from the shattered windshield— whatever he can spot. He keeps it all in this box."

"Tom told me about this," he said. But Ryan was no longer looking at the box. He was looking at Rachel. She was gently raking her fingertips over Babes's precious collection, as if it meant even more to her than to her son. It wasn't right, a mother burying her daughter.

"What really happened that night?" said Ryan.

She was still looking down into the box of broken mementos. "You bought Chelsea and Ainsley tickets for the game," she said. "But you didn't get one for Babes."

This was old ground. "It was the right decision," said Ryan. "In hindsight, it might have saved his life. He could have been killed if he'd been in the front seat next to Chelsea."

"Yes," she said, finally looking at Ryan. "Good thing he was in the back-seat."

"What?"

"It was World War Three here when Babes found out he wasn't going. The thought of missing the last game of the season sent him into a major meltdown. When Chelsea came home from the school to pick up Ainsley, I begged her to take Babes with her."

"But there were only two tickets."

"Chelsea could hold a two-year-old in her lap for the game. Babes could have the other seat."

"So Babes was in the car when it crashed?"

She nodded. "Chelsea put him in the backseat to keep Ainsley entertained."

"Did he see the car that ran her off the road?"

"No. He was playing itsy-bitsy spider with Ainsley, and all he saw was Chelsea's reaction. She swerved, lost control. The next thing Babes knew, the car crashed into an oak tree."

"Babes looked fine to me at the funeral."

"He wasn't hurt. Neither was Ainsley. It was the tree branch through the windshield that killed Chelsea. When Babes saw all the blood in the front seat, he freaked and jumped out of the car. He left Chelsea and Ainsley there and ran all the way home."

"Why has this been kept secret? Why haven't I heard this before?"

Her voice began to quake. "Babes didn't want anyone to know he was a passenger in the car. He's ashamed of the way he lost it when he saw Chelsea's injuries."

"Well, too bad. We've been spinning

our wheels for three years trying to find out what happened to Chelsea."

"Don't be angry. You know how fragile Babes is. He actually considered himself responsible for Chelsea's death. In his mind, he could have saved her if he had kept his cool and called the ambulance. She might have lived."

"He told you that?"

"Yes."

Ryan looked at Paul. It had always been obvious to him that Paul and Rachel treated Babes differently. This revelation didn't explain everything, but it meant something.

Paul said, "That night he ran home, Babes was hysterical. He was screaming that Chelsea was dead, and I—" his voice broke.

"It's okay," said Rachel.

Paul went to his wife, sat beside her on the bed, and pressed her hand into his. It was the most intimate contact Ryan had witnessed between them since Chelsea's death.

"We didn't know what to do," Rachel told Ryan. "Babes had nothing to add to the investigation, other than his own sense of guilt. So I . . . Paul and I decided to keep Babes out of it. Nobody knew that he was in the car, so we didn't even let the police talk to him. I know that must sound terrible to you, but we'd already lost a daughter. We didn't need Babes seeing his name in the newspaper, hearing people call him a coward for running from the scene, and then doing something horrible to himself out of shame."

Paul lowered his gaze. "Intellectually, at least, that's where I was. But something in my heart wouldn't let me forgive Babes for losing his head and not doing everything I would have done to save Chelsea. Until now. Now that we're in danger of losing him too, I realize what a fool I've been. I love Babes. I really do. It wasn't his fault that Chelsea died. He wasn't even supposed to be in the car, so how can you blame him for not reacting differently to a terrible, terrible situation?"

Rachel started to cry quietly, and Paul held her closer.

"You can't fault Babes for just being Babes," she said.

"No," Paul said sadly. "You can't ever do that."

Ryan gave them a moment, but then he had to ask: "Do you think this is what Babes's confession is about? Is that why he called me on the air to tell the world he killed his sister?"

Rachel wiped away a tear.

Paul said, "I'm hard on Babes sometimes, but I know my son. I think that's exactly what's going on."

Ryan rose. "Rachel, are you going to be okay here alone?"

"Yes," she said, sniffling. "Where are you going?"

"Where else?" he said, as his gaze shifted to his father-in-law. "Paul and I have to keep looking."

CHAPTER 30

On Tuesday at one PM Emma left the courthouse. Babes had yet to turn himself in, and Chief Garrisen's twenty-four-hour deadline had expired.

A warrant was issued for his arrest.

The chief still had the office operating under a strict no-comment rule, so Emma had to duck the media on her way to her car. Her cell phone rang as she was driving out of the parking lot. She recognized the number from the Rhode Island Department of Health Forensic Laboratory. It was the head of DNA testing, Bob Entwistle.

"Got some bad news for you," he said.

Emma stopped at the red light. "I heard last night," she said. "You can't construct a reliable DNA profile from the hair strands I gave you."

"That's not the problem anymore. The kit that arrived this morning took care of that."

She'd been awake most of the night thinking about Brandon's visit to her apartment, but it was still hard to believe that he'd gone through with it. "So Brandon Lomax actually submitted a DNA sample?"

"Not only that, but he told me to call you directly with the results."

"And now you're telling me that the news is bad?"

"I'm afraid so," said Entwistle.

"Are you saying there's a match?"

"No, not that," he said with the distinct chuckle of a know-it-all scientist. "We can work pretty fast if we drop everything and focus on a single case, but results this quickly would be TV-crime-show fast."

She was relieved but confused. "So what's the bad news?"

"Well, as you know, in order to create the original DNA sample three years ago, we extracted saliva from the vomit that was collected at the scene of the accident."

"Yes, and that was a fine piece of work."

"You bet it was," he said, a little defensive. "Not all departments have the equipment to extract DNA from vomit, and if I hadn't lobbied for the purchase of that new extraction kit with paramagnetic particles to isolate extremely pure DNA for use with STR analysis, we never would have had a sample in the first place."

Emma rolled her eyes. Whenever scientists felt challenged, they seemed to lapse into a level of detail more suitable for a rocket-science manual.

"Relax, Bob. I wasn't being condescending. It *was* a fine piece of work."

"Oh," he said, backpedaling. "Thanks. But now I'm even more embarrassed to tell you the news: we never got around to constructing a DNA profile from that sample. I'm sorry about that, but this was effectively a cold case with no suspects. You know how busy the lab has been with everything from forensic files in active investigations to criminal offender files for convicted felons, and we—"

"Bob, it's okay," said Emma. The guy was beyond defensive. "So there's no DNA record in the computer; is that what you're telling me?"

"That's correct."

That explained the foot-dragging Emma had encountered when she'd submitted the hair sample. "So you have to go back to the original sample in the state databank and construct a DNA profile, and then compare it to Brandon's DNA. How long is that going to take?"

"There's the problem," he said.

"Weeks or months?"

"We can't locate the original sample."

A car horn blasted behind her. Emma had watched the light turn green, but it was as if Entwistle's words had prevented her brain from telling her foot to press the accelerator.

"It's lost?" she said, as she drove through the intersection.

"I won't say lost. It's . . . missing."

"How can that be?"

"I don't know."

"But if there's no sample and no previously constructed DNA profile in the computer, there is no way to compare Brandon Lomax's DNA—or anyone else's DNA—to the DNA found at the crime scene."

"That would be correct," he said reluctantly.

Emma had tremendous respect for the professionals in the lab, but every now and then a case would deliver a painful reminder that Rhode Island had been the last state in the union to create a DNA databank. "Where do we go from here?"

"I'm double-checking. Since a drunk driver may have been involved in this crash, it's possible that someone sent out the vomit sample to test for alcohol levels."

"You can't get a reliable blood-alcohol level from vomit."

"I know, but I'm just theorizing here.

I'm also going to check to see if some-where along the line the department contracted with an outside lab to do DNA testing in this case or another one. Maybe there was a mix-up."

She stopped at another traffic light, and the car behind her nearly rear-ended her. That would have been to-day's icing on the cake.

"Do me a favor and sort this out as quickly as you can," she said.

"Will do. Like I said, I'm sure it's just a mix-up."

"I'm sure," she said, wondering if for a certain former attorney general, the mix-up was a highly convenient one.

Ryan finished the morning radio show and went straight to Cambridge. If Babes's friend Tom wouldn't answer his cell, Ryan would go straight to Tom.

Ryan took the same subway that had taken him to MIT last week, but this time he walked away from campus, toward Tom's apartment. He should have been planning his conversation with Tom, but he was still preoccupied with this morn-ing's radio show and one of the biggest jerks ever to call in to *Jocks in the Morning.* The conversation replayed in his head as he walked down Kensington Avenue.

"Hey, sport. How are you?"

Sport? Who does this guy think he is, Robert Redford in *The Great Gatsby?*

"Doug Wells, here, *Action News* in Providence. We have a mutual friend in Conradt Garrisen."

Nobody called him Conradt, especially not his friends. *You don't know Connie any more than I know the Prince of Wales.*

Ryan said, "You realize we're on the air, right?"

"Absolutely," said Doug. "I hear you're returning to baseball, so I wanted to call and let your listeners know that we here at *Action News* in Providence will be following your comeback every step of the way."

Ryan hated it when people called to promote other networks, other programs. This one was particularly bothersome, since he had not yet made his comeback a topic of discussion on the show.

"That's kind of you, Doug. Thanks for calling."

"Oh, one other thing."

"Running out of time here, Doug."

"I'll be quick. My heart goes out to you and your brother-in-law."

"Thank you."

"And Babes, if you're listening, I know it can be hard to talk to family about things you have bottled up inside. Sometimes you just want to talk to someone who isn't going to judge you. So, Babes, if you can hear me, call me at the *Action News* station or at home, and we can even talk off the record—"

Ryan cut him off.

Asshole.

Tom Bales lived in a two-bedroom apartment just a few blocks from MIT. Ryan went up the elevator and knocked on the door. A young and good-looking guy answered. He was wearing torn blue jeans, no shoes, and a T-shirt that read AND YOUR POINT *Is*? Not since his own college days had Ryan seen eyes like these, and it was a safe bet that the kid had been smoking some kind of herb since breakfast.

Some of Ryan's friends had told him to try that too, for insomnia.

"Is Tom here?"

"Tom who?"

"Tom Bales."

"Oh, my roommate," he said, laughing. For some reason, he thought that was really funny. So did the giggly girlfriend on the couch in the living room.

"Is he here?"

"Uh, no. Hey, you're Ryan James, right? The sports dude on the radio."

"That's me. You a listener?"

He fluttered his lips like an overworked horse. "Nah. Tom linked me up with your brother-in-law to do computer support for my paper on thermal plasma outflow and circulation within the Earth's inner magnetosphere. Babes has been great. This could be one of the most detailed surveys of ion pitch angle distributions ever done by—"

"I hate to be rude," said Ryan, "but I really need to find Tom."

"Honestly, I haven't seen him in about two days."

"What?"

"Well, that's not unusual. When Tom

gets into his projects, he could be working nonstop at the lab and sleeping two hours a night on the floor. If he sleeps at all."

I can relate to that.

"What about his girlfriend? Could he be at her place?"

Now the kid was really laughing.

"What's so funny?" said Ryan.

"Virgin Tom—a girlfriend?" he said, snickering. "Tom talks a good game, but I don't think I've ever seen him with a woman."

The image of Tom's chase after the Tommy Bahama girl on campus flashed in Ryan's mind.

"I'd like to leave him a message," said Ryan. He didn't trust Tom's roomie to deliver it. "You mind if I put a note in his room, where he'll get it?"

"Be my guest."

He directed Ryan to the first bedroom off the hallway, and then went back to whatever he had been doing in the living room with Giggles the girlfriend.

Ryan opened the bedroom door and almost gasped. He wasn't that many years removed from quirky college living conditions, but this was over the top. A two-hundred-inch LCD screen covered nearly the entire wall. Ryan had seen projection screens that large, but never an LCD. He'd heard of them in sports bars in Japan, and he checked the brand. There was no label. He inspected the workmanship more closely. This was no factory model. Tom had built the thing himself.

It was getting easier all the time to understand Babes's friendship with Tom.

Ryan's gaze drifted across the room to the mirror above the bureau. It was large and had an oak frame, but most of the mirror itself was covered with photographs that Tom had taped onto the glass. Ryan was too curious not to walk over and take a closer look.

They were typical college photographs—Tom with his friends having a good time. True to the remarks of Tom's roommate, however, Ryan didn't notice any photographs of Tom alone with a woman. Then his eye caught a photograph of Babes, and the image struck him.

It was a typical picture of Babes. He

wasn't smiling. He wasn't even looking at the camera. Tom was smiling. So was the other person in the photograph. It was a woman, and Ryan couldn't take his eyes off her.

The woman was Chelsea.

It was the only photograph in the room of Tom and Babes—and it included Chelsea.

Ryan took a step back and breathed in and out, not sure what mix of emotions was coursing through his body. But he suddenly wanted out of Tom's room.

He scribbled a note with his phone number—"Tom, call me IMMEDIATELY"—left it on Tom's pillow, and stole one more glance at Chelsea on his way out the door.

CHAPTER 31

Babes slept until noon. No surprise there. He had lain awake till dawn, afraid to make a move, too frightened to close his eyes.

His unexpected visitor had chewed him out royally for eating his box of vanilla wafers. How was Babes to know that the guy had been living in the Dawes family crypt—*Babes's* crypt—for the past six months? Throughout the chilly night, Babes had hoped that the man would be gone in the morning. When he woke, however, Babes saw him seated cross-legged on the floor and studying the collection of baseball cards. They were still neatly displayed, each team forming its own column, just as Babes had arranged them.

"These yours?" the man asked.

Babes rose up on one elbow, still on the cold floor. It was Babes's first look at the man in daylight, and while he avoided making eye contact, he couldn't help staring. He wore torn blue jeans, an old army coat that was too big on him, and tattered sneakers that didn't match, one black and one white. His hair was an oily dark mess, shoulder length on one side and down to the middle of his ear on the other, clearly a self-inflicted cut. A thick, snarly beard covered most of his face, leaving only his narrowed eyes and a deeply furrowed brow to convey expression. He was obviously homeless, which gave Babes a funny feeling; school kids used to tease Babes and say that he would end up that way someday.

"Hey, I asked you a question," the man said. "Are these cards yours?"

Babes nodded.

"Lots of Red Sox cards. You a Sox fan?"

"Yes," Babes said quietly.

"Too bad. I like the Yankees. Guess I'm gonna have to kill you."

Babes screamed at the top of his lungs and scurried deep into the corner.

"Hey!" the man shouted.

"Don't kill me!" shouted Babes.

"I was kidding, you idiot!"

Babes cowered and continued to wail like a mortally wounded animal.

"Stop it! I'm not going to kill you!"

Babes kept on screaming, barely taking a breath. The echo off the granite walls made the noise inside the crypt almost unbearable, and the man had no idea how to stop it. In desperation, he scooped up the columns of baseball cards into stacks and hurled one stack after another at Babes.

Babes shielded himself with his hands and screamed louder. But as cards began to fall around him and gather like snow at Fenway on opening day, his screams became a whimper. His attention was suddenly refocused. The whimper turned into a sniffle.

The man looked on in amazement as Babes, in the span of minutes, went from utter hysteria to pensive silence. Soon he began to reorganize his cards, as if the outburst had never happened. The speed and concentration with which he worked was remarkable and strangely fascinating.

The man drew closer for a better look, but Babes didn't notice.

"What order are you putting them in now?" the man asked.

"Teams, ranked according to their won-loss percentage."

"For what year?"

"Franchise history."

The man did a double take. "You know the won-loss record of every major league team from the day they joined the league?"

"Yes, well, as of two days ago. I didn't get the newspaper yesterday."

The man's mouth fell open. "You re-calculate every day?"

"Yes."

"Cool. I think. Who's in first?"

"The Yankeees. Winning percentage of .567, if you go back to the New York Highlanders in 1901."

"Ah, my boys from the Bronx," he said

with a smile. "Hey, you're doing this for me, aren't you? Cuz I'm a Yankee fan."

Babes stopped arranging his cards and looked off to the middle distance, his face expressing only confusion. It had never occurred to him that he was doing it for anyone but himself. "I suppose it could be seen that way," he said, turning his attention back to the cards.

"Who's in second place?"

"Giants, if you count both their time in New York and San Francisco. Five-thirty-nine."

"Then who?"

"Dodgers. Winning percentage of .524, Brooklyn and Los Angeles combined. St. Louis Cardinals are in fourth at .517. My Red Sox are in fourth place at .515, if you count their time as the Boston Americans. Chicago Cubs are right behind at .513, followed by the Cleveland—"

"Okay, okay."

Babes didn't hear him. He was in his zone, his mind processing won-loss percentages to the third decimal as he laid out the cards in perfect order. It took him about fifteen minutes, and it didn't bother him in the least that a homeless man was his audience. In fact, he was perfectly fine being watched. Even as a small child, his play dates had gone just fine—until the other boy got tired of watching Babes do what Babes wanted to do, and then it was a disaster.

"And in last place," Babes announced, "the Tampa Bay Devil Rays."

The homeless man applauded. "That's amazing."

Babes shrugged. "Not really."

"No, I mean it. You are one cool dude."

"You think . . . you actually think I'm cool."

"Yeah. No lie, dude."

Babes smiled, but he still didn't look the man in the eye. "Do you want to see me do it again?"

"Sure. I could watch this forever."

"You could? Forever?"

"Well, not forever. But I mean, a really long time."

"Okay," said Babes, it never occurring to him that the man might just be making conversation or saying something to be nice. "How about this time I do it by team home runs, most to least?"

"That would be awesome."

Babes scrambled the cards on the floor and eagerly started all over again.

"Hey, what's your name?" the man asked.

Babes answered without looking up. "People call me Babes."

The homeless man waited, as if expecting the question to come back at him. Babes was too into his project to care about another person's name.

The man glanced at a stray baseball card beside him, which happened to be one of the most famous Red Sox of all time. "My name's Carl Yastrzemski."

Babes froze. "Really?"

"No, you moron. But you can call me Yaz anyway."

"Okay, Yaz."

Babes finished his first column, taking extra care to make sure the cards were lined up just so.

"Hey, tell me something, Babes."

"What?"

"I meet some weird dudes under

bridges and stuff. But you . . . you're a little hard to figure out."

"I have a pervasive development disorder."

"A what?" he said, chuckling.

Depravement provides evildoers—the letters were tumbling in Babes's mind again, rearranging themselves. "A pervasive development disorder," he said, his tone punctilious.

"Okay. If you say so. What are you hiding out here in the crypt for?"

"I killed my sister."

Babes said it without emotion and with no hesitation, as if now that he'd confessed over the radio it was simply an established fact.

Yaz said, "Well, I'm sure she deserved it."

"No, she didn't."

"I was kidding again, okay? You need to work on your sense of humor, you know that?"

Babes didn't answer. He was busy building the second column of cards, his face pure concentration.

"So, how did you do it?"

"Do what?"

"Kill your sister."

Babes looked up, but his gaze was cast downward at the man's feet, not at his face. "You really want to know?"

"Yeah. I really want to know."

Babes put down his baseball cards and started plucking at his eyebrow. "Okay. Then I'll tell you."

CHAPTER 32

After nightfall, Ryan met Emma at the Townsends' brownstone in Pawtucket.

It had been Ryan's idea to tell Emma everything that Chelsea's parents knew about the night of the accident. He met her for coffee that afternoon and laid it all out for Emma exactly as Paul and Rachel had for him—from the fact that Babes had been a passenger in Chelsea's car to his frantic run home without calling 911. Paul wasn't keen on divulging so much information to the attorney general's office, at least not with a warrant still out for Babes's arrest, but

Ryan convinced him that being straight with Emma was the best course.

Selling Rachel on a face-to-face meeting with Emma was another hurdle entirely.

"I can come back later," said Emma, "if she's not up to this."

She and Ryan were alone in the Townsends' living room, Ryan seated on the couch and Emma in the armchair. Paul was in the master bedroom with his wife, trying to convince her that this was the right thing to do.

"Let's give her a little more time," said Ryan.

Silence returned, broken only by the steady tick of the clock on the wall—a reminder that time was not on their side.

Emma said, "This must be so hard for Rachel. Not to minimize what you and Paul have gone through, but it's so hard when a mother loses a child."

Ryan thought of all the joy—virtually his only joy—that Ainsley had brought him over the past three years.

"How is she doing, really?" said Emma. "I know a lot has been going on, but are you keeping your hand on her pulse at all?"

"We all try."

Emma noticed the Bible on the coffee table. "Is this Rachel's?"

"Yeah," said Ryan. "She's not overtly religious, but she seems to turn to the Bible in times of stress. It was the same way when Chelsea died."

Emma picked it up. It was a leather-bound version with silk ribbon markers. She turned to a marked page, read to herself for moment, and then seemed to stop abruptly.

"What is it?" said Ryan.

"Do you know what your mother-in-law is reading?" said Emma.

"Not exactly, no."

"The passage is marked in ink. It's from Jeremiah 31:15," she said, and then she read aloud: " 'A voice heard in Ramah/mourning and great weeping/ Rachel weeping for her children/and re-fusing to be comforted/because her children are no more.' "

Ryan recalled what Rachel had said earlier about the night of Chelsea's acci-dent—her fear that Babes would hurt

himself out of shame if the police interrogated him, her fear of losing a son on
top of a daughter.

Emma closed the book and laid it on
the table.

"Sorry to keep you waiting," said
Rachel, as she entered the room. Paul
was at her side.

Ryan took a good look at her, and he
saw a woman trying hard to be strong,
but more than anything else, he saw a
mother suffering as he'd never seen suffering before. And at that moment he
came to a realization. Yes, she loved
Chelsea, her beautiful daughter who'd
had it all—a brain in her head, compassion in her heart, an amazing young
child, and a man who would love her till
the end of time. But for all his flaws and
idiosyncrasies—maybe even *because* of
them—Rachel loved Babes every bit as
much. If not more.

Ryan greeted her with a kiss, and
Emma shook her hand. Rachel took a
seat next to Ryan on the couch, opposite Emma. Paul sat beside his wife.

Emma said, "I want to thank both of

you for letting Ryan share these latest details about Babes."

"Of course," said Paul.

"Ryan seemed to think it was the right thing to do," Rachel said cautiously.

"It was," said Emma. "But now that you have been completely open and honest with me, I am going to do the same with you. Maybe you can help me."

"I'll sure try," said Rachel.

Emma laid her briefcase on the coffee table and opened it.

Before she could begin, Ryan interjected. "Emma and I went over this earlier. Some of it's pretty surprising. Shocking even. Don't take anything you see here as fact. Think of it more as clues. If you get upset and need a break, just let her know."

Rachel nodded, though far from putting her at ease, Ryan's words seemed to have made her more anxious. Her husband took her hand, but Ryan noticed that Paul's hand was shaking a little too.

Emma removed a copy of the first anonymous tip she'd received, the three-year-old newspaper with the coded sentence.

"This was tip number one," said Emma. "Ryan and I agreed not to show it to you before, knowing how hard it would be for you to see the newspaper report of Emma's death again."

"Okay," said Rachel. "And you're showing me this now because . . ."

"I want your honest opinion," said Emma. She laid the newspaper in front of the Townsends.

Rachel looked away, then back.

"Sorry," said Emma. "But if you just focus on the article and read the five underlined words in the numbered sequence, it forms a sentence: 'I know who did it.' "

Emma looked at it. "What is it you want to know?"

"Could this have come from Babes?"

"I don't know."

"Does it look like his work?"

Paul and his wife exchanged glances. Paul said, "You would know better than I would, sweetheart."

Rachel took a closer look. Then she glanced at Ryan, who gave her a look of encouragement, telling her it was okay to be honest.

"I would say yes," said Rachel.

"Why?" said Emma.

"Babes has very poor penmanship. His numerals are even bad. Those handwritten numbers that accompany the underlined words—one through five—look like his handwriting to me."

"Anything else that makes you think it's from Babes?"

"The whole concept—numbering words and rearranging them into a sentence. That's something Babes would do. And it's logical that the three-year anniversary of Chelsea's death would prompt Babes to implicate himself."

Ryan said, "What do you mean implicate himself?"

"That's what I think he means when he says 'I know who did it.' Babes is saying that he did it."

"It's interesting you say that," said Emma, as she pulled the next document from her briefcase. "This was the second tip I received. For obvious reasons, we kept this highly confidential. I'm sharing this with you now because I don't see any other way to sort out what's happening with your son. And Ryan assured me that this information will not leave this room."

"If he assured you of that, we'll honor it," said Paul.

Emma showed it to them, and surprise immediately registered on Rachel's face upon seeing the photograph and the coded two-word sentence: "It's him."

"Brandon Lomax?" she said, her shock now tinged with anger.

"We don't know if it was him," said Emma. "This tip could be a crank. Could be a mistake."

Paul said, "I can't believe—"

"Rachel, Paul—please," said Ryan. "Don't be judge, jury, and executioner on this. Let's go one step at a time. All Emma wants to know is: Does this second tip look like it's from Babes?"

Rachel studied it, her face straining with thought. "Honestly, I can't tell. The only handwritten marks on the page are the underlining beneath two typeset words and the numbers one and two in the margin. The underlining and the

number one are just straight lines. So
the only real basis upon which to make
any kind of meaningful handwriting
comparison is the number two."

"I understand what you're saying,"
said Emma. "I've prosecuted enough
forgery cases to know that no respectable handwriting expert would
render an unqualified opinion based
upon a vertical line, two horizontal lines,
and the number two. That's part of the
reason I haven't pushed for a professional handwriting analysis."

Ryan said, "Emma just wants your impression. Does it look the way Babes
writes the number two?"

"That's really hard to say," said
Rachel. "It's difficult for Babes to write
characters the same way on a consis-
tent basis. It could be his handwriting,
but that doesn't jibe with his confession
on the radio: As Babes sees it, *Babes*
did it."

"True," said Ryan. "But the sentence
'It's him' could mean that Lomax was
the drunk driver who ran Chelsea off the
road, even though Babes considers

himself ultimately responsible for Chelsea's death."

"That's a possible reading," said Emma. "And it leads me to the third tip."

She removed a copy of the e-mail message and let Rachel read it from top to bottom—including the reference to Lomax walking up to Chelsea's car, seeing her grievous injuries, and vomiting at the scene.

Rachel needed time to collect herself upon reading it, and Paul put his arm around her.

"I'm sorry to hit you with this," said Emma.

"It's all right," said Rachel.

Emma gave her a few moments longer, then asked, "Do you think Babes—"

"Absolutely not."

"I'm sorry," said Emma. "I was going to ask if you thought Babes wrote this."

"No, no," she said firmly, then added again: "No."

Paul said, "You seem incredibly sure about that."

"I am."

Emma said, "I'm sure Babes is good with the computer."

"Yes, he works out of the house for his friend Tom Bales at MIT."

"So he would know how to create a free e-mail account under a fictitious name and send a message from a public computer, which would make it impossible to trace the e-mail back to the real sender."

"Or Tom could have helped him with that," said Ryan. "That's something I've been trying to talk to Tom about, but he won't return my calls."

Rachel shook her head. "Tom is a good kid. My opinion has nothing to do with Babes's or Tom's computer skills anyway. I can simply read it and tell it's not him. The word choice, the sentence structure, the speech pattern: It doesn't sound like anything I've ever read from Babes."

"That's important," said Emma.

"And I would never have let this happen," said Paul.

"What do you mean?"

"If Babes had been able to identify the

drunk who ran Chelsea off the road, I would have forced him to go to the police. That night he ran home from the accident, he swore to me that he never saw anything or anybody."

Rachel said, "That's the only reason Paul and I were able in good conscience to protect him and, for his own good, not let the police interrogate him."

Ryan could see that Emma's line of questioning was beginning to take a toll on them, particularly Rachel. "I think that may be enough for one night," he said.

Rachel breathed a sigh of relief. "I hope that was helpful."

"Very," said Emma.

Paul and Rachel rose and said good night. Ryan and Emma held their discussion until they heard the bedroom door close at the end of the hall.

"What do you think?" said Ryan.

"Two possibilities," said Emma. "One, Babes did see someone that night, and he lied to his father when he swore that he hadn't. Or—"

"Two," said Ryan, finishing the thought for her: "Someone else did."

"Someone else?"

"There's a rocket scientist I still need to talk to," said Ryan—and he was thinking of Tom.

CHAPTER 33

Yaz was going to kill himself.

All day long, baseball. On into the evening, more baseball. Didn't this Babes ever get tired of talking about the same damn thing, hour after hour? No doubt about it: if there'd been a pistol to suck on, Yaz's brains would have been all over the wall.

Yaz found a comfortable gravestone and sat down in the moonlight. His food run into town had taken only half an hour. It was amazing what ended up in the Dumpster behind a subway shop. He took one last bite of an only slightly spoiled turkey loaf, put it back in his

coat pocket, and started back to the
crypt.

Babes would be there waiting for him.
Yaz had tested him all afternoon to
make sure he wouldn't run. Yaz told him
to shut up or he'd cut off his ear. Babes
shut up. Yaz ordered him to stand on
one foot for five minutes or he'd slit his
throat. Babes stood on one foot. And
before leaving the crypt, he told Babes
to sit in the corner until he got back, or
he'd kill his entire family. That one had
made him cry, but Babes went straight
to the corner.

This is too easy.

The crypt was one of the most impressive memorials in the old North Burial Ground. A full moon and the shadows of sprawling oaks created the eerie,
horror-film feeling that Yaz loved. He
turned the broken latch, and the iron
gate creaked open. It was pitch dark inside the crypt, so he struck a match before entering. Sure enough, Babes was
huddled in the corner, exactly where Yaz
had left him.

"Good boy, Babes," said Yaz.

Babes didn't move.

"You hungry?"

Babes refused to look at him—the guy never seemed to make eye contact—but he nodded. Yaz tossed him the half-eaten turkey loaf. Babes fumbled it, and the hunk of processed meat fell to the floor.

"Five-second rule," said Yaz, meaning that if you picked up dropped food quickly, it was still okay to eat it. Babes seemed to take it more as a command—a *rule*—than a joke.

This guy is so literal.

Babes picked up the turkey, sniffed it, and took a tiny bite.

"Good, huh?" said Yaz.

Babes made a face and took an even smaller bite.

Yaz struck another match and lit the candle on the bench in the center of the crypt. Then he took a seat, and watched Babes eat.

"You'll do anything I say, won't you?" said Yaz.

Babes chewed in silence.

"Yes, sir," said Yaz. "I bet you'd even kill for me, wouldn't you?"

Babes stared at the floor.

Yaz rose and walked over to the vacant niche, the makeshift storage closet that had held everything from Babes's baseball cards to Yaz's vanilla wafers. He removed the cover, took an old blanket from his collection of stuff, and spread it out across the floor.

"You're like a child. An innocent, gullible little child." Yaz chuckled, then turned serious. "Come here, Babes."

Babes shrank even farther into the corner.

"Come on, little boy," said Yaz, his eyes narrowing in the flicker of candlelight. "Come lay down on my blankie. *Now.*"

CHAPTER 34

Midnight was decision time for Brandon Lomax. Another sixteen-hour day of speeches and glad-handing was over. He and his campaign manager were the last remaining souls in his Providence campaign headquarters. They were seated in the back row of the telephone bank, Lomax with his tired feet up on a battered metal desk. His jacket was off, the shirtsleeves were rolled up, and his tie was loosened in his signature style. On the wall behind them was a red, white, and blue banner proclaiming his original (and since rejected) cam-

paign slogan: TO THE MAX—*LOMAX*—
FOR U.S. SENATE.

"What do they know so far?" said Lomax.

"My read is nothing," said Josef. "But
you never know with the media."

Lomax took a final gulp of cold decaf
and glanced at the desktop telephones
behind them. "The phone would be ringing off the hook if anyone had a clue
about a lost DNA sample that could
prove I was involved in the Chelsea
James crash."

"Or proved that you weren't," said
Josef.

"Yes, but that wouldn't be news, now
would it—if I wasn't involved."

"I suppose not. Which raises the
question: Do we leak the fact that you
willingly submitted a DNA sample to be
compared to DNA found at the scene?"

"I think it can only be helpful," said
Lomax. "A guilty man would never vol-
unteer to do that."

"It still all depends on how the media
spins it," said Josef.

"What's the worst they can say?"

Josef paused, as if taken by the size

of the question. "It's sticky, since you were the attorney general when this evidence was gathered. Some reporters might suggest that the department never constructed a DNA profile from that evidence because you prevented it from happening. Or they might speculate that the disappearance of that sample wasn't recent. It vanished years ago, while you were still AG, a calculated destruction of evidence on your part to make sure the shit didn't hit the fan after you left."

"That's preposterous."

"Is it?"

The men locked eyes. "Yes," Lomax said coolly.

Josef blinked. "And then there's the Garrisen connection."

"What about it?"

Josef chose his words carefully, as if trying not to antagonize his boss any further.

"Connie Garrisen is one of your biggest supporters—could well be the next U.S. surgeon general if you're elected to the Senate. His wife is the current chief of the Criminal Division.

Glenda Garrisen might have some questions to answer about DNA evidence disappearing under her watch."

"It's not really *her* watch. The DNA bank is maintained by the Department of Health."

"The media doesn't always point out those finer distinctions."

Lomax mulled it over. "If we don't leak anything, how will this play out?"

"As long as Emma Carlisle doesn't go public with the anonymous tips that name you, Brandon Lomax is nowhere in the Chelsea James story. The media is left only with Chelsea's troubled younger brother going on the radio to confess that he killed his sister."

"I think we leave it right there," said Lomax.

"I do too. He's the only suspect. Police are out there in full force looking for him."

"And if he has an Asperger's meltdown that forces some trigger-happy cop to make 'I killed my sister' his last words, it wouldn't necessarily be a bad thing."

Josef looked at him in disbelief.

"What?" said Lomax.

"I just wish I hadn't heard you say that."

"Oh, come on. I wasn't serious."

Josef sighed. "It's getting hard for me to tell anymore."

"What do you think I'm going to do next, hire some mob guy to take him out?"

"No," said Josef, rising. "But do me a favor, will you?"

"What?"

"Before you get there, fire me."

Lomax wasn't sure if he detected a hint of a smile on Josef's face or not, but asking to be fired before the candidate hired a hit man was a dangerous thing for a campaign manager to joke about.

"I'll let you lock up," he said, rising. He grabbed his jacket and left through the front door. His car was at the curb. He got in and caught almost every green light on the way to his house on Benefit Street. He stopped at the traffic light in front of the same convenience store he'd visited the other night to get the warm milk—the one with the pay phone he'd used to call Sal Vanelli.

Speaking of hit men.

It occurred to him that he hadn't spoken to Sal since he'd botched the attempted interception of the anonymous tipster at the Modern Diner. Josef's snide remark was playing in his ear, and a wave of panic suddenly washed over the candidate. Sal had totally screwed up the assignment. What if he felt like he still owed his friend Lomax a favor? What if he tried to make it up to him and did something *really* stupid.

Lomax steered into the parking lot, parked in front of the outside pay phone, and dialed Sal at the bar.

"It's POTUS," he said, feeling a little silly about the spylike code stuff.

"Hey, boss. I didn't want to call you, for obvious reasons, but I'm really sorry about the way things went screwy the other day."

"Forget about it. It's not a problem."

"Let me make it up to—"

"No, *no.* That's what I was afraid of. You don't owe me anything."

"You sure? Because I'm really a smart guy. In fact, I've been putting two and two together here, and it seems to me that you could use some help."

Lomax froze. He'd been very careful about how much to tell Sal. "What do you mean?"

"Well, it's pretty clear to me that this kid Babes who's been in the news is the tipster I was supposed to meet at the Modern Diner. My job was to buy him off and keep him quiet, right?"

Lomax didn't answer.

Sal said, "Now he's blabbing his mouth all over the radio. And just today—did you hear that guy from *Action News* call in to *Jocks in the Morning*?

"I heard about it."

"Well, I'd be worried about that if I was you. So long as Babes is talking on the radio to his brother-in-law, you can keep track of what he's saying. But what if he takes up this offer from Doug Wells? If Babes calls him on a private line and they talk off the record, you got no idea what Babes is telling the media. That doesn't sound like a good situation for you."

"What are you saying?"

"I say we take things up a notch.

Somebody should give Dougy boy a little visit."

Lomax's stomach was suddenly in knots. "No. Absolutely not."

"Won't cost you anything."

"I said no. Don't go there."

"Okay. I'm not going to argue with you. But if you change your mind, you know how to reach me."

"That I do," said Lomax, and he hung up the phone.

CHAPTER 35

Yaz needed ice.

His left eye was throbbing. That lunatic Babes was strong as an ox when he freaked. He was docile, gullible, obedient—as long as you didn't touch him. The slightest physical contact, however gentle, was like an electric shock to the genitals. All Yaz had done was run his fingertip back and forth along Babes's lower lip. Babes bucked like a bronco, fists flying, legs kicking. The hardest blows went straight to Yaz's face. He had no mirror, but he was sure that his shiner would be big and purple.

Crazy son of a bitch.

Yaz tore another strip of cloth from his dirty blanket and twisted it into a make-shift rope. Babes's ankles and wrists were already bound together with a dozen other strips, but Yaz tied this last one extra tight.

"That ought to hold you," he said.

Babes grunted, but he'd lost his will to fight.

Yaz stopped to collect his thoughts, his plan fully conceived. It was now only a matter of execution. The idea had come to him after Babes's tell-all monologue about the night of his sister's death. A drunk driver had been involved. It wasn't clear to Yaz how Babes knew the driver's name, and the name didn't mean anything to Yaz anyway. The important point was the car—anyone who drove a big Mercedes-Benz had to be rich. Yaz saw dollar signs. Driving drunk. Leaving the scene of a fatal accident. Maybe even vehicular homicide. If it were Yaz's ass on the line, and if he were a respectable member of society who drove an expensive Mercedes, he'd cough up serious dough to stop an eyewitness like Babes from calling the police or the newspaper.

Ten grand. At least.

It was one o'clock in the morning, but what better time was there to catch someone at home? Yaz powered up Babes's cell phone and called nation-wide directory assistance. Babes had been absolutely certain about the name and spelling. There were three separate listings in New England, and Yaz chose the one with the familiar area code.

The operator offered to dial it for him at an extra cost of thirty-five cents.

"What the heck?" said Yaz, smiling thinly. "I'll be rich soon enough."

There was an answer on the third ring.

"Yes, is this the killer of Chelsea James?" said Yaz in his most official tone.

There was a click on the line.

Yaz smiled. This was fun. This time he dialed the number himself. He knew he'd planted a seed. The guy had to be shitting his pants right now. Yaz gave the pansy ass six rings, tops—that's how long it would take him to pick up again.

It rang five times.

"Hello."

"I saw you vomit," said Yaz. "I know you did it."

This time Yaz hung up—and waited. He was confident that a man of this stature would have some kind of call screening that had logged Yaz's incoming phone number. He checked the flashing time and temperature on the bank marquee across the street. It was 1:17 AM. He predicted a callback before 1:20 AM.

Ninety seconds later, Yaz's phone rang. It was the mark.

"Got your attention?" said Yaz.

"What do you want?"

Yaz felt like he had found the proverbial genie in the lamp. "Money."

"What do I get in return?"

"Silence."

"How much do you want?"

"Ten thousand dollars."

The man paused to consider it. "I can have it tomorrow."

"Excellent," said Yaz. "Meet me—"

"Under the I-95 bridge over the river in Pawtucket."

Yaz took a moment. It seemed perfect. "I know it well."

"Eleven o'clock tomorrow night."

"I'll be there," said Yaz. "Pleasure doing business with you."

He closed the flip phone, and the deal was sealed.

CHAPTER 36

Ryan was putting his life on the line.

This morning he'd decided to add to his exercise regimen by jogging to the radio station. Unfortunately, he chose a route through the South End that involved crossing Tremont Street at Worcester Street, where drivers confused survival of the fittest with the law of the crosswalks. A speeding BMW nearly flattened him between the lines. Ryan didn't catch the license tag, just the bumper sticker: "Life's too short not to be Italian."

A pedestrian was a dangerous thing to be in Boston, even at 5:20 AM.

Emma was waiting at the radio station when he arrived. They'd agreed to meet before the show to plan their on-air strategy with Babes. To his surprise, she came dressed in exercise clothing.

"Don't tell me you ran here from Providence," he said.

"Don't tell me I *look* like I ran here from Providence."

He smiled. The word that came to mind was hot, but not in the sweaty and overheated sense that applied to his own appearance.

"You look . . . fine," he said.

"Fine?" she said. "Is that neither-here-nor-there fine, or more like nineteen-seventies *Super Fly* 'Ooh, that girl is *fine*'?"

Ryan's mouth opened, but the words didn't come. With Chelsea, he'd never fumbled the how-do-I-look question. But he hadn't expected it from Emma.

"Ryan, snap out of it. I'm yanking your chain, okay? If I drive straight from here to my gym, I can still be in court for a nine-thirty hearing. So let's get started."

"Sure."

Ryan grabbed two bottles of water

from the kitchen fridge and led her back to the studio. It was small with no windows to the outdoors, but a large interior window looked out into the hallway, and another one looked into the control room. The walls were acoustically padded and drab gray, and the carpet had probably absorbed more coffee spills than sound.

"Have a seat," he said, offering Emma his chair. He moved the boom microphone out of the way and pushed the headsets to one side of the table for a clear work area. His cohost typically arrived at 5:59 AM for the six o'clock broadcast, so he and Emma had time alone. That meant no chance to shower before the show, which made him a little self-conscious in such a small room. He grabbed a clean T-shirt from his workout bag, made a quick change, pitched the dirty one out into the hallway, and closed the door.

Emma looked mortified.

"Sorry," he said. "I guess I just sort of undressed in front of you."

"Forget that. You just threw a dirty T-shirt into the hall."

"You . . . want me to bring it back?"

She gave him a curious look, definitely not one of judgment or disgust, but a much more complex one that Ryan was having trouble reading.

"Poor Ainsley," she said.

"What?"

"Nothing," she said. "Is your producer still OK with your making a direct appeal to Babes?"

"Yes," said Ryan, as he took a seat in his cohost's chair. "I have the first three minutes."

"That's plenty. When did you last try Babes's cell?"

"This morning, before I left the house. The call went straight to voice mail, which tells me that either the battery is dead, or his phone is turned off."

"Then your show is still our best chance of reaching Babes," she said, and then she seemed to shift gears. "By the way, I am so sorry about the way Doug Wells made a complete ass of himself on your show yesterday, trying to get Babes to call him."

"Television reporters. What can you say?"

"I had plenty to say—to *him.* I want you to know that I had nothing to do with that. In fact, I told him I don't ever want to see him again."

"Really?" said Ryan.

"Yes. So now that we have that out of the way, let's make sure you say the right things when Babes calls again. Have you written anything down?"

"I'm a baseball might-have-been who cohosts *Jocks in the Morning.* I haven't written anything down since college."

Emma took a notepad from her briefcase. "I am *so* glad I came."

"Me too," said Ryan.

She seemed to sense something in his tone, but she let it pass. "Can I borrow a pen?"

Ryan lent her one, and during the next fifteen minutes they worked out a script word by word, line by line. She helped Ryan organize his thoughts, but she also had a subtle way of helping him sort through his feelings about Babes, his confession, and the danger he was now in. He tried to focus all of his energy on the radio message, but another message was coming through. Everything from the way Emma looked to the way she had driven all the way from Providence before dawn to help him this morning made it impossible for him not to notice things that for the past three years he'd been unable to see. Emma was kind, smart, sensitive—and yes, she was even nineteen-seventies *Super Fly "fine"* in her workout clothes.

Emma was underlining a word in the text when her pen dropped to the floor.

"I'll get it," they said simultaneously, and the ensuing head butt nearly knocked them both unconscious.

"Hey, dudes," said Ryan's cohost as he entered the studio.

Jock Grogan had a full head of shock-white hair and a serious coffee buzz that propelled him into the studio like the *Silver Streak.* He took one look at Ryan and Emma, who were grimacing in pain and rubbing the emerging knots on their foreheads, and he stopped short.

"What the hell have you two been doing? Zinedine Zidane imitations?" he said, referring to the French soccer player's infamous head butt that handed

Italy the 2006 World Cup Championship.

Emma didn't get the joke. Ryan was in too much pain to laugh.

"Thirty seconds," the producer said, as she appeared in the open doorway. She left quickly and reappeared on the other side of the glass inside the control room.

"I'll wait in the hall," said Emma.

Ryan moved over to his chair, and Jock took his seat. Ryan gathered up his script, put on his headset, and adjusted the microphone. The engineer did a quick voice test, and on audio cue from his producer, Ryan was ready to go.

"Morning, knuckleheads. Ryan James here with the incomparable Jock Grogan, and this is *Jocks in the Morning,* the numero uno sports talk show in the Hub."

Ryan glanced at Emma, on the other side of the glass, who could hear the broadcast on speaker. With her nod of encouragement, he continued according to their script.

"We're starting on a serious note today," said Ryan. "Those of you who were listening to the show a couple of days ago heard a pretty remarkable phone call from my brother-in-law, a very special person who our family refers to as Babes. Three years ago, when my wife Chelsea was killed in a car accident, I thought my own life was over. But it wasn't only tough for me. Chelsea's little brother took it very hard too."

Ryan paused. This was proving to be more difficult than he'd thought it would. He glanced toward Emma on the other side of the glass. She shot him another subtle vote of confidence, and it gave him more strength than she'd probably intended. He was suddenly no longer tied to the script.

"When something like this happens to you—man, you can't describe it. At first, it's like a lightning bolt. No way could this be true. You think you're going to wake up, and it will all be a bad dream. But it's not a dream, and you're so angry you could . . ."

Ryan was completely off script now, speaking from the heart, no going back.

"Well, you just want to find the bastard who did this and make him pay. But then you realize that no amount of justice or revenge—whatever you want to call it—is going to bring Chelsea back. That's when the bottom falls out. I mean, sometimes you can't even breathe. You know you should get down on your knees and thank God that your daughter is still alive, but then you ask yourself: Why the heck did He let the accident happen in the first place? Why did He have to take Chelsea? And it's not just because you've lost the best thing that ever happened to you. You actually feel guilty, because you have your whole life ahead of you, and Chelsea's life is over, except in your heart. Which is so unfair, even ironic. Because your heart is frozen, and why should a person as warm and loving as Chelsea have to live on in this emotional tundra?"

Ryan drew a breath, but something inside wouldn't let him stop.

"So you wake up every day resenting the fact that somehow this cold and frozen *thing* keeps on beating, forcing you to live with the pain, forcing you to hear people tell you that time heals all wounds. But time has a flipside. You're getting older, and what's worse, your memories get old too. You might even start to forget exactly what her voice sounds like, and the anger comes flooding back, and suddenly you're drowning all over again."

He paused, collected himself. "Sorry. This probably isn't making any sense to you. What I'm trying to say, Babes, is this: I talked to your mom. She told me everything. I know why you think you killed your sister. But I'm here to tell you that you did nothing wrong. Chelsea's death," he said, his voice quaking, "was not your fault. It's just not your fault."

Ryan swallowed hard. It was difficult to say those words aloud, but not because he didn't believe them. Listening to his own voice, it was for one surreal moment as if Ryan were speaking to himself, trying to get the message through his own thick head once and for all, after so much time, that he had done nothing wrong either, that he had not caused Chelsea's death, and that there was nothing he could have done to save her.

There was complete silence on the air as the truth sank in for Ryan.

Finally, his cohost prompted him: "Ryan?"

It was clear from Jock's expression that he thought Ryan had merely zoned out or lost his train of thought. Jock didn't understand. Then Ryan looked again toward Emma, who was still on the other side of the glass, watching and listening. The compassion in her beautiful eyes told him that she *did* understand. Maybe it took the heart and soul of a woman who dealt with violent crime and victims every day, but Emma understood *him*—completely. In a split-second flashback that reached to his very core, it was as if he were simultaneously back in his kitchen with Ainsley and staring straight into the sun—the nearest star to earth—while Emma whispered to him without words that the answer was always closer than you thought.

Ryan reached inside for the strength to finish. "Babes, we all want you to come home. Please, just come home."

Ryan could speak no longer. He signaled to Jock, who took it from there.

"Ryan, we're all with you, pal. Hope it works out. Okay, dudes," he said, shifting gears. "Let's talk sports."

The current winning streak of the Red Sox was the farthest thing from Ryan's mind. He removed his headset and pushed the boom microphone away. His gaze shifted once again toward Emma, and their eyes met. She looked as if she wanted to tell him something, and there was definitely something he wanted to say to her.

She gave him a complicated smile, then she turned and left—quickly. Too quickly, Ryan thought.

Ryan started after her, but his producer caught him in the hallway. She was smiling widely, excitement in her eyes.

"That was fantastic, Ryan. Absolutely great radio!"

Ryan heard the ding of the elevator from the lobby. Emma was leaving, and he let her go.

"Yeah," he said. "Great stuff."

CHAPTER 37

Yaz was not about to let Babes go any-where.

Last night's phone call had gone re-markably well. Yaz was downright proud of his performance. Blackmail was his game. The price was ten thousand dol-lars. He could have been more heavy-handed, but it was clear enough that if the sum wasn't paid in full, he would go straight to the newspaper to tell all— and name names. The meeting was set: tonight at 11:00 PM, under the I-95 bridge at the Seekonk River, Yaz would take delivery of the cash.

The last thing he needed now was Babes crying to go home.

"It's a trick," said Yaz.

Together they'd listened to *Jocks in the Morning* on Babes's radio. Ryan's plea came through loud and clear. Yaz had serious damage control to do. Babes seemed to like repetition, so every hour or so, Yaz would rehash the same conversation, brainwashing him.

"Yes, sir," said Yaz, "your brother-in-law is definitely working with the police."

Babes was sitting in the corner of the crypt with his knees drawn up and his back to the stone wall. He kept his eyes forward, looking only at the floor.

Yaz said, "If you go home, the cops will be waiting for you. And you know what they're gonna do?"

Babes shook his head.

"What are you, stupid? You went on the radio and told the whole world that you killed your sister. They're going to arrest you and throw your ass in jail. You ever been to jail, Babes?"

"No," he peeped.

"I have. I seen plenty of guys like you

in jail too. You know what happens to boys like you in jail, Babes?"

Babes blinked twice, much harder than usual, and then it was suddenly as if he couldn't stop blinking.

"The really big men steal packs of cherry Kool-Aid from the prison kitchen," said Yaz. "And it's all for you. Do you like Kool-Aid?"

"Doesn't everybody?"

"Well, it's good that you like it. Because they're gonna love you. See, they don't mix it into a drink. The men take the pure powder and smear it on your lips. Gives them a bright glossy red color. You didn't like it very much when I touched you on the lips, did you?"

"No," he said firmly.

"I know you didn't. But here's the thing. In jail, you have to take off your clothes every night and go into the shower with a whole bunch of other naked men. And what do you think happens when a nice-looking young man like you walks stark naked into the shower with those beautiful and sexy cherry-red lips?"

"I'll wash it off."

"No, you won't," he said, laughing. Then he turned serious. "Because if you do, they'll beat the living hell out of you. Some of those men have been in jail a very long time. They want those lips. They want 'em real bad."

"Shut up!" said Babes, as he covered his ears.

Yaz smiled. "It's okay. I won't touch you again. I won't lay a finger on you. So long as you stay here in the crypt and don't go anywhere, you're safe. How's that sound?"

Babes didn't answer. In fact, he didn't say another word the remainder of the day. He just listened to his radio, ate the rest of the turkey loaf that Yaz had given him, and took a bathroom break when Yaz decided it was time.

At dusk, Yaz lit the candle on the bench. The hours were passing slowly— partly because he had nothing to do, but also because he was so eager with anticipation. Blackmail had a way of getting his adrenaline flowing. He'd done some con before he was homeless. Years ago, it was a Medicaid scam that had landed him in jail on fraud charges. He hadn't realized how much of the game was still in his blood.

He couldn't be late for his meeting. The only way to check the time was on Babes's cell phone, but he needed to conserve the battery. He waited as long as he could, turning it on and off every so often to check. At 10:40 PM, the time had finally come.

"I'm going out," said Yaz.

Babes was silent.

"I know you're not crazy enough to run," said Yaz, "but I have to tie you up anyway."

Babes did not resist as Yaz bound his wrists and ankles with the strips he'd torn earlier from his blanket. The bindings were probably sufficient to keep him from going anywhere. A little fear would be all the insurance Yaz needed.

Yaz went to the stack of Babes's baseball cards on the bench. By the light of the candle, he sorted through them until he found what he wanted: Carl Yastrzemski.

"My namesake," he said, showing it to Babes.

He held the card over the lit candle.

"Stop!" said Babes.

The corner turned black and then burst into flames.

"No, don't!" Babes shouted.

Yaz pulled it out of the fire and blew out the flame, but the corner had burned off.

Babe was angry and in tears. "What'd you do that for?"

Yaz came close. He was looking into Babes's eyes, but Babes wouldn't—couldn't—look back into his.

"I'm taking the cards with me," he said, as he stuffed them into the deep pockets of his army coat. "If you're not here when I get back, I'll burn every last one of them."

"No, don't burn them! I'm not going anywhere!"

Yaz smiled. "Good dog, Babes. We'll teach you to roll over yet."

He blew out the candle and headed out into the night, leaving Babes alone in the blackened crypt.

CHAPTER 38

Ryan had a visit from Ivan around ten-thirty. The Red Sox road trip was over, and he was back in Boston for the next eight days.

Had it been the off-season, Ryan might have hired a babysitter and headed over to the Beantown Pub, across the street from the final resting place for Samuel Adams and two other signers of the Declaration of Independence, the only place to enjoy a cold Sam Adams within a stone's throw of a cold Sam Adams. As it was, the two men drank a couple of nonalcoholic beers in the living room while Ryan brought Ivan up to speed.

"So you heard nothing today?" said Ivan.

"Nada. Jock and I did the rest of the show as normal. Every time the phone line lit up, I thought it might be Babes. I spent the rest of the day with Chelsea's dad driving around, searching. Even went out toward Sabin Point in East Providence this time. There's a flock of geographically confused parrots that Babes likes to watch up on the wires—not up close, of course, since all that squawking can set him off sometimes. Saw the birds, but no Babes. I'm honestly running out of places to look."

"Have you tried organizing the community, getting a group search going?"

"That would be a great idea if the police didn't have an arrest warrant out for Babes. Neighbors have a way of not wanting to get involved when you're looking for a wanted criminal."

"I see your point," said Ivan. "I'm not the starting pitcher again for at least two more days. I can help you tomorrow."

"Thanks," said Ryan. The offer was genuine, Ryan knew.

"So," said Ivan, "when you gonna tell me about the elephant in the room?"

"What elephant in the room?"

"The dead one. What the hell is that smell?"

"Oh, that," said Ryan. "It's scented oil called summer safari. It's supposed to help my insomnia. Aroma therapy."

Ivan chuckled the way only a best friend could. Ryan didn't dare tell him that some insomniacs swore by sniffing dirty socks before going to bed.

"You want aroma therapy?" said Ivan. "Let yourself get close enough to a woman to breathe in her perfume. It's time."

Ryan looked off to the middle distance, peeling the label off his bottle. "What do you think of Emma Carlisle?" he said.

Ivan did a double take. "In what way do you mean?"

"Just as a person. What do you think of her?"

"Did something happen while I was gone?"

"Not what you're thinking. I'm just getting to know her better."

"Really? Let's hear it, dude."

Ryan sighed, not sure how to explain. "It's funny. About six months ago, I went to Boston Brewery for dinner. I was by myself, watching ESPN. Out of the corner of my eye I spotted Emma with some of her friends. It looked to me like she was about two dart tosses away from setting a record for the most bull's-eyes under the influence of four cosmopolitans. It was the first time I'd seen her just being herself, not doing anything having to do with, you know, the accident. I thought about going up and saying something. But then I thought, no, she's out having fun. I'm her work. So I watched for a few minutes, figuring maybe she'd see me. Then she could decide whether to just wave from across the bar or come over and say hello."

"So what happened?"

"She hit another bull's-eye, and some guy came over and gave her a big hug and a kiss. And I left. But it's weird. Every now and then, I find myself thinking about that night, and for the first time since Chelsea has been gone, I sort of . . . wonder. Do you know what I'm saying?"

"I'm pretty sure I do."

"Do you think it's too strange, her being the prosecutor and all?"

Ivan considered it. "I'll answer that question, but only if you promise not to take it the wrong way and get pissed at me."

"All right. That's fair."

"If you're going to go this route," said Ivan, "I think you should try something."

"What do you mean?"

"Don't ever make her feel like a walking reminder of the worst day of your life."

Ryan was suddenly thinking about this morning at the studio, and the image of Emma leaving in such a hurry flashed in his mind. She'd practically run to the elevator after his on-the-air soul baring, gone before he could say a word to her.

Ryan raised his bottle in salute. "Thanks, Ivan. You're a pretty smart guy. Some of the time."

Ivan tipped his bottle back at him. "You're welcome, dude. All of the time."

The whine of speeding cars on the interstate told Yaz that he was near the drop point. It was a familiar sound to him. Before he found the crypt, he'd lived beneath this particular bridge where I-95 crossed over the Seekonk River.

Ten thousand dollars. It was a nice piece of change. He wasn't thinking about the money, really. He was thinking about what he'd do with it. Ten grand would buy him plenty of first-class beatings—one for each bastard who'd ruined his life. Slow and painful was the way he wanted them. His ex-wife would be first. The bitch never smiled, so what did she need teeth for anyway? Next on the list was the little Puerto Rican stud who was banging her. Battery acid on the balls for Mr. Hot Nuts. His wife's divorce lawyer—now there was the guy who'd really put Yaz on the street. That one called for some real creativity. Yaz could still see that stuffed prick standing in the courtroom so smugly, all decked out in his Ivy League bow tie, the red suspenders stretching over his fat belly, his thumbs in his belt loops. Always with the thumbs in the belt loops. The son of a bitch was going to have a hard time doing *that* with no thumbs. That kind of maiming might cost an extra five or six hundred bucks. But what was money for? Yaz was loving this game. The old con artist in him was back, with the emphasis on artist.

Yaz stopped directly under the bridge. The two-mile walk from the cemetery had winded him slightly, and even with the anticipation driving him, he needed a moment to catch his breath. It was dark in the shadow of tons of formed concrete, but the city glow provided just enough light for his eyes to adjust. The place hadn't changed much. His old shopping cart with the broken wheels was right where he'd left it. The remnants of cardboard boxes were strewn about, tattered remains of homes for the homeless.

A man emerged from behind one of the massive concrete pillars. Yaz's adrenaline was pumping.

"Looks like I'm right on time," Yaz said to him.

The man didn't answer. He walked straight toward Yaz in silence.

"Did you bring the money?" said Yaz.

No reply. The man was ten yards away and approaching steadily, a discernible confidence in his step. Yaz couldn't see his face in the darkness, but he was much bigger than Yaz had expected.

"You better have brought the money," said Yaz, but his voice betrayed him—it cracked, exposing his concern.

The man kept coming. Yaz saw no bag or briefcase—nothing to carry the cash in—and his concern quickly turned into fear. Instinct told Yaz to run, but before he could move, the man closed in and struck him with a club that he'd concealed behind his arm or torso. The low and lightning-quick blow took Yaz's legs out from under him.

Yaz screamed with pain and fell to the ground. It felt as if his kneecap was broken.

"Don't, please don't!" said Yaz.

"Where's your buddy?" the man said.

It was definitely not the voice Yaz had

heard on the telephone. This guy was a hired professional, and Yaz knew he was in serious trouble.

"What friend?" said Yaz.

Again the man whacked him with the club, a direct blow to the left shin. Yaz screamed at the sound of his own leg breaking. The man stood on the broken bone, sending Yaz into near convulsions.

"The guy whose cell phone you called on," the man said. "The one they call Babes."

"He's hiding," said Yaz, tears running down his face, "in the old North Burial Ground. There's a crypt there that nobody ever visits."

The man slammed the bat across his ribs. "You're lying!"

"No," said Yaz, struggling to force the words out through the pain. That last blow had cracked his ribs and smashed Babes's cell phone. "It's for a family named Dawes. Babes is there. Go now, you'll find him. I promise."

Yaz didn't see the final blow coming, and the next few moments were a complete blur. He heard a dull thud, felt a hot explosion on the side of his head, and fell face first to the ground. He saw the club land right in front of him, and he heard footsteps as his attacker walked away.

Then his world went black.

CHAPTER 39

Babes was free of his bindings. Removing them hadn't proved difficult. With no rope, Yaz had torn an old woven blanket into narrow strips, but the fabric was threadbare and rotting. Babes had more than enough leg strength to break through the ankle ties first, and the restraints on his wrists didn't take much longer.

But he still lacked the courage to leave the crypt.

Moonlight shone through the arched entranceway, and the long shadow of a Baroque-style wrought-iron gate extended all the way to the marble bench in the center of the crypt. The dark and light pattern on the stone floor was one of the most intricate and beautiful things Babes had ever seen. The gate's gentle curves, the symmetry of design, and the precision of the lines, as captured in the shadow of moonlight, seemed to emphasize that the iron was more decorative than protective. In a way, it reminded Babes of those maze games he used to play as a kid, where the object was to get all the way to the exit without lifting the pencil tip from the page and without having to double back from a blind alley. Babes retreated into his dark corner and imagined that he was four inches tall, walking through the ornamental maze—to the exit.

But he didn't move. The crypt was his refuge, the only safe place in Rhode Island. It was exactly as Yaz had warned: the police would arrest him the minute they spotted him. And leaving Pawtucket sure wasn't an option. Babes couldn't count the number of family vacations he had ruined. Every year it was the same thing: his father and mother hoping that Babes had outgrown his anxieties, packing the family into the minivan, checking into a roadside motel for the night—and then checking out and heading straight home before bed-time because Babes was freaking out.

What was that?

Babes was suddenly on high alert. He could have sworn he'd heard a noise outside the crypt.

There it is again!

It was a crunching sound, like footfalls on a gravel path. Babes listened hard. He closed his eyes tightly, as if that would improve his hearing. There was only silence, but he was certain he had heard something earlier. He needed to check it out. On hands and knees he crawled across the stone floor toward the gate, taking care to stay in the pro-tection of the dark shadows, just be-yond the bright streak of moonlight. He lay flat on his belly, making himself as invisible as possible as he peered out through the iron bars and into the ceme-tery.

His heart skipped a beat. A man was approaching.

Yaz?

He hoped so. The man was near the path but walking on the grass now, as if he'd realized that the crunch of gravel beneath his shoes was making too much noise. The white beam of a flashlight helped him to navigate around headstones. Babes didn't remember Yaz owning a flashlight that actually worked. Maybe he'd found one.

The flashlight cut off. Why would Yaz switch off the light before he reached the crypt? Yaz wouldn't. And this silhouette was much bigger than Yaz.

That's not Yaz!

Babes had to think fast. Hide—but where? The interior of the crypt was a simple rectangular room. There was only one place for the living. But the two long walls were lined with plenty of places for the dead—or for anyone who didn't want to die at this particular moment.

Babes hurried across the crypt to his secret hiding place, the vacant niche where he used to stash his baseball cards. It was at the bottom of the column near the entrance, right below *Daisy Dawes, born August 9, 1847, died*

April 21, 1935. He removed the polished granite marker that had been intended for another member of the Dawes family. The crypt accommodated caskets as well as urns, so the niche was plenty big for Babes.

He took a deep breath for courage and crawled inside.

The sound of footsteps outside the crypt grew louder. Babes had less than a minute to pull the granite marker back into place and fully disguise his whereabouts. But Babes was frozen. Being inside the crypt had never bothered him before. Actually lying inside an internment niche was another matter. It was the difference between being among the dead and being *one of* the dead.

The iron gate rattled.

He's here!

Babes was shaking. He struggled to hear his mother's sweet voice: "Think only pleasing thoughts," she would have told him.

Suddenly he was Christopher Plummer in *The Sound of Music*. These weren't dead people around him. They were the Trapp family. That guy rattling the gate was Rolf. And everyone knew that Rolf was a dolt.

Babes pulled the marker into place, sealing off his niche from the intruder. The edges were routed, so even without fastening bolts, the granite fit snugly. Inside it was dark beyond the blackest night, but four unused bolt holes, one in each corner, allowed enough air inside for him to breathe. If Babes craned his neck just so, he could peer out through one of the holes.

He heard the gate creak as it swung open. The click of the man's heels echoed off the stone walls. Babes calmed his breathing and waited.

Through the open bolt hole, he saw the sweep of the flashlight. The man walked to the far corner where Babes had been hoveled. He inspected the bindings that Babes had broken. The beam of the flashlight traveled to the marble bench in the center of the crypt. The man inspected the burned candle and sat on the bench. And then Babes saw it: the gun. The man definitely had a pistol in one hand.

Something bad had happened to Yaz—he was sure of it.

Babes considered making a run for it, but that was a foolish thought. He fought off the urge and lay perfectly still.

The man rose from the bench. The sweep of his flashlight went from one end of the crypt to the other, brightening row after row of dead Daweses. Finally, it swept past Babes, and he cringed for a split second as the white light shone like lasers through the four bolt holes.

But the man hadn't noticed.

Or had he?

The clicking heels grew louder. The stranger was coming closer.

Babes held his breath. The footsteps stopped. A pair of shoes was less than a yard away from Babes's head, just on the other side of the granite. Then Babes heard the most welcome sound imaginable. The gate creaked, and Babes could breathe again.

He's leaving!

The gate closed with an unmistakable metal clank. The man was definitely go-ing away. Babes had fooled him. The danger was gone. He'd narrowly escaped death, but he didn't dare move. He couldn't leave his hiding spot too soon. That had been the Trapp family's near fatal mistake. And Babes didn't have singing nuns to help him escape. Even if he did, he wouldn't trust them.

I'm on my own. And I can never go home.

CHAPTER 40

A noise outside his bedroom window woke Doug Wells from a sound sleep. The clock on the nightstand said 3:40 AM.

Doug was too tired to reach over and turn on the light, let alone get up and investigate. He was determined not to lose any sleep over that bitch Emma dumping him—for good, this time. So far, he'd been fabulously successful. Sleeping like a baby. A stupid bat flying into the window or a branch brushing up against the building wasn't going to change that pattern. His head sank back into his pillow, his eyelids slowly closed, and he felt his mind drifting back into dreamland.

Another bang at the window—this one was so sharp that it sent him sitting bolt upright in the bed.

What the hell?

He listened, but there was silence. Part of him wanted to go back to sleep, but that last noise was a little too close to home. He climbed out of bed, crossed the dark room, and went to the window. The blinds were shut. He wasn't sure why—he'd never been afraid to live alone—but something made him think twice about opening those blinds. He did it quickly.

The glass was black with night.

He reached for the lamp and switched it on—and what he saw gave him a start. It was right in front of his eyes, stuck to the window. A piece of paper. A note. Handwritten. He leaned closer to read it.

"Open the door. Let's talk again. Babes."

Doug felt tingles. He wasn't sure what "again" meant, but Babes must have considered Doug's pitch on the radio as their first talk. His stunt on Ryan James's show had worked.

In your face, Emma.

Doug ran to his closet and grabbed his robe, but he threw it aside. Not exactly the power look. He rummaged for real clothes: a shirt and pants. The adrenaline was flowing. This was big. Sure, his J-school professors would have cringed at his tactics. They taught the future reporters of the world never to make themselves part of the story. But some of the biggest names in the business had made their careers by ignoring that rule—and not just in recent history. Did anyone criticize Woodward and Bernstein for selling the movie rights to Hollywood for *All the President's Men*? Did anyone ever tell Dan Rather that he should have gone off camera to confront the Chicago police at the 1968 Democrat National Convention? Even the right-as-rain *New York Times* had cooperated with law enforcement and published the Unabomber's rambling manifesto.

Now it was Doug Wells's turn.

He pulled on his shoes and raced down the hall.

It seemed a little strange that Babes hadn't just knocked on the front door. Maybe he had, but Doug had slept through it. Either way, Babes was here now and had the full attention of the rising star at *Action News.* Doug turned the deadbolt and pulled open the door.

The force that hit him was like a charging bull.

Doug tumbled head over heels into the hallway. The door slammed shut. Before he could react, a huge hulk of a man was on top of him.

"Don't move," he said.

Doug felt the barrel of a gun pressing up under his chin. One squeeze of the trigger and a bullet would shatter his jaw, rip through his brain, and come out the top of his head.

"Don't shoot," he said, barely moving his mouth.

"Don't resist."

The man turned him over with ease, partly because of his strength, partly because Doug was so compliant. He pulled Doug's hands behind his back and fastened them with plastic hand-cuffs. They were cinched too tightly, and the narrow bands of flexible plastic cut into his wrists.

"Now, I want you to get up slowly."

Doug complied. The man had an accent, Doug noticed. *Russian?*

"We're going to the bedroom."

The bedroom. A million thoughts ran through his head, none of them pleasant.

Doug felt the barrel of the gun against the back of his head. With his hands behind his back and an armed Russian grizzly bear breathing down his neck, fighting didn't seem like an option. Slowly he walked down the hallway toward his bedroom. The Russian was right behind him. He stopped at the open doorway.

"Inside," the man said.

Doug entered, and the gun felt glued to the base of his skull. He was standing at the foot of the bed when the Russian finally told him to stop.

Doug closed his eyes, then opened them slowly. His throat was going dry. *This* was not what he'd had in mind when he decided to take the plunge and make himself part of the story.

"What do you want?" Doug said.

"Shut up."

The response cut through him like a knife. The man had a frightening edge to his voice, one that spoke of no negotiation.

"Turn around, slow."

The thought of coming eye to eye with his attacker sent his pulse rate off the charts. Only a killer would let the victim see his face. Doug turned so slowly that he almost lost his balance. He didn't want to look but—*thank God!*—the Russian's face was unrecognizable, utterly distorted by the nylon stocking pulled over his head. Maybe he didn't plan to kill him after all.

A good thing.

"Kneel," the Russian said.

A bad thing.

Slowly, with obvious reluctance, Doug lowered himself to his knees. He looked down at the man's shoes.

"You seemed very excited to talk to Babes."

Doug didn't know what to say—

couldn't even begin to guess what the right response might have been.

"Have you talked to him?" the man said.

"No. Never."

"Liar. That's why I wrote 'Let's talk *again.* If you never talked to him, you would have known the note was bogus."

"I just figured that the way I reached out to him on the radio show counted as our first talk. That's what I thought he meant by 'again.' "

"Nice try. But I still say you're lying."

"It's the truth."

"What did he tell you about Chelsea James's car crash?"

"Nothing. I've never talked to him. I swear."

He grabbed Doug by the throat. His Adam's apple was suddenly in a vice grip, and his lungs yearned for air.

"I'm going to give you one more chance: What did Babes tell you?"

The Russian released his grip, and Doug coughed in his struggle for air.

"I swear," he said, coughing again. "We never talked."

"I wish I believed you. I really do."

Doug looked up. The Russian had a rope in his hand.

"What are you going to do?"

"You ever heard of a garrote?"

Doug shook his head with trepidation.

The Russian went to the night table beside the bed, picked it up, and smashed it to pieces on the floor. He grabbed one of the broken legs with one hand and held the loop of rope in the other.

"Let me show you."

He dropped the loop over Doug's head. It hung around his neck like a noose. Then he fed the table leg through the rope and turned it quickly, tightening the slack.

"I never met Babes!" said Doug. "I'd tell you everything if there was anything to tell. I never talked to the guy!"

"Let's see if you're still saying that five minutes from now."

He gave the table leg another turn.

Doug's head tilted back, and the noose gripped his neck. He tried to talk—plead with the Russian—but he had no voice. His groans turned to wheezing. His vision blurred.

Another half turn of the garrote.

Doug could no longer bear it. His body twisted, his feet swept out from under him, and he rolled to the floor. The Russian grabbed him from behind, maintaining pressure on the garrote as he buried his knee in Doug's spine. Doug was pinned face down on the floor, completely at the Russian's mercy. His head pounded with congestion, like the worst sinus headache imaginable. The eyes bulged. His face flushed red. It was as if he could hear nothing but his own desperate grunts, but then he heard something more.

The Russian was shouting at him.

Doug struggled to make out the words, wanted to answer if it would end this suffering. But it was all running to-gether.

The garrote tightened further. Doug tasted blood in his mouth as small bleeding sights erupted in the moist, soft mucosa of the lips and mouth.

The shouting continued, except that to Doug's ears it no longer seemed like shouting. It sounded like . . . singing. The Russian was singing to him at the top of his lungs.

Then Doug's eyes closed, and the singing stopped.

CHAPTER 41

A phone call at 4:25 AM was never good news, especially from the police. Emma sat up in her bed at the sound of Lieutenent Adler's voice. Probable homicide. A battered body had been found under Pawtucket bridge number 550.

"*What* bridge?" she said. Emma had lived in Rhode Island all her life, so street names—much less bridge numbers—meant nothing to her when it came to directions. Landmarks were all that mattered: *Turn right at the Dairy Queen, then go another mile past the redbrick building that used to be the A&P but closed about ten years ago.*

"It's where I-95 crosses the river," said Adler, "south of old Slater Mill."

"Got it," she said.

Emma reached the crime scene before dawn and was glad to have her overcoat. Autumn had not yet officially arrived, but on the breezy waterfront at five AM, it felt as though winter had.

The Seekonk River begins at Pawtucket Falls, just a hundred feet or so north of the I-95 bridge, also known as Pawtucket bridge number 550, but only to Lieutenant Adler and perhaps one or two retired bureaucrats from the Department of Transportation. The Seekonk was fed by the historic Blackstone River, which cut through the heart of Pawtucket. As early as 1790, enterprising Americans had turned the waterway into a working river, with Slater Mill the first successful water-powered cotton-spinning factory in the United States. The area was truly the cradle of the Industrial Revolution, but two centuries of dyes, heavy metals, varnish, solvents, and paints had transformed the river into an industrial sewer. Cholera outbreaks were common in the mid-nineteenth century, and a hundred years later mobsters joked that the quickest way to make someone "disappear" was to drop him into the river—alive. Great strides toward cleanup had been underway since Emma was a little girl, after a report to the U.S. Congress declared the river totally polluted and not suitable for bathing.

The warnings never seemed to deter the homeless.

Emma followed a footpath along the east bank. A deadly combination of early morning commuters and all-night partiers zoomed overhead on six lanes of interstate. Skimming upriver in a needlelike scull was a rowing crew of eight from Brown University, or perhaps from one of the local clubs, the team of oars dipping in rhythmic silence. A media helicopter hovered overhead, the first on the scene. In another thirty minutes remote broadcast crews from Providence and possibly even Boston would turn the surrounding area into a wintry forest of tall metal towers topped with microwave dishes.

I'm surprised Doug Wells isn't here yet.

For now, the scene was all about police work. Uniformed officers and yellow crime tape closed off the entrance points to the riverfront on either side of the interstate. Emma stopped at the tape and watched for a moment as the crime scene investigators tended to the body beneath the bridge. It was like a well-oiled machine—swabs taken, photographs snapped, evidence gathered.

"This ain't no peep show," said one of the cops.

Emma met his sarcasm with a flash of her credentials, which got her past the outer perimeter. The temperature seemed to drop another five degrees as she entered the underbelly of the old bridge. It was a tired cantilever steel structure nearly 100 feet wide and spanning 695 feet across the river and two riverside streets. It badly needed replacement, but it got high marks from some of Rhode Island's homeless, who didn't seem to mind the buzz of 172,000 vehicles a day.

Emma caught the eye of Lieutenent Adler, who recognized her.

"Got an ID of the victim yet?" she said.

Adler had the look and demeanor of a homicide detective who had seen far too many murders. He was perpetually tense and angry, his upper lip leathered from chain smoking, a clenched fist of a man.

"No," he said. "Pretty obviously homeless. Really bad teeth—I'm guessing not just from lack of flossing. Probably meth addiction."

"How long has he been dead?"

"Foo-owwas," he said.

Emma had to translate in her head. Adler had one of those "Roe-Dyelin" accents that even natives had a hard time understanding.

"A few hours—so not much rigor mortis beyond the head and neck, I presume?"

"Nah much."

Emma glanced toward the cloth-draped corpse. The examiners were getting ready to lift it onto a gurney. "Cause of death?" said Emma.

"Blunt trauma. Someone absolutely crushed the side of his head."

"You have a murder weapon?"

"Yeah. Baseball bat was right next to the body. Traces of blood and human hair on it."

Mere mention of anything "baseball" hit Emma like ice water. It was suddenly clear why she had been summoned to the scene. "I see," said Emma.

Adler said, "Pretty careless to drop the bat right beside the body. If you're not going to take it with you, at least throw it in the river."

"People panic, they do strange things," said Emma.

"Especially if they have one of those autism syndromes."

Emma tried not to push back too hard. "I understand where you're going with this. But just because a homeless man is beaten to death with a baseball bat doesn't mean the killer was Ryan James's brother-in-law."

"I'd agree with you, except that this particular baseball bat happens to be signed by Ivan Lopez. I listen to Ryan's radio show every morning. He and Ivan are best friends."

More ice water. Emma knew it was true. "Anything else pointing you in that direction?" she said tentatively.

"We found baseball cards in the victim's coat pockets. Some are probably collectors' cards, fairly valuable. There's one of Carl Yastrzemski's rookie season with the corner burned off. Possible evidence of motive there."

"Motive?"

Adler shrugged, theorizing. "A guy like Babes is probably a loner, not many friends. He runs away from home, taking only his prize possessions: his baseball cards and an autographed bat. He calls into Ryan's radio show, tells the world he killed his sister"—*sistuh*—"and doesn't know where to hide. He gets chummy with some homeless guy under a bridge. Homeless guy steals his baseball cards. Babes bashes his brains out with a baseball bat."

"Makes sense," said Emma. Almost too much sense. "Any witnesses?"

"So far we've talked to two other homeless folks. But they were clear on the other side of the river. Didn't see anything, and with all this traffic noise, Lord knows they didn't hear anything."

"How about fingerprints?"

"Picked up some clean ones from the cards and the bat," said Adler.

"We have Babes's prints in the data-bank," she said. "The lab lifted one from my BlackBerry earlier this month."

"Good to know. We'll run it. Victim also had a cell phone on him. Stolen, presumably. Body blow from the bat bashed it to bits. Not sure if we'll get any latent prints or not, but our techies will track down the owner. If it belongs to Babes, that only strengthens my the-ory. Should have our answer before breakfast."

"Doesn't sound like you're expecting any surprises," said Emma.

"Been doing this too many *yizz*," said Adler, looking off toward the river. "I'm done with surprises."

CHAPTER 42

Babes was terrified.

He hadn't slept a wink inside the niche. It took hours for the first signs of daylight to shine through the small bolt holes in the granite marker. Still, he waited. To be absolutely certain that the man with the gun was gone, he had to remain out of sight until he could stand it no more. It was his bladder that finally betrayed him. He pushed out the granite marker and crawled from his hiding place.

To his relief, he was alone in the crypt.

Babes quickly stepped outside to answer nature's call, then hurried back inside. He didn't want to go anywhere, but he was starving. Yesterday, Yaz had raided the Dumpster outside his favorite Italian restaurant and scrounged up a half-eaten Stromboli and garlic rolls for dinner, but there was nothing left for breakfast. Babes probably could have fooled himself into believing that Yaz would show up any minute with a loaf of bread or some granola bars—whatever they handed out at the downtown homeless shelter. Realistically, however, Babes knew that it wasn't going to happen. The mean-looking man with the gun last night had made this much clear: Yaz's blackmail scheme had backfired on him. He was now running from serious trouble, or he was already in it. Either way, Yaz wasn't coming back to the Dawes family crypt. Even worse, Babes understood that he, too, had to leave now—before the man with the gun came around again.

Babes slumped into his corner and considered his next move. Trusting Yaz had been a huge mistake. He should never have told him about Chelsea's crash. But after three years of bottling up the truth, he needed to tell someone what he had seen—and *whom* he had seen. It just so happened that Yaz had been there to listen. The thought of blackmail had never entered Babes's mind.

What'd you have to go and do that for, Yaz?

Babes took a breath. He needed to get moving, but he wasn't ready to start walking. He put on his headphones and switched on his pocket radio.

Ryan's voice was in his ear.

"I think the Patriots go thirteen and three this season, and that's more than good enough to win the Eastern Division," said Ryan.

Babes switched stations. He hated when people talked about football when baseball was just reaching the most interesting part of the season, but more than that, he was not yet ready to hear Ryan's voice—at least not until he'd figured out what he was going to do.

"All news, all the time," said the next announcer.

Babes was about to turn the dial again when "the top story" caught his attention: "A homeless man was found dead in Pawtucket early this morning, the apparent victim of a brutal homicide."

Babes froze.

"The man, who has yet to be identified, is described as a white male, approximately thirty-five years old, with black hair that is longer on one side than the other. He was wearing an old army coat."

Yaz!

"The body was found beneath the I-95 bridge over the Blackstone River. Police say that the man was beaten to death with a baseball bat. A number of old baseball cards were also found in his coat pockets. Fingerprints taken from both the bat and the cards reportedly match those of Daniel Townsend of Pawtucket."

"What?" said Babes, his words coming aloud like a reflex.

"Townsend is the brother-in-law of former PawSox star Ryan James, whose wife died in a car crash three years ago, and who currently hosts a popular radio show in Boston. Town-

send, who goes by the name Babes—
has been on the run since phoning in to
James's radio show several days ago
and confessing that he killed his sister.
Anyone with information as to the
whereabouts of Daniel Townsend or the
identity of his alleged victim should no-
tify the police. And now for this traffic
update, we go to—"

Babes killed the radio. He wanted to
scream, but he maintained control and
began to process the news.

Yaz was dead. No doubt about it.
Babes was the prime suspect. It made
perfect sense that his prints were on the
baseball cards. He could explain that to
the police. But how did they end up on
the baseball bat? The radio station must
have gotten that wrong. Definitely. That
was it. Reporters mixed up their facts all
the time.

Babes closed his eyes, feeling only
pain. Surely the cops had intensified
their search after his on-air phone call to
Ryan's radio show. It was bad enough
that he'd killed Chelsea. If they had him
pegged for Yaz's murder as well, law en-

forcement was going to be everywhere. His photograph would be all over the newspapers, the television, the Internet. He could even end up as the featured fugitive on *America's Most Wanted.* There might even be a reward for his capture—dead or alive.

This is going to kill Mom.

He wanted to call her, but no way could he drag his mother into this. She'd try to talk him into turning himself in, and if he turned himself in, the police would throw him in jail, and if he went to jail, it was big naked men in the shower and cherry-red lips of Kool-Aid for Babes.

Don't touch me!

Babes pulled his hair, two tight fists on either side of this head, and he let out a noise that was somewhere between a groan and a scream. He had no idea what to do, but he had to act fast. The world, or at least the cops, needed to hear how he had met Yaz and how he'd had nothing to do with his murder. Yaz had taken his cell, but his mom had always made Babes carry a prepaid phone card in his wallet for emergencies, just in case he lost his cell or the battery died. All he had to do was find a pay phone.

It was time to call Ryan again.

CHAPTER 43

The studio door swung open. Ryan kept talking into the microphone—"looks like he's been scarfing down too many Fenway Franks lately"—as he read the expression on his producer's face.

"Line three," she said, mouthing the words more than speaking: "Babes."

"Oops, we lost Mike in Worcester," said Ryan, as he hit disconnect. Just switching lines made his pulse quicken. "Let's go to Babes in . . . where are you, Babes?"

"Stop it," he said. "You know I can't tell you."

Ryan did know. Emma had called to

fill him in before his show, and at every commercial break, Ryan had darted off to read the latest copy for the station's newscasters. The fingerprint match on the murder weapon was especially devastating news. Ryan wanted to be in Pawtucket with his in-laws, but Emma had talked him into staying on the air. Her hunch that Babes might call was playing out.

"Babes, let me go to a commercial so you and I can talk in private."

His producer was borderline apoplectic, arms waving and her head shaking in silent but emphatic disagreement.

"No!" Babes shouted. "I want everyone to hear this. Especially the police. I want to be on the radio!"

Ryan had never heard so much fear in Babes's voice. "All right," said Ryan. "We'll do it any way you like. Just calm down a little, and don't hang up on me."

"Calm down? How am I supposed to calm down? Somebody killed Yaz!"

"Who's Yaz?"

"He burned my baseball card!" said Babes—his never-ending obsession.

"Help me out a little. Was it Yaz who

the police found down by the river this morning?"

"Well, *duh.* Those were my baseball cards in his pockets. He took them."

"Did that make you mad?"

"He burned Carl Yastrzemski. Wouldn't that make *you* mad?"

Mad enough to kill him?

It was the next logical question, but Ryan didn't dare ask it on the air. He glanced through the glass at his producer, whose body language told him to take as much air time as he wanted.

"Let's start at the beginning," said Ryan. "How did you meet Yaz?"

"That's what I'm trying to tell you, okay? I'm trying to explain everything."

"Go right ahead. I'm listening."

"When I left the house, I went to my secret place. I haven't been there in a long time. Unfortunately, it turned out that Yaz was living there. He's homeless."

"Where is this place?"

"Stop it, Ryan! I said it was secret!"

"Sorry. I promise I won't do that again. So you met Yaz in your secret hiding spot."

"Right. We got to be—not really friends, but we got to talking. He wanted to know why I was hiding, so I told him about Chelsea."

Mere mention of Chelsea's name sent chills down Ryan's spine. "What did you tell him?"

"I told him about the crash."

"What about it?"

"Everything, Ryan. I told Yaz *everything*."

Ryan was at a crossroads again. A motive for murder just came to mind. "Did Yaz laugh? Did he make fun of you?"

"No, not at all."

"Did he not believe you?"

"He believed everything, of course. It was all true. That's the problem."

Ryan wasn't sure where to go with that remark. "I don't understand. Why was there a problem if he believed you?"

"It was Yaz's idea, not mine."

"What was Yaz's idea?"

Babes voice was cracking on the line, his words running together, as if he couldn't get them out fast enough. "It never occurred to me to blackmail anybody, but Yaz used my cell phone to make the call, and then he tied me up and went out to collect the money—ten thousand dollars—but he didn't come back, and then this guy came looking for me, a guy with a gun!"

"Whoa, slow down," said Ryan. "Who did Yaz try to blackmail?"

"The man I saw that night. The night Chelsea died."

A tightness gripped Ryan's chest. "Babes, I've talked to your parents. I know what happened that night."

"No, you don't!"

"Yes, I do. You said you were in the car. When you saw what happened to Chelsea, it scared you so much that you ran all the way home. You panicked. That's okay. Lots of people would panic. I understand why you think you killed Chelsea, but you didn't kill—"

"No, you don't understand! Mom and Dad don't understand either! Nobody understands anything!"

Ryan gripped the phone, fearing that Babes was about to hang up. "You're right. We can't understand until you explain it to us. So go ahead. What are we missing?"

"You're missing the part that I told Yaz."

"Do you want to tell it to me now?"

"Yes—*yes*! Just stop being the talk-show host. Shut up and listen to me! Nobody ever listens to me. Only Yaz did, and then he . . ."

Ryan could tell that Babes was either crying or on the verge of it. "Don't hang up, Babes. Tell me what you told Yaz."

Babes's sigh crackled on the line. "When I saw what happened to Chelsea, I knew she was hurt really bad, but I didn't know what to do. I just ran into the park and hid in the trees. I don't know how long I was there, but it's not like I told Mom. I didn't run straight home."

"What did you do?"

"I sat there, hiding. Because I didn't know *what* to do. The car was smashed into a big oak. There was a branch right through the windshield. Chelsea's door was hanging open. She was bleeding like crazy. Ainsley was screaming in the backseat. I couldn't—I just couldn't handle it."

"It's all right," said Ryan. "Tell me what happened next."

"Then this car pulled up."

Ryan froze. This was new. "What kind of car?"

"The same car that was coming at us on the road. The guy swerved right in front of us. That's when Chelsea lost control."

"You saw that car?"

"Yes. And he came back. He stopped on the side of the road. A man got out. He was kind of frantic as he ran to the car. Chelsea's door was flung open from the crash. He took one look at Chelsea and saw how bad she looked. He threw up right there."

Ryan didn't want to interrupt, but for some reason, Babes had paused. "Are you okay?" asked Ryan.

"Yeah," he said, his voice more distressed. "This is the really hard part. Chelsea—she wasn't dead, you know. She was still alive."

For Ryan, this had suddenly moved beyond painful. "I know. She was alive when the ambulance brought her to the hospital."

"See, that's the thing. If the ambulance had gotten there sooner, maybe it would have been different."

Ryan knew that was true. It was one of the big ifs that would torment him for the rest of his life. But he didn't want to lay it on Babes. "It's not your fault that—"

"Shut up, Ryan! Just listen! I was there, and I'm the only one who knows whose fault it was. It was dark out, but the guy's headlights were shining right on Chelsea, and I could see everything. She was still alive, I could tell. She was barely conscious, but she was digging in her purse for her phone. She had it in her hand when the drunk guy came up to her."

"She *what*?" said Ryan, almost unable to comprehend.

"Don't you get it? She was trying to call for help, but she couldn't dial the phone. Her face was so bloody she probably couldn't even see it."

Babes was definitely crying now. Ryan wasn't far behind him. "Stay with me," said Ryan. "Tell me what the man did?"

"He did exactly what I should have done in the first place. I didn't have my own cell phone three years ago. Mom thought I wasted too much time playing the games. But I should have taken Chelsea's phone and called nine-one-one."

"Are you saying that the man took her phone?"

"Yeah. He took it out of Chelsea's hand. That's what I should have done, Ryan. I should have taken her phone and dialed nine-one-one. If I hadn't run like a coward into the woods, if I'd just kept my composure and stayed to help Chelsea dial nine-one-one on her phone, she would have lived. Even the drunk guy who caused the accident had enough sense to do that. He didn't kill her. I did. He came back to help. I'm the idiot who freaked out and ran instead of helping her before it was too late."

Just listening to this story was taking Ryan's breath away. Could Chelsea have been saved if Babes had dialed nine-one-one? He could have allowed his mind to go there, but he felt only compassion for Babes. The anger was flowing in another direction.

Ryan said, "Did you get a good look at the man who took Chelsea's phone?"

"Yeah," he said quietly. "I did."

"Do you know his name?"

"I can't tell you his name."

"Babes, it would really be helpful—"

"I'm not telling you his name! I told it to Yaz. He made one phone call, and now look what's happened to him."

"That's not going to happen to you," said Ryan. "Just tell me the man's name, and come home where it's safe."

"I can't come home. The police will never believe me. They'll throw me in jail, and then they'll make me put Kool-Aid on my lips!"

Kool-Aid?

Babes was coming unglued, which concerned Ryan. "Don't get upset," said Ryan. "Trust me on this. You need to come home. You can't keep running."

"I didn't kill Yaz!"

"I know you didn't. And when you explain all this to the cops, I'm sure they'll understand too."

"There's a police car! I just saw one turn the corner. They're looking for me, I know they are. Did you send them?"

"No."

"You're tracing this call! Are you working with Emma Carlisle? How could you do that to me? I trusted you! I don't even have a new hiding place yet!"

"Babes, don't—"

Ryan stopped himself in midsentence. It was too late.

Babes was gone.

CHAPTER 44

Ryan practically flew out of the radio station to head for Pawtucket. Two minutes into his journey he pulled a U-turn toward Brookline to pick up Ainsley from school early. The route back to the expressway was a maze of road construction, and somehow they ended up on chic Newbury Street, which turned into a traffic jam straight out of *The Twilight Zone.* At one end, a naked young woman covered only with body paint was protesting against the fur shops. At the other end, picketers railed against the citywide trend of ice-cream trucks announcing their arrival not with the familiar jangle of bells but the blasting of calliope music from loudspeakers.

Is there anything they don't march against in Boston?

"Daddy, can I have an ice cream?"

"Not now, Ainsley."

"I'm gonna tell Grandma you showed me a naked red woman on the street."

Ryan hit the brakes, got out of the car, and bought two soft-serve cones with chocolate jimmies. The whole time, some creepy instrumental version of "Islands in the Stream" blared at nightclub levels from the ice-cream truck.

Maybe the protestors have a point.

Thirty minutes later they were speeding down I-95. Ryan put in a phone call to the station manager at *Action News.* The more he thought about Doug Wells's stunt on the radio yesterday, the angrier he got. He called to make a formal complaint, and the station manager seemed surprisingly sympathetic— Doug had missed an appointment that morning, and he wasn't answering her calls.

Probably too embarrassed to show his face.

Ryan hung up and retreated into thought. Ainsley was mesmerized by *Shrek 24* or some such movie on her portable DVD player. They were well into Rhode Island when Ryan's cell rang. It was Emma.

"Were you never going to call me?" she said.

"Sorry. I'm driving to Pawtucket. I'm still processing."

"That's what I'm here for. Can you talk?"

He checked the rearview mirror. Ainsley had her headphones on, still into her movie. Ryan put the phone aside and said, "Ainsley, which of the Wurster twins did you say you were going to marry—Timmy or Jimmy?"

No response. The Wurster boys drove her crazy. If that didn't elicit a squawk, she couldn't possibly hear what he was saying.

"Okay," he said into the phone. "I can talk."

"Good. I heard the call, if you're wondering."

"You were listening?"

"No, I was in court. But the police are

monitoring your show. I wasn't the only one who thought Babes might call in again. I listened to a tape."

"What do you think?"

"I think the police are going to put a tracer on your phone. If Babes is going to continue calling the radio station, they'll want to pin down the pay phone he's using."

"I don't think the station will have a problem with that. We all want to find Babes before he gets hurt. But that's not my point. What do you think about what he told me?"

"I want to know what you think," she said.

Normally, Ryan wouldn't have let anyone turn the conversation around that easily. But he wanted to tell Emma how he felt.

"For three years," he said, and his voice cracked. It embarrassed him, but he didn't know why.

"It's okay," she said. "Tell me."

"The paramedics told me that Chelsea was conscious when they arrived on the scene. The doctors never came right out and told me, but it was always the unspoken truth that they could have saved Chelsea if she had been brought to the hospital sooner. It wasn't the impact of the crash that killed her. Every minute counted, and she bled to death."

"I know," said Emma.

Ryan checked his speedometer. Too fast. He moved into the slower lane.

"After she died, I took all her belongings home from the hospital. There was no cell phone. She *always* had her cell with her, especially when she made that commute from Boston to Pawtucket. For three years, it has driven me absolutely crazy that she didn't have it with her that day. I even checked her billing records—that's one of the things that blindside you after your wife dies. The funeral's over, the friends and relatives have all moved on with their lives, and you're still getting phone records and credit card statements that help you reconstruct everything she did in those final days before she died."

"That's so hard, I'm sure."

"But that's not my point," said Ryan. "I

checked Chelsea's phone bill, and the last time she used her cell was around midday, hours before the crash. We always just assumed that she'd lost it sometime during the afternoon, because the phone never turned up. It was just one more stroke of bad luck that had led to Chelsea's death. If only she hadn't lost her cell phone, Chelsea could have dialed nine-one-one, the paramedics would have arrived in time, and she wouldn't have died on the operating table."

"But her phone wasn't lost," said Emma.

"Exactly," said Ryan. "Babes just blew the 'lost-cell theory' out the window. He saw it with his own eyes. Chelsea had it and was trying to dial nine-one-one. That drunk took the cell phone right out of her hand."

"So when Babes says the man dialed nine-one-one—"

"Babes completely misconstrued what he saw. Babes thought that the man was helping her. But the phone records show no call to nine-one-one from Chelsea's phone. It was a passing motorist who saw the wreck and finally dialed nine-one-one."

"Which means the guy took Chelsea's cell phone, and—"

"He did nothing," said Ryan. "He was standing there drunk, having just run another car off the road, looking down at a woman who was barely clinging to life . . . and he chose *not* to call nine-one-one."

"He realized he was looking at DUI charges, for sure. Possibly even serious jail time for vehicular homicide."

"So he took Chelsea's phone, and he left. He ran like a coward."

"He let her die," said Emma.

Ryan spotted the first exit sign for Pawtucket. They were coming up on the bridge over the Seekonk River, where Yaz's body was found.

"No," said Ryan. "He killed her. Because dead people and two-year-old girls in the backseat make lousy witnesses for the prosecution."

He checked the mirror again. Ainsley was into her movie, but she seemed to sense that her daddy was upset.

"Ryan?" said Emma.

He reeled in the anger. "Yeah?"

"It's a whole new ball game."

"You got that right."

CHAPTER 45

Ryan recognized the gaudy Hawaiian shirt the minute he walked in the back door. Seated at the Townsend's kitchen table was Babes's friend from MIT, Tom Bales.

"Wassup, dude?" said Tom.

Ainsley sprinted off to the bedroom in search of her grandma. Ryan went to the kitchen counter, looked at Tom, and said, "I was going to ask you the same thing."

Tom was eating the last few bites of a grilled cheese sandwich. "I just finished the morning shift."

"The morning shift of what?"

"Looking for Babes."

Ryan took a half step closer, letting Tom feel his presence. "I've been calling you since Monday afternoon. I even went to your apartment and talked to your pothead roommate. Where the hell have you been?"

Tom smiled. "Do you remember that brunette I spotted on the green when you and I were talking last week?"

"The girl with the Tommy Bahama backpack?"

"Yeah, isn't she cool? We really hit it off."

Ryan recalled what Tom's roommate had said about Virgin Tom. "Are you trying to tell me that for three days you've been with the Tommy Bahama girl?"

His grin got even cheesier. "Well, I hate to kiss and tell."

Ryan was deadpan. "I don't believe you."

The tone took Tom aback. "It's true," he said, as he pulled out his cell phone. "I got naked pictures and everything. Check this one out."

Ryan looked away, not in need of that much proof. The guy did have the unmistakable giddiness of a schoolboy with his first notch in his belt. "Okay, I believe you. Put the pictures away."

Tom seemed disappointed not to be able to share, but he tucked his cell away.

Rachel entered the kitchen with Ainsley riding piggyback. "Tom has been kind enough to help out while you're on the radio."

"Good," said Ryan, checking out Tom's shirt again. This one was various shades of blue, green, yellow, and orange, depicting pineapples, women in bikinis, and just about everything else Hawaiian. "Babes will certainly be able to see you coming."

Ainsley said, "Can I have one of those?"

Ryan hoped she meant the grilled cheese, not the shirt.

"Sure, I'll make you one," said Tom.

"Yay!"

That was fine with Ryan. He and Chelsea's mother went into the den to talk alone. She sat on the couch, and Ryan sat facing her on the ottoman.

"When's the last time you slept?" he said.

"Seems strange for *you* to be asking *me* that question."

She had a point, but it was impossible for Ryan not to be concerned. Each time he saw her, Rachel looked a little less like herself, a shell of a human being.

"Do you think Babes killed that man?" she asked.

"No. I really don't."

She didn't reply.

Ryan said, "Do you?"

Her gaze was cast in Ryan's direction, but she wasn't really looking at him. It was as if she were looking through him. "It's strange," she said in a vacant voice. "My first thought was no way. There was no way that my Babes could possibly have beaten a homeless man to death with a baseball bat. But then I started to think about it. All of us—you included, Ryan—have at one point or another witnessed a meltdown by Babes that frightened us."

"I've never seen Babes hurt anyone."

Her eyes finally met Ryan's. "I have. Once."

Ryan was almost afraid to ask. "Go on."

"It was that night, the night of your baseball game. Babes came out of his room wearing his PawSox hat and his baseball mitt, all ready for the big game. I told Babes he wasn't going, that you got tickets only for Chelsea and Ainsley. Well, let me tell you. He was out of control."

"What did he do?"

"I—I don't think he meant to hurt me."

"He hit you?"

She shook her head. "He pushed me out of the way. No, *pushed* is not the right word. He grabbed me and threw me against the wall. I was okay. But honestly, I thought he'd broken my arm. And it was at that moment when I finally realized: Babes is a man. For all his childlike limitations, he was strong enough to really hurt someone."

"Babes didn't kill that homeless man," said Ryan.

"I think you're right about that. But

I've been thinking about who really killed Chelsea. Babes took his share of responsibility on your radio show. But don't I have some responsibility too? When Chelsea came home that night, she was so stressed. Apparently, the entire faculty had a very upsetting meeting at the school that afternoon. Instead of putting her at ease, I practically ordered her to take Babes with her and Ainsley. Who knows what was going on inside that car when Chelsea crashed?"

Ryan pulled the ottoman closer to his mother-in-law and took her hands in his. Now was not the time to tell her that her daughter, effectively, had been murdered, but he couldn't let her go down this path of self-destruction.

"Don't *ever* blame yourself for what happened. A drunk driver killed Chelsea. Not Babes, and certainly not you."

Ryan didn't feel as though he'd uttered anything profound, but he could see the words register on Rachel's face. Her expression was complex, to be sure—a combination of "thank you" and "why hasn't *anyone* ever taken the time to take me by the hand, look into my eyes, and tell me this before?" She leaned forward and gave Ryan a hug that told him how much she appreciated it.

Finally, they separated.

Rachel wiped away tears. "What's going to happen to Babes?"

"I'm hoping that he'll keep hunting down pay phones and calling in to my show, and I'll talk him home."

"He has his phone card. I've been paranoid about making sure he carries one ever since Chelsea's accident. Just in case he lost his cell."

"That's a good thing."

"But how do we convince the police that he's not a killer?"

"The hardest thing to explain is the murder weapon. It's a baseball bat signed by Ivan. It has Babes's prints on it."

"His signed bat from Ivan is gone."

"You're sure?"

"Positive. He kept it on the shelf right above his bed. It's not there, and I've

turned the house upside down looking
for it."

Ryan reached for his cell phone.

"Who are you calling?" she said.

"Emma. I want her to get the police
out here."

"What for?"

"Somebody had to steal it and then
used it to kill the homeless guy. The police are better at detecting signs of
breaking and entering than we are."

Rachel gently took his hand, closing
Ryan's cell phone. "I wouldn't hold out
any hope for signs of breaking and entering."

"Why not?"

"Once, when Babe was in high
school, he ran away from home. He
came back at three AM, and the door
was locked. He panicked, put his fist
through the window, and sliced open his
arm. It took nearly thirty stitches to keep
him from bleeding to death. Ever since
then, we don't lock Babes out."

"So the doors have been unlocked
since Babes went on the run?"

"Yes. We don't have an alarm either.
We had one about five years ago—for

about two days. First time it went off, Babes totally lost it. I'm afraid we couldn't have made it easier for some-one to take Babes's bat, or anything else he wanted."

"Okay, let's go about this another way. Since the anniversary of Chelsea's death—when Emma got her first tip—who has been in the house? That you know of."

"Paul and I, of course. You and Ains-ley."

"Housekeeper, repairman?"

"No. No one. Just Tom."

"Tom," said Ryan. "How many times has he been here?"

"Twice. He was here the day of the an-niversary, when I asked him to go out and look for Babes. And then again to-day."

"That first time he was here—did he spend any time in Babes's room?"

"I don't know. I can't really remember. It's possible."

"Where did he go after he was here?"

"Back to Cambridge, I presume."

"With or without Babes's signed bat?"

"Oh, come now. You don't really think Tom would do anything to hurt Babes."

"He's been avoiding me for days. He says he's been with this new girlfriend, but surely he knew what was going on from the news. He could at least have returned my phone calls."

"I know he's been avoiding you. He's been avoiding Paul and me too."

"Doesn't that make you suspicious?"

"Not at all. Tom and Babes have a very special friendship. He's been avoiding all of us because, if Babes called him, he wanted to be able to say—truthfully—that he had not spoken to his parents or anyone else. That's the way Babes and Tom have always operated. He's the one Babes goes to when he can't go to family, so it's important for Tom to keep separate from the family."

"I suppose that makes sense."

"Of course it does. Don't let yourself think that way about Tom."

A flash of color went through Ryan's mind, as vivid as Tom's Hawaiian shirts. For an instant, it was as if he could see the feelings that Tom had once had for Chelsea—feelings Ryan had sometimes thought went beyond a mere boyhood crush.

"I don't know what to think," said Ryan.

CHAPTER 46

The Checker was alone in his hotel room.

A deadbolt and chain secured the door. The lights were out, the shades were drawn, and he was exhausted. But he couldn't shut off his mind and close his eyes. Normally he would sleep for a day after a contract killing, particularly after lunch in Providence's Little Italy. But even with a bellyful of traditional red-sauce fare from Angelo's Civita Farnese, he was restless.

Technically speaking, Doug Wells wasn't supposed to die.

The garrote was one of the Checker's

specialties. He couldn't say that he'd learned much from the Spaniards, but this favorite method of execution under the Francisco Franco regime was a gem. The Checker had used it many times with proven results. The beauty of the garrote was that it didn't have to be fatal. You could take a man to the brink of death, release the tension, and revive him. They *always* spilled their guts when they regained consciousness.

If they regained consciousness.

The Checker had pushed Doug Wells further than the boss's orders. Clients, however, didn't always know best. The Checker knew how to deal with nosy journalists. Threats never worked. You had to eliminate them. He could have cited any number of homegrown Russian examples: the Murmansk television reporter who had been critical of local politicians; two journalists from Togliatti who got too close to the local mafia; Paul Klebnikov, the American editor of *Forbes* magazine's Russian edition who knew too much about Russia's oligarchs. Even the head-in-the-sand Americans had heard about Anna Polit-

kovskaya, Russia's best-known journalist. Threats and an attempted poison-
ing hadn't stopped her from criticizing
the Chechen War. She was finally shot
in broad daylight, her body found in
the elevator of her apartment building
alongside the gun that was used to kill
her—standard practice for Moscow's
arrogant hit men.

Arrogance, however, wasn't behind
this execution. Doug Wells needed to
go. Period. Still, the client was the boss,
and the boss wasn't happy, as his client
made clear to him over the pirated
iPhone that the Checker had provided
him.

"You went too far," the text message
read.

The Checker didn't even try to justify
his decision to eliminate Wells. Someday the boss would thank the Checker
for overriding the order and doing what
had needed to be done. For now, at
least, no one would ever find the body—
he was professional enough to have
made sure of that.

"Shit happens," he replied.

"I don't pay the big dollars for shit re-sults."

"Job one went fine." Job one was the elimination of the blackmailer.

"I could have done that myself," was the reply. "His balls were obviously big-ger than his brain."

Typical. After the work was done, clients *always* thought they could have done it better themselves. The Checker didn't go there.

"Job two—so far, so good," he text-messaged.

Job two was to have eliminated the blackmailer in a way that made Babes look like the killer. Getting his (gloved) hands on Babes's baseball bat had been beyond easy, and then it was sim-ply a matter of leaving it at the crime scene after a home run swing on a hu-man head.

The reply came quickly: "Job three—more bumbling."

The Checker took that one personally.

Job three was to kill Babes in a way that looked like suicide—a troubled young man with some kind of disorder, overcome by the reality of his horrible acts. Everything had been falling right into place. The Checker was sure that he'd beaten the truth out of the black-mailer before delivering the death blow. Without question, he'd found the right family crypt, and Babes had definitely been hiding there. But the bundle of un-tied bindings that the Checker found in the corner told the rest of the story: Babes had freed himself and made a run for it. He was out on the streets somewhere, brave enough to have phoned into his brother-in-law's radio show that morning, quite possibly on the verge of naming names on the next live broadcast.

Skunked by a fucking retard.

"It will get done," he text-messaged back.

"Be sure it does," was the reply, and the call was over.

The Checker switched on the lamp, then lay back on his bed, thinking and staring at his reflection in the big mirror on the ceiling. It was *that* kind of hotel. He was wearing chinos but no shoes, and he liked the way his sleeveless un-dershirt showed off his considerable

muscles, even if he was alone. Two hundred push-ups, five hundred sit-ups—
every morning. It had nothing to do with
fitness. Over the years, plenty of whores
had run from his bed with a busted lip or
a black eye for not making enough of a
fuss over his body. One way or another,
the Checker always got what he paid
for.

So did his clients.

His real name was Vladimir Beria. He
was Georgian—not from the American
South, but the former Soviet state. It
wasn't true, but Vladimir liked to tell
people that he was a descendant of
Lavrenti Beria, the notorious head of the
KGB under much of Stalin's rule. Lavrenti eventually went the way of many
early members of the Soviet politburo:
tried for conspiracy and executed by fir-
ing squad on the same day. But it was
the beginning of Lavrenti's career, not
the abrupt end, that intrigued Vladimir.
Lavrenti got his start in the Georgian secret police, the Cheka.

Vladimir fancied himself a student of
Georgian history, and being in need of
a nickname in his chosen life of or-

ganized crime, he called himself The Cheka. As fate would have it, Vladimir was in Rhode Island when he coined his name, so even though everyone was right on board with the pronunciation—The Cheka—what they thought he was really trying to say was The Checker.

A rose is a roser. Or something like that.

Vladimir walked to the bathroom, splashed hot water on his broad face, and lathered up his whiskers. He never used creams or gels. Soap and a straight razor, nothing more, and he shaved while listening to his favorite *muziek.* Vladimir's taste in music was unusual, even if measured by the standards of a hotbed of counterculture like Providence. He was into traditional Georgian polyphonic songs, especially those of Svaneti. His very favorites were those sung in their original forms, which employ intervals and chords that simply do not occur in the diatonic scales of familiar Western music, such as the "neutral" third, which falls roughly between a minor and a major third. The technicalities of it were unimportant to Vladimir.

His business was all about the effect—
and there was nothing like an old Georgian work song and a straight razor to
get the desired effect. Vladimir would in-
sert his earbuds, get caught up in the
music, and then perform his magic with
the razor, or the garrote while singing
along at the top of his lungs, an a cap-
pella nightmare that must have sounded
like something out of a horror movie to
his contract hits.

Doug Wells had certainly looked
blown away.

The straight razor, not the garrote,
would be the implement of choice on
Babes—just as soon as Vladimir got his
hands on the little twerp. But he would
have to resist the urge to overdo the
slashing. The hit, after all, was supposed to pass for suicide—self-inflicted
wounds.

His BlackBerry chimed, signaling another text message. Vladimir wiped the
soap from his face and went to the
nightstand. The message was just a
phone number, different from the number that had been used to send the text
message. Whenever possible, people

took a few extra steps when communicating with the Checker, just in case anyone ever tried to follow the trail.

Vladimir dialed the number.

Syndicated crime in Russia was not a model of organization, but the type of criminal activities that various groups engaged in was often determined by the former soviet state of their origin. Georgians were among the most feared. They were the hit men, so effective that even the Mafia had taken to contracting out its hits to Georgians. The hit on Babes was the first and only job that the Checker had ever botched.

He already knew his client was unhappy.

What now?

The man on the other end of the line spoke in broken English. An intermediary—another layer of protection between the Checker and his real client.

"New plan," the man said.

Vladimir sat on the edge of the bed. "Talk to me."

"Forget it should look like suicide. Just take Babes out."

The reason for the intermediary was

now clear: A direct order for a hit that used the target's name. No way to couch it in the rubric of "job one" or "job two."

"Consider it done."

"And the big mouth, Ryan James. Enough talk on the radio. Boss man's afraid somebody gonna mention his name."

Vladimir smiled, tapping the flat side of his straight razor against his thigh. "I'll be sure he gets the message."

CHAPTER 47

Around eleven PM Ryan planted a good-night kiss on Ainsley's forehead. She was sound asleep in her grandparents' guest room, and he could smell the bubblegum-flavored toothpaste on her breath. Her toes were pressed up against the headboard, and her head was pointed in the general direction of the foot of the bed, which meant that she was deep in dreamland. It would be midnight by the time Ryan returned to Boston, and he didn't see any point in waking her just to strap her in a booster seat for the long car ride home.

"Tell Ainsley I'll be back in time to take her to lunch," he told Rachel.

His mother-in-law was standing on the covered front porch of their brownstone, her arms folded tightly in the chilly night air.

"Are you sure it's okay for her to miss school tomorrow?"

"Relax," said Ryan. "This is a legitimate family crisis. At Brookline Academy, they give kids an excused absence to catch the 'Last Call' sale at Neiman Marcus."

"Really?"

"No," he said, smiling.

Rachel swatted him playfully and offered a little smile in return. It was the first hint he'd seen of her sense of humor since Babes had disappeared.

"Drive carefully," she said, parting words that had special meaning in their family. Then she gave him a kiss on the cheek and went inside.

Ryan's car was parked on the street around the corner, about a block and a half away. He followed the stepping stones across the tiny front lawn to the tree-lined side street. A rush of wind stirred the leaves overhead. A few fluttered downward and fell in Ryan's path, but it was still a bit too early for Rhode Island's red maple trees to surrender to autumn.

Ryan dug into his pocket for his car keys, stopped, and glanced over his shoulder. He thought he'd heard footsteps behind him, but no one was in sight. Up ahead, the sidewalk darkened in the shadow of older, larger trees. Gnarly old roots had caused entire sections of the sidewalk to buckle over the years. Low-hanging limbs blocked the light of the streetlamps, forcing Ryan to locate his car more from memory than sight.

Again, he heard footsteps. He walked faster, and the clicking of heels behind him seemed to match his pace. He stepped off the sidewalk and down off the curb, as if he were going to cross the street. The sound of the footsteps behind him changed along with his own, from heels on concrete to heels on asphalt. He returned to the sidewalk and heard the clicking heels behind him do the same.

He definitely felt he was being followed.

Ryan stopped and turned. In the pitch darkness beneath the trees, he saw no one, but he sensed that someone was there.

"Rachel, is that you?" He was pretty sure it wasn't, but it seemed less paranoid than a nervous "Who's there?"

No one answered.

Ryan reached for his cell phone. Just as he flipped it open, a crushing blow between the shoulder blades sent him flailing, face-first, to the sidewalk. The phone went flying, and the air rushed from his lungs. As he struggled to breathe and rise to one knee, an even harder blow sent him down again. This time he was too disoriented to break the fall. His chin smashed against the concrete. The salty taste of his own blood filled his mouth.

"Why . . . are," he said, trying to speak, but it was impossible to form an entire sentence.

He was flat on his belly when the attacker grabbed him from behind, took a fistful of hair, and yanked his head back.

"One move and I slice you from ear to ear."

Ryan froze. A steel blade was at his throat. The man's voice sounded foreign, perhaps Russian. More important, the threat sounded real.

"Take it easy," said Ryan.

"Shut up," the man said. "And consider yourself warned."

"Warned—about what?"

"No more calls on the radio from your brother-in-law."

"I can't control that."

"*Take* control," he said, as he yanked Ryan's head back harder. "If he calls, you hang up. Stick to sports, or stay off the air. Understand?"

"You don't—" Ryan stopped in midsentence. The blade was pressing harder against his throat.

"Yes or no, big mouth? Do you understand?"

"Yes."

"Make sure you do," he said, then he slammed Ryan's forehead into the sidewalk.

Ryan fought to stay conscious, but he was barely hanging on. He saw nothing, heard nothing, as his world slowly turned darker than the night itself.

CHAPTER 48

Emma was dressed for bed, relaxing on her couch, and watching the *Late Show with David Letterman* when her doorbell rang. Her first reaction was that Letterman should do the top ten reasons not to answer your door after 11:30 PM.

It rang again. She pulled on her robe and looked through the peephole, both relieved and surprised to see Ryan.

"Can I come in?" he said as she opened the door.

Her hesitation wasn't intentional, but the nasty bruise on his forehead had taken her aback. "What happened to you?"

"Occupational hazard. Someone doesn't like my radio show."

Emma took him by the arm and led him to the couch. Ryan didn't so much as sit down as fall onto the overstuffed cushions. The way he looked gave her no time to worry about her own appearance—dressed in her favorite old robe, no makeup, her long brown hair up in a chip clip.

"How did this happen?"

He started to tell her, but she interrupted. "You're going to have a knot the size of a walnut," she said, gently touching his forehead. "Let me get some ice. But go on—what happened?"

Ryan told her as she dug around in the freezer. She returned with a quart-sized bag of ice in one hand and bag of frozen peas in the other.

"Personally, I like the peas," she said, "but if you're like most men with green vegetables, we can go with the ice."

Ryan almost laughed, but even the act of smiling seemed to hurt.

"Lie back," she said, as she helped him swing his legs up onto the couch. Ryan lowered his head onto the cushion, and Emma gently placed the cold bag of peas on his forehead.

"How long were you unconscious?"

"Maybe just a few minutes. Last thing I remember was some guy with a Russian accent telling me to stop talking to Babes on the radio."

"Did you call the police?"

"My cell went flying off somewhere in the attack, so I didn't have a phone. My first thought anyway was to check on Ainsley and her grandparents, so I sort of hobbled back to the brownstone. Rachel and Ainsley were fine. Paul was still out looking for Babes, but we got him on his cell, and he was fine too. This was directed only toward me, as a radio host, not at the family."

She lifted the bag of frozen peas to check his knot. "Oh, that looks wicked painful."

Wicked—another Roe-Dyelin thing. Winters were wicked cold, oysters were wicked fresh. Ryan hoped never to meet anyone who was wicked wicked.

"Folks at the studio are going to think I got drunk and fell down," he said.

"Tell them Rhett Butler slugged you."

"What?"

"That's a Carlisle family joke. My grandmother was the only southerner in the family—from Atlanta. She got drunk one New Year's Eve, started parading around the house like Scarlett O'Hara, and then fell down and broke her nose. From then on, we called her 'Gone with the Gin.' "

Ryan laughed, then groaned. It was his ribs this time. "Please, don't make me laugh," he said.

"You think you should see a doctor?"

"I thought I should see you first."

"Me? Sorry to disappoint you, but I have more in common with Clarence Darrow than Florence Nightingale."

"No, I was hoping that you might have some advice on how to handle this thug. Prosecutors must get threats often enough. What should I do?"

She nudged the bag of frozen peas back into place. "You should go on the radio and tell the world about the threat."

"He specifically told me to stick to sports on my show."

"You asked for my advice. As a prosecutor, I've butted heads with some scary characters. The best way to handle a threat against your own safety is to go public with it immediately."

"You really think that advice applies here?"

"Absolutely. The more public you are about the threat, the harder it is for your attacker to carry it out."

"Okay," said Ryan. "So at six AM, I open *Jocks in the Morning* with the story of what happened to me tonight."

"Exactly. Spare no detail. If you want, I can be there in the studio with you."

"That's probably a good idea. The first problem is figuring out how to get back to Boston. With this blow to the head, I'm not sure I should drive. I cabbed it over here from Pawtucket."

"You think you should go to the ER?"

"If I'm feeling worse in the morning, I'll see a doctor. Honestly, I don't like going to hospital emergency rooms."

"Of course you don't," she said. Especially the one in Pawtucket. *God, you're an idiot sometimes, Emma.*

Ryan sat up, seeming to sense that she was silently chiding herself over the

ER comment. "I guess I should get going," he said.

He handed her the bag of peas, and
as the frozen vegetables changed
hands, Emma saw past the bruising on
Ryan's face and found something else
entirely. There was a hint of the same
expression she'd noticed for the first
time at the Marble House fund-raiser,
and that she'd seen again yesterday
when Ryan had glanced at Emma
through the glass wall in the studio. It
was a look that had nothing to do with a
need for sympathy or justice. Emma
didn't know where this was headed, but
it suddenly occurred to her that she'd
been way too nice for too long to guys
like Doug Wells.

"I wouldn't be much of a friend if I sent
you out on the road in this condition,"
she said.

"I can cab it back to Pawtucket."

"But we haven't even started on the
frozen corn."

He chuckled again, right through the
pain.

"I'll get a pillow and blanket," she
said.

She went to the linen closet, grabbed the bedding, and quickly made up the couch. Ryan was standing off to the side when she finished. Their eyes met—and held.

"What?" she said.

"Thanks," he said.

"No problem."

"Not just for tonight. I mean for everything. All three years. Thank you."

She started to answer but she stopped herself. Her usual response— "It's all part of my job"—just didn't fit in Ryan's case. Not even close.

"Get some rest," she said. "Alarm goes off at four-thirty."

"Funny," he said, as his head hit the pillow.

"What?"

"I think I might actually be able to fall asleep tonight."

She smiled and turned out the light. "Good night, Ryan."

"Good night, Emma."

CHAPTER 49

At six AM Ryan was at the microphone. Emma was in the studio with him, Ryan's cohost having surrendered his chair to her for the first segment of *Jocks in the Morning.* The producer gave the signal, and Ryan began the show with his own twist on the lines Emma had scripted.

"Any Bruins fans out there?" said Ryan.

Emma shot him a curious look, but Ryan put her at ease with a smile that said he would get around to the script—eventually.

"As a boy from Texas," he told his listeners, "I didn't dream about growing up to be a hockey player. Baseball was in my blood. My granddaddy played catcher for the Alpine Cowboys in the heyday of semipro ball, back when just about any town in Texas with more than two gas stations had a team. If you called my daddy right now, he'd tell you how his old man took him out to the barn when he was a boy, stuffed his catcher's mitt with pecan shells, and threw fastballs until his little hand was tough enough to catch Nolan Ryan with the wind at his back.

"But living in New England, you learn to love hockey as much as baseball. Any old-timers out there remember a Boston Bruin tough guy named Eddie Shore? In a game long ago, Shore didn't like the way a Toronto player stood him up at the blue line, so he got even with a vicious hit from behind to a player named Ace Bailey. Bailey slammed headfirst to the ice and fractured his skull. Folks said it sounded like a watermelon splattering on pavement. The benefit game played in Bailey's honor the following season evolved into today's NHL All-Star Game, and Ace went on to the Hall of Fame. But he would never play hockey again. That cheap shot from Shore ended a spectacular career.

"I woke up feeling a little bit like Ace Bailey this morning, and I have a purple knot on my forehead to prove it. In just a few minutes, Jock and I will take your calls about the worst cheap shots in sports history. But right now, let me tell you about the one I took last night."

Ryan's producer was suddenly signaling him with two raised fingers. Several phone lines were lit up, but the expression on her face and the timing of the interruption made caller number two's identity clear.

"Looks like my story will have to wait. Got a call I need to take," he said, as he hit the button. "Babes, is that you?"

"Yes," he said. "Tell the police not to bother tracing this call. I'm at a pay phone, but I'll be long gone by the time they get here."

It seemed like paranoia, but when Ryan glanced at Emma, she seemed to confirm that the trace was already under way.

"Don't worry about that," Ryan said into his microphone. "But—"

"You have to help me," said Babes, his voice strained. "I'm hungry, I'm tired, and I don't know where to hide anymore."

"I can help you," said Ryan.

"I just want you to tell the police to stop looking for me."

"I can't do that, Babes."

"I didn't kill Yaz!"

"We know. That's why you should come home," said Ryan.

"I can't. He's going to kill me."

"Who is going to kill you?"

Babes's voice was racing, the words coming too fast. "Him. The guy. That man who killed Yaz. Why else would he come looking for me at the—" he stopped himself.

"At the what?" said Ryan.

"I can't tell you my hiding space. I might have to go back there."

Part of Ryan wanted to pursue the location of the hiding spot, but something else was more pressing. "Babes, do you have any idea who the man is who came looking for you?"

"No."

"Did he sound Russian?"

"I never heard his voice."

"Is it the same guy you saw at the crash?"

"No. Totally different guy."

"If you saw that man again—the drunk driver who took Chelsea's cell phone out of her hand—could you identify him?"

"Yes. I told you all this last time. That's what got Yaz into so much trouble with the blackmail. I know exactly what the guy looks like. I know his name."

"Can you tell it to me?"

"No! Do you want me to end up like Yaz?"

Perhaps Ryan was pushing too hard for information from Babes, putting pressure on him to reveal information that he was not ready to divulge. But Ryan couldn't help it.

"I need you to tell me his name, Babes."

"I can't! He'll kill me!"

"Not if you say his name on the radio

he won't. Once the cat's out of the bag, there's no point in killing you."

"Are you sure?"

Ryan glanced at Emma, but he already knew what she was thinking. "You have to go public. He killed Yaz to keep his name a secret. So let out the secret, and then there's nothing he can do."

"Okay," said Babes. "You should . . ."

"Should what?" said Ryan.

"You should . . . look for . . ."

"Look for who?" said Ryan.

Babes took a moment, as if the wheels were turning in his head.

"Go ahead," said Ryan.

"Look for . . . a nicer nose ring," said Babes.

He hung up, and there was silence on the air.

Ryan was sure that his listeners had interpreted Babes's remark—"a nicer nose ring"—as the equivalent of "Go fly a kite." But Ryan knew better.

"We'll break for a commercial now," said Ryan. "Jock will be here to take your calls when our show returns. I'll see you knuckleheads tomorrow morning."

He switched off the microphone and looked at Emma.

"We have some work to do," he said.

"We?"

"Yeah," said Ryan. "How good are you at anagrams?"

CHAPTER 50

Brandon Lomax's hand was shaking on the steering wheel. He needed a drink, but he refused to feed that beast. He had to keep a clear head—and not solely because he was cruising up the interstate toward Boston.

Babes was going to name him—he could feel it.

His campaign manager had called at 6:30 AM to tell him about *Jocks in the Morning*. By the grace of God, Babes had chickened out and told Ryan to go pick his nose, or something like that, when Ryan pushed for the name of the drunk driver. But it was only a matter of time until Babes would find his nerve and blurt out the name.

And then it would be over for Brandon Lomax.

His cell rang. It was on his truly private line, a call from his wife, Sarah.

"I thought you were going to a staff meeting," she said.

"I . . . uh."

"The truth, Brandon. You rushed out claiming to have some early meeting that you'd completely forgotten about. Twenty minutes later your campaign manager calls the house and wants to know where you are. What's going on?"

Caught. More lies would have been pointless. "I need to talk to Ryan James. Man-to-man."

Sarah didn't argue, but the reservations were palpable in her voice. "Are you sure you want to do that?"

"I'm not going to talk to him about the anonymous tips. I have the inside story there already. But this blackmail stuff is preposterous. Babes has to be making that up."

"Do you think . . ."

"Do I think what?"

"Could the blackmailer have called someone in your campaign? Someone who spoke on your behalf—without you knowing about it, I mean."

Lomax checked the exit signs on the interstate. He was getting close. "Do you mean Josef?"

"It's just a theory. He has an awful lot invested in your winning. Then along comes Babes and his anonymous tips, and all could be lost."

"All is *not* lost," he said, his tone harsher than intended. "That's why I need to speak to Ryan James and get this straight."

"But Ryan must know all about the tips that say you were the drunk driver. If Babes hasn't told him, Emma probably has. What are you going to do if he confronts you with that?"

"I can handle it, Sarah."

"I'm not sure you can, sweetheart. Not when your answer is that you were in a state of drunken blackout and don't remember anything about the night of the crash. I'm your wife, and I'm not even sure I . . ."

He waited for her to finish, and if he

hadn't been speeding down the interstate at that very moment, he would
have closed his eyes to absorb the
blow. "Not even sure you believe me—is
that what you were going to say?"

"It's not that I think you're lying.
Maybe you're suppressing something—
subconsciously, I mean—for reasons
that have nothing to do with alcohol. I
don't know. I just don't know."

He sensed her struggle, but he wasn't
about to change his mind. "It will all
work out. I'll call you when I leave Boston. Love you," he added, and then he
said good-bye and hung up.

Lomax checked his GPS monitor. He
was nearing the point where the north-
bound interstate and several other major thoroughfares ran parallel to an
equally wide swath of railroad tracks,
seeming to create one big congested
artery that fed into endless road construction. The mechanized voice from
his dashboard was directing him west,
toward Ryan James's house in the
South End. To the east was South Boston, which some might say had about as
much in common with the South End as

South Africa had with South America, other than the word *south.* Lomax switched off the GPS and took Exit 20 into South Boston. He had a specific bar in mind, but he wasn't in search of a drink.

He wanted his memory back.

South Boston—Southie to its residents—had a long Irish Catholic history, and even with recent arrivals of Albanians, Lithuanians, and other ethnic groups, it would hardly be unusual to see a hand-painted mural on a building that read WELCOME TO SOUTH BOSTON in English and FÁILTE GO MBOSTON DHEAS in Irish. The east side, closer to downtown, had seen some gentrification, but the west side remained a hardscrabble neighborhood. Some of America's oldest public housing was in South Boston, including three of the six most dangerous in the entire city. One was on West Broadway—not too far from a bar called The 6 House.

Lomax stopped his car across the street and gazed out the driver's side window. Last year's Christmas lights were still hanging from the front canopy, but they were unlit. The 6 House was closed.

It was here that Lomax's trouble had begun—three years earlier, on the night of Chelsea James's accident. Back in the day, The 6 House was known as the Triple O's, a hangout for James "Whitey" Bulger, a Southie native, the older brother of the Massachusetts State Senate president, and a notorious organized-crime boss who fled with his favorite mistress and about forty million dollars on the eve of his indictment for racketeering. Even after the Bulger era, the Irish American mob kept a tight grip on local bookies and gambling. Once upon a time, Brandon Lomax had felt that grip—almost literally—around his throat. At a table behind those darkened windows, he'd pleaded for more time to pay. His debt collectors were a couple of muscle-bound thugs with Southie accents straight out of *The Departed,* and even though the old Triple O's bar was gone, Lomax had been well aware of the fact that he was in the same building where Bulger's heavy-handed debt collector, Stephen "the Rifleman" Flemmi, used to deal with deadbeats who couldn't pay. Lomax had arrived wearing a hat and sunglasses, praying to God that no one would recognize the Rhode Island attorney general. Those smart asses had been so smug.

Goon number one: Tell your daughter to suck my dick and we'll call it even.

Goon number two: Say what? Lick-'em-and-leave-'em Jenny doesn't do you for free?

The bastards had laughed in his face, given him another "twenty-four hours," and walked out, leaving him alone at the table to figure out how he was going to come up with the cash. Lomax ordered a scotch. Another one. Several more. A bottle. That was the last he remembered.

Seeing the bar again this morning didn't jog anything loose from his selective memory. He still had no idea how he and his car got from South Boston to Providence on the night of Chelsea's accident.

He cranked the engine and headed west over the Broadway Bridge, literally to the other side of tracks, beyond Interstate 93 toward the South End. He drove past the *Boston Herald* building, and he could only imagine what they would print about another Rhode Island politician headed for the slammer. The era of former Providence mayor Buddy Cianci, his tomato sauce, bad toupees, and RICO conviction had long passed. They needed fresh meat.

I'm screwed, he thought, as he sat at the traffic light.

His blackout aside, logic, if not the lost DNA evidence, pointed to Brandon Lomax as the drunk driver. Why else would Babes have waited three years to contact Emma? Only recently was Brandon Lomax's face all over the television screens as a front-running candidate for the U.S. Senate. Seeing Lomax over and over again must have finally prompted Babes to tell Emma "I know who did it." On the other hand, according to Lomax's sources, the subsequent e-mail message—complete with details about the vomit, yet lacking any of the pedantic verbiage that was typical of Babes's writings—could not possibly have come from Babes.

All of which left the proverbial sixty-four-thousand dollar question: If Babes wasn't pointing the finger explicitly at Lomax, who was?

Lomax parked on the street and headed up the sidewalk. Braddock Park was a typical leafy residential square in the South End, where even a resident might walk into the wrong redbrick, nineteenth-century row house if he didn't check the address. The uniformity of the bowfront architecture gave the neighborhood its character and integrity. Added personality could be found in the ornamental details of doors, windows, and wrought-iron balustrades and railings. Small gardens and balconies lent more charm. Lomax was oblivious to it all as he climbed the steep stoop to the second-floor entrance of the James residence.

He rang the doorbell and waited. No one answered. Ryan had announced on the air that he was finished for the day, and when Lomax called the radio station, the receptionist confirmed that Mr. James had left early.

Lomax was about to ring the bell

again when he heard footsteps inside. The lock clacked, and the door opened. An attractive Latina with sweat on her brow and a warm but tired expression on her face was looking back at him. Lomax assumed she was the house-keeper.

"Can I help you?" she said.

"I'm looking for Ryan James."

She suddenly appeared nervous. Lomax assumed that she recognized him from his campaign commercials or the news.

"Mr. James is not here."

Lomax was about to ask the next logical question, but a brain hiccup put him on an entirely different track. He suddenly realized that the woman wasn't nervous because she recognized him. She was afraid that he would recognize *her.*

"You work for Connie Garrisen," said Lomax.

"*Sí.*"

"You were there," he said.

"Excuse me?"

"Yes. You were with Connie Garrisen three years ago."

She smiled awkwardly. "Three years is a long time, *señor.*"

"You were definitely there," he said, the memory flooding back to him. "And Connie came to get me."

"*No sé,*" she said, her English suddenly escaping her. But Lomax knew it was only out of loyalty to her boss.

"Thank you," he said, and he sincerely meant it. Then he turned and headed down the stoop.

"*Señor,* you want me to tell Mr. James you were here?"

"No," said Lomax. "There's someone else I need to see."

CHAPTER 51

"I feel like smashing Connie's face in," said Ivan.

Ryan was dressed in street clothes and seated on a padded bench press watching Ivan peel off sit-ups on the floor mat. The before-work exercise crowd had already showered and left the gym for downtown office buildings. Ryan and Ivan practically had the place to themselves, save for a handful of new mothers who would spend the next four hours on the treadmill working off the latest pregnancy. He'd told Ivan everything, ending with the discovery that "a nicer nose ring" was an anagram for "Connie Garrisen."

Ivan stopped in the up position and toweled off his sweaty face. "Really," said Ivan. "I could hurt him. Bad."

"Don't go there," said Ryan.

"What are you going to do?"

"Emma Carlisle is still the prosecutor overseeing the investigation."

"So?"

"She's working out a strategy as we speak."

"So?"

"I promised Emma I wouldn't take matters into my own hands."

"So?"

"Stop looking at me like that. And why do you keep saying 'so'?"

Ivan rose and went to the rack of free weights. "Blame it on my Dominican blood," he said, as he grasped the fifty-pound dumbbell. "But I don't care what you promised Emma. I'm asking the question you need to ask yourself, dude."

"Which is what?"

Ivan pumped the weight up over his head, speaking to Ryan's reflection in the mirrored wall. "What'd you promise Chelsea?"

Brandon Lomax drove himself to Louisburg Square—to Connie and Glenda Garrisen's house on the Hill.

The Beacon Hill neighborhood was Boston of another age. Traffic thinned out, streets narrowed, and even though downtown was just a short walk away, city noises faded. Aside from the vehicles parked along the street, the feel was of a nineteenth-century village of redbrick houses and cobblestone squares, hidden gardens, and graceful bay windows. Flower boxes brimmed with color. A canopy of elms shaded the sidewalks on sunny days, and gas lamps lit the way by night. The tidy rows of Federal houses were by no means ostentatious displays of wealth—their original Brahmin owners were known for their self-restraint, even if they did hire Bulfinch to design them—but no other Boston neighborhood had quite the heritage and pedigree of Beacon Hill. Henry James (no relation to Ryan) clearly went too far in calling it "the only respectable street in America," but it was impossible to stroll down Mount Vernon Street and not imagine yourself passing Oliver Wendell Holmes or Louisa May Alcott, or perhaps even tripping over Edgar Allan Poe after he'd been thrown out of a party for drunkenness. It was a virtual time warp for any visitor.

For Brandon Lomax, it was also a chance to roll back the clock, even if it was just three years.

"I need answers," said Lomax.

From his car, Lomax had phoned Garrisen at the hospital and told him that they needed to meet in absolute privacy. Lomax didn't trust the hospital walls. The Garrisens lived about a quarter mile from Massachusetts General— Connie Garrisen was hardly the first chief of staff to reside on Beacon Hill— and Glenda Garrisen was at work in Providence. The two men were alone in the walnut-paneled study, where in days gone by they had killed off countless bottles of expensive scotch.

"What's with the hostile tone?" said Garrisen.

"It has finally come back to me. Three

years ago. The night of Chelsea James's accident."

Garrisen showed little expression, but the silence was telling enough.

Lomax continued. "It started with the worst meeting of my life. I was in a bar in South Boston, and I don't know how I even made it to my car, I was so wasted. I needed to get home, but I was afraid to call a cab. I was sure that somehow it was going to hit the newspapers that the Rhode Island attorney general stumbled dead drunk out of a Southie bar that was once the hangout of Whitey Bulger. So I called you. I knew you'd be heading to Pawtucket for the last PawSox game of the season. I asked you to come and get me and drive me to Providence. I waited in my car on West Broadway, trying to stay awake. You finally showed up with your housekeeper—what's her name?"

"Are you referring to Claricia?"

"Yes, Claricia. She was at Ryan James's house this morning. And when I saw her, it was like a light going on. I remembered how you and Claricia pulled me out from behind the steering

wheel and laid me in the backseat. But I
also recalled that during the whole time,
you two were arguing with each other.
You told her to drive your car back to
Beacon Hill, and you were going to drive
me to Providence. She was furious with
you. Do you remember what she said?"

Garrisen did not respond.

"She said: 'Sir, you have too much
drink in you to drive.' At the time, I
thought she was talking about me. But
now I think she meant you. *You* had
been drinking too. But you drove me
back to Providence anyway. The next
morning, I woke up in my own bed at
home. My car was in the driveway. You
must have driven me home in my car,
left it at my house, and then taken a taxi
back to Boston. But something terrible
must have happened while you were
driving to Providence."

Garrisen's eyes narrowed. "Are you
accusing me of killing Chelsea James?"

Lomax drew on every bit of his prosecutorial experience and kicked into his
cross-examination mode.

"When did you first hear about the
anonymous tip to Emma Carlisle?"

"When the media reported it. Same as everyone else."

Lomax chuckled with skepticism. "I don't think so. The press release was very general."

"So was my knowledge."

"Hardly. You're married to the chief of the Criminal Division, so I'm guessing that you were one of a privileged few who knew that the tip came in the form of an old newspaper clipping. You knew about the underlined words and the number code that the tipster used to construct his message. And when you learned what it said—'I know who did it'—you panicked."

"Why would I panic?"

"Because you were afraid that the anonymous tipster was about to identify *you* as the driver who ran Chelsea James off the road."

"Have you been drinking again, Brandon?"

"No," he said. "I'm thinking very clearly now. It was you who adopted the tipster's style and sent Emma my photograph with the second coded message: 'It's him.' "

"That's ridiculous."

"You sent the anonymous e-mail message identifying me as the drunk who vomited at the scene. You knew all those details, because it was actually you who threw up, not me."

"Enough, Brandon."

"You knew that you'd have to submit a DNA sample for comparison once the real tipster identified you as the drunk driver. That's why the three-year-old DNA sample disappeared. Did Glenda help you with that?"

"Don't drag my wife into this."

"You're right. That was unfair. DNA evidence is maintained by the Department of Health. You're chief of staff at Mass General. Maybe you had your own way of making it disappear."

Garrisen's face was turning red, but he took a deep breath to calm himself. "Even if I were the drunk driver, there was never any reason for me to implicate one of my friends to hide my own guilt."

"I was an easy target, though, wasn't I? The press would be eager to nail a guy like me, someone with an even bigger public profile than yours. And even better for you, I had no alibi for the night of the crash, because you knew I was passed out in the backseat of the car while you were driving."

"A friend doesn't do that to another friend."

"Spare me the friendship angle," said Lomax. "I'm not buying it. Nobody wants to go to jail for vehicular homicide—especially not the chief of staff at the most storied hospital in the world, who has aspirations of being the next U.S. surgeon general. Desperate men do desperate things."

The two men locked eyes, but it was Garrisen who spoke first.

"For the sake of argument, let's say it's true: I pointed the finger at my friend Brandon Lomax, the former attorney general, before Chelsea's brother could point the finger at me, who happens to be married to Glenda Garrisen, the current chief of the Criminal Division. Wouldn't that be the perfect way to discredit the anonymous tipster?"

"What are you talking about?"

Garrisen smiled wryly, obviously trying

to take some of the edge off of Lomax's anger. "Anyone who looked at your theory objectively would say it was never Connie Garrisen's intent to peg Brandon Lomax as the driver."

"Your tips named *me.*"

"Only to paint the real tipster as a liar with a vendetta against the attorney general's office. Maybe the angry relative of a convicted defendant. Or perhaps someone like Babes who thought the prosecutors had let down the victim's family. In any event, *someone* who acted on a grudge by leveling false accusations first against the former attorney general and then against Glenda Garrisen's husband. Anyone with such an obvious ax to grind and such a propensity for changing his story would have absolutely zero credibility. No one would ever believe that *either* Brandon Lomax or Connie Garrisen was involved."

Lomax watched him closely, and then his gaze slowly swept the room. The Garrisens' old study held plenty of memories, the most recent of which was a meeting Garrisen had arranged between his old friend and some of the wealthiest out-of-state contributors to the Lomax Senate campaign.

"You're expecting an awful lot from a friend," said Lomax. "Chelsea James's family has suffered, and you're asking me to cover up a crime."

Garrisen flashed a thin smile. "I'm not just doing this for me."

"Meaning what?"

He leaned closer, as if to underscore the importance of his words. "You can count on the fact that no one will ever know how you staggered out of that Southie bar. And all that mumbling in the backseat about being up to your eyeballs in gambling debts to the Irish Mafia? Well, that secret is safe with me too."

The threat was hardly subtle.

Garrisen settled into his high-back leather desk chair, rocking steadily, his confidence growing. "I'd offer a toast, but I know you don't drink anymore."

Part of him wanted to accept the offer just so he could throw the scotch in

Garrisen's face. It was the same feeling that had swelled up inside him three years ago, when those thugs insulted Lomax's daughter and told him to cough up the money in twenty-four hours. Back then, however, he didn't get to throw anything in anyone's face. He simply drove back to South Boston the next day and handed over the deed to his sailboat—his pride and joy—to cover the gambling debt.

This time, it was Garrisen who was trying to force reality upon him.

"One thing I don't understand," said Lomax. "To drive to my house from Boston, you wouldn't get off the interstate until the second Providence exit. But the accident happened in Pawtucket."

"I exited early. I needed to talk to Chelsea."

"Before the game?"

Garrisen's expression turned very serious. "Before the bitch destroyed me."

The answer surprised Lomax, and that kind of candor told him that Garrisen's confidence was at an all-time high, his grip on Lomax even more secure than Lomax himself realized.

"Why would Chelsea have wanted to hurt you?"

Garrisen leaned forward, as if he were about to reveal the world's best-kept secret. And then he told him.

CHAPTER 52

Ryan was feeling small.

The Brookline Academy kindergarteners were in "movement" hour, a fancy pants term for some combination of physical education, dance, and recess. Ryan was alone with Sloan Walsh in the classroom, seated in desk chairs that were designed for five-year-olds and Lilliputians. Finger-painted self-portraits adorned one wall. A collage of autumn-colored leaves covered another. Hand-made stars and planets dangled from the ceiling, and at the center of it all was the sun, reminding Ryan of the good advice his daughter had (in her own innocent way) imparted: the answer is closer than you think.

"I'm guessing you didn't come here to chat about Ainsley," said Sloan.

Ryan shook his head. He had always liked Sloan, and her handling of a school crisis last year, when she was Ainsley's teacher, had cemented his respect for her. Brookline Academy had a preschool tradition of 'My Special Day,' when each student had his or her own day to dress up in a costume, and parents could also come into the classroom to tell a story or play a game with the kids. By year's end it had evolved into a can-you-top-this phenomenon in which parents converted the classroom into shrines to their children. After one mother showed up with live swans, potted palm trees, and a professional event coordinator reminiscent of Martin Short in *Father of the Bride,* Ainsley came home and gave her daddy her piggy bank so that he would have more money, "just like the other parents." Ryan would have pulled her from the school if Sloan hadn't been the one faculty member to step up and help the headmaster reestablish the preschool environment that Chelsea had wanted for Ainsley. With that kind of backbone, it was easy for Ryan to understand how Chelsea had been so fond of her.

Supreme loyalty to her best friend was another of Sloan's virtues.

"It's about Connie Garrisen," said Ryan. "It's been hard for me to put my finger on it, but you and I have talked many times about the day Chelsea died. Lately, I've had this growing sense that there is something you haven't told me."

Sloan crossed her legs and folded her arms. It didn't take a degree in psychology to see the defensiveness in her posture. "About Dr. Garrisen?"

"Yeah," said Ryan. "Specifically, about the meeting he had with Chelsea before she died. I was talking with Rachel yesterday, and she mentioned that meeting again—how upset Chelsea was when she came home." Ryan glanced toward the Styrofoam sun hanging from the ceiling like a disco ball. He was so close to the truth he could feel it. "You were Chelsea's best friend. And I . . ."

Ryan was suddenly having difficulty.

"It's okay," said Sloan. She broke out of her defensive posture, leaned forward, and touched him on the forearm. But Ryan noticed that her hand was shaking.

"We're friends," she said. "Go on."

Ryan looked her in the eye. "I think you know what I'm saying. Something happened that night before Chelsea left Brookline Academy. I *need* to know what."

"It's no secret. That was the afternoon Dr. Garrisen met with the entire faculty and announced that tuition remission was being eliminated. No more free ride for children of faculty members. People weren't happy."

Ryan's gaze intensified, and he could even hear it in Sloan's voice now—she was holding something back. "I mean after the meeting," said Ryan. "I think something happened *after* that meeting."

She returned his gaze, but Ryan could see her coming around. It was almost as if she wanted to tell him—had wanted to tell him for a long time—but he had never pushed hard enough before.

"Chelsea was really upset about losing free tuition. Ainsley was only a year away from enrolling in the three-year-olds program, and Chelsea planned to teach at least until she got her law degree and passed the bar exam. That was three, maybe four years of private education for Ainsley, tax free. That's almost a six-figure benefit. Without remission, there was no way Ainsley could go to school here."

"Did she say that at the meeting?"

"Nobody but Dr. Garrisen spoke at the meeting. It was an announcement, not a discussion. Chelsea and I talked afterward. She told me that she was going to go to Dr. Garrisen and make a plea of hardship."

"So did she meet with him? That afternoon, I mean?"

Sloan swallowed hard. "I told her that it wasn't a good idea."

"Why?"

"I just knew that Dr. Garrisen would misconstrue her message."

"I don't follow," said Ryan.

Sloan averted her eyes, clearly struggling. "Chelsea seemed too desperate, as if she was willing to do anything to get Ainsley into the school."

"What do you mean, 'anything'?"

"I mean that Dr. Garrisen might see . . . an opportunity."

"You thought he would come on to her?"

"You can just tell about certain men."

Ryan felt his anger rising. "So did he hit on Chelsea?"

Sloan shifted uncomfortably in her chair. "No."

"Are you sure?"

"Yes. He never got the chance."

"What do you mean?"

Sloan breathed in and out. "Chelsea went back to the administrative offices to see him. He doesn't have an office there—he's a trustee, not an administrator—but whenever he's on campus, he makes a point of checking out the administrative side of things. It was after hours, and it was like a ghost town back there, but Chelsea knew he was there somewhere. She tried the headmaster's office, the assistant headmaster. No one was there. Then she tried the visiting professor's office."

"And?"

"The door was closed. Chelsea was about to knock when it suddenly opened. A student wearing one of our high school uniforms walked out. A girl."

"From the visiting professor's office?"

Sloan nodded. "Chelsea didn't really see anything explicit. It was more a feeling she got. It started with the look on the girl's face. At first she was shocked to see Chelsea. Then it turned into this silly kind of expression that school girls get when they've been naughty, if you know what I mean."

"Who was inside the office?" said Ryan—he wanted to hear it from Sloan's mouth.

"Dr. Garrisen," she said quietly. "And the lights were off."

Ryan was more confused than stunned. "How would he get to know a student well enough to hit on her?"

"He's never been your usual trustee. Dr. Garrisen volunteers as a guest lecturer in our high school honors science classes. The kids love him. He's very willing to work one-on-one with students who show an interest in medicine.

For lack of a better term, he's very hands-on, very accessible."

Most pedophiles are, thought Ryan, and he was suddenly feeling ill. "What did Chelsea do?"

"She got flustered and left."

"She didn't say anything to Connie?"

"Not at that time. She caught up with me and told me everything. She was in a state of disbelief, not really sure if she had seen what she thought she had seen. But from what Chelsea saw, the expression on Dr. Garrisen's face was even more incriminating than the girl's."

"Chelsea may not have caught them in the act, but I don't think there was much doubt about what was going on."

"Still, the evidence was pretty thin."

"At the very least, legitimate questions come to mind when the chairman of the board and a high school student are found inside the visiting professor's office after hours with the lights off. Any school with a legal compliance program would be obligated to investigate the matter. And once Chelsea was able to identify the girl by name and they interviewed her, chances are she would confess. Garrisen would stand to lose everything."

"I'm sure Chelsea realized that. But without a smoking gun, I know she was conflicted."

"How?"

"In addition to being chairman of the Board of Trustees at Brookline Academy, the man owned the Pawtucket Red Sox. Naturally, Chelsea feared that would be the end of your career."

"So did she tell Garrisen that she was going to report him or not?"

"I don't know," she said.

"Think hard, Sloan."

"I think so. Most likely yes. That's probably why she was still so upset when she got home to Pawtucket."

The big picture was suddenly becoming clear. Ryan rose from his little chair and began to pace. "Why didn't you tell me this before?"

"After Chelsea died, I didn't see the point."

"The man was having sex with a high school student. A teenager."

"But I had no idea who the girl was," said Sloan. "Chelsea didn't tell me her name. I'm sure Chelsea didn't know her name. Over three hundred girls are enrolled in our high school, and they all wear the same uniform. What was I supposed to do—tell our legal counsel that Chelsea may have seen something suspicious before she died and that every girl in the high school should be interviewed to find out if any of them have ever had sex with Dr. Garrisen? People would say I was starting a witch hunt."

Ryan didn't like the answer, but he did see her point.

"Believe me," said Sloan, "I did keep my eyes and ears open. If Dr. Garrisen was going to step out of line again, I wanted to be the one to nail him."

"Well, now you can leave that to me."

Ryan began to pace, the pieces of the puzzle finally coming together. The turning point had been Chelsea telling Garrisen that she was going to contact legal counsel. Garrisen saw his world crumbling—fired from the Board of Trustees at Boston's most prestigious academy, relieved of duty as chief of staff at Mass General, and probably facing a divorce. Possibly even statutory rape charges if the girl was under the age of consent. Possibly even *rape* charges if he'd used his position of power to coerce her consent.

"The guy must have freaked," said Ryan, speaking to himself, completely unaware of how confusing his words were to Sloan.

Ryan was deep in thought, and in his mind's eye he could see Garrisen steadying his nerves with a scotch or several, trying to figure out how to stop Chelsea. What other choice did the man have? He drove to Pawtucket to make one last desperate attempt to persuade her to keep the matter quiet. Before reaching the house, he saw her car approaching and ran her off the road. Maybe it was intentional. Maybe he was trying to flag her down and get her to stop and talk to him. Either way, at the crash site he found a badly injured Chelsea with her cell phone in her hand. As a renowned medical doctor, he must have understood that Chelsea would die if she did not get immediate medical attention. He took her phone—and in a very bad state of mind, out of fear of

losing everything he had worked his entire life to achieve, he made a terrible
decision: instead of dialing 911, he
stuffed her phone in his pocket and left
her there to die.

"Ryan, are you okay?"

He stopped pacing, oblivious to the
path of anger he'd nearly scorched onto
the classroom floor.

"I'm fine," he said. "But I really have to
go now."

"Where?" she said.

In the back of his mind echoed the
words of his friend Ivan: *What did you
promise Chelsea?*

"There's something I need to do," he
said.

CHAPTER 53

Babes was ready to jump out of his skin.

It was Friday at ten AM. Time for his standing appointment with Dr. Fisch. It had been a week since their last session, not counting Babes's unscheduled invasion of his office after the Modern Diner. Seven full days since they had done any real therapy. One hundred sixty-eight hours. Ten thousand eighty minutes. Check that: ten thousand eighty-*one* minutes. There had been a time in his childhood when being one minute late would have triggered a forty-minute tantrum.

What to do, what to do, what to do?

He huddled in the corner of the abandoned railroad car, hugged his knees, and started rocking back and forth. He wasn't crazy about his new hiding spot, an old freight car where the tracks ran beneath the Smithfield Avenue bridge, less than a quarter mile from the North Burial Ground. Ten years earlier, when he'd named his newest discovery the Sox Boxcar, it had been a decent hangout. Now it smelled like rotten wood and wet straw. And with the sliding door stuck in the half-open position, it would surely get chilly at night. But the pistol-wielding man at the Dawes family crypt hadn't come knocking just to tell Babes hello, so he had to avoid going back there at all costs.

His leg tremors resumed. Babes hugged his knees tighter and rocked a little faster, trying to stop the shaking.

Medication had always been a hot-button issue in the Townsend household. There was no magic pill for Asperger's syndrome, but anxiety was one of the comorbid conditions that could be treated. Starting as far back as elementary school, before his condition had been correctly diagnosed, Babes overheard countless knock-down, drag-out arguments between his mother and father.

I just don't believe in drugs.

It's not about your beliefs; it's about what's best for Babes.

It's masking who he really is.

No, it's revealing who he really is.

In the great parental compromise, Babes had been medicated only during the most stressful periods of his life. A change of schools. The death of his sister. Just about any crisis short of what could be worked out in weekly sessions with Dr. Fisch, the rare medical professional who understood Asperger's syndrome and who could actually make talk therapy or role-playing work within Babes's limited self awareness, social understanding, and theory of mind.

You need Dr. Fisch.

No, you need meds.

Drugs are the easy way out.

Something as big as a cat scurried past his feet. It wasn't a cat.

A rat!

Babes ran to the opposite corner,

grabbed two fistfuls of hair, and pulled until he screamed. He wanted to jump out the door, but he was too frightened to move. He tried the breathing exercises Dr. Fisch had prescribed. Deep breath. In and out. In. Out. Being on the run was tough for anyone. For Babes, whose life revolved around the routine and the familiar, it was becoming unbearable. Maybe it was time to go home. But that would mean going to jail.

Do you like cherry-red Kool-Aid on your lips. Babes?

He shrank into the dark corner and rocked back and forth again. Jail was a death sentence. But with the cops everywhere, the only other hiding place he could think of was the Dawes crypt, which was no alternative at all. Some guy had once managed to live for almost two years, undetected, in vacant space at the Providence Mall, but Babes could never have pulled that off. This stinky old freight car would have to do. He just had to stay put, rats and all.

And pray that the night would never come.

*   *   *

Ryan was fuming by the time he reached Beacon Hill. At some point he would apologize to Tom Bales for thinking he'd had anything to do with this nightmare, but at the moment the real target was in his sights. Rather than ring the bell, he beat on the front door. To his surprise, Brandon Lomax answered.

"Connie isn't here," he said.

"What are you, his house sitter? I called the hospital. His secretary said he went home."

Lomax hesitated. "He went out. To the bank."

It was an obvious lie. Ryan climbed the short stoop and shouted through the half-opened door. "Connie, I know you're here! I need to talk to you!"

Lomax grabbed Ryan's arm and spoke in a coarse whisper. "For your own good. Leave. *Now.*"

The door swung open all the way, and Garrisen was suddenly standing right behind Lomax. "Come in, Ryan."

Garrisen's even tone forced Ryan to reel in some of his anger. Still, he threw Lomax a sharp look as he entered the old row house. Both men followed Garrisen down the narrow hallway to his study, and Garrisen invited them into the walnut-paneled room.

"This is between Connie and me," said Ryan.

"Brandon stays," said Garrisen. "I don't like your body language. I feel like I need a witness."

Ryan didn't argue. Lomax's presence might well prevent him from doing something he'd regret.

Garrisen closed the door and offered Ryan a seat. He chose to stand. Garrisen sat behind his desk, and Lomax took the armchair off to the side.

"What's on your mind?" Garrisen said coolly.

Ryan knew better than to confront Garrisen in this emotional state, but all the pain of Chelsea's death was rising up within him, preventing him from holding back.

"It was all an act, wasn't it?" said Ryan.

"What was?" said Garrisen.

"The way you pretended to be my biggest supporter in the Red Sox organization. Even the scholarship you created in Chelsea's name so that Ainsley could attend Brookline Academy."

"I don't know what you mean."

Ryan took a step closer. "It would have been bad enough if a total stranger had gotten drunk and killed Chelsea on the road."

Ryan leaned forward, planting his palms atop the desk. "It would have been bad enough if you had gotten drunk after your extracurricular activities with a high school girl and run Chelsea off the road. But it's so much worse this way."

"I have no idea what you're talking about," said Garrisen.

"I'm talking about the fact that you could have saved Chelsea if you had called for help after the accident. The fact that you didn't just fail to help her, but you actually took the cell phone out of her hand. The fact that you let her die—killed her—to protect your own reputation."

"I hope you don't plan on saying that on the radio," said Garrisen.

"It's already been on the radio. When Babes told me to look for 'a nicer nose ring,' it was an anagram—for Connie Garrisen."

Finally, Garrisen flinched. It was clear that Ryan alone had figured out Babes's play on words.

Garrisen regained his composure. "If that's the case, your station had better issue a retraction immediately. Because you are about to be on the receiving end of the biggest slander suit in the history of communications law."

"Lawyers? Shit. Now I *am* scared. Worst case, I thought you might send that hired thug to beat the crap out of me again. Or maybe the guy you hired to beat that homeless man to death."

Garrisen glanced at Lomax. "Are you listening to this? I think he's lost his mind."

Ryan said, "Babes told his homeless friend everything. The guy tried to blackmail you, and you had him killed."

Garrisen showed no reaction, but Ryan noticed that the politician in the room was visibly shaken.

"This has gotten way out of hand," said Lomax. "I heard on my way over here that Doug Wells may have gone missing. Connie, you were standing right beside me at my fund-raiser at Marble House when Doug said he was going to help Emma get more media attention for the Chelsea James investigation."

"Shut up!" said Garrisen. "This makes no sense. If I were such a ruthless killer, I would have eliminated Babes a long time ago."

"Yes, you would have—if you'd known that Babes was a passenger in Chelsea's car. But only his parents knew that. Babes was already freaked out and hiding in the woods when you drove up to inspect the damage you'd caused. You were like me: you didn't know *anyone* had seen *anything* until Babes sent Emma the anonymous tip three years after the accident."

Lomax rose and said, "I think it's time to give it up, Connie."

"Sit down!"

Lomax froze, but he didn't sit. "My advice to you—"

"Just shut up, Brandon! I don't need your advice. I'm tired of covering for you."

"What?" said Lomax.

"Ryan, I am so sorry," said Garrisen. "I've known all along, and I should have told you. I hope you can forgive me for trying to protect my friend."

Lomax said, "That's not going to work. Ryan, talk to Claricia. She'll tell you that she and Connie put me in the backseat of my car and that Connie drove me home to Providence."

Ryan glanced at Lomax, then took a long look at Garrisen. For the first time, Ryan saw serious worry, almost panic, in his expression. It was as if Ryan could hear him running through his options, thinking of everything he had to lose: his license to practice medicine, his distinguished career as chief of staff at Mass General, his possible appointment as the next U.S. surgeon general, the pending sale of his cosmetics company, his seemingly happy marriage.

It was too much to give up.

Garrisen pulled a gun from his desk drawer and pointed it at Ryan.

Lomax rocked back on his heels.

"Don't move," said Garrisen. "Either one of you."

He picked up the phone and punched three buttons. Ryan could only presume that Garrisen was dialing 911, but that realization only confused him further. Lomax looked equally perplexed.

Garrisen's expression changed abruptly as he spoke in a phony voice of urgency. "This is Dr. Connie Garrisen, owner of the PawSox. We need an ambulance right away! One of my former ballplayers, Ryan James, barged into my house saying wild things about my friend Brandon Lomax, accusing him of killing his wife three years ago. He came at us and," he paused as if swallowing the lump of disbelief in his throat, "I had to shoot him. Please hurry!"

Garrisen hung up and kept the gun trained on Ryan. Sirens blared in the neighborhood. The cops and the ambulance were on the way.

"Don't do this," said Ryan.

"Brandon, are you with me on this?" said Garrisen.

"It's over," Lomax said, as he stepped in front of Ryan. "Unless you're willing to shoot me first."

The crack of a single gunshot filled

the room, and Lomax fell to the floor. Ryan instinctively dove behind the armchair. He could hear the front door burst open and what sounded like an army charging down the hallway.

"Police, freeze!"

Garrisen dropped the gun. Two cops rushed in and cuffed him. Two others went to Lomax.

"Damn," said Lomax, "I didn't think he'd actually shoot."

Ryan saw no blood, just a bullet mark on Lomax's suit coat.

"You're wearing a vest?" said Ryan, not quite understanding.

"Emma insisted," said Lomax, grimacing.

"Emma?" said Ryan. "This was a setup?"

"She and I cooked this up after I spoke to your housekeeper. That's why I told you to leave when you got here."

"I bet you're wired too, you bastard," said Garrisen.

"No, I preferred not to arm my political opponents with a taped conversation about my drunken night in South Boston. In hindsight, I wish I had let Emma wire me up. Cops would have been here before you shot me. But thanks to the vest, I'm still alive and well enough to testify against you."

The police read Garrisen his rights as they took him from the room. The paramedics rushed in. Ryan helped them get Lomax to his feet, and a paramedic helped him remove his coat.

"What's this made of, Kevlar?" said one of the paramedics.

"Level II-A polyethylene," said Emma, as she entered the room. "It's thinner and easier to conceal."

Lomax grimaced as he lowered himself into the armchair. "It still feels like I got kicked by a mule."

Emma went to him and hugged him the way she'd hug a father. "You were really brave," she said.

Then she turned to Ryan and after a slight hesitation, gave him a hug as well. At first it was the kind of hug she might have shared with any member of a victim's family. This embrace, however, lasted for an ambiguously long time. Finally, she pulled away.

Ryan said, "Now it's time to bring home the bravest one of all."

"You mean Babes," she said.

"I mean fast," said Ryan.

CHAPTER 54

The Checker had unfinished business.

He sat on the edge of the mattress and lit a cigarette. It was a habit he'd picked up at the age of twelve, back in the days of Soviet cigarettes that self-extinguished if they weren't puffed constantly. Now he could afford cigarettes that didn't have him drawing on his cancer sticks like a baby on a bottle, but he rarely smoked anymore. In fact, the hotel room was nonsmoking, as he had requested at check-in. Lighting up was a sure sign that he was upset.

Professional failure was the one thing that upset him most.

Connie Garrisen was a tier-one client. Garrisen and his team of managers traveled extensively on business, building international markets and trying to secure the requisite foreign government approvals for his company's line of skin and beauty products. Kidnapping for ransom was a legitimate concern for businessmen in emerging markets, and the smart ones hired bodyguards who knew how the criminal mind worked.

Vladimir, however, had never been called upon to do wet work for Garrisen before.

Frankly, it had surprised him when the contract came in. Supplying him with a pirated iPhone so that he could send off an untraceable e-mail to Emma Carlisle was more typical of the work that the Checker did for a man like Garrisen. But the Checker never questioned a job from a valued client. He provided "full-service" corporate security. If that meant a first-class ass kicking for a big-mouth radio host like Ryan James or a suck on the business end of a Beretta for his weird-ass brother-in-law, so be it.

He'd even thrown in the disposal of

Doug Wells's body for free. And a job well done it was: as far as he could tell, no one had even reported Wells missing yet.

Vladimir took another peek inside the big envelope that was beside him on the bed. It contained five thousand dollars in cash—President Ulysses S. Grant, one hundred times over—paid in advance.

The bathroom door opened. A tall, naked redhead sauntered across the room. With that hairy brown bush and hardly a freckle on her olive skin, the Debra Messing hairdo was obviously a dye job. She went to the bureau and removed a brush from her purse. Vladimir watched in the mirror as she combed through the tangles in her long, wet hair. He had to smile. Even after a long shower, her ass was still red from where he'd spanked that naughty bitch.

He grabbed her clothes from the foot of the bed and threw them at her.

"Get lost," he said.

She sorted through her clothing and pulled on her panties. "Aren't you forgetting something?"

He selected a crisp fifty-dollar bill from the envelope and held it up length-wise between his middle and index fingers. "Come and get it."

She pulled her dress on over her head and fastened her stiletto heels. "Sorry, pal. That mess you made in my hair doubled the price."

Vladimir didn't argue. It was money well spent. He took another fifty from the envelope. "Now, beat it."

She crossed the room with attitude, snatched the cash from his hand, and started toward the door. Vladimir rolled across the bed and beat her to it. She seemed surprised that he would open the door for her, but that surprise turned to concern when he leaned his shoulder against it to prevent her from leaving.

She smiled nervously. "You want to go again?"

He shook his head.

"Well, if you have any friends who—"

"I don't have any friends."

She swallowed hard. "Okay. But if you change your mind, you know how to reach me."

He grabbed her jaw tightly and forced

her to look at him directly. "That's exactly right," he said, his expression deadly serious. "I know how to reach you. I know where to reach you. I know when to reach you. So forget you ever met me."

His tone was so chilling that she nearly dissolved before his eyes. He released the vicelike grip on her jaw.

"Okay," she said, barely able to talk. "Whatever you say."

Vladimir unlocked the deadbolt, stepped aside, and opened the door. She left with the haste of a freed hostage, and just as soon as she was gone, Vladimir secured the door with both the chain and deadbolt.

It was time to get back to business.

He went to his leather bag, removed his .22 caliber with silencer, and laid the tools of the trade on the bed. The gun was a familiar model to him, but this one was brand-new—stolen from a gun shop in New York. It would be used once and then discarded, preferably in deep water. It was his weapon of choice for execution-style killings: barrel in the mouth or to the back of the head, the low-caliber bullet entering the cranium and ricocheting off the inside of the skull, no exit wound, turning the brain to scrambled eggs. Just in case things went wrong, he also packed a 9mm Glock with two ammunition clips.

Unfortunately, there was no way of knowing where his prey might be. Vladimir couldn't search every corner of Pawtucket and Providence. But a guy like Babes wasn't too savvy. All Vladimir had to do was pick a spot—a logical place that Babes would run to—and wait.

The Checker crushed out his cigarette, leaned back on the bed, and drew a mental map of his return to the North Burial Ground and the Dawes family crypt.

CHAPTER 55

It was after sunset when Emma reached the morgue.

All afternoon she had been negotiating with Garrisen's criminal-defense attorney, trying to get Garrisen to give up the name of the thug he'd hired to kill Yaz, beat up Ryan, and silence Babes. No dice. Garrisen wasn't talking.

But by sundown, Emma had a break of another kind.

The assistant medical examiner was waiting for her in the autopsy room. A wave of ice-cold air flooded in from the air-conditioning ducts overhead, forcing Emma to keep her raincoat on. Beneath the white sheet, laid out on the gurney, was Yaz's battered body.

The door opened. Two detectives from the sheriff's office entered. The woman with them was a dirty blonde—literally. She was dressed like a bag lady in construction boots, flannel shirt, ankle-length skirt, and an old knit beret. A scar from a knife or a nasty fall ran across her chin, and on her neck was a bad tattoo of a long-stemmed rose. The officers led her to the gurney and stopped on the side opposite Emma. The expression on the woman's face was somewhere between scared and sad.

"Thank you for coming," said Emma.

The woman nodded.

The senior detective spoke up. "She came by the station this afternoon. Said her friend was missing. From the way she described him, we thought it might be our John Doe."

Or Yaz Doe, thought Emma.

"Are we ready?" the medical examiner asked.

The woman nodded again.

The ME started to lift the sheet, but

Emma stopped him. "Ma'am, I have to warn you. He suffered a severe blow to the head. This may be disturbing."

"I'm ready," she said softly. From her voice, Emma guessed she was much younger than she looked.

The ME pulled the sheet back to reveal Yaz's face.

The woman gasped and covered her mouth. "It's him," she said, and then she quickly looked away.

The examiner put the sheet back.

Emma gave Yaz's friend a moment to regain her composure. "I know this is difficult for you," said Emma. "But can you tell us his name?"

"Cookie is what we called him. He loved vanilla wafers. I never knew his real name."

"Where did Cookie live?"

"Here and there," she said with a shrug.

"Did he have a favorite place?"

"Well, I ain't never been to it. But every now and then, I heard him talk about an old crypt in the North Burial Ground."

Emma felt like she'd struck gold. "Did he mention any crypt in particular?"

"If he did, I don't remember it. Cemeteries give me the creeps."

Emma asked a few more questions, but the woman had nothing to add. Emma thanked her and left the remaining follow-up to the detectives. From the parking lot, she dialed Ryan on her cell and told him the news.

"I can be in the North Burial Ground in an hour," he said.

"The cemetery is closed after dark," she said, as she reached her car. "I'm going to send the police."

"Don't do that," said Ryan.

"Why not? Babes seems to crave familiar surroundings. It makes sense that he would return there."

"I agree," said Ryan. "But if he sees the cops coming for him, he'll panic."

"It will be fine," she said. "With Garrisen in custody, Babes is no longer a wanted man in connection with the death of Chelsea or Yaz. The responsibility of the police is not to swoop in and apprehend him. Their sole mission is to bring him home safely."

"But Babes doesn't know that. It's clear from his phone calls to the radio station that he's terrified of the police coming to arrest him. He could hurt himself or someone else."

Emma considered it. Ryan had a point. "We could just call the curator of the cemetery to check out the crypts."

"That's even more problematic," said Ryan. "Babes is already afraid that someone came looking for him after Yaz was killed. What if he bought or stole a weapon to defend himself?"

"What do you suggest then?" said Emma.

"I'll go. No cops or curator with me to send Babes into a frenzy. Babes knows and trusts me."

"I'm nervous about that," said Emma.

"Don't be," said Ryan.

"I think you're overlooking something. Whoever killed Yaz and then went looking for Babes is still out there."

"He must be halfway across the country now that Garrisen has been arrested."

"I wouldn't bet on that," said Emma. "A professional finishes the job. The fact that Garrisen is in jail doesn't call off the contract. In fact, if there is a possibility that Babes is going to testify against him at trial, that only makes the hit more urgent."

There was silence on the other end of the line. Emma could almost hear the wheels turning in Ryan's head.

"Let me do this," he said.

Her instincts were saying no way, but she could hear how important this was to Ryan. "Meet me at the entrance to the burial grounds," she said, as she climbed into her car. "We'll take it from there."

CHAPTER 56

Nightfall only heightened Babes's fears. His new hiding spot in the railroad car was spooky enough in the daylight hours. Babes had taken some comfort in the narrow rays of sunlight shining through the slats and cracks in the old wood. One by one, they were erased—first by a late afternoon rain, and then by dusk, which turned the walls completely black. The sliding door was partly open, but the distant glow of city lights reached no more than a few feet inside the boxcar. He tried to calm himself by thinking of the *Boxcar* books his mother used to read with him as a child, but

that was fiction, and the harmless ho-
bos of the 1930s had long since given
way to child molesters and serial killers.
This place was a veritable haunted
house on rails, worse than a cemetery.
At least the crypt had candlelight.

"What was that?"

Babes didn't always talk to himself
aloud, but sometimes the sound of his
own voice could calm his fears.

He listened carefully, straining to hear
the noise again. The abandoned railroad
car was parked under a bridge, and he
heard only the steady whine of vehicles
overhead. It suddenly occurred to him
that perhaps he hadn't heard anything.
He'd *felt* something. Motion. Forward
movement.

The train is leaving!

He jumped up from his dark place in
the corner and stood perfectly still, arms
out, balancing himself like a surfer. But
he felt no motion beneath his feet. The
boxcar hadn't moved. It hadn't gone
anywhere in more than a decade.

Calm down, scaredy-cat.

The whine of traffic continued overhead. It sounded like a pulsating white

noise. But if he really focused on it, he could appreciate the rhythm. Each passing vehicle made the same noise. Coming, it was the hiss of rubber tires on slightly wet pavement: *eshh* . . . Going, it was the vibration of the bridge, a slightly fading pitch: *eer* . . .

Car after car: *Eshheer, eshheer.*

It was as if they were talking to him. *Eshheer.*

Or to someone else. *Esh-heer.*

About him. *He's here, he's here.*

Betrayed by machines and their secret-coded anagrams. They might as well have shouted *kill him, kill him, kill him.*

Babes screamed in the darkness, ran to the door, and leaped through the side opening at full speed. Arms flailing and heart pounding, he flew through the air, and he didn't stop screaming until he hit the ground and tumbled across the gravel. The fall stunned him. His head hurt and his leg was throbbing. He noticed a tear in his pant leg. The darkness beneath the old bridge made it difficult to see, but he could feel the warm, wet blood. He reached inside and touched his knee. The skin was badly scraped, but not split open. No stitches needed. That was good news.

Babes pushed himself up and tried to stand on two feet. The injured knee delivered a pain so sharp that it stole his breath away. He took a step. It hurt again, but not as much as before. It was like what the team managers always told their ballplayers: "Walk it off, Babes."

He put one foot in front of the other and started down the old railroad tracks, working through the pain. He'd had enough of that old boxcar. Going home was not an option, but he could easily retrace his familiar steps to more friendly surroundings.

Babes started back to the Dawes family crypt.

In an old stone chapel atop the cemetery's highest hill, the Checker waited and watched.

The rain had stopped about an hour earlier, but moisture hung in the air like a cold, wet blanket. A sliver of a moon was trying to break through the clouds, but for the most part the night was as dark as the crypt itself.

Vladimir had been casing out the cemetery since sundown. He'd made a careful pass and inspection upon arrival, which confirmed that Babes had not yet returned to the crypt. Logic and instinct told him that Babes would be back—sooner rather than later. The chapel perched atop the hill seemed like the ideal place to wait. The Dawes family crypt was at the bottom of the hill, less than thirty yards away. A night-vision monocular with built-in infrared illuminator gave Vladimir a decent view of the North Burial Ground up to about forty yards. He'd picked up the toy from a GI Joe Store in Providence for about two hundred bucks. Given the weather conditions, he wished he'd spent the extra dough for better equipment, but it was good enough to stake out the crypt. Every twenty minutes or so, the moon would make a brief appearance through the clouds, and he could get a fuzzy view of the parking lot in the distance. He kept one eye on the comings and goings at the main gate and the other on the Dawes family crypt.

He knew about Garrisen. It was pure luck that he had caught the report on the evening news back at the hotel. He didn't care for American television, and the local crap was particularly dreadful. He'd killed most of the afternoon reading a Russian crime novel by his favorite author, Alekseyeva Marina Anatolyevna. Only after finishing it was he desperate enough to switch on the tube and catch the lead story: Connie Garrisen—prominent Boston surgeon, owner of the Pawtucket Red Sox, and husband to Rhode Island assistant attorney general Glenda Garrisen—was under arrest. The reported charges revolved entirely around the death of Chelsea James three years before: vehicular homicide, voluntary manslaughter, and leaving the scene of an accident. There was no mention of the contracted killing of a blackmailer or the disappearance of Doug Wells. Vladimir had no way of knowing whether anyone had uncovered those pieces of the puzzle or whether, for strategy reasons, the police had simply withheld from the media all information about the black-mail.

The Checker had only one reaction: it didn't matter.

As far as he was concerned, the hit was still on. Past clients in worse predicaments than jail had not called off a contract, and he had heard nothing from Garrisen or his cohorts. In Vladimir's business, no news meant full speed ahead. And this mission had become a matter of pride for him: Babes was the only contract he had ever failed to execute without a hitch.

It was downright personal.

Finally, he detected motion in the distance. A shadow in the dark was coming toward the crypt. He adjusted his night-vision monocular, focused, and smiled to himself. His calculations had proved correct.

Like a hapless housefly, Babes was returning to the spider and his web.

CHAPTER 57

Ryan reached the North Burial Ground even sooner than he had expected. Emma was waiting for him in the main parking lot. So were a dozen police officers and six squad cars. A seventh car, albeit unmarked, pulled up behind Ryan. Sirens weren't blaring, but police beacons were flashing, their red-and-blue swirl of authority glistening off the puddle-dotted pavement. Ryan stepped out of his car and went straight to Emma.

"What's with the police armada?" he said. "I thought we agreed that I was going to approach Babes alone."

"I requested police backup, just in case something went wrong. I didn't expect this much show of muscle."

Ryan looked out toward the cemetery grounds. The sea of gravestones and monuments brightened with each sweep of the police beacons.

"This is enough to wake the dead," said Ryan.

"They're just being cautious. We are talking about the chief witness in a murder-for-hire case against the assistant attorney general's husband."

"We're talking about Babes," said Ryan. "If he isn't freaking out right now, it's only because he isn't here."

Emma seemed to share his concern. She walked over to the sergeant on the scene, and Ryan could hear the frustration in her voice.

"Can we kill the lights, please?" she said.

The sergeant gave the order, and the parking lot went dark.

Emma was still talking with the sergeant when Ryan's cell vibrated. He didn't recognize the number, but he took the call.

Babes was on the line—and frantic.

"Are you with them?"

Ryan recognized the voice, but the incoming number had thrown him. All he could figure was that Babes had borrowed or stolen someone else's cell. "Babes?"

"Answer me right now! Are you with the police?"

Ryan glanced across the parking lot. Emma was too far away to overhear him, but he got inside his car and closed the door anyway, just to make sure.

"What police?" said Ryan.

"Don't play games with me! I saw all the cars in the parking lot. Did you bring them?"

The swirling lights had obviously pushed Babes to the edge. Ryan prayed that they wouldn't push him over it. "Calm down, all right? Take a deep breath and tell me where you are."

He paused, seeming to struggle. "I have to hang up now."

"Don't hang up!"

"If the police are gone, I'll call you back in five minutes. If they're still here . . ." he said in a voice that faded.

Ryan braced himself, afraid of what Babes might say.

"If the police are still here," said Babes, his voice cracking, "you'll never hear from me again."

The words chilled Ryan, but before he could respond, the call was over. Babes had disconnected.

Ryan had to think fast. He wasn't sure if Babes was suicidal, but the pressure on him had been tremendous over the past few days, and Ryan couldn't take any chances. He jumped out of the car and ran to Emma and the police sergeant.

"I just got a call from Babes," said Ryan. "We're in the wrong place."

"Where is he?" said Emma.

Ryan searched his mind, but damned if he could come up with the name of the other burial ground in the area. "He's hiding in that big cemetery on the river," he said. "Closer to Providence."

"Swan Point?" said the police sergeant.

"Yes, exactly," said Ryan. "That one."

* * *

Vladimir tucked his phone into his coat pocket. It was a pirated cell—not as nice as the pirated iPhone he'd gotten for Connie Garrisen, but still effective—so he wasn't worried about the call being traced back to him. Through the night-vision monocular, he watched from the old chapel atop the hill. At this distance, his equipment wasn't good enough to get a perfect view of the parking lot, but with all the lights swirling, he didn't need night vision to figure out what was happening.

The police were leaving.

"Excellent job, Babes," he said.

Up until twenty minutes ago, plan A had been going just fine. Vladimir had watched Babes enter the Dawes family crypt, figuring that he would wait an hour or so, until Babes fell asleep. Then he would skulk his way down the hill, enter the crypt in utter stealth, and finish the job with a single efficient bullet in the head at close range. When the swirling police lights appeared in the parking lot, however, he'd been forced to formulate plan B on the fly.

He checked his watch. "Two more minutes."

"Then what?" said Babes, his voice a pathetic whimper.

Vladimir pressed the silencer to the back of Babes's head. After fumbling the first attempted hit on Babes, he was determined to give his client more than his money's worth.

"If you do as well on the follow-up call to your brother-in-law, I'd say Dr. Garrisen gets himself a twofer."

CHAPTER 58

Emma was the last to leave the parking lot. Except for Ryan.

Half of the squad cars had fallen off and gone back to their regular routes. The others were ahead of Emma on the road to Swan Point Cemetery. Ryan was supposed to follow her, but she didn't see his headlights behind her. That was curious enough, and her suspicions were only heightened by the fact that his story didn't ring true to her. Supposedly, Babes didn't want Ryan to come. He wanted his mother, and Mrs. Townsend would be waiting at Swan Point for the

police to escort her into the dark cemetery to find her son.

Oh, really now?

She pulled a U-turn, drove back to the
old North Burial Ground, and parked in
the lot. Ryan's car was still there, never
having moved. She got out of the car
and walked to the driver's side window.
Ryan was nowhere to be found.

Just as I thought.

Emma went back to her car. She still
had the grounds map that the curator of
the cemetery had given her before
Ryan's arrival. Only the oldest section of
the cemetery boasted private, chapel-
style family crypts that would have
made a suitable home for a street person or a hiding spot for Babes. The curator had circled the five most likely
prospects on the map. Emma retrieved
a flashlight from her glove compartment
and planned her route.

On paper, things looked easy enough.
But as she stepped out of her car and
surveyed the cemetery grounds, the
darkness was foreboding. She reached
for her cell and dialed Ryan's number. It
rang several times and went to voice

mail. He'd chosen not to answer—probably didn't want to talk to her. Emma couldn't blame him. She felt as if she had let Ryan down, after he'd pleaded with her to keep the police out of it, only to have seven squad cars waiting for him in the parking lot. The least she could do was help him find Babes before something else went wrong—even if cemeteries did give her the creeps.

Emma felt a raindrop on her cheek. Then another. She looked up at the sky, and the rain started falling harder.

Naturally, she thought.

She cinched up her raincoat and took a deep breath. Then she started down the path, her footfalls crunching in the pea gravel, a flashlight guiding her toward the black forest of oak trees and old stone monuments.

Ryan was battling the dark and worrying about the weather. Rain was not going to make it any easier to find Babes.

More than five minutes had passed, and Babes had yet to call back. Ryan was deathly afraid for Babes, fearful of what he might do alone, at night, in a dark and scary cemetery. He was concerned enough to venture out into the cemetery without specific directions.

The weather changed again—it was one of those weird nights, when the sky wasn't sure what it wanted to do. A sliver of a moon had broken through the clouds, but it didn't offer much guidance. Ryan kept a flashlight in the trunk of his car but—Murphy's Law—the batteries were dead. As best as he could tell, however, there seemed to be a limited number of large family crypts, and the old cemetery wasn't *that* big. This was Rhode Island, not Texas. If he stuck to the gravel path and let his eyes adjust to the darkness, he was confident he could find Babes.

His cell vibrated in his pocket. He checked the number. It was Emma again. He let it ring through to voice mail, just like the last call. With Babes already on edge, the last thing he needed was the return of a half-dozen squad cars with beacons swirling.

Ryan followed the curve of the path behind a stand of beech trees and came upon the first large crypt. The impressive stone structure looked to be centuries old, and it was definitely large enough to serve as Babes's hideout. He approached with caution.

"Babes?" he said in a gentle voice. "It's me, Ryan."

There was only silence. He checked the family name that was chiseled into the frieze: BROWN. He wondered if it was the same Brown as the university.

His cell vibrated again. But this time it wasn't Emma. The number that flashed was the one from before—the one Babes had called on. Ryan answered quickly.

"Babes?"

There was no reply, but Ryan sensed that someone was on the line. "Babes, is that you?"

The silence was palpable.

"The police are gone," said Ryan. "I told them you were at Swan Point Cemetery, and they bought it. It's just you and me, I promise. Talk to me, Babes."

His phone chirped. The call ended.

Babes was gone.

* * *

The Checker was furious.

Babes had completely shut down on the follow-up phone call. He was supposed to have given Ryan directions to the Dawes family crypt, but the retard froze up.

"A nicer nose ring," said Babes, "you need a nicer nose ring."

Vladimir tucked his phone into his pocket. "Will you shut up, already?" he said sharply.

Babes was crouched in the corner, rocking forward and back, and clutching his knees to his chest. He was driving the Checker absolutely nuts, mumbling the same nonsensical sentence over and over, like a yoga and his mantra.

"A nicer nose ring; you need a nicer nose ring."

"I said shut your trap!"

Babes fell silent, but he continued to rock back and forth.

Vladimir raised his monocular and surveyed the grounds. Minutes earlier he'd watched the squad cars leave the parking lot. His vision was less than ideal, but as best he could tell, all but one vehicle—presumably Ryan's—had

taken to the road and headed toward
the river. The last phone call had not
gone well, but at least it had explained
that delightful turn of events: Ryan had
fooled the police with the Swan Point
ruse.

Pretty slick, Mr. James.

In the distance, Vladimir spotted an
approaching light. He strained to make
it out, but the visibility was worsening.
Just when it had seemed that the night
was going to clear, the clouds returned
and the intermittent rainfall resumed.

The bright yellow beam faded and
reappeared beneath the canopy of
trees. The approach of autumn had
claimed a fair number of leaves over the
past week or so, and more had fallen in
the afternoon rain. But the old section of
the cemetery contained hundreds of
mature trees, and in the dead of night
the autumn-colored leaves were every
bit as capable of limiting Vladimir's visibility as were the green ones. The tall
conifers didn't help matters. Even with
his night-vision monocular, he couldn't
get a clear enough line of sight to determine who was coming—at least not

with certainty. In fact, every time the flashlight pointed right at him, it over-loaded his infrared illuminator. He could tell only that it was someone wearing a raincoat. But who else could it have been?

It almost made him laugh.

Could you possibly make yourself an easier target, James?

CHAPTER 59

Babes wedged himself as deep into the corner as possible.

Inside the old stone chapel it was even darker than night, but Babes's pupils were adjusting. He could see the Russian across the room. At the front of the chapel the stained-glass window in the shape of a rose medallion was colorless in the absence of light, but Babes could tell that several panes were broken or missing. The Russian was peering out one of the openings, using his night-vision monocular. Babes could have jumped him, had he been able to find the courage. His captor seemed no more worried about Babes than about the bodies in the surrounding graves.

Arrogant jerk.

Who did this hotshot with the fancy gun and silencer think he was, threatening him and Ryan with a twofer? Babes had seen plenty of movies and television dramas—even *The Sopranos.* Did this joker really think Babes was so stupid that he didn't know a contract killer when he saw one? And Yaz—easy prey for the Russian—was an even bigger idiot. If Yaz hadn't concocted the extortion scheme, the Russian would never have found him or Babes. The irony was that a homeless guy like Yaz probably didn't even care about the money. He just wanted to show some rich guy how clever he was.

Another arrogant jerk.

The more Babes pondered it, the madder he got. But he couldn't fool himself. More than anything, Babes was mad at Babes—for everything that had ever gone wrong for anyone he had ever known in his entire life. As always, he was to blame, and now it was time to pay the price for his screwups.

Bad things happened to bad people, whether or not his father was around to punish him. That, of course, was something his father had been telling him all his life, or at least whenever Babes acted up. His mother had the patience of a saint, but his father was all about tough love. Babes always knew when the hand of discipline was coming. "You're enabling that boy," his father would say. "He needs to learn that there are consequences for his actions."

Consequences. They were Babes's biggest fear—and fear kept him cowering in the corner. Fear felt like ice to Babes, and when it mixed with the heat of his anger, his emotions swirled inside him like a spring tornado.

Babes recoiled into his comfort zone—knees to his chest and rocking back and forth. He worked it slow and steady for a while, but as the storm inside him intensified, his pace quickened. The night was growing colder by the minute, but Babes was actually breaking a sweat. He breathed in and out like a long-distance runner. The rhythm helped him focus, but his emotions were too complex to sort out. Without a doubt, he had failed Chelsea on the night of her accident. All he'd needed to do was take her cell phone and dial 911. A child could have saved her. But not Babes. It was disgraceful, and now that he'd gone on Ryan's radio show and told the world about it, the shame was more than he could handle.

Babes kept rocking. It was all he could do to keep his emotions in check. The fear remained. He could never get rid of it entirely. But only the anger continued to grow, and in one key respect, Babes could feel his resolve strengthening.

He was determined not to fail Ryan.

Babes suddenly stopped rocking. He thought he'd heard something. Keeping his body perfectly still was self-inflicted torture, but he forced himself to listen.

He heard it again. It was coming from outside the chapel—a crunching noise, very faint and in the distance. It sounded like a giant monster chewing ice cubes. No, someone was walking. Footsteps in pea gravel.

Someone's coming!

Babes took a good look at the Russian. The man was on one knee, still peering out the broken window. It was impossible for Babes to see the expression on his face in the darkness, but his movements seemed different now—smoother, more purposeful and controlled. The Russian bent down to retrieve something from a leather bag on the floor beside him. It took a moment, but finally Babes discerned the shape in the shadows. It was a gun—a pistol of some sort, different from the one with the silencer on it. Slowly the Russian raised his new weapon and put the barrel through the hole in the window.

He's going to shoot Ryan!

There was a moment of confusion for Babes—the hot and the cold swirling inside him, the anger combining with the fear of losing Ryan. What happened next seemed to take a very long time for Babes, but it all happened in less than a split second. The tornado within him took over, propelled Babes from his cocoon, and sent his body flying across the room. He broadsided the Russian with the force of a charging rhinoceros, but it was like running into an oak tree. Babes felt a sharp pain in his shoulder and a jolt to his spine on impact. The Russian oak fell over, but not before he managed to squeeze off a single shot that reverberated like a canon inside the stone chapel.

Babes rolled across the floor, and he heard the gun sliding across the concrete floor somewhere beside him. He'd knocked it from the Russian's hand, but Babes didn't look for it, didn't want to get anywhere near it. He was barely aware of his screams as he hurried toward the door, pushed his way out of the chapel, and ran faster than he'd ever run before, disappearing among the tall trees and crumbling tombstones of the black burial grounds.

CHAPTER 60

Ryan heard the gunshot, followed by screaming.

Babes?

The first two family crypts had turned up nothing for Ryan. He wasn't sure where to go next in the darkness, and the search for Babes was slow without a flashlight. Then, through the woods, he'd spotted the glow of a flashlight moving steadily across the grounds, like a ship on the horizon. Ryan had been following it until the gunshot had stopped it cold.

The beam of light was now aiming straight up at the clouds.

"Babes!"

All along, suicide had been Ryan's biggest fear. Providence was like any other big city: it wasn't difficult to get a handgun illegally—even for someone like Babes, who had no idea how to use one. The screams immediately after the gunshot told him only that Babes had botched the attempt, and in his mind's eye, Ryan saw him running frantically through the cemetery with powder burns on his scalp—or worse.

Ryan raced through the darkness toward the glowing flashlight. The screaming had stopped, and the utter silence only exacerbated his fears. A hundred-yard dash through a cemetery was a tricky thing in the dark. The rain was letting up, but the grass was wet and slippery. Ryan tripped once over a low-lying gravestone, got up immediately, and continued toward the light. The second stumble came just twenty yards farther along, as Ryan stepped into a hole. This time he'd turned his ankle, but he sprinted through the pain. He was breathing heavily when he reached the flashlight, but what he found there turned his fears to confusion.

"Emma?" he said.

She was lying on the wet grass, her body in a strange pose, almost a twisted heap. She'd obviously fallen—dropped—to the ground. Ryan grabbed the flashlight and knelt at her side. Then he saw the blood.

"Oh, God," he said.

She looked up at him, her eyes clouded. "Is it as bad as it feels?"

There was so much blood. The bullet was in her upper right torso. Ryan hoped it was the shoulder.

"You're going to be okay," he said, trying to reassure her.

The ground was cold with dampness, and Ryan worried that she might go into shock. He removed his jacket and laid it on top of her for warmth, and he removed his shirt as well. The rain was now more of a mist, but it felt cold on his bare skin.

"What are you doing?" she said.

"Don't try to talk."

Ryan was no paramedic, but years ago one of his neighbors back in Texas had been accidentally shot on a hunting trip. Ryan seemed to recall people saying that applying pressure to the wound had stopped the man from bleeding to death.

"This is going to hurt," he said.

Ryan rolled his shirt into a ball and pressed it directly to the wound.

Emma's mouth opened, but no sound emerged. It was as if the pain had transported her to a place that was beyond screaming.

"Hang in there," said Ryan. With his free hand, he dug his cell from his pocket and dialed 911.

A gunshot rang out, and Ryan dove to the ground.

"Babes, it's me, Ryan! Stop shooting!"

Another shot ricocheted off the tombstone. Ryan didn't want to move Emma, but he had no choice. He took her by the left arm and, gently as possible, dragged her about five feet, where they both found cover behind a much bigger stone monument.

"Kill the flashlight," said Emma, her voice weakening.

Ryan grabbed it and switched off the

light, which made them far less conspic-
uous to the shooter. Only his cell phone
glowed in the darkness.

The 911 dispatcher was on the line:
"What is your emergency?"

"I'm not the one shooting!" Babes
shouted. He was somewhere nearby, invisible in the night.

It took a moment for Ryan to process
things—bullets flying, Emma wounded,
Babes hiding.

"Nine-one-one, what is your emergency?"

Ryan spoke into the phone. "There's a
shooter at the North Burial Ground.
Emma Carlisle has been shot. Send the
police and an ambulance—and hurry!"

CHAPTER 61

The Checker spotted the greenish glow of a cell phone and assumed that Ryan was dialing 911. The police would arrive soon, which meant that a gunfight was unavoidable.

It was time to take stock.

He tried to scan the cemetery one more time with his night-vision monocular. No go. His cheapo equipment was definitely broken. That idiot Babes had hit him like a Mack truck and sent the monocular flying onto the concrete floor. He didn't need night vision to beat these amateurs anyway. Ryan—he'd identified himself as Ryan when shouting to

Babes—had taken cover behind a stone monument. Obviously, that first target in the trench coat had been someone else. Probably Emma. Maybe she was hit. In any event, she was out of sight, down somewhere in the sea of gravestones.

Vladimir checked his ammunition. Under ideal conditions, he would have needed just one bullet for each target, but with rainfall coming and going, he would have to count on a few more misses. He had one extra magazine for his Glock pistol—another fifteen rounds in addition to the dozen remaining in the first magazine. Plenty of firepower. The Beretta was also fully loaded, but it wasn't very accurate at a distance of more than thirty feet, and unless he had the barrel of the gun pressed up against the victim's skull, the Checker never counted on a .22-caliber weapon to deliver a fatal blow. From here on out, the 9mm Glock was his ticket out of this mess.

"Ryan, where are you?" shouted Babes.

"Stay down and stay quiet!" Ryan shouted back.

"Watch out for the Russian!"

Vladimir used the voices to pinpoint his targets. Ryan was still down low, out of the line of sight.

But Vladimir had an open shot at Babes.

Babes was only fifty feet away, much closer than Vladimir's earlier shot at the trench coat. Even a sliver of a moon peering through passing clouds was enough light to complete this hit. Babes's body was concealed, but most of his head was exposed above a waist-high stone monument. He reminded Vladimir of a young deer: alarmed and alert enough to look up but lacking the experience to realize that it was time to run away.

Easy pickings, even without night vision.

Vladimir took careful aim. A simple squeeze of the trigger would have ended it. But he backed off.

Sirens blared in the distance—barely audible at this point, but approaching. The cops were indeed on the way. Matters were getting complicated. Vladimir needed to rethink his escape.

A hostage.

He might need one. But only *one.* Between Babes and Ryan, Babes would be easier to subdue. Vladimir could also be certain that Babes was unarmed. The same could not be said about Ryan.

The police sirens were growing louder. No time to waste. It was settled. He'd retake Babes. And then he would kill the guy who had dragged the police here in the first place and screwed up Vladimir's entire night.

Ryan.

CHAPTER 62

Babes gripped the gravestone tightly as he crouched atop some dead Puritan's final resting place. The marker didn't exactly crumble in his hands, but it felt strangely fragile. Despite the stress—or because of it—the numbers called out to him, and he studied the dates on the monument. It was more than two centuries old, discolored, cracked, and decaying from the elements.

He wondered if Vladimir's bullets could cut right through them.

Babes felt a strong urge to draw his knees up to his chest and rock, but he forced himself to remain as still as possible. The slightest movement could reveal his whereabouts, which would have been deadly. He listened. The busy interstate bordered the western edge of the cemetery, and even though Babes couldn't see beyond the trees, the rain had made passing vehicles audible. Speeding tires on wet pavement sounded just like the traffic on the bridge over his boxcar.

Eshheer.

He's here.

Babes heard the approaching sirens too. The police. They were coming for him. Surely a guy like the Russian would know how to escape, but Babes feared that his own luck was running out. If the cops caught him, they would pin Yaz's murder on him and throw him in jail. Then the big men without women would smear his lips with cherry Kool-Aid and have their way with him.

Footsteps!

Babes could have sworn he'd heard footsteps. Someone was coming. Maybe it was the police. Or the Russian. He wasn't sure which would have been worse. Either way, he had to escape.

Babes got down on his belly and, like a snake, slithered between the monuments, keeping low and making himself invisible.

Watch out for the Russian. That last warning from Babes was burning in Ryan's ear. It had to be the same thug who had laid out Ryan on the sidewalk outside his in-laws' house last night.

"He's coming," said Ryan, whispering.

It was purely instinct speaking. In the darkness he couldn't see the Russian, but the silence told him that something was under way.

"Either that, or he's going after Babes," Ryan added, thinking aloud.

"Take my gun," said Emma.

It hadn't occurred to Ryan that she would be armed, but it was no surprise that a female prosecutor who went up against rapists and murderers on a daily basis would be licensed to carry a firearm.

"Lucky me," said Ryan. "My first shootout, and it has to be with a trained killer."

"Don't tell me you're the only boy from Texas who doesn't like guns."

He didn't bother telling her that his dormitory at UT had boots, knives, and guns sculptured onto the frieze. Or that by the age of fifteen he could have shot the cap off a bottle of Dublin Dr Pepper at fifty paces. "I know guns," he said.

"Good. It's holstered on my left side."

Ryan released the pressure on her wound, which made Emma cringe with pain. Change of any kind obviously didn't agree with her at the moment. He reached carefully inside her coat, where everything was wet with blood. It had soaked all the way over to her left side, which scared him. The bullet's entry point was too high to have hit a vital organ, but any wound that bled this much could be fatal.

Emma seemed to pick up his concern. "Am I dying?" she asked.

Ryan froze, and even though his hand was on the gun, he could feel her heart beating. In a strange but powerful way, he felt connected to her. "No," he said firmly. "You are *not* dying. Not tonight. Not any time soon."

Ryan slid the gun from the holster and wiped it clean on his shirt.

"It's a SIG-Sauer," she said. "Nine millimeter."

The sirens were getting louder. Ryan guessed that the police and the ambulance were three minutes away. The bad news was those three minutes felt like three hours.

"You have ten rounds in the magazine," said Emma.

Ryan cocked the hammer with his thumb, then pulled the slide back and released it, loading a live round into the barrel.

"Let's hope we don't need that many," he said.

The Checker had lost sight of Babes. One minute the twit was an easy target, the next—poof. He'd vanished amid an overcrowded collection of tall markers that stood side by side, almost on top of one another, a veritable forest of chiseled granite.

You're a total pain in the ass, you know that, Babes?

It didn't seem possible, but the night

was growing darker. Once again the cool mist was turning to cold rain, and the last band of clouds had moved in and swallowed the light of the crescent moon entirely. Vladimir had worked under far worse conditions. If not for the approaching police sirens, he would have relished the challenge of this little search-and-destroy mission. In about three minutes, however, the cemetery would be crawling with cops. He'd had enough. To hell with Babes and the notion of taking a hostage. There was no telling where he was hiding, and Vladimir didn't have the time to smoke him out. It was best just to drop that screwball at the first opportunity.

He changed direction and doubled back toward the place where his first round of gunfire had dropped the body in the trench coat—back toward Ryan.

"Ryan, watch out!" Babes shouted.

In one fluid motion, Vladimir turned, fired two quick shots in the direction of Babes's voice, and immediately dove to the ground, taking cover behind a marker.

"Babes!" Ryan shouted.

Babes did not respond. The night was deadly silent.

Vladimir smiled to himself. Ryan's last shout to Babes had confirmed his suspicion: Ryan had stayed near the body of the Checker's first victim.

Gun in hand, his body low to the ground, Vladimir used the monuments as cover as he made his way toward his final target.

CHAPTER 63

Silence pierced by sirens—the sound was haunting to Ryan.

The night was beyond black. Emma lay at his side, and the darkness was so profound that it was even difficult to see her face. For an instant—a bizarre and confusing moment in Ryan's mind—Emma became Chelsea, and Ryan was at her side as the ambulance approached too slowly, too late to stop the bleeding and save her life.

Ryan shook it off. He could hear Emma breathing. She was struggling.

"Only a couple minutes more," he whispered.

A shot rang out, and then another. Ryan hit the ground as the bullets ricocheted off the marker behind him. The second one had whistled right past his ear. Surely the squad cars were pulling into the parking lot by now—they sounded closer than ever. Still, help was a quarter mile away on foot, and the officers would have to find their way through the cemetery's maze of winding footpaths. If Ryan didn't take out the Russian before they arrived, one of those cops might lose his life.

Ryan was going to have to put Emma's gun to use.

Suddenly he felt ready—on so many levels, and for so many reasons. At that moment, the need to save Chelsea's brother was more powerful than was the need to avenge Chelsea's death. And if Babes was already gone—silenced by those last gunshots in the dark—there would be at least as much justice in taking out the Russian as there had been in bringing down Connie Garrisen.

Emma emitted a gurgling sound. Her breathing was growing more difficult with the passing of each precious minute.

Ryan sat up slowly, his back pressed hard against a granite monument. He was still shirtless, and the polished stone felt like a block of ice against his bare back. Saying another word to Emma was out of the question, fearful as he was of drawing more fire. He simply reached out in the darkness and squeezed Emma's hand to reassure her.

Then, in total silence, he raised his head above the marker and searched for his enemy. And his heart sank.

He saw only the black of night.

The Checker approached with the confidence of an assassin. Time was short. The police were coming. The target was near at hand. His heart was pounding.

I can't see shit.

The darkness, however, was strangely exhilarating. Ryan had yet to fire a shot—perhaps he didn't even have a gun—but Vladimir had to assume he was armed. He *always* assumed that his targets were armed, and if that body in the trench coat was Emma Carlisle, he was experienced enough to know that prosecutors often carried weapons. Commonsense insights and assumptions had enabled him to keep the upper hand throughout his career. More than a dozen hits—way more—without a hitch. His keys to success were simple: Know your target. Know your surroundings. Know your way out. Tonight he was breaking the rules, battling the darkness, venturing into uncharted territory.

And he had never felt more alive.

Sixty seconds more was all the time he had. He could almost feel the police closing in, and soon he would have to make his escape.

Vladimir moved to the next marker, stopped, and listened. If he couldn't see Ryan, he knew that Ryan couldn't see him. But Vladimir had the advantage. Ryan had already given away his position by calling out to Babes. All Vladimir had to do was avoid making any noise—and keep his ears open.

The next man to make a sound would die.

* * *

Ryan felt it in his bones that the shooter was nearby—perhaps just a few stone markers away. But he couldn't see a thing in the pitch darkness.

Where the hell are the cops?

They had to be on the way, but maybe they had charged off to another section of the cemetery. Ryan had told the 911 operator that there was a shooter at the North Burial Ground. In the confusion of the moment, he couldn't recall whether he'd mentioned the Dawes family crypt. Surely the police had the common sense to realize that the Dawes crypt was in Emma's original plan and that Dawes was what Ryan had meant to say.

Who knows what they realized?

Ryan wanted to redial 911. But that was risky. The light from the cell phone's display would make him a glowing target in the darkness. He could keep the phone in his pocket and punch out the numbers by feel, but that was a stupid idea. How would he talk to the operator without getting shot?

A touch of irony gripped him. He couldn't call 911 to save Emma. Connie

Garrisen had failed to dial 911, which
had killed Chelsea.

Ryan raised his weapon, pointing the
barrel upward in the ready position. The
SIG-Sauer was among the smaller 9mm
pistols, and it felt comfortable in his
hand. He'd been away from guns since
leaving Alpine, Texas, for the most part.
There was a time after Chelsea's accident when anger had gripped him, and
he'd taken up target practice at a shooting range in South Boston. The target
was a black-on-white image of a man,
and Ryan would cast the dark silhouette
as the faceless drunk who had run Chelsea off the road. He'd squeeze off hundreds of rounds, all to the head and the
heart, kill shot after kill shot.

Ryan bristled. He heard something.
The shooter? No. Just the wind.

Where are the fucking cops?

He tried to focus. His ears were his
only ally. This was a game of sound and
silence. Make a sound, and you'd be silenced. Like Babes.

Please, God. Not Babes too.

Goosebumps suddenly covered his
upper body. Ryan was naked from the

waist up, but the chills had nothing to do with the cold. It was a confluence of thoughts. On one side of his brain were Babes, Chelsea, Emma, and 911. On the other side were the shooter, the silence, the danger of making noise. Like a flash of light in the night, it came down to one common denominator.

The phone.

It was his only chance against a professional killer.

With his left hand, he reached into his pants pocket, pulled out his phone, and pressed it face down in the grass so that it would emit no light. With the tip of his finger, entirely by touch and memory, he found the rectangular Menu button on the right and pressed it. He found the corresponding OK button on the left. He pressed it. Then he found the round Talk button in the middle. He punched it— and held his breath.

The next three seconds felt endless. If all had gone right, Ryan was dialing the last number to have called him.

A phone chirped in the darkness.

Instinct took over, and in a total blur of adrenaline-driven motion, Ryan rolled to his right, sprang from behind the cover of the granite marker, and rapid-fired three shots—*pow, pow, pow*—aimed directly at the ringing cell phone. The noise, the vibration in his hands, the recoil in his forearms—every bit of it seemed to overload his senses and touch his very core. He wasn't just squeezing off gunshots. He was squeezing out three years of grief, anger, sadness, and every other emotion that had kept him staring at the ceiling night after night since Chelsea's death.

He heard a thud—a body hitting the ground.

Then silence.

Ryan moved forward, one stone marker to the next, maintaining a position of cover. Just five gravesites away, beside a tall stone monument, he found what he was hoping for.

The Russian lay face down in the wet grass.

Ryan reached out and put two fingers to the Russian's jugular. No pulse. Another silhouette, another kill shot.

Right beside the body lay a professional killer's tool of choice: the pistol that could have killed Ryan and Emma. The pistol that might already have claimed a life tonight.

"Babes!" Ryan called into the darkness.

CHAPTER 64

"Ryan?"

The voice in the night was like music to Ryan's ears.

Babes was alive.

Ryan hurried in the general direction of the lonely voice, sidestepping gravestones along the way, praying to God that Babes wasn't down from a gunshot and bleeding onto the grass.

"I can't find you," said Ryan, searching frantically in the darkness. "Where are you?"

"Forty-one degrees, forty-four minutes north; seventy-one degrees, twenty-six minutes west."

Ryan smiled. Only a healthy and un-harmed Babes could have reached into his memory bank of Rhode Island trivia and pulled out the exact latitude and longitude for north Providence.

Ryan leaped over a gravestone and found Babes hiding behind a tall monu-ment. He was huddled into a ball, pulling his knees tightly up to his chest.

"Are you hurt?" said Ryan.

"Where's your shirt?" said Babes.

Ryan had almost forgotten that he was naked from the waist up, but a question like that from Babes only con-firmed that he was just fine. Ryan went to him and hugged him tightly. Babes bristled. Hugs had never been Babes's thing, not even with Chelsea, but at the moment, Ryan couldn't help himself. He was that glad to see him.

There was a commotion in the woods. Flashlights swirled, and the approach-ing footsteps sounded like a herd of charging buffalo.

Babes cowered. "What's that?"

"It's okay," said Ryan. "It's the police."

"No, no! No cherry Kool-Aid!"

Ryan had no idea what Babes was

talking about. He tried to hold him, but Babes's fears had taken over. His arms were flailing, his feet were kicking, and Babes was able to wriggle free. He sprang from his hiding place and ran off wildly, screaming in a voice that pierced the night.

"No cherry Kool-Aid!"

"Police, freeze!"

"Don't shoot!" Ryan shouted.

The beam of a high-powered flashlight had caught up with Babes, adding to his confusion and anger. He turned and ran straight toward the police, still screaming.

"Freeze!" another cop shouted, his weapon drawn.

Babes kept charging toward the police, yelling at the top of his voice, a total outpouring of emotion more than the verbalization of any specific thought.

"Babes, stop!" shouted Emma.

Maybe it was coincidence. Maybe it was the hand of God. Or maybe it was just the sound of a woman's voice in the darkness.

Whatever it was, Babes stopped.

Two officers grabbed Babes and ordered him onto his belly. Babes was sobbing, facedown on the wet grass, when Ryan caught up with them.

"Please, leave him alone," said Ryan. "The shooter's dead. You need to help Emma Carlisle. She's been hit."

Ryan was pointing. The officer aimed his flashlight and found Emma.

The old cemetery grounds were too wooded and too crowded with grave-stones for emergency vehicles to pass, but a team of paramedics was rushing up the gravel pathway on foot. The offi-cer called out to the paramedics and led them to Emma. The area around the Dawes family crypt was suddenly aglow with emergency lighting. Ryan stayed a moment longer with Babes, watching from a distance as the paramedics tended to Emma and her wound.

"Is she going to be OK?" said Babes.

The paramedics were working quickly, already infusing her.

"I think so," said Ryan.

The paramedics lifted Emma onto a gurney, but she stopped them before they could whisk her away. Ryan noticed her hand moving. She was gesturing—calling him over.

"Wait right here," he told Babes.

Ryan approached quickly. A paramedic stepped aside so that Emma could speak to him.

"Closer," Emma said softly.

Ryan stepped up close to the rail on the gurney, and she curled her index finger to call him closer still. He leaned over. She reached up, cupped the back of his neck with her hand, and pulled his face toward hers.

For a moment, Ryan thought she was going to kiss him, but she pulled his ear to her lips.

"Nice abs," she whispered.

Ryan smiled.

Emma was going to be OK. Just like Babes.

They would all be OK.

EIGHT MONTHS LATER: MAY

CHAPTER 65

It wasn't opening day for Major League Baseball. It wasn't even the first home game of the season for the Boston Red Sox. But it was the biggest first in the career of Ryan James. He was wearing one of the most classic and recognizable uniforms in all of professional sports—and he was playing third base at Fenway Park.

Ryan could scarcely believe he was standing on such hallowed ground.

For almost a century, virtually every boy in America has dreamed of playing at Fenway—some as the Beantown hero, others as the clutch hitter for an archrival who would ruin another Boston "summah." Fenway was a battle-tested constant in a hi-tech world of disposable everything. It was a place where the perfect symmetry that defined every ballgame—four bases exactly ninety feet apart—played out amid truly unique charm. Seats intimately close to the manicured field of Kentucky bluegrass. A thirty-seven-foot-high Green Monster of a wall in left field with its manually operated scoreboard. The towering lighted Citgo sign a block away but as much a part of the stadium as home plate. Diehard fans, thick Boston accents, Fenway franks, cold beer, and on and on. The park was so beloved that even the foul poles had names (Fisk in left field, Pesky in right). Sure, its thirty-six thousand seats were cramped; "rubbing elbows" was no figurative expression at Fenway. Lines at the bathrooms had been known to force beer-chugging fans to run across the street to use the facilities at neighboring restaurants, and the concession stands probably could have been better. But this familiar old shoe of a ballpark wasn't built for comfort. It was built for New Englanders.

And for boys from Alpine, Texas, with a dream.

Ryan felt right at home—even if he was 0 for 3 at the plate, still looking for his first major-league hit.

"Next batter for the Red Sox," said the stadium announcer, "number eleven, the third baseman, Ryan James."

Virtually every Sox game was a sellout, and thousands of fans cheered as Ryan stepped out of the on-deck circle and approached the batter's box. Of course, one voice stood out.

"Let's go, *baaaabe.*"

Babes had a choice seat right behind home plate, which meant that he was actually closer to the batter than the pitcher was. Only at Fenway.

"Come on, Daddy!"

The score was tied, and the game had gone into extra innings. Ainsley was out way past her bedtime, but no kindergartner ever had a better excuse for it. Ryan glanced at his little girl and gave her a wink. She waved.

So did Emma. She and Ryan had

been dating since Christmas, but only recently had Ryan taken the bigger step of making Emma part of his daughter's life. She and Ainsley were sitting together, right next to Babes.

On a cool spring night, beneath the hot white lights at Fenway, the events of last September seemed like another lifetime to Ryan. For a time, the media in Boston and Rhode Island were all over the story, stoking the fires for the next big "trial of the century," the prosecution of PawSox owner and Beacon Hill blueblood, Connie Garrisen. It ended with a quick plea bargain, triggered no doubt by the discovery of Doug Wells's body. A tourist in Providence spotted it in the murky waters of the Blackstone when workers ignited the huge cedar-filled urns for the popular river fires. Garrisen was sentenced to six months probation for leaving the scene of Chelsea's accident; twelve years in prison for hiring a hit man to murder Yaz, the homeless blackmailer; and another twenty in connection with Doug Wells's execution-style killing. The press decried the deal as too lenient, but Ryan was OK with it,

knowing that it was better than putting
Babes through a trial as a witness.
Brandon Lomax was happy with it too.
With the senatorial election looming, he
just wanted all the talk of Connie Garrisen to go away, even if his cooperation
in nabbing Connie Garrisen was seen as
heroic. In the end, however, his oppo-
nent was able to exploit Lomax's gambling debts and alcoholism, which were
part of the Garrisen saga. Some said it
was another sad chapter in the state's
corrupt political history. By "Roe Dyelin"
standards, it was barely a footnote.

"Another rookie, another strikeout,"
the catcher said.

Ryan ignored him and stepped into
the batter's box.

Ryan was by no means the megastar
his friend Ivan had become, but no one
had worked harder to make the team.
The training was intense, but it was
amazing what a difference a good
night's sleep could make in the life of an
athlete. A little luck didn't hurt either.
Three weeks into the season, the Sox's
starting third baseman broke his wrist in
a motorcycle accident. Ryan was called

up from Pawtucket. He was supposed to be a backup infielder, but the manager liked the way he swung the bat against left-handed pitchers. Tonight, facing a southpaw, he made Ryan a starter.

"*Stee*-rike!" shouted the umpire.

It was a good pitch, but it wasn't the one Ryan wanted.

The pitcher stepped off the rubber and went to the rosin bag at the back of the mound. Ryan stepped out of the box and tapped the dirt from his cleats with his bat. Thirty-some thousand spectators watched and waited.

The pitcher was in his stance. Ryan assumed the ready position—elbow up, knees bent slightly, and bat cocked.

The pitcher went to his windup and hurled a fastball—straight at Ryan's head.

Ryan dived to the ground. The true test of how fast the human body can move is when a rock-hard, nine-inch sphere—cork, rubber, and 369 yards of tightly wound yarn covered with cowhide—is rocketing toward your skull at ninety-eight miles per hour.

It missed him. But it hit his bat.

"Strike two," said the umpire.

The crowd booed. The Sox's third-base coach shouted a few choice words at the pitcher that, hopefully, Ainsley didn't hear.

Ryan pushed himself up from the dirt and dusted himself off. The pitcher turned his back to home plate and gazed out toward centerfield. Ryan wondered if he was chuckling to himself.

Baseball isn't one of those sports, such as football, where anger is almost always an asset, an emotional tool that takes a player to a higher level. Sometimes, however, it does help, and nothing made Ryan madder than a head-hunting pitcher.

"Come on, *baaaabe.*"

Ryan's adrenaline was flowing, his heart thumping. He gripped his bat, then eased off. Nice and comfortable, not too tight.

The pitcher reared back for his windup. Ryan was guessing curve ball—something off-speed to screw up his timing after a blazing fastball that had nearly killed him.

He'd guessed right, and the next few moments unfolded like a slow-motion highlights film.

The pitch.

The swing.

The crack of the fat barrel of the maple bat colliding with the ball, the air seemingly sucked from the stadium as the crowd rose to watch a deep fly ball to left field—a ball that just seemed to keep going up and up, a towering blast that showed no sign of ever coming down. It soared over the Green Monster between the Fisk foul pole and the giant Coca-Cola bottle. It sailed over the tiered seating atop the monster, the most expensive seats in Fenway.

Ryan knew it was gone before he stepped out of the batter's box. He rounded the bases with a slugger's trot. The home crowd was jumping up and down at their seats, screaming wildly. The Red Sox dugout cleared, and the entire team was a pulsating mob waiting for him at home plate, ready to maul him after his game-winning blast.

It was Ryan's first home run at Fenway.

And it was all the way *out* of Fenway.

Ainsley was asleep when Ryan carried her into her room and laid her on the bed. He peeled back the fluffy red comforter with the Red Sox logo on it, tucked her in gently between the sheets, and kissed her good night.

The excitement was still coursing through his veins. A walk-off home run in his first game as a Red Sox player put Ryan into a small club. Babes, of course, was immediately able to tell him how small: "One. You're it, Ryan!" Ryan would listen to *Jock in the Morning*—his friend Jock was again doing the show alone—to see if Babes was right. Ivan had said some equally nice words about him to the team in the clubhouse. The hugs from Ainsley and Emma were the icing on the cake. It had been a perfect night, except for one thing.

No one had found the ball.

Ryan could only surmise that when it sailed out of the park and into the city street, it had rolled into a storm sewer.

"Daddy?"

The sound of her little voice made him smile. He turned to face her in the darkness.

"I thought you were asleep."

"Almost. But I was thinking."

"About what?" he said.

She propped herself up on an elbow. "Will anyone ever find your home-run ball?"

"I don't know," he said.

"Are you and Uncle Ivan going to look for it?"

"Probably not. It's not really important. We'll always remember it. That's all that matters."

She laid back into her pillow. "I guess that's right."

He went to her and kissed her forehead. "I love you. Now go to sleep."

"Love you too."

He was standing at the door and about to close it when he heard that sweet voice again.

"Daddy?"

He stopped. "What?"

"Do you know what I think?"

"Tell me, honey."

"I think Mommy caught it."

Her words touched Ryan in a way that, eight months earlier, he could never have felt. He smiled at Ainsley's thought.

"Maybe so, sweetheart. Maybe so."

Acknowledgments

Some stories percolate in a writer's mind for years before pen ever meets paper. For me, *Intent to Kill* is one of those stories. I mention this up front because I can't possibly remember everyone who helped me with it over a period of so many years. I apologize to all you unsung heroes.

As with *Lying with Strangers,* my first book-club exclusive, Markus Wilhelm, Richard Pine, and Carole Baron are at the top of my list of those to thank. Countless others who worked many years for the book clubs also have my sincere gratitude.

Thanks also to Eleanor Rayner who, over the last fifteen years, read each one of my manuscripts. *Intent to Kill* will stand as her last. She will be missed terribly.

As you might imagine, the research for this novel was great fun—much of it done simply by observing, drinking beer, and root-root-rooting for the home team. Several friends deserve special mention. Rob Murphy helped me experience (vicariously) a ballplayer's journey from minor-league to major-league baseball and, ultimately, to Fenway Park. I received especially gracious treatment from folks in Austin, namely, Joe R. Alba, special services coordinator with the Office of the President, who gave me a first-class tour of the University of Texas at Austin; Mark Franklin, Longhorn team manager, who provided an insider's look at University of Texas baseball (and who scored me a signed baseball from Augie Garrido, which I promise *never* to sell on e-Bay); and De-Laine Ward, from the Austin Bar Association, who helped to arrange all of this fun (with the exception of the body shot at some bar on Sixth Street). Gordon Van Alstyne was extremely patient and did his best to help me understand everything from silencers to body armor.

As always, any mistakes are mine.

Tom Bales lent his name and his Hawaiian shirts to a character in *Intent to Kill.* His generosity at a character auction will benefit the children at St. Thomas Episcopal Parish School in Coral Gables, Florida. Maybe one (or more) of them will end up at MIT too.

Finally, I want to thank my wife, Tiffany. There is nothing sexier than a mother of three who has never looked better in her life.